12:00

WHITE
GHOST

Also by Steven Gore

WHITE GHOST

A GRAHAM GAGE THRILLER

STEVEN GORE

wm

WILLIAM MORROW
An Imprint of HarperCollins*Publishers*

This book is a work of fiction. The characters, incidents, and dialogue are drawn from the author's imagination and are not to be construed as real. Any resemblance to actual events or persons, living or dead, is entirely coincidental.

FIRST EDITION

Designed by Diahann Sturge

Library of Congress Cataloging-in-Publication Data has been applied for.

ISBN 978-0-06-202508-1

16 17 18 19 20 OV/RRD 10 9 8 7 6 5 4 3 2 1

For Ranjana Advani, M.D.,
Katy Pose, P.A.-C, and
Alan Yuen, M.D.

Last night I dreamed a dreary dream
Beyond the Isle of Skye,
I saw a dead man win a fight—
And I thought that man was I.

—*The Battle of Otterburn* (1388)

Character List

China
Dong, owner, Tongming Tiger
"Old Wu," owner, Efficiency Trading
Ren, Qidong PLA port commander
Thomas Sheridan, Peter's father
Zhang Xianzi, general, People's Liberation Army

Golden Triangle
Cobra, Bangkok-based investigator
"Eight Iron," Bangkok-based methamphetamine trafficker
Kai, Gage's longtime friend
Kasa, Eight Iron's Shan bodyguard
Kew Wai Su, Wa State Army general

United States
Cheung Kwok-ming, "Ah Ming," United Bamboo leader
Fong Hai-tien, "Ah Tien" associate of Ah Ming
Jack Burch, international lawyer
Lew Fung-hao, Ah Ming's assistant
Linda Sheridan, Peter Sheridan's mother
Lucy Sheridan, Peter Sheridan's sister
Chau, owner, Sunny Glory Import, San Francisco and Taiwan

WHITE
GHOST

T he slug's impact wasn't anything like in the Hong Kong movies. It didn't throw Peter backward or knock him off his feet or send him twisting and flailing.

No, it wasn't like that at all. His body just . . . went . . . limp.

And it made no sense.

He'd known for certain nobody would get hurt. *It's an inside job. Nobody gets hurt on an inside job.* That's what Big Brother said when he chose him, when he let him use the name Ah Pang and handed him the gun.

A voice pierced through the gunfire and the screams and the running feet and the tumbling boxes.

"Ah Pang's shot Ah Pang's shot Ah Pang's shot."

A hand gripped Peter's shoulder and wrenched his head from the floor. His eyes jerked into motion and spun past the desks and shelves, the distant walls, the fluorescent lights, the high raftered ceiling, finally coming to rest just inches away from the face of a kneeling Dog Boy.

Peter saw his minute reflection in his friend's eyes and his image magnified in Dog Boy's terror—until he turned away and pushed himself to his feet. Peter then heard soles pounding concrete, accelerating into the distance, and voices yelling.

"Go—Go—Go."

What did Big Brother say they should do if something went wrong?

Run to the truck.

That's what Dog Boy had done, but now only Peter's thoughts ran. The unconscious flow of thought into action had been severed, and even if he could will his legs to move, there was nowhere left to run, for the enveloping stillness told him the others had faded into the void from which they had emerged only minutes earlier.

Peter's eyes caught sight of frightened Chinese workers peering over boxes and peeking around desks, then each recoiling at the sight of the black revolver in his hand. Even the security guard, the pudgy old white man who'd shot him, stood twenty yards away, face flushed, wide-eyed, body trembling.

Peter's gaze settled on the butt of his gun an arm's length away, dwarfing his skinny wrist, pinning his fingers to the concrete floor. Only moments before it had been awesome and alive, but now it was just cold dead metal.

He felt the confusion at the heart of his life mushroom into an unexpected form. He didn't know the word for it, but he was certain that his sister would, for Lucy knew all the words.

Peter heard rustling as clerks reached for their cell phones and whispered from a dozen hiding places.

"Help ... please ... shooting ... guns ... robbers."

Robbers.

Peter now saw himself through the terrified eyes watching him. He was a robber. He'd been Ah Pang among those he came with, but who was he now that they were gone? And what had he been before?

Lucy would know that, too.

Getting shot wasn't at all what he'd expected. And lying on the concrete floor as it warmed to the temperature of body and blood, he found that dying wasn't what he'd expected either. It was just a pounding heart . . . the sound of his breathing . . . and . . .

CHAPTER 1

G raham Gage's cell phone rang as he walked into his third-floor office in his converted redbrick warehouse. He lowered the window shade against the early spring sunlight ricocheting off San Francisco Bay and connected the call.

"I need your help with something."

"Hello to you, too, Jack."

"It's not a hello-to-you-Jack kind of morning. A client's son was killed during a computer chip robbery in San Jose yesterday."

"His parents must be devas—"

"It's a lot worse than you think. The kid wasn't the victim, he was the bloody robber."

International lawyer Jack Burch's reversion to the Australian idioms of his youth told Gage that his friend was floundering. Strategic ambiguities in law and finance had always fascinated and enthralled Burch, and his mastery of both had made him the Fortune 500's choice to navigate the turbulence of international business. But certain kinds of ambiguities and discontinuities in life frustrated him, sometimes paralyzed him. And Gage could hear in his voice and in his tone and in his clipped speech that this was one of them.

Before Burch could continue, Gage said, "Hold on a second," and covered the mic.

A wave of nausea first crept, then exploded through Gage's body, leaving his face burning and a metallic taste in his mouth. He eased himself down onto his chair and rested his head in his hands until he felt it all receding.

"Sorry." Gage picked up a file from his desk and slapped it down loud enough for Burch to hear. "Somebody came into the office to drop something off. And your client is . . ."

"Thomas Sheridan. Manufactures cell-phone components in China for Nokia and Motorola. Manages the plants from Hong Kong. He's a British ex-pat, but his wife is Hong Kongese. He sent her and the kids over here ten years ago when he was finally convinced the Chinese takeover was ending life as he knew it."

"Instead, life as he knew it ended here yesterday."

"And for his wife. She's the reason I called. She's seen your name in the Hong Kong papers over the years and wants you to find out what happened."

"What could she have read that would make her think I do street crime investigations?"

All of Gage's work in China that had been covered in the press had to do with corruption, fraud, intellectual property theft, copyright infringement, and currency manipulation, not robberies and homicides.

"I asked her the same thing. She'd read an article that said you were once a San Francisco police detective. That was good enough for her. And since they pay us a half a million a year in fees, I—"

Gage gasped as the nausea surged again.

"You okay? That didn't sound so good."

"I was just picking something up off the floor."

"Yeah . . . right."

"You think I'd lie to you?"

"Of course you would, but you wouldn't lie to Faith and she inadvertently let on how bad it's gotten."

"Where'd you find time to turn my wife into an informant?" Gage forced a laugh. "Aren't there mergers that need merging or acquisitions that need acquiring, or maybe joint ventures that need jointing?"

Gage's words sounded hollow, even to himself. An escape or an evasion. And the silence at the other end of the line told him Burch recognized it.

The high squeak of Burch's chair jabbed at Gage's eardrum. He imagined Burch rising to his feet in his financial district office tower, his already ruddy face reddening, the broad muscles across his shoulders tightening.

"It would be a lot simpler if you'd stop answering with questions, and start answering with answers."

"Whatever it is will pass; everything does."

"That's still not an answer."

Gage pictured Burch's clenched jaw, and his fist tightened around his phone. Burch wasn't a courtroom lawyer, but he was a man who expected his questions answered and headed a firm of a hundred attorneys who always answered them.

"Have I ever told you that your stoicism is really annoying?"

"Not this week."

Burch took in a long breath, then sighed. "I give up."

"Thanks. What do these people want from me that the police and the FBI can't give them?"

"Sheridan wants the gangster behind the whole operation and doesn't believe law enforcement can reach him. And, get this, he claims to know who he is."

"How could he know—"

"He didn't want to talk about it on the phone."

"Sounds a little paranoid."

"A little, maybe. Wary, for sure, in the way commercial predators are. And when he thinks he needs something, he gets it; and his wife has convinced him he needs you."

Gage's thirty years, first as a detective who had spent time working in Chinatown, then as a private investigator working in Asia, thumbnailed Sheridan and his wife.

"It sounds to me like a combination of a mother with a cultural suspicion of governmental authority and the grief-driven delusion of a father who thinks he can buy anything."

"I don't know about her, but you're dead-on right about him, and I'm sorry to put you in the middle of it, especially now."

"Now." The word shook Gage for a moment. He wasn't sure what *now* was, for that meant understanding both the past and the future—what had made him sick and what it would do to him.

Now only meant what illness always means: feeling trapped in the present.

"Bring Sheridan by tomorrow and I'll find a way to deal with him."

"He won't get here for another forty-eight hours. It'll be his wife and daughter. Ten A.M. okay?"

"Make it two. I'll be locked into something until then."

CHAPTER 2

T he coastal hills a few miles away were still shadowed as Gage lay on a sliding table at the Stanford Hospital radiology clinic waiting to be fed into a roaring metal doughnut whose internal workings would produce hundreds of cross-sectional views of his body.

But he had no reason to believe the scan would be any more revelatory than the tests preceding it in the last three weeks; at least that seemed to be the meaning of his doctor's shrug when he'd ordered it.

Gage thought of Faith sitting in the waiting room and knew she felt the physicians' diagnostic failures as her own. She'd called and e-mailed fellow anthropologists throughout Asia, Africa, and South America where he'd worked during the previous months, describing his symptoms and seeking instances of diseases that might have caused them. She begged her graduate students doing fieldwork overseas to report not just on their research, but on illnesses they observed.

And the possibilities poured in. From African sleeping sickness to West Nile virus to dengue fever to scrub and Queensland tick typhus, even to plague. But his doctors had excluded each in turn.

A technician approached Gage from behind.

"Ever have an allergic reaction to iodine contrast material?"

"Just the warm, fuzzy feeling everybody gets. A surgeon needed to figure out how to dig some lead out of me without doing more damage." He smiled up at her. "Don't worry, I was the good guy."

She smiled back. "I suspected you were."

She swabbed the inside of his right elbow with alcohol, inserted the IV into his vein, and then swung a metal arm above him. A clear plastic plunger hung from the end and attached to it was a flexible clear tube. She snapped the dangling end of the tube onto a plastic nipple extending from the needle, then raised both his arms, extended them, and brought them to rest behind his head.

"We'll be making three passes, about thirty seconds each," she said. "You'll need to hold your breath during each one."

Gage heard her step into the observation booth and close the door.

A male voice emerged godlike out of the silence. "I am now beginning the IV."

Gage watched the plunger drive down, shooting the iodine into his arm. His body warmed and an edgy chemical taste mixed with the barium he had consumed three-quarters of an hour before the procedure began.

The voice spoke again. "Hold . . . your . . . breath."

The scanner whirled as the table eased forward, sliding him into the doughnut as far as his chin, then back out to his hips.

"Breathe."

At the start of the third pass, a wave of nausea shuddered through him. His faced flushed and his fists clenched.

"Hold ... your ... breath." 30 ... 29 ... 28 ... 27 ... 26 ... He gritted his teeth and stiffened his body. 25 ... 24 ... 23 ... 22 ... 21 ... He could feel a damp warmth under his back as sweat soaked through his blue medical gown pressed against the white sheet covering the table. 20 ... 19 ... 18 ... 17 ... 16 ... The wave passed. He stopped counting.

"Breathe."

"DID YOU GET A CHANCE to talk to the radiologist?" Faith asked as Gage drove them from the hospital toward the tree-lined streets of downtown Palo Alto.

"All I got out of him was a weak smile, but at least he didn't shrug."

"You almost lost your balance when you got out of bed this morning." Faith glanced at the Brooks Brothers store as they passed Stanford Shopping Center. "And I looked at your belt last night and saw where you used to buckle it."

It was Gage's turn to shrug.

"I'm sure we'll have the answer in a few days."

Faith sighed and looked down at her hands folded in her lap.

"How many times have we told ourselves that?"

Gage looked over. The cloudless May sky allowed the sun's rays to fill the car, highlighting the few strands of gray among the auburn hair that framed Faith's tense face and strained eyes and flowed down to her shoulders.

He laid his hand over hers.

"For all we know, a couple of weeks with the right antibiotics or some foul-tasting, take-on-a-full-stomach syrup and it'll be gone. Maybe today was the last test I'll need."

Gage pulled the car to the curb near the University Cafe, and a few minutes later they had worked their way between the sidewalk tables and past the brass and cast-iron coffee roaster to the counter.

"Jack telephoned yesterday," Gage said, after they'd ordered coffee and bagels and sat down.

"How'd that go? The uncertainty of this thing scares the hell out of him."

They both knew Burch had yet to recover his balance after he was shot as part of a securities fraud cover-up and after the breast cancer that nearly took his wife's life. For Burch, it had been less that these were confrontations with mortality and more that for the first time he felt his world and his life slip from his grip, torn away first by the rude mechanics of a biological process and then by a man with a gun.

"Why'd he decide to face the abyss and call you himself?"

Gage withheld his answer until after an approaching waiter passed by.

"A wealthy client's teenaged son hooked up with a gang and was killed during a robbery."

Faith looked down, shaking her head, then back up.

"How could a privileged childhood end up like that?"

"I don't know. But I suspect the kid wanted more out of the crime than just money."

Gage thought of the Navajos he grew up with on the Arizona and Mexican border near Nogales, the older people talking about going to war having been a young man's rite of passage, and he remembered a friend's older brother who'd enlisted in the Marines in 1968 while not even knowing where Vietnam was. For him, the pretenses of the ceremonial dances, the reenactments of others' heroism, hadn't been enough. He believed he needed to fight to feel alive, to feel real in his world. And he'd died trying.

But Gage doubted Sheridan's son's death was about that, about feeling alive and real. Like the other immigrant and cross-cultural children of his generation who populated the Asian gangs, the kid probably had more of life than he could handle.

"What do you think he wanted out of it?"

Gage gazed over at the traffic passing on the street and the tree-shadowed sidewalk. "I don't know, but someone else will have to find that out." Then back at Faith. "I'm only meeting with the family to make sure they don't destroy themselves in a misguided attempt to discover on their own what that was and who was behind it."

CHAPTER 3

When Gage arrived in his office reception area, he found Jack Burch sitting on a couch next to a slim Eurasian woman. Her back was straight, her eyes forward, her hands locked together as though her grief could be contained by force of will. Her gray suit and the string of pearls hanging around her neck seemed to Gage to be camouflage, like the feather pattern on an owl that imitates bark or stone.

"Graham," Burch said, as they rose for introductions, "this is Lucy Sheridan."

"I'm very sorry about your loss." Gage took her hand and glanced toward the double glass doors facing the parking lot and the bay. "Wasn't your mother—"

"She needed to take care of some things." Lucy looked away for a moment. "She sends her apologies."

Burch caught Gage's eye with an expression that said, *Her mother isn't ready to deal with this.*

Gage passed on their drink requests to his receptionist, then led them down a hallway agitated by clicking keyboards, whirling printers, and voices echoing against the redbrick walls and into a conference room.

"I spoke to the FBI lead agent," Gage said, after sitting down across from them. "He says the kids they caught were just—"

Gage hesitated. The meeting had just begun and he'd already caught himself moving too fast toward its inevitable end. He looked from Burch to Lucy. He was surprised she held his gaze.

"You can say it. I'm ready. I might not be in ten minutes or in an hour or in a day. But I am now and I need to know."

Gage watched her grip the edge of the table in front of her in apprehension, preparing herself both to hear the words he would speak and to brace herself against their meaning.

Finally, Gage spoke. "The kids the police captured are called throwaways."

Lucy blinked but kept her eyes fixed on Gage.

"A *dai lo* picked your brother for the robbery." Gage glanced toward Burch. "*Dai lo* means big brother." Then back at Lucy. "Peter was known as Ah Pang."

Lucy winced, pained by the words and what they meant for what her brother had become. "That's a character Peter liked in a Hong Kong gang movie, *Dragon's End.*"

"They pick a name to give themselves a sense of identity, but it actually makes them anonymous. That's something the big brothers understand and the underlings don't."

The receptionist knocked and then entered carrying a drink tray. She served Lucy tea and Burch and Gage coffee.

Gage slid a San Jose Police Department offense report across the table and watched Lucy's eyes work their way down the text, pausing, and then pushing forward.

> 18:05HRS . . .
> Asian male, Suspect (1), 24 to 25 years old—
> business office of PL Computers—
> handguns—
> Victim (1) and Victim (2) . . . tied up—

    8 Asian males entered the warehouse—
    loaded boxes of microprocessors into a van—
    security guard shooting—
    Suspect (5) fell to the floor—
    males jumped into the back of the truck—
    responding officers located Suspect (5)—

Gage saw Lucy's eyes widen, then her brows furrow as she grasped that Suspect (5) was her brother and that he was about to die before her eyes.

    deceased in the warehouse—

Lucy's jaw tightened and she swallowed.

    Suspect (6) and Suspect (7) were found hiding in
a dumpster—
    the loss was approximately $4,500,000—
    Suspect (5), later ID'd as Peter Sheridan, 16 years
old, was released to the Coroner at 01:55HRS.

Lucy wiped away the tears that had formed as she read.

Gage could tell that she'd never seen a police report and hadn't anticipated how it would read and hadn't known to brace herself for its synthesis of the brutal and mundane.

She straightened in her chair, then folded her hands on the table.

Gage wondered where her strength came from, suspecting it hadn't come from her absent mother.

"My father knows who was behind it."

"Knows? Or just thinks he knows?"

"He met the man once, a few months ago. Peter was with him. Peter . . ."

Lucy raised a finger as if she'd arrived at an unmarked trail-head and was lost in a vertiginous moment, struggling to decide whether to backtrack or press forward. Gage understood she wasn't ready to start at the end, that she hadn't yet caught up to the present. Even more, he knew she needed Gage to understand Peter's life, not just his death, the throwing away. With a nod of his head, he gave her permission to start at the beginning.

"Peter was just six when we arrived here. I was fourteen. We only saw our father when he came to the United States for the holidays and when we visited him in Hong Kong during summer vacation. And Mother . . ." Lucy looked back and forth between Burch and Gage. "I know at times like these people blame the mother."

"No one here is placing blame," Gage said, wondering whether by people Lucy meant herself.

"Mother was always something of a mystery. My father once said this was what infatuated him when they met. But it really wasn't mystery. It was distance. She was as psychologically dis-tant as my father was geographically." She glanced at Burch. "I know some people refer to her as reclusive."

Burch's face reddened.

Lucy pushed on. "She is, but I don't think it's only because of her disability. It's a lot deeper, way beyond just the awkwardness of her limp."

"She refused to come to my office when we were doing the corporate reorganizations," Burch said, attempting to recover his position of confidence, "even though she's a shareholder and board member in all their companies."

Lucy stiffened as though someone had leaned against her in a crowded elevator, then pushed on.

"As a child, Peter was as naïve and trusting as a puppy. But by middle school he began to close himself off, just like our mother. He'd disappear for days, sometimes weeks. My parents made him move to Hong Kong to live with our father, trying to break his ties to his friends here and regain some control over him."

Gage shook his head. "I don't see how that could've worked. I doubt that his problems were geographical."

She nodded. "My father couldn't control him either. Things escalated. He became what they call a *fei jai*." She looked again at Burch. "A junior gangster. My father hired a private detective in Kowloon who tracked him to Temple Street where gamblers were using him as a lookout. My father had no choice but to send him back to the States. And Peter took up where he left off, and then ran away for the last time when he was fifteen. My mother—" Lucy's voice caught. Her hand rose to cover her heart. "My mother is just devastated, so bewildered, so . . . I mean, no one expected . . . she . . . we . . . couldn't grasp what was happening."

Lucy looked down at the police report as if it represented the completion of her thought, then gripped her teacup in both hands and held it close to her chest.

"Do you know where he was living before the robbery?" Gage asked.

"With other first-generation kids, moving from place to place. East Bay. South Bay. San Francisco."

Lucy set her cup down and focused on Gage.

"Peter came home on my birthday two months ago. He was surprised to find my father visiting from Hong Kong. They got into an argument and Peter yelled, 'You're nothing to me' and then mumbled the name Ah Ming as he ran out of the house." She paused and then sighed. "And that was the last time I saw him."

"Lucy's father was too embarrassed to tell me about it," Burch said, "so he hired a private investigator out of the phone book. A contact in the San Francisco Police Department told the investigator that Ah Ming's real name is Cheung Kwok-ming and that he came to the States in the mid-'90s and built a chain of Asian supermarkets. I'm sure you've seen them. They're called East Wind. In no time he became a big man in the Chinese community. One of my associates did some research and found he's on the boards of a couple of benevolent associations and gives a huge amount to Chinatown charities."

Lucy took the story back. "My father decided his only chance to get Peter back was to confront Ah Ming, so he asked the investigator to take him to Ah Ming's mansion in Hillsborough."

Gage looked at Burch, who shook his head with a disheartened expression, foreshadowing how it would end.

"Peter was standing in the front courtyard with some other boys when they drove up." Lucy's eyes went vacant, as though the imagined scene was developing in her mind. "Peter ran inside and Ah Ming's men grabbed my father as he stepped across the threshold and threw him back down the front steps. It took twenty stitches to close the gash in his scalp."

"Did your father call the police?"

Lucy blinked herself back into the present and shook her head. "He thought it would be counterproductive. Peter would've gone into hiding where we'd never find him . . . and that was the last we heard about him until the police came by the day before yesterday."

Burch let a few moments pass, then said to Gage, "That should give you an idea of what the Sheridans have in mind."

Gage did, but he didn't believe in grasping at phantoms, especially when he had a real enemy of his own. He leaned forward, crossing his forearms on the conference table.

"Actually," Gage said, first looking at Burch. "I'm not yet sure they have a clue what they'd be getting into." Then at Lucy. "And I'm also not sure that Peter's presence in the company of Ah Ming two months ago necessarily means Ah Ming was behind the robbery."

Uncertainty washed over Lucy's face. Gage knew that what she'd missed, what the grief-stricken always miss, is that suffering reduces their perception of the complexity of the world. They're taken captive by a picture and the force of its irresistible logic, and the chaos of possibility gets distilled into a syllogism limited by a narrowed sense of relevance:

Sheridan last saw Peter with Ah Ming.

Peter died in a robbery.

Therefore, Ah Ming was behind the robbery.

Gage knew he needed to drive the point home even though the focus of her anger, the anger that made her grief bearable, might transfer to him.

"What about the dozens of other people Peter might've been seen with if your father had been there to look? Who knows how many big brothers he came in contact with at safe houses or on Chinatown street corners or in Vietnamese coffee shops."

Lucy's face flushed like she was suffocating. Gage recognized it as the expression of a rape victim after she's been told the DNA didn't match the man she had picked out of the lineup; it was born of the fear that somewhere out there the man who really attacked her was on the street. And it was also born of the realization that she was wrong about something about which she'd been positive.

"And even if Ah Ming really was behind the robbery, I'm not sure we'll be able to connect him to it. All the human links between him and the kids who were arrested are probably gone."

"How's that possible?" Lucy's face flushed and her voice rose. "There has to be some kind of trail. Doesn't there?"

Gage knew her unfinished thought was: *And isn't it your job to find it?*

"The short answer is no."

Gage picked up a pen, then grabbed a yellow legal pad from a stack at the end of the table.

"Look at the numbers. Let's assume they net two million dollars from the stolen chips. A hundred thousand goes to whoever set it up. Fifty thousand goes to the *dai lo* who managed the robbery—recruited the kids, rented the car and the van, bought the guns. A few hundred dollars each to the underlings, say five thousand dollars total. They can spend another fifty thousand scattering everyone between the top and the bottom around the country and still net one point eight million dollars. And even the fifty thousand in traveling money isn't wasted because they now have people available to work wherever they land."

Lucy nodded. "I understand."

Gage shook his head. "Not yet. The death of your brother is even more than felony murder; it's murder with special circumstances. The law doesn't distinguish among those who die in a robbery. Robber or victim. So fifty thousand dollars or even five hundred thousand isn't too much to spend to blow up a bridge to death row. And while I may not know the road map of this particular crime, my experience tells me the bridge was blown just minutes after your brother died."

"Are you saying there's no—"

"Wait," Gage said, holding up his hand. "There's more. Do you think whoever is behind this is going to have the computer chips delivered to him, unloaded at his house, stacked in the corner?"

Gage shook his head, answering his own question.

"These guys are insulated with front companies and intermediaries, suit-wearing pillars of the community who connect the aboveground to the underground, but never get their hands dirty."

He leaned back and spread his arms.

"Why does Ah Ming give to charity? Out of the goodness of his heart?" Gage thumped the table with his forefinger. "His heart beats only to keep his blood moving. Charity buys cover."

"Are you saying it's hopeless? That Ah Ming is untouchable?"

"That's not the question we're faced with."

"Then what is?"

"We need to know whether your father is targeting Ah Ming because he really thinks Ah Ming caused the death of your brother, or simply because Ah Ming humiliated him."

Lucy looked down at her tea, now cold in the half-empty cup.

"The thought of Ah Ming is eating away at him." She took in a long breath and shrugged. "But if it isn't Ah Ming, we have to know that, too."

"Where do we go from here?" Burch asked, his tone suggesting to Gage that he was so caught up in a desire to find out the truth, he'd forgotten the point of the meeting, which was to find a means to sidetrack the Sheridans from self-destruction.

Gage locked his eyes on Burch, who reddened and said, "I mean—"

Gage cut him off with a raised hand and looked over at Lucy.

"Give me a couple of days," Gage said, finding himself speaking as though to a client whose tragedy he had taken on, instead of a person he was trying to divert.

At the beginning of the meeting he'd felt he was protecting Burch by taking the burden onto himself, but now realized it was something else, and he wasn't sure what.

"Let me try to find out more about Ah Ming. There's a lot of intelligence out there: business competitors—"

His previous thought lingered, leaving him both puzzled and anxious to find an answer.

"FBI and DEA analysts looking at Asian gangs and triads, IRS criminal investigators on the lookout for money laundering, ICE agents trying to stop human trafficking, even other gangsters looking for an opportunity to take over new territory."

All this was true, but it was composed of the sort of acronyms and names he doubted Lucy had ever uttered, elements of a world that was alien to her, and one she deserved to be insulated from.

And he knew he shouldn't have said any of it, for he hadn't told her anything that would help her find her feet. He just tossed her into a borderland with neither a map to locate her brother's place in it nor a GPS to find her way out.

Looking at Lucy's now drawn face and the uncertainty and confusion in her eyes, Gage realized he needed to restore her balance, to ensure that the consequence of her current helplessness wouldn't cause her life to forever pivot around the moment of her brother's death.

Even though he was sure he wouldn't, Gage asked, "I may need your help down the road. What Chinese languages do you speak?"

"Cantonese with my mother and my friends in Hong Kong," Lucy said, "and I studied Mandarin in college."

"Do you have a Chinese name?"

Lucy's face brightened as if she had recognized an old friend across a crowded room and had been acknowledged in return. Or maybe met someone in a strange land who knew her culture.

"Siu-cheng."

"And at home . . ."

A shy smile. "I was sort of an awkward child."

"Which means your mother called you . . ."

"Chicken Feet."

BURCH DIRECTED LUCY toward the lobby as they filed out of the conference room, and then he and Gage paused at the door.

"You surprised me," Burch said. "This is the first time I've seen that kind of intensity in you since this medical problem began." He glanced toward Lucy's receding figure. "But I'm wondering whether you were a little rough on her."

"I worried about that, too, but she deserves to know where

she stands. And for the moment I'd rather her anger and frustration be aimed at me rather than Ah Ming. It's safer for her, and her father."

They watched Lucy turn from the hallway into the lobby.

"I'm afraid that in her father's grief and guilt," Gage said, "he's twisted it around in his mind so that if there isn't a great evil behind what happened, a great evil that's finally brought to justice, then Peter's death means nothing."

Gage paused, looking at the empty hallway, listening to his investigators' speaking on their phones chasing facts, trying to discern truths behind appearances.

"But there might not be a greater meaning. All there might be behind the robbery is a punk who wanted fast money and got two million dollars' worth of lucky."

"But you don't think so."

Gage shook his head.

"You think she's bought into her father's story?"

"Not completely. But I think she's brave enough not only to accept the truth, but to make her parents accept it, too."

"But there's something else, isn't there?"

Gage felt Burch's eyes on him, then looked over and nodded.

"I don't know whether Ah Ming was behind the robbery. And I don't know yet who Ah Ming is, but I sure know *what* he is." Gage pointed at Burch. "You know how some people are called expendable? Well, Ah Ming is the guy who expends them. Sheridan didn't call the police because he was afraid it would drive his son into hiding. The kid was already hiding. Sheridan was as terrified as if he'd seen an awesome god. And when he finally reached out to you, he was afraid to talk."

Burch held up his palms toward Gage, as if trying to block his path.

"Hold on. I know what you're thinking. I can see it in your eyes. You already picture the world without Ah Ming in it, and all that remains for you is to figure out a way to make the world match the picture."

"I'm not going to rush into anything," Gage said, eyes softening. "I've got to get this medical thing figured out and I think I'm too old to face down dead-eyed little thugs to get to him."

Burch nodded. "I'd rather have you stay out of harm's way for a while."

Gage reached over and put his arm around Burch's shoulders.

"We're always in harm's way, Jack. It's just that we're usually looking in the wrong direction."

CHAPTER 4

Alex Z appeared at Gage's office door an hour after Burch and Lucy left.

Gage thought of Alex Z as the office genius, a view he knew wasn't always apparent to corporate clients distracted by his tattoos of Popeye and Olive Oyl, rings through soft tissue body parts, and clothing too tight, and too old. But even those among his staff of former state and federal agents who prayed in the darkness their children wouldn't follow Alex Z's fashion hoped they'd have his mind.

Gage pointed at one of the two chairs in front of his desk. "What did you find out?"

Alex Z slid a folder toward Gage and sat down. "Ah Ming's a cash man. No loans, no mortgages, no equipment bought on time. No lines of credit."

"Anything in his name?"

"Nope. His house is owned by a Hong Kong company, which in turn is owned by a Cayman Islands company."

"And the Cayman Islands company?"

"For real?"

Gage smiled. "Yes, for real."

Alex Z shrugged. "I have no idea."

"Yet?"

"Yet."

"What about East Wind?"

"Same gimmick, different islands. I'll keep working cyberspace," Alex Z pointed down toward the two floors of investigators below. "You want some folks to scout around and see what they can find out?"

"Law enforcement is doing enough of that. I don't want to risk provoking a reaction from Ah Ming because he feels pressure from an unexpected direction."

Gage started to push himself to his feet, then felt a wave of exhaustion and settled back.

"You okay, boss?" Alex Z asked, inspecting Gage's face.

Gage nodded, then leaned over and opened a desk drawer.

"Just forgot something I needed."

GAGE DROVE SOUTH along the four-lane Embarcadero, first past new condos, and then old warehouses, and finally onto the freeway bordering the San Francisco Airport that would take him to the industrial park where the private investigator Sheridan hired had his office. He wanted to ask him a question that had bothered him since he'd spoken to Lucy: How had SFPD learned Ah Ming's real name?

Gage doubted the SFPD dispatcher's log ever reported that "Ah Ming called to complain about a homeless person sleeping in his office doorway." Or that "Ah Ming called to have an abandoned car towed." Ah Ming was an underworld name and if law enforcement had learned it, they'd earned it, and Gage wanted to know how and why without tipping off the department. He was too well known, and knowledge that he was interested would make others interested in finding out why.

Gage found the investigator sitting at his desk in his one-person office. The bare walls, the absence of a receptionist, the single file cabinet, and the dusty Golden Gate Bridge paperweight all made it seem like he was working in a purgatory between failure that always threatened and success that was forever out of reach.

The man's eyes widened when Gage walked in, then he stood up as if at attention. It seemed to Gage to be a performance. They both knew their relative positions in the industry, and Gage saw no reason for the investigator to act out his role.

Gage nodded toward the desk chair and the investigator dropped into it. Gage remained standing while he laid out the Ah Ming problem, and then asked, "Who clued you in?"

"A guy I know in patrol; we worked security together years ago at a Target store. The East Wind warehouse is on his beat."

If the name had been passed down from the intelligence unit to street cops, Gage knew that there must have been a broader investigation involving uniformed officers tasked with making pretext stops and running drivers' licenses and plates to identify members of Ah Ming's organization.

"How did your guy know that Cheung's nickname was Ah Ming?"

The investigator shrugged. "He didn't say."

Which meant to Gage that he hadn't asked.

The investigator caught the meaning in the silence that followed, then shrugged again and said, "You know how it is; you can't push an informant too far."

But they both knew that he hadn't pushed far enough.

AS GAGE DROVE BACK TOWARD HIS OFFICE, he telephoned Nancy Kramer, a criminal defense attorney who worked the San Francisco courts, always avoiding the press and putting her clients' interests before her ambitions. She'd represented scores of gangsters over the years, but her refusal to speak to the media helped her avoid the mob lawyer label. Gage and other investigators in his office referred clients and witnesses to her who had criminal cases they needed disposed of quickly and quietly. He'd made dozens of referrals just in the last few years, which meant Kramer owed him.

"You remember anyone with the nickname of Ah Ming in any of your tong or triad cases? He may be big."

"I can't think of any, but there must've been. I think these crooks have used up every nickname or alias ever invented." She laughed. "I heard a hilarious one the other day. Hung Pho."

"Pho as in Vietnamese noodles?"

"Exactly. Noodle Hung. Swear to God. A gangster named Noodle Hung. He owned a café in Little Saigon."

"Owned?"

"He was a contract killer who had what goes around come around, right into the back of his head . . . I take it Ah Ming is still alive."

"So I've been told.

"What are you looking for?"

"Wire intercept data, surveillance logs, DEA and FBI reports. I'd rather not approach anyone in law enforcement until I get a sense of how his operation fits together."

"You mean you want to know more than they know before you go knocking on their door."

"Something like that. And if anything turns up, I may want to talk to a few of your clients."

Kramer called Gage back a couple of hours later. He was at his desk, thinking he really was the wrong person to be doing this, frustrated by the realization that he'd lost contact with the local Asian gang world. His had been a white-collar practice for decades: securities fraud, trade secret thefts, embezzlements, bid rigging, foreign corruption. Arms trafficking had brought him in contact with the Russian underworld and extortions in contact with Italian organized crime, but his knowledge of the identities of those who populated Ah Ming's world was so dated he felt less like an investigator than an anthropologist returning to study a tribe after a generation had passed.

"I've got some good news and I've got some bad news," Kramer said. "You can have the paper and plastic, the hard copy reports and DVDs of the data, but none of my boys are willing to sit down and talk with you."

"But they know Ah Ming."

"You betcha, but you'll never hear them say his name. He's way too big. Way, way, way too big." Kramer fell silent for a moment, then continued. "I don't know what you have in mind, but if it's taking him down, don't even think about it. From what they're telling me, nobody's ever going to sneak up on the guy, and you've been too visible over the years to even risk trying."

"Don't worry. This is just about helping a friend with a little information. When can we pick up the stuff?"

"I'll be in my office until six. But be careful with it and don't tell anyone where you got it. I don't want anybody blaming the messenger."

lex Z removed a file box from the chair next to him as Gage walked into the secure room in the basement. The FBI and DEA data-packed DVDs inside rattled as he set it on the floor.

"I downloaded all the wiretap data from the last eight years. Ah Ming was never a target, and he was only mentioned five times in over a hundred thousand calls and text messages." Alex Z looked past Gage for a moment. "Now that I think about it, there isn't much that connects all of them together. They all might not even be about the same guy. He can't be the only Ah Ming in the Chinese underworld."

"Show me."

Gage sat down as Alex Z typed "Ah Ming" on his keyboard. He pointed at the transcript excerpts that appeared on his monitor.

"The earliest one is about some guys saying an Ah Ming flooded the market with something called Double UO Globe, but I can't tell what it is."

"China White heroin."

"With a brand name?"

"And a trademark. Two lions leaning on the earth. Buyers need to be able tell a Rolex from Timex. It's been around for almost half a century."

"What about knockoffs?"

"There aren't any. Trademark infringement is always fatal."

Alex Z scrolled down and pointed at the references to Triple K and 555. "And these?"

"Brands that came after Double UO Globe. It's made by the Wa State Army—"

"Wa?"

"An ethnic hill tribe in the Golden Triangle. They've been fighting for independence from Burma and China for generations. They use heroin trafficking to raise money to buy weapons."

"Like Pashtuns in Afghanistan?"

"Exactly. Years ago, the Wa became strong enough to grab most of Double UO Globe's share of the trade, and their brands began to dominate the world market."

"And if it's the same guy they're talking about, Ah Ming went with the flow and started buying from the Wa."

"Not directly. Through a heroin broker." Gage made a downward cutting motion with his hand. "Everyone has an interest in keeping the source end and the distribution end separate."

Alex Z peered at Gage. "How do you know all this? Since I've been here all we've done is white-collar stuff."

"It's just residue from a past life."

A fragment of a memory came to Gage of the last time he heard of Double UO Globe. It wasn't that long ago. A hint it was making a comeback. A report from the Chinese Xinhua news agency he'd read in Beijing. Ten kilos off-loaded at an Australian port from a North Korean ship that had stopped in Yangon, Burma, on its way along the Pacific Rim.

Alex Z paged down.

"Here's a conversation from six years ago. People going back and forth about how Ah Ming brought a guy named Ah Tien to the Eight Dragons Café in Chinatown."

"It was a hangout for tong and triad members, maybe it still is. It probably means that Ah Ming wanted to give Ah Tien face so the other gangs would know that Ah Tien represented him."

A stronger memory. Thirty years earlier, still with SFPD, doing surveillances outside of Eight Dragons, working with the gang task force, trying to figure out who was coming up. In civilian life, a generation is twenty-five years; in the world of Asian street crime, it was usually four or five. And only a few were powerful enough and insulated enough to span more than one or two generations.

Gage gestured toward the monitor. "Anything about computer chips involving Ah Ming or Ah Tien?"

Alex Z shook his head. "But there's talk about somebody wanting to do something big, and being pissed off because Ah Ming did it first."

"Did they say where or when?"

Alex Z shook his head again. "But there was one about East Wind, which means it was somehow connected to our Ah Ming. A guy says he almost got caught with two stacks and wished he had an East Wind. Is stacks heroin, too?"

"Most likely money. Whatever else East Wind is, it's probably Ah Ming's money laundering operation."

Gage paused for a moment, thinking about how to turn what they'd learned into leads and the fact that their route into the unknown might only be through Ah Tien.

"Does Ah Tien's name come up anywhere else?"

"Once when somebody called a number and asked for him. A kid said he wasn't in and hung up."

Gage cocked his head toward the box of DVDs from which Alex Z had downloaded the data.

"Is there a telephone subscriber database in there?"

Alex Z nodded.

"See if you can find an address."

FIVE MINUTES LATER, Gage's phone beeped with the arrival of a text from Alex Z:

> Boss:
> This is the address that goes with the telephone number the person called looking for Ah Tien:
> Fong, Hai-tien
> 990 25th Avenue
> San Francisco

Gage replied:

> Cheung Kwok-MING: Ah Ming
> Fong Hai-TIEN: Ah Tien
> Good work

Sorry I'm late," Gage said as he entered Abe's Fly Shop in San Jose an hour later.

Standing near the front counter, FBI Senior Special Agent Joe Casey glanced up from the rooster cape he held in his hands.

"No problem. I just walked in a minute ago."

Casey fanned the outer vane and then returned it to its plastic sheath. As he set it back on the display rack, he looked over at Abe behind the counter.

"You got any coffee?"

Abe nodded and pointed toward the rear of the store.

Gage led Casey into the back room and then poured two cups. They sat down in folding chairs near Abe's workbench piled with the thread, hackles, hooks, and fur for the custom-made flies he sold up front.

Casey inspected Gage's face. "You've lost a little weight. You been on a diet?"

"I picked up a bug somewhere, maybe Africa. I got tied up there on a platinum price-fixing scheme a couple months ago."

Gage smiled and shrugged. "I needed to lose a few pounds anyway."

"Don't we all." Casey took a sip of his coffee. "What's going on?"

"I've decided to look a little further into that computer chip robbery I called you about."

Casey frowned as he picked up a streamer from the table and tested the hook against his thumbnail. "If you want my opinion, it's a dead end. The task force they set up the other day is just a publicity stunt." He tossed down the fly. "It's like when they call us in after a child kidnapping. We never find the kid alive. Never. We're just the advance detail for the coroner." His forefinger thumped the table. "And every time the brass in Washington insists on another one, we end up failing twice: the crime is never solved and the task force fails trying to solve it. It's just a—" Casey raised his hand, ready to punch the air, then caught himself and shook his head. "Sorry. I've been getting more and more frustrated with this stupid routine and with the press making my people the fall guys."

"Maybe this one will be different; my client thinks he knows who was behind it."

Casey smirked. "Gee, I guess I was wrong. It looks like the task force just had its first success." He slumped back in his chair. "Sorry again, this time for the sarcasm, and for directing it at you. It's been a long couple of days chasing little gangsters around. What does he know?"

"*Thinks* he knows."

"Is your client the insurance carrier?"

"The father of the kid who was killed in the robbery."

"Sheridan? I'm not sure how a corporate type in Hong Kong—"

"He came here a few months ago. He had a run-in with a guy named Ah Ming."

Casey flushed with anger. "Why the hell didn't he tell us about it?"

"Fear of Ah Ming. And even if he could've gotten over it, there might have been a problem with his wife. She's Hong Kongese and may be a little suspicious of law enforcement." Gage gestured toward Casey's face. "Why the explosion?"

"Because he's . . . he's . . . maybe you better tell me what else you know, first."

"All I've learned so far is that Ah Ming has been around awhile, has had heroin connections in the Golden Triangle for at least the last fifteen years or so, and uses East Wind to launder the profits. But I still can't tell if he's involved in computer chips."

"It's never come up before. We weren't even able to put a face to the name until eighteen months ago. It took us a long time even to get that far. He made the smartest move a heroin trafficker can make. He realized that whites, especially suburban ones, were the biggest market for heroin and the DEA's focus on blacks and Hispanics left open territory. And they'll pay the difference between Mexican or Afghan black tar and his China White."

"And then he insulates himself with layers of Asian gangsters that white drug dealers are so afraid of they won't inform against them if they get caught."

Casey nodded. "And when we've stuck his photo under the nose of any of the Asian gangsters who do start to cooperate with us, all we get are thirdhand stories from what are always second-rate sources. Just say his name and these punks start squirming and forget how to speak English or Chinese or Vietnamese or whatever language they lie in. And they've got good reason to be scared. He puts the 'god' in godfather. Old Testament. A vengeful, but unseen presence."

"That's the tone you use when you point out a big fish rising."

"He's bigger than big."

"And just out of casting distance."

"Worse than that. It's like shark fishing with a four-pound tippet."

"What about leads from the robbery, something that might connect back to him?"

"Nothing. We found the U-Haul they used torched outside of Modesto. No usable forensics. It had been rented by a generic Asian female with a fake driver's license and a forged credit card. And the gun we recovered was stolen three years ago in Des Moines. There were prints, even some on the shell casings, but they all belonged to the kid."

"Sounds like you're at a dead end."

"But that's not something the task force will admit—yet. We like to time the announcements of our failures for big news days so they'll get lost in the noise."

"You mean even if Ah Ming was behind the robbery, you're not going to get him."

Casey shook his head. "We're not going to get him."

ON THEIR WAY BACK TO THE ENTRANCE, Casey retrieved the rooster cape and paid for it. They walked out into the parking lot and stood next to his car. A jet rush of airplane that had just taken off from the San Jose airport passed over them, leaving a hollow silence behind.

Casey looked down at the asphalt, then up at the high scattered clouds, for the moment blocking the sun. "Man, I'd sure like to be on the river right now." He glanced at the keychain in his hand and flipped the remote back and forth, then peered at Gage. "Are you sure you're up for messing around in Ah Ming's world? I mean, if he's the guy. Whatever you've got seems to be taking its toll."

Gage shrugged. "It'll pass."

"And that's not the only reason. Ah Ming is old-school. You

know what his nickname was when he first showed up in the States?"

"I haven't got that far."

"Hak Guai."

"Black Ghost?"

"He's not the kind of guy who's gonna die in his sleep. When he goes, he'll be taking people with him, and I wouldn't want you to be one of them." Casey wrapped his hand around his keys, then fixed his eyes on Gage's. "About six months ago we developed an informant high up in the U.S. branch of the United Bamboo triad, I mean *really* high up. He was going to work off a monster heroin case by setting up Ah Ming." He rubbed his neck on both sides of his Adam's apple. "Remember the severed head that was tossed onto the steps of the federal building? That's what happened."

Gage reached out and gripped Casey's shoulder for a moment.

"Don't worry. I'll keep my head. I won't be sticking it out very far. I only need to understand enough to give the kid's family some advice."

"And then you'll walk away?"

Gage nodded.

Even as he responded, Gage was thinking back on his conversation with Burch at the conference room door, remembering his anger that was long in fading and later that morning noticing stiffness in his hands from his clenched fists.

"I'm too old for this kind of thing and you've got youngsters in your group who—"

Casey squinted at Gage, causing him to let his sentence die unfinished.

Gage realized his face must have given away what he was really thinking and why he'd been thinking it: there was a tragedy beneath the mechanics of the crime and it was pushing up into it and into him.

"But there's something else, isn't there?"

"That confused kid never should've been in that warehouse. It's a shame he didn't live to figure out what brought him there, even if he had to do it in the California Youth Authority." Gage paused as an image came to him of Peter lying on the warehouse floor. "Makes me wonder what he was thinking about at the end, and whether that was it."

Casey didn't answer right away, just stared at an airplane rising into the sky from the airport. Finally, he shook his head and said, "Whatever it was, I hope it wasn't that."

Casey unlocked his car door and climbed in. He sat for a few seconds, then said, "The warehouse security guard came by to see me yesterday. Didn't call. Just showed up. Needed somebody to talk to who he thought might understand. He'd heard my name in news reports about that thing with Judge Meyer."

That thing was a gunfight in a San Francisco warehouse that put an end to a massive political corruption scheme. Gage had killed a crooked former CIA operative and Casey had killed his enforcer while rescuing the judge from a conspiracy that had turned against him.

"He told me Peter was scared, terrified, jerking the gun around. He was afraid the kid was about to panic and start firing, so he emptied his gun at him first."

"What did he want from you?"

"Something I couldn't give him," Casey said, now looking up at Gage. "Something nobody could give him. A time machine."

CHAPTER 7

A h Ming pulled down the shades over his office windows facing the warehouse floor, shielding himself from the ordered chaos of laborers and forklifts and order-taking clerks. He removed his suit jacket and loosened his tie, then looked out at the rear parking lot and at the low fog that had been oozing over the western hills and down into the flatlands all afternoon. He watched as a tendril wormed in through the driveway, furtive in its movement. He felt an amorphous threat, a vague but almost physical presence creeping up the alley, slipping along the walls and between the Dumpsters.

What were they calling that kid? Ah Pang? That's right, Ah Pang. The kid with the crazy father.

The sense of threat faded as Ah Ming focused on the broken chain of causes and effects: Ah Pang was the only link between him and the robbery, and the kid was dead. But uneasiness remained. He knew it was only coincidence that Ah Pang had been at the safe house when the *dai lo* picked the crew, but he recognized it was the kind of coincidence that still might lead him to the needle end of a syringe in the death chamber at San Quentin prison.

Ah Ming turned at the sound of the light double knock of his assistant, Lew Fung-hao, and the opening door.

"The police found where the two captured boys were staying before the robbery." Lew's thin seventy-three-year-old face was no more expressive than if he'd announced the arrival of a container of processed garlic at the loading dock. "But otherwise they're flailing around. Their informants have been trying to start conversations in the Vietnamese coffee shops in San Jose and the task force is chasing little *fei jai* around, but they haven't identified anyone connected to us."

Ah Ming glanced at his watch. It was 4 P.M.

Lew anticipated his next question. "The chips are already on their way. That's the schedule Ah Tien gave me before he left."

"I'm worried about Norbert Louie." Ah Ming pointed at a *Tsing Tao* newspaper on his desk. "He's overplaying his part, acting like the stolen microprocessors were his kidnapped children. For the two hundred thousand dollars we paid him, he should've just played it straight."

Ah Ming's mind returned to the thoughts Lew had interrupted.

"Where's the *dai lo* who fucked up the robbery?"

"Ah Tien sent him to Toronto."

Ah Ming looked down at the newspaper again. "The prosecutor keeps talking about the death penalty. I don't want this *dai lo* to roll on us if the police up there catch him." He pointed toward the south. "Contract with someone in LA to go up and break the trail back to Ah Tien."

CHAPTER 8

C ustoms broker Alan Lim was sitting at a window table when Gage arrived at the New World Restaurant near the San Francisco Airport, a lunch hangout for the import-export trade. As he shook Lim's hand, Gage was surprised to find that Lim didn't look much older than he had a decade earlier when Gage had cleared him as a suspect in a shipping container hijacking scheme. He was still thin and angular, forehead higher, but unlined, and his fifty-year-old shoulders remained unrounded.

Hired by a group of Silicon Valley high-tech manufacturers whose offshore subsidiaries had been victimized, Gage sent investigators to Hong Kong, Kuala Lumpur, and Rotterdam, each of whom had traced the conspiracy, and the tens of millions of dollars of losses, back to Lim's company.

After greeting Gage, but before he'd sat down, Lim ordered three kinds of dim sum from a waitress passing by with a cart, then continued the conversation he and Gage had begun on the telephone a few hours earlier.

"A friend I went to school with in Taiwan referred Cheung to me, but I never dealt with him after our first meeting. Only with his assistant, Lew Fung-hao. A mainlander who learned the trade in Hong Kong."

Lim paused, his eyes darting as he thought. It was those quick eyes that had made him seem guilty when Gage had confronted him years earlier.

"Interesting guy, Lew. He was a history professor in Guangzhou before the Cultural Revolution. Suffered one humiliation after another before he escaped to Hong Kong. He strikes me as a bitter man who submerges himself in the technicalities of the trade to try to insulate himself from a world that must still seem irrational."

"Maybe it's to keep from killing himself. One of my wife's students did a study of suicides by aging Red Guard victims. The rate was the same as among Holocaust survivors."

Lim shook his head and sighed. "If my grandparents hadn't fled in the 1950s . . ."

Gage remembered the dead informant on the courthouse steps.

"Since he didn't choose suicide, how about homicide?"

"Lew?" Lim's eyes widened, then his brows furrowed as he peered over at Gage. "Homicide?"

"That's part of what I'm trying to find out."

"I don't see him hurting anyone, even lashing out. He seems more defeated than angry. He's . . ." Lim bit his lip for a moment, his eyes darting again, as though searching for a word. "He's almost robotlike."

Gage didn't express the thought, but in Ah Ming's business, a man who executed orders without thinking was an asset.

Lim looked down at Gage's motionless chopsticks. "You aren't eating much. You okay?"

Gage smiled and patted his stomach. "I'm trying to lose a few pounds."

Lim made a show of surveying Gage's body. "I think you already have."

"A little." Gage deflected the conversation back to Ah Ming. "Has East Wind ever had trouble with ICE?"

"No more than anyone else. A paperwork problem or a missing country of origin or phytosanitary certificate—they import a lot of ginger and garlic—and containers get held and searched. And we're in a position to know. We're the only customs broker he uses. Once in a while we hear that some of his people have been seen going into InterOcean, but I don't think East Wind has ever done business with them. They aren't big enough to handle the volume. Maybe they just have friends there."

"You ever suspect any underworld ties?"

Lim stiffened. In that reaction Gage saw him make a connection back to the subject of homicide. He leaned across the table and lowered his voice. "A few years ago I found out that the friend who sent him to me had become a member of the United Bamboo triad. They've become huge in Taiwan. But I've never heard anything implicating either Lew or Cheung. And I think I would have." Lim gestured toward the suited men sitting at nearby table. "These people don't like him because he always undercuts them in higher profit items, but no one has ever even implied that he has organized crime connections." He shrugged his shoulders. "But sometimes these things are hard to see."

Despite his quick eyes, Lim had failed to notice the infiltration of his own company's overseas branches by gangsters inserted by his wife's brother.

Lim spooned a piece of *ma po* tofu onto Gage's plate. "You should try this. Not too many calories."

Gage snagged it between his chopsticks, then changed the subject. "Have you heard from your brother-in-law?"

"Last year he asked me to visit him in prison. He finally apologized for using our business—using me—as a front. For the first time he took responsibility for what he did, instead of blaming his gambling like it was a separate person making him do things."

"Was he being honest or did he just learn in a prison therapy group what to say so you'll give him a job and the parole board will let him out early?"

Lim smiled. "I don't know. Maybe I'll hire you to go talk to him and find out. You were right about him last time."

GAGE'S CELL PHONE RANG as he pulled away from the curb in front of the restaurant. It was Thomas Sheridan.

"I'm sorry about your son."

Sheridan ignored the condolence and announced in a hammering British accent, "Burch promised me you'll get Cheung."

Gage knew that Burch had neither made that promise nor said anything that could be construed into that promise, but he didn't challenge Sheridan.

"We first need to link him to the robbery and we can't do that yet."

"Then do it," Sheridan said, and then disconnected.

Gage stared at the road ahead. He was tempted to call Burch to get him to back Sheridan off, but decided against it. He could absorb Sheridan's misdirected grief for the few more days until he'd fulfilled his obligation to Burch. After that, it would be up to Burch what he did with Sheridan. Gage guessed that soon enough the balance would shift and the money Burch's firm was making from Sheridan wouldn't be worth the annoyance.

h Ming glanced down at the beeping cell phone lying on his desk displaying a text message from Ah Tien.

Father died. Must come home.

Ah Ming texted back:

Too risky. Stay where you are.

Standing in his New York hotel room overlooking China-town's Hester Street, Ah Tien felt his body turn molten in horror and anger as he read the words. A principle at the heart of his life was at stake:

Eldest sons bury their fathers.
I am the eldest son.
I will bury my father.

From the moment his grandfather died almost a generation earlier, he'd understood this obligation, and it wasn't one he could shake off.

Although his eyes stared at the cell-phone screen, his mind

saw his grieving mother and younger brother sitting at the kitchen table in their little bungalow in San Francisco, surrounded by the blue-gray smoke of incense, waiting for him to return and fulfill his duty.

Even Ah Ming, once a fugitive hiding in Thailand in the mid-1980s, had bragged that he'd snuck back home to Taiwan to bury his father.

He hadn't left his mother to weep alone.

And wasn't that the point—the whole point—of Ah Ming telling me the story? That duty always trumps risk?

But, Ah Tien now realized, Ah Ming had only meant duties owed to him.

The question Ah Tien asked himself as he turned off his phone was simple.

Am I my father's son or not?

Three hours later, Ah Tien answered that question by boarding a flight from Kennedy International Airport back to SFO.

As Ah Tien stepped out of the taxi in front of his mother's house that night, he glanced over at the two young Vietnamese men down the block with their heads shadowed by the raised hood of a white two-door Acura. The scene gave him a feeling of familiarity and predictability, of normalcy. Modifying cars was so much a rite of passage in the neighborhood that the driveway of nearly every house and the pavement in front had been blackened by oil and transmission fluid.

Ah Tien paid the driver, then retrieved his carry-on and briefcase from the trunk and climbed the concrete stairs, the heaviness of his step, weary and grieving, bearing the weight of his duty.

The Vietnamese men alerted to Ah Tien as he emerged into the bright funnel of the streetlight. They watched him glance their way as he ascended the concrete steps to the front door. After he disappeared inside, Minh Duc Le slid into the passenger seat of the Acura and made a call. Moments later, a black cargo van crept up the street and stopped in front of the house. The driver signaled to Le and his partner, who then approached the front door.

When Ah Tien responded to his knock, Le pointed a 9mm at his stomach and said, "Someone wants to talk to you."

Ah Tien knew who and he knew why, and he'd practiced what he'd say during his flight back from New York.

When he glanced down at the gun, he saw that the porch light illuminated a familiar tattoo on Le's wrist: *Tien*. Money. He didn't doubt that Le's sleeve hid four others: *Tinh, Toi, Thu,* and *Tu*. Love, Crime, Revenge, and Prison.

Le and his partner bracketed Ah Tien as they urged him down the stairs toward the van's open side door. Just after Ah Tien climbed in, they pushed him to the floor, then bound and blindfolded him.

Whatever fear Ah Tien felt was muted by grief and by the confidence that the loyalty he'd shown over the years would serve as a bulwark against Ah Ming's anger.

As they drove, Ah Tien heard the silence broken only by the bump and rush of the tire tread on the pavement, the whoosh and rumble of passing cars, and Le's voice directing the driver's turns.

Thirty minutes after they started moving, the traffic sounds began to fade. Ah Tien imagined that they'd driven into the Bayview warehouse district, maybe even to East Wind itself.

The van stopped and then rocked as the side door slid open.

Ah Tien felt himself wrenched from the floor. Cool ocean air struck his face as he tumbled to the sidewalk. His head thudded against the concrete. Hands gripped his upper arms and yanked him onto his knees. Through the nausea and daze of a concussion, Ah Tien heard footsteps approach, certain it was Ah Ming coming to confront him. He searched for the words he'd practiced, the ones that would resonate with their past bond, the culture they shared, and the obligations weighing on them that he knew would save his life.

CHAPTER 10

As his wife drove the winding road up the canyon after teaching her evening graduate seminar, Gage sat by the fireplace of their East Bay hillside home, an unopened book in his hand. The metallic rumble of the automatic garage door broke through Gage's insulation of exhaustion. The sound pushed him to his feet and walked him to the front door.

"Any news?" Faith asked, as he took her jacket.

"Dr. Goode's office called. They'll have the radiologist's report by tomorrow. They want us in the day after."

Faith inspected his face. "How do you feel?"

"The usual. How was class?"

Faith smiled. "The usual."

Gage poured her a glass of wine, then joined her on the couch. They sat in silence, looking toward the bay and the lights of San Francisco beyond. After a few minutes, he leaned back and closed his eyes. Moments later he was asleep.

Faith gazed over at him, then ran her fingers through his hair, looking through the shadow of the coming appointment back at how their life together began.

She never thought she'd ever date a cop, even an ex-cop,

much less marry one. She didn't like guns, didn't like uniforms, and didn't like the rigidity of thought that these entailed.

But this one had been different.

Older than the others in the Berkeley graduate philosophy seminar, he'd sat silently, week after week. Listening. Thinking. The fifteen students were intimidated by him. And it wasn't merely that among those who wanted to believe their pens were mightier than others' swords, he was the only one who'd ever carried a gun. Rather, it was that he wasn't driven to speak by nervousness, by a desire to impress the others, or by a need to ask ingratiating questions of the professor.

The others whispered about him, concluding in the end that he must be brilliant, that somehow he knew it all already.

Faith took a sip of wine and smiled to herself as she remembered the first words he spoke, six weeks into the quarter.

"I'm not sure we've really grasped what Hobbes was trying to tell us."

He then described a homicide he'd investigated, a rape and murder of a child. He wove together passages from *Leviathan, On the Body,* and *Human Nature* with what witnesses had told him, the evidence the crime scene people found, his interview of the murderer, and finally a rival gang stabbing him to death in prison.

Faith remembered the silence in the room when he'd finished. What he said had terrified them, for they'd discovered the state of nature in their own hearts: they'd all wanted to knife the murderer themselves.

It hadn't been the analysis that had captured her, it was how he'd begun.

I'm not sure.

And that was true. He wasn't. He only knew that somehow, if he thought deeply and carefully enough, he'd better understand what had led to those two dead human beings, those two wasted lives, and understanding all that made a difference to him.

Until that moment, Faith assumed that Gage, like the others in the seminar, would go on to an academic career. But it was clear after he'd spoken that this was a man who needed to be in the world and that for him, right and wrong would never be matters only for academic debate. He'd only be in graduate school long enough to get what he came for, and that wasn't long.

He left after two years and went back into the world.

Faith looked out toward San Francisco, the lines of traffic crossing the Bay Bridge, the necklace of lights circling Lake Merritt in the foreground, tugboats guiding tankers into the port. She sipped her wine, enjoying the last of the warmth flowing from the graying coals in the fireplace, and wondering whether there was a wife sitting next to her husband on a couch in San Francisco, looking at the lights sparkling in the hills, and worrying what life-changing words a doctor might say two days later.

She finished her wine and then reached for the two afghans knitted by Gage's grandmother that lay draped on the back of the couch. She covered him with one and wrapped the other around her shoulders, and as the embers faded, she joined him in sleep.

hen Gage looked up, he saw Alex Z entering his office wearing the expectant expression he acquired when he discovered a fact that at least for a fragile moment had deprived the world of its confusions.

"Heard something on the radio just as I pulled into the lot. A homeless guy named Lester Hardiman found Hai-tien Fong murdered last night. Pretty gruesome. Shot in the face. He was ID'd from prints."

The death ambushed Gage like quicksand. He'd hoped to walk through or over Fong to find a connection between Ah Ming and the robbery and then out of the case.

Gage shook his head. "We should've gotten to him."

"No chance, boss. SFPD is saying he'd been out of town on business for four days and only got back last night, less than an hour before he was killed."

Gage and Alex Z both looked over at the wall calendar and came to the same conclusion. Alex Z said it aloud.

"Ah Tien left town the same day as the robbery."

"So did about twenty thousand other people. Call Sylvia. Ask her to get down to the Hall of Justice."

An hour and a half later former SFPD homicide detective Sylvia Washington called back.

"I've been working over my old partner. You were right, Fong's gang name was Ah Tien. He hasn't come up on the task force radar for a long, long time, but they're still thinking it's gang related because he was shot in a way that sends a message, but there's been no mention of Ah Ming."

"You didn't—"

"I figured you'd want to keep that name to yourself."

"Was he killed where he was found?"

"Looks that way. Most of the blood spatter was absorbed by the blindfold, but there was some on the warehouse wall behind him. It must've been small caliber. The slug didn't come out the back of his head."

Gage heard her flipping pages in her notebook.

"It looks like the killer rolled the body back and forth to strip him of ID. Emptied everything from his pockets. Cleaned him out."

"Anybody hear the shot?"

"The beat cops did a neighborhood canvass and turned up a shipping clerk working late who heard a pop. But that was about forty minutes before Hardiman found the body. The witness thought it was a distant backfire. Homicide thinks it's unrelated, but it seems to me it's too early in the investigation to conclude anything."

"Me, too. Where's Hardiman now?"

"In booking. He failed to appear on a trespassing charge a few months ago, so he needs to clear a warrant. As a reward for his cooperation, they'll be citing him out and giving him a court date in a couple of weeks."

"Wait for him. Take him out for breakfast and pump him with coffee. Promise him you'll get him a hotel room for a couple of days, then bring him here."

"No problem. Except I'll have to stop on the way to buy him some shoes. The detectives took his so they won't confuse his tread with the shooter's."

"Thanks. You did a great job."

"Them sharing a little information with me is part of my retirement plan. I gave them twenty-three years, eight months, and four and a half days of my life. It's the least they can do."

next to Sylvia Washington's solid five-eight and one-forty, the man she directed into the conference room an hour later looked to Gage like a scarecrow she'd yanked out of a Dumpster.

Lester Hardiman was short, skinny, hairy, red-nosed, exhausted, and somewhere between forty-five and fifty. He also smelled like three uninterrupted months on the street, and the odor ratcheted up the nausea that now infused Gage's life.

Gage had Sylvia take away Lester's oil-and-grease-caked army surplus jacket and then sat him in a wooden chair on the opposite side of the conference table. He didn't want Lester to leave his grime and stench behind on a cloth one.

"Lester," Gage said, "I know you're just a guy trying to get along, support yourself, and stay out of trouble."

Lester grinned. "Low profile. That's me all the way."

"And you wouldn't do anything that might interfere with us finding out who killed the guy."

Lester nodded.

"So we understand each other?"

"Sure."

"Now, you know what happens when someone gets shot in the head?" Gage didn't wait for an answer. "The bullet goes in, bounces around, then the person dies because his brain stops working."

Lester nodded again.

"And what else happens?"

Lester shrugged.

"Have you heard of blood spatter and blowback?"

"I know what blood splatter is."

"Blood spatter. It's called blood spatter. You know what blowback is?"

"No."

"Blowback is the fine particles of burned gunpowder and blood and brain that explodes back out of the wound. It floats around for a while, and then settles down. It's almost invisible. But it transfers to anything that rubs against it."

Sylvia returned and sat next to Gage.

"Let me ask you something else. You know that someone out there heard the gunshot, right?"

"I overheard the police talking. They was saying it was a backfire."

"I know that's what they were saying, but you know it wasn't."

"I don't know that."

"Of course you do. We both know what really happened."

"You don't know shit." Lester sat up, now trying to stare down Gage.

Gage leaned forward and pointed his forefinger between Lester's eyes.

"Don't try to play the tough guy. You don't have it in you."

Lester blinked, then drew back. His eyes remained fixed on Gage's hand as he lowered it to the table

"First you heard a shot, then the sound of a car drive away."

Lester looked up.

"You searched until you found where the sounds came from. You went up to the body and kicked it with your shoe. When it didn't respond, you got down on your knees and rolled it back and forth so you could get to all his pockets and strip off his watch and rings."

Lester swallowed.

"What gave you away is that you cleaned him out, even took all the change. You shouldn't have taken the change. Real tough guys don't take the change."

"You're lying." Lester's voice rose, then hardened. "I didn't take shit."

"What do you think we're going to find when we check your jacket for blowback?"

Lester reached with his right hand and grabbed his left forearm as if to wipe it off, but all he touched was shirt. He bit his lip and his face twisted.

"What really happened is that you gathered up everything, hid it far enough away so the police wouldn't find it, then came back, found a phone, and called 911. That's the forty-minute gap."

Lester glanced toward the door.

"Don't even think about looking to grab your jacket and making a run for it. It's already bagged and gone."

Lester looked at Sylvia as if for rescue. She stared back. His frightened eyes returned to Gage.

"Are you gonna turn me in?"

Gage shook his head. "You can even keep the dead guy's money, but I'm keeping your jacket and you'll give Sylvia everything else you took. She'll buy you a new coat, rent you a hotel room for a few days, then we're done."

"You gotta promise not to turn me in," Lester said, the desperation in his voice as thick as a prison wall. He swallowed again and rubbed his hands together. "I mean, I can't have this coming back on me. I did a lot of stupid stuff when I was young so I got two strikes. I can't take no more cases."

"We won't volunteer anything to the police, but if they figure it out on their own, you'll have to fend for yourself."

Sylvia motioned with her head for Lester to move on out.

After they left, Gage realized he was sweating under his jacket. He removed it and found that perspiration had soaked through his shirt. In his concentration on Lester, he'd been oblivious to it. He heard a door close down the hallway and wondered whether Sylvia had noticed it, and how he would explain it away.

inety minutes later, Gage entered the second-floor conference room next to Sylvia's office where she was laying
out Ah Tien's possessions.

Sylvia's hand tracked the rows of items as she described what
she found. "Credit cards, address book, business cards in English
and Chinese, a letter in Chinese, an invoice from a luggage outlet
at Kennedy Airport, house keys, a New York hotel bill, and few
pieces of paper with English and Chinese handwriting."

Gage felt Sylvia inspecting him as he scanned the articles,
but she made no comment about the condition of his shirt at
the end of their meeting with Lester or why he'd changed into
a fresh one.

Sylvia pointed at a business card. "If this is legit, he worked
for the LA branch of a company called Great Asia Import and
Export. They also have offices in Taipei and Bangkok." She
turned it over. "Interesting thing. He only used his Chinese
name, Fong Hai-tien, even on the English side of the card. No
Henry or Harry Fong."

"Which means he probably didn't have any non-Asian customers."

"But it sure looks like he has lots of Asian ones." Sylvia reached for the address book. "Lester found this hidden in Ah Tien's sock."

"That's pretty old-school. Maybe he figured the government would break into his contact list on his phone and didn't want to take the risk."

"There are a couple of hundred names in here. Most written in Chinese, but some in English and some transliterated from Chinese into English."

Gage flipped through it. He spotted a name and a Hong Kong address and telephone.

"Some of the numbers are coded. The country code for Hong Kong is 852, not 498."

Gage paged Alex Z, who walked in a minute later.

"See if you can get the country codes to make sense." Gage handed him the address book. "Maybe the rest will follow."

Gage returned to examining Ah Tien's possessions as Alex Z left. Staring at the remnants of the man's life, things of meaning once warmed by the man's body heat and now forever cold, like the man himself, sent a chill through Gage.

"No cell phone?"

"Lester denied even seeing one, even after I told him I'd buy it if it just happened to turn up." Sylvia gestured toward the papers she'd laid out. "What do you want me to do with these?"

"Scan them and have Alex Z put them on the network, and then run everything over to SFPD."

"How will I explain where I got it?"

"Say you were doing surveillance in the area on an insider trading case and spotted the stuff. They won't believe you, but there's nothing they can do. If they lean on you, tell them we're working for Burch's firm and what we're doing is privileged. I'll clue Jack in to be ready if they call him."

"If I was still in homicide and all this turned up now, I'd

be wondering whether Lester stole it and then got scared and dumped it. That means they'll be wanting to talk to Lester again."

"That's the reason I didn't make him any promises. Call Nancy Kramer if he gets busted. She'll figure out a way to make the case go away or at least kick it down the road until our part in this is done."

Sylvia turned toward Gage. "You sure you don't want to tell SFPD about the possible Ah Tien–Ah Ming connection?"

Gage shook his head. "They'll race headlong at Ah Ming and he'll bury anything or anyone who could incriminate him. And SFPD is a sieve. We first found out that Ah Ming is Cheung because a babbling cop told the private investigator Sheridan hired. When the time comes, we'll go see Joe Casey. This is better in the FBI's hands."

The conference room phone beeped. Sylvia answered and put Alex Z on speaker.

"Hey, boss, I got it. It's a plus and minus six system. Plus six on the first number and minus six on the next, then back to plus, and so on. The guy made it too easy. He picked the Chinese lucky number for prosperity. I conferenced Annie Ma in to translate and made a call to Taipei. Bingo. It was the office voice mail of the guy whose name was in the entry."

Gage stood up to leave as Sylvia disconnected. "It looks like six didn't turn out to be such a lucky number after all." He looked down at what remained of Ah Tien's life and shook his head. "What a waste."

CHAPTER 14

D r. Mitchell Goode, head of the Infectious Diseases Department at Stanford University Hospital, pointed at a CT scan displayed on a monitor in the corner of the examining room. The grayscale image showed twenty cross sections of the lower neck and upper shoulders of Gage's body.

Gage sat with his shirt unbuttoned on the end of the exam table. Faith stood next to him, sharing his view of the screen.

Goode pointed at misshapen globs of tissue nestled among the bony structures of Gage's neck.

"These are enlarged lymph nodes. They should be a quarter of the size they appear here."

Goode turned from the monitor and pressed his fingers into the depression between Gage's clavicle and neck muscles.

"Take your fingertips and push down like I did and you'll feel a lump. That's one pushing up against the muscle."

Gage found it as Goode stepped back to the monitor and pointed at the larger of the gray blobs.

"If they'd been bigger or in more accessible places closer to the skin, we'd have noticed them sooner and gone right to the CT scan."

"What does it mean?"

"Not much in itself. But let me show you a few more images."

Goode paged through the scans until arriving at one that displayed a slice of Gage's lower lungs and spine. He pointed with his pen at three globs of tissue suspended in Gage's chest cavity.

"You can see a few more enlarged lymph nodes in this area." Goode gestured toward an elongated mass. "And this is your spleen. Also enlarged."

Goode looked at Gage, his brows furrowed. "Is your appetite a little depressed lately?"

"Some."

"A lot," Faith said.

Goode selected another scan and enlarged it on the monitor.

"This shows your liver and your abdomen. These small bodies are a cluster of enlarged lymph nodes. You won't really be able to make it out, but this area"—Goode circled Gage's mesentery with his pen—"shows some density that is usually associated with inflammation. It may account for the nausea you've had."

Faith reached around Gage's shoulders and hugged him. "So it's just an infection, just like we thought. And the lymph nodes are just reacting to it."

Gage turned his gaze from the scan to Dr. Goode. "Is it the dog wagging its tail, or the tail wagging the dog?"

Goode shrugged. "I don't know."

"What?" Faith dropped her arm from Gage's shoulders and bent down toward the monitor.

"What he means is that he doesn't know which is the cause and which is the effect."

Faith peered at the image and ran her index finger over the light gray lymph nodes and the darker area of inflammation as though she could trace the link between cause and effect.

"We'll need to do a biopsy to find out," Goode said.

Faith turned back. "Cancer? You think it's cancer?"

"No, not necessarily."

"But that's what biopsies are for."

"They can also exclude it and reveal other possibilities, other diseases, even other infections."

"When can we do it?" Gage asked.

"Given your symptoms, I think the sooner the better. Let me make a call."

Goode pulled the door closed behind him as he left the room.

Gage slipped down from the exam table, buttoned his shirt, and stepped over next to Faith still standing in front of the monitor.

"What do you think?" Faith asked.

Gage pointed at the inflammation, then at a lymph node. "I don't think this tail is wagging that dog."

Goode returned a few minutes later.

"I just spoke to one of our head and neck surgeons. He suggested the safest approach is to go after the ones below your collarbone. I told him you'd stop by his office after you left here."

"No problem. If he's going to have a knife at my neck, I think I'd like to size him up."

After Goode left, Gage and Faith walked over to the Ear, Nose, and Throat Department, where Gage identified himself to the receptionist.

A half hour later, a nurse escorted them into Dr. Michael Norman's office. He directed them to sit down, then leaned back against the edge of his desk, facing them.

"I know this may appear to be relatively minor surgery," Norman said, "but there are some risks."

Faith placed her hand on top of Gage's.

"The main one is damage to the accessory nerve, causing numbness and a reduction in your range of motion."

Norman turned his monitor toward them. He pointed to the target lymph nodes.

"The ones we're going for are tucked in right here." Norman placed the tip of a pen on the two overlapping gray spheres on the right side of the cross section of Gage's neck.

"What about a needle biopsy?" Faith asked. "Like for breast cancer."

"We'd have no guarantee we'd capture enough cells for genetic analysis, which is key to choosing the right treatment. We really have to go in."

"Why nerve damage?" Gage asked.

"I'll have to cut through a lot of tissue, move some muscle. It's a critical spot in your body. Neck, shoulders, and arm all link up."

"Aren't there others you could go after?" Faith asked.

"They'd require major surgery and are either near Graham's spine or dangerously close to some major organs, maybe even involved with them."

"When do you want to do it?" Gage asked.

"In the next day or two. I'll have my scheduling nurse call you this afternoon. The operating rooms are heavily booked, but we'll squeeze you in. I don't want this thing lingering."

ylvia, Alex Z, and Annie Ma, were waiting in the conference room when Gage arrived after dropping Faith off at her office on the Berkeley campus. Alex Z slid a spreadsheet across to Gage as he sat down.

"Ah Tien had coded numbers for two inside lines at East Wind," Alex Z said. "Alan Lim confirmed they belonged to Cheung and Lew. They have been the same all the years since Lim started handling their shipments. There wasn't a cell-phone number for Ah Tien, but there was for Lew, and there were both coded and uncoded numbers for import and export companies and for other customs brokers and freight forwarders."

Alex Z reached out toward Gage and pointed at an entry on the list.

"The most interesting one at least as far as microchips are concerned is a coded number for a company named ChinaCom in Shanghai."

"It's a computer and electronics manufacturer in China," Annie said, "for the domestic market."

"Sure makes Ah Tien look like a key guy in the chip operation," Sylvia said. "Steal them here, use local freight forwarders, and smuggle them to ChinaCom."

Alex Z displayed a map of northern China on a monitor hanging on a far wall.

Gage's gaze fell first on Shanghai and held fast. A memory came to him of a visit he made to a Chinese herbalist twenty-five years earlier, looking for a flu remedy before Western medicine had entered the Chinese market. A bespectacled man had collected leaves, twigs, and powders and wrapped them in newspaper. Gage took them to the hotel kitchen where a cook boiled them. Gage first had winced at the acrid odor, then gulped it down, hoping it wouldn't roar back up. As he stared at the map now, he wondered what those herbs, or others like them, might do for whatever his biopsy would find.

"Graham?"

Sylvia's voice brought him back to the present.

Gage blinked, then looked up. "Sorry. I was just trying to figure this out." He pointed at the monitor. "The most direct route to ChinaCom would be to smuggle the chips in through the Pudong container port across the river from Shanghai."

He thought back over the material Sylvia collected from Lester.

"Didn't Ah Tien have an invoice from a luggage store at Kennedy Airport?"

"For a briefcase."

"Maybe he carried back some paperwork inside. It could be in his house. But we'll need his family's cooperation in order to get it."

"What if they're involved in this thing, too?" Alex Z said.

"I don't think they are." Sylvia slid a page across the conference table toward Gage. "This is Annie's translation of a letter Ah Tien's brother wrote to him last—"

"An actual letter?" Gage asked. "Not an e-mail or text?"

"Ah Tien really appears to be a low-tech guy. Old-school in this just as he was with his address book."

"It makes me think even if we find his phone, there won't be much stored on it."

"The kid's name is Winston. There must be about a fourteen-year age gap between them. He's an accounting major at UCLA. It's mostly adolescent complaints about their parents and about Ah Tien, too, for always taking their side."

"The handwriting is a little juvenile," Annie said. "Winston probably learned how to write Chinese characters in an afternoon school over here. Ah Tien's writing is proficient enough that he might've learned in China."

Gage read over the letter. "It looks like they grew up in different worlds. Winston is making fun of Ah Tien for letting their parents choose his wife." He smiled. "There's a line in here about them building a bridge to the thirteenth century and Ah Tien falling through it." He looked at Sylvia. "I don't see this kind of kid being involved in his brother's crimes. See if he's willing to talk to us."

Sylvia and Alex Z remained in the conference room after Gage and Annie left.

"Did he look all right to you?" Sylvia asked.

"A little tired, I guess. Maybe a little distracted. But when he's really into something, he sometimes shuts out the world for a minute or two until he gets what he's looking for fixed in his mind."

"I think it's more than that. He looks gray. And I know he's lost weight. In the few months I've been here I haven't gotten to know him well enough to ask him about it."

"It isn't a matter of knowing him well enough. He's not the kind of guy you ask personal things. And he's not going to tell you anything about himself unless it affects your work. If it doesn't, you'll never know about it." Alex Z shuddered. "Once he called me from Ukraine to check on something and didn't even mention that he'd been stabbed in the back an hour earlier."

CHAPTER 16

Gage's receptionist beeped him at the end of the day, telling him that Jack Burch and Lucy Sheridan were on the phone. He pressed the blinking button and caught Lucy saying, "My father had to leave for Hong Kong this morning."

"I thought your mother would join us," Gage said.

"She decided it would be simpler if she didn't, but I don't understand what she meant. She asked me to pass on how grateful she is that you agreed to help us."

"How does it look?" Burch asked.

"It appears that Ah Ming was involved in something pretty significant recently, but I don't know if it had anything to do with what happened to Peter."

"You mean he's a criminal," Burch said, "but maybe not the right criminal."

"And I'm not in the business of playing Lone Ranger. Unless we can connect him to the robbery, there's no reason to stay with this."

"What did Ah Ming do?" Lucy asked.

"I'd rather not say. My thinking is based too much on assumption and speculation. I'd like to follow up on a couple of leads. Depending on what we find, we may want to hand it over to the FBI and let them finish it up."

"When will we know?' Lucy asked.

"Let's talk in a few days."

"A few days?"

Gage sensed the beginnings of frustration in Lucy's voice.

"That's the best we can do. Hang in there."

Gage's cell phone rang moments after he hung up from the conference call. It was Burch.

"So what did he do?"

"I told you it is mostly speculation."

"So speculate. I won't pass it on to the Sheridans until you say it's okay."

Gage outlined what he learned about Ah Tien.

"That's a lot more than speculation."

"My guess is that if Peter hadn't died during the robbery, Ah Ming would have killed him later. The kid was probably chosen for the robbery by mistake, kind of like a clerical error. And that clerical error was his death sentence."

"And you're thinking it might be better if Lucy and her parents never find out how trivial and inevitable Peter's death was."

"That's part of it."

"What's the other part?"

"Faith and I have spent most of our marriage ten time zones apart. I think we're both tired of living that way. I can see myself lying in a hammock, reading a book in some jungle camp while Faith does her fieldwork. And the only way to do that will be to turn the firm over to my employees."

"Did you get some medical news you're not telling me about?"

"No news at all. And even if there were, it wouldn't affect what I'm thinking."

"And that means that you're going to let this Sheridan thing go?"

"Maybe. Maybe not. Taking down Ah Ming wouldn't be a bad way to end. And I think I can come up with a way to do it."

"If you're healthy enough."

"The symptoms have backed off a little. It might get better on its own."

"Does that mean they're close to figuring out what it is?"

"Almost. One more test and I think this'll be over with."

"What's that?"

"Nothing. Don't worry about it."

"Tell me or I'm going to call Faith."

"A little surgery."

"What kind of little surgery?"

"A biopsy. A minor one."

"There's no such thing as a minor one. Where are you having it done?"

"Stanford Hospital. I'll just be there overnight. In and out. No big deal."

"Of course it is. I'm going to make some calls."

"Jack, don't—"

But Burch had disconnected.

CHAPTER 17

Lew Fung-hao stood near one of the last remaining phone booths in San Francisco's Chinatown reading a nightclub playbill pasted to the side of a fish market. He cocked his head when the telephone rang as though puzzled by why it was ringing with no one standing by to answer it. He shrugged toward the fruit and vegetable vendors a few yards away, then reached for the receiver.

"Hello?"

"Me and my friends are in the other city."

It was Le.

Lew lowered his voice. "Did you destroy Ah Ming's cell phone?"

"Yes. What now?"

Lew smiled at the vendors.

"Go to Tai Ping Travel and ask for Tat Mo. He's expecting you."

Lew hung up, then shuffled away like an old man with no-where to go and nothing to do. He wound through the China-town alleys, then back out to a commercial street of restaurants and offices. He walked until he found a cellular outlet and bought a pay-as-you-go phone. He then stepped into the recessed doorway of a residential hotel and sent a text message to Ah Ming:

All is well.

AH MING READ THE WORDS, then leaned back in his chair and looked at the calendar. All he needed to do was replace Ah Tien, he told himself, and everything would continue as planned, and as it always had. But he knew he was deceiving himself for he was on the needle end of two capital murders: Ah Pang and Ah Tien.

Tension pushed him to his feet. He held out his hands and stared at them. At moments like these he saw them for what they were and recalled the day thirty years earlier when they transformed from flesh and bone into weapons, when they'd beaten a gambler to death in Taiwan who hadn't paid a debt to United Bamboo.

At the time the act had seemed like a kind of metamorphosis. He later came to understand it was more a moment of revelation about himself to himself. For he'd come to recognize it hadn't been guilt he'd been feeling as he looked down at the man's body, but rather an almost incomprehensible combination of power and shame. He'd had the gambler under control with the first blow. There'd been no reason for a second, even less for the fatal third one.

Ah Ming turned his hands over and inspected the lines on his palms, troubled not by the deaths of that man or of Ah Tien or of the dozen others over the years, but by Ah Pang's. He was certain he could dominate men, the killings were proof of that, but the coincidental was uncanny and unnerving, and too much like a fortune-teller's prediction that mirrored a reoccurring nightmare.

'm just pulling away from Winston Fong's house," Sylvia said in a call to Gage. "I snagged him when he walked to the corner store. He's nervous and wants to meet in a public place outside of San Francisco. I suggested Jack London Square."

At 7:45 P.M., Sylvia and Gage were sitting at a wrought-iron table watching the tourists, the seagulls, and the moneyed high-tech young intermingle on the Oakland waterfront.

At 8:00 she tilted her head toward Winston emerging alone from the underground garage. Gage rose and once again offered his condolences to a grieving sibling.

"We're looking into a number of things," Gage said, after they sat down, "and one of them is the death of your brother."

"The detective came by this morning to look around Hai-tien's room," Winston said, "but he didn't spend much time and didn't take anything." He smirked. "I guess when he didn't find drugs or guns or a gang sweatshirt and matching cap he lost his enthusiasm."

Gage let the sarcasm pass. He knew part of the reason SFPD was stumbling around in the investigation was because he had yet to share what he knew with them. And he couldn't. Spike Pacheco, the last of his generation in the homicide unit, had retired and Ramon Navarro, the best of the new generation, had been cross designated as a federal agent and sent to Michoacán to help the Mexican police and DEA in investigating cartel murders.

Delay would do no harm anyway. Gage never accepted what was called the forty-eight-hour rule when he was in homicide, and even if there was such a rule, he knew that discovering the truth about Peter Sheridan's death would be the exception.

"Did the detective ask you anything?"

"Not this time. The night my brother was killed he asked if Hai-tien had any enemies or gang affiliations. But it was less like he was investigating a crime and more like he was drawing a line on a flowchart or filling in a blank, and ignoring the possibility that the answer might be none of the above."

Winston inspected Gage's face through his wire rim glasses. "Are you trying to fill in a blank, too?"

Gage shook his head. "Our focus is on who killed your brother and why, not on blank filling, and we have some ideas we're working on."

"Which are?"

"I'm sorry, but I'm not ready to share them."

Winston reddened, opened his mouth to speak, then hesitated. Finally he nodded and said, "I did some Internet research about you after Sylvia left this afternoon, so I know the kind of work you do. And I called a friend's father who's a lawyer with a big firm in Beverly Hills. He said they hired your firm last year on a government contracting fraud case in Iraq and that you recovered something like forty million dollars. He was surprised you were interested in just a homicide."

"There's no such thing as *just a homicide*. A life is a life."

Winston shrugged. "You know what I mean. Because my brother did some things he shouldn't have almost twenty years ago, the police seem to be blaming him for his own death."

Gage imagined Ah Ming had been thinking the same thing, that Ah Tien brought it on himself.

"We'd like your help, but we don't want you telling anyone what we're doing. If the wrong people start thinking we've figured out this homicide might be connected to something they want hidden, they'll come after us."

"Okay."

"Not even your mother?"

"Okay."

"Not even your friend whose father is a lawyer in Beverly Hills?"

Winston smiled and nodded. "What do you need?"

"To start with, your brother may have brought a briefcase back with him from New York."

"There's one in his room, but I don't know how long it's been there. The detective looked inside, but he just left it. I guess he didn't find anything important. You can have it if you want."

"Does your brother have an office at the Great Asia Import and Export in LA?"

"Just a cubicle in a room with other sales reps. I'm going back to UCLA tomorrow and I can see whether his supervisor will let me take what's there that belongs . . . I mean . . . belonged to him."

Gage tilted his head toward Sylvia. "She'll fly down with you and bring it all back, and maybe you can get her into the place where he lived down there."

"I can get the spare key he left with us, but the house is pretty bare. Monklike. A lot like him, or at least how he became in the last five or ten years."

"Became how?"

Winston hunched forward, paused for a moment, then spoke.

"I guess you could say that in some ways he was more in my parents' and grandparents' generation than mine. He went to a trade fair in Shanghai a few months ago, then down to Guangzhou to meet a woman my folks had picked out for him to marry, like it was 1930."

"Is that where your parents are from?"

"And where he went to elementary school. My parents know a lot of people in Southern China who have daughters they want to send to the States and they wanted a daughter-in-law that spoke Cantonese, like them."

Gage smiled. "Has your mother been looking for a wife for you?"

"That's a whole different problem that Chinese culture hasn't prepared her for. I've read all the old texts, but there don't seem to be arranged marriages for gay people."

"Lucky you."

"Lucky me."

Gage circled back. "You know whether he traveled anywhere else in China besides Shanghai?"

"I don't think so, unless taking the five-minute ferry ride across the river to Pudong counts as going somewhere else. I know he was there because he wrote me a postcard from the top of the Oriental Pearl Tower talking about how much of Shanghai he could see. He never said much about his work. I think the only reason he told me about Shanghai was because I needled him about picking his own wife."

"What about Taiwan?"

"I know he was there a few years ago, when I was still in high school. He showed me some Taiwanese money when he got back."

"You said the police are still taking a hard view of him because of things he did when he was young."

Winston pointed his thumb toward San Francisco across the bay, now overlaid by the evening's fog.

"You remember when the Wo Hop To triad came from Hong Kong and tried to take over Chinatown?"

Gage nodded. That was almost twenty years earlier.

"My brother was in the Stockton Street Boys. Until Wo Hop To showed up, all they did was stand around and look tough. If the police hadn't taken them seriously, not that many people would have."

In fact, that wasn't true. The Stockton Street Boys were the muscle protecting gambling dens and houses of prostitution, extorting protection money out of restaurants, and committing takeover robberies of Chinese homes down the peninsula.

But Gage didn't challenge him.

"Everything changed when the Wo Hop To guys came from Hong Kong and recruited the Stockton Street Boys to join them. They couldn't just look like hard guys, they had to do stuff or get pushed off the streets. There was a shoot-out where a couple of rival tong heavyweights got killed. The police always believed my brother was involved."

"Did he get arrested when Wo Hop To finally got rounded up?"

Winston nodded. "But he wouldn't snitch and there wasn't enough evidence to prosecute him, so they had to let him go. I think the arrest may have scared him out of the life. I never saw him with any of his old Stockton Street friends after that. He went to work at East Wind and then moved down to LA. My folks were really proud of him, and grateful, too. A few years ago he bought the house we live in."

"Even with the best intentions," Gage said, "some guys have a hard time leaving that life behind. The adrenaline rushes. The money. The women. The power."

"He wanted all that stuff when was young, but after the shootings, he became just a face in the crowd. A lot of Stockton Street Boys hooked up with United Bamboo, 14K, and Big Circle, the triads that filled the vacuum Wo Hop To left, but Hai-tien turned into a working guy."

"He make any money at it?"

"A lot." Winston looked away for a moment and his brows furrowed, then he shook it off and said, "But it didn't seem like he was under a lot of pressure. Wasn't always scratching for clients. He had his regulars, and it looked to me like he was satisfied with those."

"You ever meet anyone he worked with?"

"I went by his office a couple of times and he introduced me to a few people, but I don't remember their names."

Gage leaned forward, folding his arms on the table.

"Now, here's the tough one. Why do you think your brother was killed?"

Winston shrugged. "I don't know."

"You think you'll be ready for the answer if we find it?"

"I don't know that, either." Winston took in a breath and blew it out. "I think I can live with it, but I'm not sure my mother can. Losing her husband and son back-to-back has really torn her apart."

"DON'T YOU THINK Winston has a theory about what happened to his brother?" Sylvia asked as they walked toward her car in the underground garage.

"The kid is an accounting major. He knows there's no such thing as a free lunch, and Ah Tien wasn't working very hard for what he got. My guess is that Winston fears what we know. By refusing to cooperate with the police against his bosses in the Wo Hop To, he proved he was a stand-up guy. Somebody noticed and he got himself promoted."

"And that's why Ah Ming walked Ah Tien into the Eight Dragons Café."

"Exactly."

Sylvia unlocked her car doors and they got in.

"You want to meet tomorrow when I get back from LA?" Sylvia asked, turning the ignition.

"I'll be busy. Let's do it the day after."

She looked over. "Are you going out of town?"

Gage avoided her gaze. "No. I'll be local. You can reach me by phone."

"Anything wrong?"

"No. Just something I need to take care of."

CHAPTER 19

G age and Faith arrived at the Stanford Hospital reception area at 7 A.M., an hour before his scheduled surgery. They found that the OR was as busy as Dr. Norman had predicted, and Gage was wait-listed, a standby passenger for a trip to the unknown.

He surveyed the room. The surgical patients wore their private hopes and terrors on their faces as they waited to be distributed among the operating rooms. Based on age, sex, fragments of quiet conversations, and the tears, grunts, and limps that accompanied them as they entered, he guessed what had brought some of them to this place: a mastectomy along the wall to his left, a hip replacement across from her, a heart bypass in the corner—

And a biopsy biding his time at the near end.

It wasn't until the early afternoon that Gage finally got his turn.

IT SEEMED TO GAGE that it was only moments after the anesthetic took effect that he awoke in the recovery room. He lay there unfocused, trying to recall what had brought him into this confusion of light and steel. He felt an itch under his chin, then reached up and worked his fingers over the gauze wrapped around his neck and down a plastic tube protruding from the incision.

Now I remember, Gage thought to himself. *Today's the day they're going to decide the course of the rest of my life.*

Gage tried to look around to see if there was anyone to give him the answer he'd come for, but his head felt sewn to the pillow. He struggled against it and tried to sit up.

A hand gripped his shoulder from behind and locked him in place.

"Whoa there, partner," a male voice said, "you're not quite ready for a walk in the park. Hang on a little longer. We're gonna be rolling you outta here in a few minutes."

Gage looked up at the nurse, a skinny man who looked to be about thirty-five with a farm-boy face. "I was thinking I would step out for some coffee, Tex."

Even to himself, his words sounded slurred, but the nurse's smile told Gage he'd understood.

"There are just two problems with that. One, despite this being California, the coffee in this place is lousy, and, two, you'd fall flat on your face."

After the nurse released his grip, Gage felt himself drifting off again, and then arriving in a Costa Rican rain forest he and Faith had once visited. Lying in the hammock, he could feel the humidity, hear the rustle of leaves on the jungle floor, and smell the loamy soil. Faith was dressed in a floppy brown hat and was walking among the ferns beneath the tree-formed canopy listening to the chirps and songs of the birds, and peering down among the heliconias and up into vermilion poró trees.

He opened his eyes to see Faith standing above him.

"Graham? Graham?"

Gage blinked against the bright fluorescent lights. "What time is it?"

"It's about six."

"When did we . . . How long have I been . . ."

"They brought you in here a few minutes ago."

Gage blinked again and looked around the pale green hospital room. Dr. Norman was standing next to Faith.

"The operation went fine," Norman said. "I was able to get into the tight areas and take out two lymph nodes more easily than I'd anticipated. I don't think there was any nerve damage."

"I think that was my second question."

Gage caught Faith's eye. She never could lie to him. He knew the answer and looked back at the doctor to receive it.

"I'm sorry. It's lymphoma. Non-Hodgkin's. I had pathology examine a sample during the operation. I think the nature of your work and where you've traveled interfered with our coming to the correct diagnosis sooner. It pointed us in the wrong directions like a broken compass, toward places where you might've encountered pathogens, instead of internally. It looks like you've had a slow-growing form for quite a while without knowing it, and then it transformed and turned aggressive. We'll have a more specific diagnosis by tomorrow."

Gage looked over at Faith, "I guess the tail wasn't wagging the dog."

Norman looked back and forth between them. "The what?"

"It's nothing, it's just the way he predicts the future."

"Which is?" Gage asked.

"We can't know that until we do some staging to see how far its spread."

FAITH RETURNED FROM WALKING DR. NORMAN to the hallway in time to see Graham drift off again.

She'd also guessed that the tail wasn't wagging the dog. She'd thought she was prepared for the results, but she wasn't, and wasn't sure how anyone could ever be. She stared at his sleeping figure, then sat down by his side, laid her head on his chest, and wept.

She'd already searched the National Cancer Institute Web site and applied the research skills she'd mastered over a lifetime to the diagnosis.

There wasn't a cure.

CHAPTER 20

After the nurse checked him out the next morning, Gage and Faith walked the long sidewalk from the hospital to the Stanford Cancer Center. They entered to find a series of glass-walled rooms—and he saw his future in the faces of those who'd arrived ahead of him: thin, pale, hairless victims of radiation and chemotherapy seated alongside their wives or husbands or children, some waiting for their doctors to take the measure of their lives, others waiting in their sickness to learn whether they were healthy enough to continue chemotherapy, still others deadened by failed hopes.

Gage gave his name to the receptionist, then he and Faith found two chairs along the wall.

"Hey, it's the coffee drinker," a man seated to the right of Gage said in a familiar drawl.

Gage looked over. "Tex? I mean, what is your name?"

"Tex'll do."

"What are you doing here?"

"This is what got me into nursing. I got leukemia about ten years ago. Came out here from Dallas for treatment. I loved the place, loved the people. Felt like it was time for a career change.

So here I is." Tex smiled. "This is what I call sweaty palms Wednesday. Every couple of months I walk over here and they check me out."

"How many times you been through chemo?"

"Twice and a bone marrow transplant."

"And how do things look now?"

Tex shrugged. "I'll find out in a few minutes."

Gage watched Tex's eyes go vacant for a moment. He suspected that Tex knew more than he was saying.

Tex changed the subject. "I heard from the surgeon that the grim reaper is looking you over, too. You here to get signed up for treatment?"

Gage shook his head. "This is just an oops-made-a-mistake-so-sorry-you-don't-have-cancer-we'll-all-do-lunch-and-laugh-about-this-later appointment."

"That's what we call a big mistake meeting, and they don't have those here."

"How about a small mix-up meeting instead?"

"They had that yesterday."

"When's the next one?"

"There isn't a next one, they're always yesterday." Tex tilted his head toward the bandage covering Gage's incision. "Which kind you got?"

"Non-Hodgkin's. It was slow growing for a long time, then it went a little nuts."

"Ouch. That's the tough one. Even if they clear out the wild stuff, you're still gonna be left with the creeping cancer you started with—and it's gonna get ya."

"You know if they take trade-ins?"

Tex smiled again. "Only on small mix-up days."

A nurse carrying a file folder called out Gage's name.

"See you around, Tex."

"Good luck, partner. I'll be pulling for you."

The nurse escorted Gage and Faith to a counter where a clerk sat in front of a computer monitor.

"You've been assigned to Dr. Stern. She'd like to see you right away. I should be able to squeeze you in this morning."

"Anytime is fine."

"I think maybe by 11:30?"

"That sounds pretty close to anytime. We'll be here."

"Stop by on your way out and I'll give you a radiology requisition form for an MRI of your head. You'll need to get it done in the next few days."

Gage felt Faith's hand tighten in his. They both guessed that the point of the MRI was to determine whether the cancer had reached into his brain. They walked back to the main hospital building, bought coffee at the café, then went outside to sit on benches in the flower garden near the entrance.

"You didn't seem surprised by the diagnosis," Faith said, "and it wasn't just because of the anesthesia hangover."

Gage shrugged. "We'd pretty much run out of other possibilities. I figured that's what it had to be, so I decided I'd better just get used to it."

They drank in silence watching patients and those with them coming and going, knowing that they, too, would be among them for the rest of Gage's life. After fifteen minutes, Gage stood up, tossed their empty coffee cups into the recycling bin, and looked back at Faith.

"You ready?"

Faith leaned forward and rested her arms on her thighs. She then took in a long breath, let it out, and rose to her feet.

"Ready."

Gage took her hand and they walked back inside.

ylvia and Alex Z were waiting for Gage in the conference room when he arrived at the office the next day. Even though he wore a turtleneck sweater under his sports jacket to conceal the tape-covered incision, he could tell when he entered that Ah Tien wasn't the first item on their agenda.

"What's going on, boss?" Alex Z asked.

"I do the same thing for a living that you do," Sylvia said "and I know something is up."

"I was going to talk to you about it in a few days. But I guess now is okay."

"Thanks," Alex Z said, "we've really been worried about you."

Gage closed the door behind him and sat down.

"But let's keep this among ourselves; the rest of the staff doesn't need to know yet. Everyone's jobs are secure, and I don't want them distracted from their work."

"It's not our jobs we're worried about," Alex Z said.

"I know." Gage folded his hands on the table and tapped his thumbs together. "I've got lymphoma. It's a blood cancer that attacks the immune system. It seems I've had it a long time, but it's only now showing itself."

Alex Z and Sylvia leaned forward.

"Have they decided on what kind of treatment you'll get?" Sylvia asked.

"Not yet. I have more tests coming up."

"But it's going to be all right," Alex said. "I mean, they're going to stop it, aren't they?"

"There'll be some ups and downs, but it'll be okay in the end."

Alex Z exhaled. "You had me scared for a minute."

Gage watched Sylvia's gaze lower and he knew what she was thinking. Unlike Alex Z, who'd spent years only questioning data, Sylvia had spent her career questioning people, listening to them lie.

Sylvia slammed her fist on the table, then looked up again. "It's not fair. How come the scumbags live forever and it's the good people that get hammered like this."

Gage shrugged. "There are a lot worse kinds of cancer. I wish I'd found out sooner, but that's life."

Alex Z looked at Sylvia. "What do you mean?"

Gage answered for her. "She just means that it may be a tough road."

Sylvia didn't respond for a moment, and then said, "Yeah. Sure. That's just what I meant."

GAGE WATCHED HIMSELF as they returned to the conference room after filling their coffee cups in the kitchen. He felt a hollowness, as if work had become abstract and he with it. He knew he'd always had a tendency to see the world in relationships, almost graphically, but now he felt himself to be at once the artist, the object, and observer.

He sat down across from Alex Z and Sylvia. "Why don't you take us through what you picked up from Winston."

Despite the gray haze of cancer that filled the room, Sylvia began.

"The key things seem to be Ah Tien's passport, a visa application, part of a cell-phone bill, and a bunch of incomplete invoices and bills of lading for a company called Sunny Glory and shipping instructions to InterOcean customs brokers."

Sylvia slid over a packet of forms.

"These bills of lading are for garlic from a Sunny Glory branch in Taiwan to their branch in the U.S. There are more for rare mushrooms, but the names of the companies are left blank. Ah Tien listed someone named Chau at Sunny Glory in Taiwan as a reference on his business visa application when he renewed it a couple of months ago."

"What about his passport?"

"It reads like a road map. Taiwan, Hong Kong, China. Five trips in the last five years. The passport control stamps show he always entered China through Shanghai."

Gage examined the papers lying on the conference table. He didn't want to try to draw too many conclusions from them, but one thing seemed clear.

"Either he was too grief-stricken to know what he was doing when he packed his briefcase or he was trying to send a message that only someone looking for it would understand."

He tapped the Sunny Glory forms.

"And my guess is the latter. He knew he was taking a risk by coming back to San Francisco. He held Ah Ming's whole offshore operation in his hands. He's the guy the FBI would want to catch and roll. He knew it and Ah Ming knew it."

Gage imagined Ah Ming as a wolf caught in a steel trap, chewing off one of his own arms to escape. Except he knew Ah Ming was the sort of monster who could grow another one.

"If Ah Tien was able to bury his father and get out, then these papers wouldn't mean anything. Even if Ah Ming happened to get a look at them, it would only appear that Ah Tien had been sloppy."

"Why didn't he just send a letter to somebody he trusted outlining the scheme?" Alex Z asked. "Like in the movies. Don't open unless something happens to me."

"First, because it would be evidence of disloyalty. Ah Tien might've been wrong about Ah Ming's intention to kill him. And second, it's a matter of face, not face like *mianzi,* what the Chinese call prestige, but *lien,* moral character, personal responsibility. He would've risked the life of whoever he sent it to."

"*Moral character?*" Sylvia said, her tone rising in sarcasm. "Tell that to Peter Sheridan's mother."

"Take it easy." Gage raised a palm toward her. "You need to look at this from within Ah Tien's world and try to understand what he was thinking and what he was likely to do." He pointed at her. "You really think he'd put it all in a letter?"

"Based on what we know now . . ." Sylvia shrugged. "Not very likely."

"And there's something else. If we go out hunting because we wrongly believe a letter exists, Ah Ming will find out and start looking, too. And if the letter doesn't exist, the body count could get pretty high while he fails to prove the negative."

"And Winston and his mother will be lying on the bottom of the pile." Sylvia bit her lower lip for a moment. "I think I screwed up. I should've set up security for Winston."

"The time may come, but it's too soon. Ah Ming has no reason to think anyone has focused on him in connection with either Ah Tien's murder or the chip robbery."

Gage gestured toward the papers.

"Ah Tien left us a road map. The question is whether it represents the road he already followed or the road we're supposed to follow to catch his killer."

"There's another question," Sylvia said. "Don't we need to turn all this stuff over to SFPD?"

"They had a chance to take the briefcase and chose not to.

We're under no obligation to give it to them. That's the law. For now it's ours. If Winston tells us the detectives have come back for it, then we'll return it to him to turn over to them."

"You're talking like you'll be able to finish this," Sylvia said. "You think you'll be able to?"

Finish.

The word startled him. He almost didn't hear the question that followed it. He knew what she meant: finish Ah Ming. But he knew that in her sense he hadn't even begun. He'd told himself from the start he was only going halfway. Just far enough to make the link between Ah Ming and the robbery, then get out.

He thought of his coming medical appointments, the staging of the disease to determine how far it had spread, and the coming decisions about treatment.

He knew that either way, the answer would be the same.

"That's out of my hands."

"ny change from last time?" Dr. Louisa Stern asked Gage after she entered the examining room in the cancer center.

Her words echoed in the sparse room. Cabinets. Pneumatic exam table. Sink. Chairs. The click of hard heels and the squish of soft soles on the linoleum-floored hallway beyond the closed door.

"Not as bad."

"Nausea?"

"A little."

"Dizziness?"

"Occasionally."

"Unbutton your shirt. Let me check for any changes in the lumps."

Stern felt along the inside of Gage's collarbone, under his chin, and pressed hard into his armpits.

"Where's Faith today?"

"She had a class to teach. I told her I'd bring her back a sucker."

Stern laughed. "Sorry, I'm fresh out." Then she tilted her head toward two bone marrow biopsy syringes laying on the counter. "You ready?"

"Have you been working out?"

"Every day."

"Then I guess I'm ready."

"I can give you a muscle relaxer. That may make it easier."

Gage shook his head. "I'll pass. I need to be alert later. I'm working on something."

Stern pointed toward the end of the exam table.

"Take off your belt and unbutton your pants, then lean over and slide yourself up. I need good access to your lower back and hip."

Gage did as instructed.

Stern pulled down Gage's slacks just far enough to expose his hips, then rubbed alcohol over his right hipbone and injected a local anesthetic.

"I'm going after some of the liquid, then after the bone marrow itself."

Stern poked at Gage's anesthetized skin with the needle and asked, "Can you feel that?"

"Only pressure, no pain."

Gage then felt all of Stern's hundred and thirty pounds lean into his hip and the corkscrew motion of the needle. He caught his breath as the hollow needle broke through the outer shell of the hipbone and drove into the marrow. She aspirated some of the liquid marrow, detached the plunger from the syringe, and set it on the counter. He then heard her attach another one.

"Now comes the hard part. Try to stay relaxed."

Stern began rotating the needle, driving it harder, forcing a sliver of bone and marrow up into the needle.

"Hang in there, I've almost got it."

Then she released the pressure.

Gage breathed out and pain iced through him as she extracted the needle.

"Jeez . . . I didn't expect that."

"That's the one you're supposed to get the sucker for. Too bad I'm—"

"Fresh out."

Gage belted his pants, then took a few steps around the examining room, testing his right leg.

"I don't think you're the squeamish type. You want to see what I took out?"

Stern held up a liquid-filled glass vial in which there stood an inch-and-a-half sliver of bone and marrow about the thickness of a small nail.

"Don't worry, it'll grow back."

"I'm not worried." Gage flashed a smile. "I didn't figure you'd break something you couldn't fix."

"I'll have the results the day after tomorrow. Then I'd like to bring in a few youngsters and put together a treatment plan."

"A little show-and-tell?"

"We're a research and teaching hospital after all and we need the Graham Gages to keep the kids entertained."

Gage eased down onto a chair next to Stern's. "I've been doing a little research myself. No one seems to know why normal cells mutate into cancer cells. It seems like an evolutionary misfire."

"All evolution, good and bad, is fundamentally a matter of mutation. It's just that this mutation makes a particular individual less able to survive in the environment."

"I think that's what Charles Darwin called extinction."

"It would be, except he didn't know about chemotherapy."

"But why lymphoma? I can't find anyone who claims to have found what causes it."

"There is no known cause. Not pollution, smoking, diet. It's nothing you did to yourself."

Gage smiled again. "So it's like a guilt-free cancer?"

"No one has ever described it that way before, but you're right. A guilt-free cancer."

"Lucky me."

Stern smiled back. "No one has ever said that, either."

CHAPTER 23

Gage picked up Faith at the Montgomery Street BART Station in San Francisco to drive to the closing dinner of the annual meeting of the International Fraud Investigators Association.

"How was class?"

"Like pulling teeth, but at least no one was drilling into my bones."

"Intro?"

"Yeah. And I finally figured out why all those football players registered for it. They signed up when they thought Alistair was still going to teach it. Looks like he's been giving free honey to the Golden Bears for the last ten years. By the time he got suspended for that ménage à trois in the library, it was too late for the team to drop the class." Faith laughed. "One of them is a smart aleck with a neck and face like a walrus. He asked me if he could do a term paper on what he called the function of voluntary associations in generating team loyalty in major college athletics."

"You mean he wants to study cheerleaders?"

"You betcha."

"Will you let him?"

"Why not? I might learn something. I've never understood that whole pom-pom thing."

A few minutes later, Gage pulled into the driveway of the Mark Hopkins, a Spanish renaissance hotel on the crest of Nob Hill overlooking the city. He retrieved a file folder from the backseat, then handed his ignition key to the valet.

Jacques Matteau, the association president and director of the French *Brigade Centrale de Répression des Fraudes Communautaires,* spotted them as they entered the lobby.

"Why the limp?" Jacques said after kissing Faith on each cheek and shaking Gage's hand. "I hope you haven't gone back to fighting crime with your body instead of your mind."

"It just got a little rough on the basketball court yesterday. A pick-and-roll that didn't work out right."

The Peacock Court room was nearly full with the thousand conference attendees seated at the round banquet tables or milling about in the spaces in between, glasses of wine in their hands. As Jacques guided Gage and Faith toward the head table, members waved at Gage or came forward to greet him.

Jacques seated Gage and Faith to the right of the podium on the elevated, flower-adorned table, then walked to the microphone and banged a gavel. The gunshot-like cracks of mahogany on oak shut mouths and turned heads toward the front.

"I'd like to welcome all the members and guests to this closing dinner and thank everyone who made this conference such a success. Represented here tonight are the premier fraud investigators in the world, representing hundreds of law enforcement agencies and investigative and security firms from over sixty countries. The most representative group ever. I know you're anxious to hear from our keynote speaker, but first things first."

Jacques signaled the waiters poised at the doorways, then seated himself to the right of Faith. Gage overheard them talking as he ate his salad and reviewed his speech, writing in some changes. He sensed Faith peeking at him, then set down his pen, reached under the table, and rested his hand on her thigh.

It's okay.

Later, when his dinner plate had been removed, Gage's eyes fell on the evening's agenda.

Opening remarks
Dinner
Awards
In Memoriam: Juan Cortez-Sanchez

In Memoriam. Gage had forgotten about that part of the annual program. With a couple of thousand members worldwide, some die every year. Usually they retire and leave the organization before they do, so nothing is said. But Juan, Spain's most skilled terrorist financing investigator, was still a member and way too young to die.

Keynote Speaker: Graham Gage

Gage suffered a morbid dyslexia. The text morphed, appearing to read "Keynote Speaker: Juan Cortez-Sanchez. In Memoriam: Graham Gage." He forced himself to look away, trying to focus on the chandeliers hanging bright and heavy from the ceiling. But he could just as well have been looking up at a rain cloud, and for a moment he wished it was and that he and Faith were back in Costa Rica.

As Jacques resumed his role as master of ceremonies, Gage felt his mind wandering off, abandoning his body.

"Juan was a twenty-year member . . . a friend to many in this room . . . selfless . . . brilliant . . . too young . . . long bout with cancer . . . his wife is here to accept . . ."

"Graham Gage . . . our keynote speaker . . . youngest recipient ever of the Lifetime Achievement Award . . . received last year at the Paris meeting . . . I present to you the man I like to call the diagnostician of deception and the philosopher of fraud."

Jacques moved back from the podium and gestured Gage to approach. No one in the room could have failed to notice Gage's smile transform into a grimace as pain attacked his hip when he straightened up. After he stepped up to the podium, he steadied himself by gripping the raised edges of the top until he felt his leg hold firm.

Jacques leaned over and pulled the microphone toward him.

"If Graham is going to insist on continuing to play basketball, perhaps we can add another training session to next year's schedule: The proper execution of the pick-and-roll."

Gage felt his face redden in response to the crowd's laughter. He wondered which was worse: being rightly known to be undergoing a painful search for the extent of his cancer or being viewed as physically incompetent. He shook off the thought, then held up his hand, acknowledging the laughter.

Gage adjusted the mic, then looked about the room at the many familiar faces. An image of Juan slid into his consciousness. Blanket covered, hunched over in a wheelchair at a Spanish hospice, gray, shriveled, hollow eyed, waiting to die. He felt a restlessness in the crowd, opened his file folder, and began.

As Gage came to the end of his prepared speech he realized he couldn't remember much of what he'd said. He recalled moments of applause and laughter and, more than anything, two thousand eyes peering up at him and him wondering what they were seeing, or maybe who they were seeing, for he knew that he wasn't exactly the same man they had seen in Paris.

Jacques approached the podium clapping. He put his left arm on Gage's shoulder and said, "How about a few questions?"

Without waiting for a response, Jacques pointed at a young woman at the nearest table, whose words were lost in the mumbling crowd.

Voices from the back yelled out, "We can't hear . . . speak up."

"Let me repeat the question," Gage said. "It was about my references to the evolution in fraud and the methods used by crooks. And did I have something deeper in mind." Gage paused, the thought still unfinished in his mind. "The short answer is, yes. The slightly longer answer goes something like this: We typically catch crooks because most frauds, in fact most crimes, are cookie-cutter jobs. They're based on paradigms, so to speak. The crooks who are a little smarter than the rest combine these paradigms, sometimes in unusual ways."

An image of Ah Ming flickered in his mind.

"The smartest crooks, the most dangerous ones, adapt these paradigms to a changing environment. That is, crime evolves. That's not news. However, my evolution reference points toward something else. It's this: Every adaptation is also a liability. Let me say that again: Every adaptation is a liability. Why? Because it creates a new dependence on the environment."

Gage looked down at the questioner. She reminded him of Sylvia Washington as a young San Francisco detective. Intent. Earnest. Serious.

"And when the environment changes, the adaptation fails and . . . sorry, I don't know your name . . ."

"Cynthia Fairbourne, National Criminal Intelligence Service, London."

"Cynthia, you can complete the sentence, the adaptation fails because . . ."

"We're part of the environment."

"Exactly. We're part of what the crooks adapt to and once we figure out the adaptation, we can make it a liability."

"But what if we can't adapt," Fairbourne said. "Like now,

criminals are using encrypted e-mails and text messages. Since we don't have the computing power to break in, we don't know what they're saying. What then?"

"We just have to work smarter. And we don't necessarily need to know what's in them in order to focus our investigations."

Gage looked away from Fairbourne and let his eyes sweep the crowd.

"How many of you worked narcotics in the 1980s?"

A hundred hands went up.

"That was before cell phones were common. All the dealers used pagers and pay phones, too many to intercept. We didn't know what they were saying. Every crime seemed to be a black box. But we learned the paradigms and became experts in surveillance. When Crook A did X we learned that Crook B would do Y."

He paused and punched the air with his forefinger for emphasis.

"Remember, once they commit themselves to e-mail, even encrypted ones, they're dependent on the environment they have adapted to. Just like a letter or text message, every e-mail has to start somewhere and end somewhere. We got lazy in the '90s and the early 2000s when the crooks got addicted to cell phones. All we needed were wiretaps and they kept snitching themselves off. But those days are over. So . . ."

Gage raised his eyebrows and nodded at Fairbourne, and she completed the sentence:

"Learn the paradigms and work smart."

CHAPTER 24

Instead of taking the bayside freeway through San Francisco south past the airport and the industrial flank of the peninsula toward Palo Alto, Gage cut inland across the commuter traffic and mall-ridden flatlands and broke out into the coastal mountains. He and Faith let their minds drift as they watched the deer grazing on the hillsides and hawks circling against the blue sky and the light shimmering on the distant reservoir. A twenty-five-minute vacation from worry—

That ended when he turned east and they spotted the sign for the Stanford Linear Accelerator Center.

They both made the same association: accelerator-nuclear-radiation-cancer.

The vacation was over.

A half hour after Gage had blood drawn, a nurse escorted them into a conference room in which Dr. Stern was waiting, along with a male oncology resident and a female research fellow.

After Stern introduced them, the resident shook Faith's hand and smiled at her.

"I'm sure you don't remember me, Professor."

"I'm sorry?"

"I took one of your classes, about ten years ago. It was wonderful. I spent the whole quarter lost in fantasies of traveling the world, going to remote places like you. I almost changed majors."

"Thanks, but right now I'm truly grateful you didn't." She reached out and touched the young man's shoulder. "We'll be needing your help."

Stern directed Gage and Faith to one side of the conference table, the doctors to the other.

"Before we start," Stern said, "let me say that we've discussed these results with the tumor board. I called a multidisciplinary case conference at the radiation oncology department this morning."

Gage felt himself launched by the phrases "Tumor board and a multidisciplinary case conference" into a world structured by people and facts and titles and organizations and events that were as alien to him as a physics lab. And he knew he'd better find his bearings or risk losing himself to what he didn't understand. He'd done it before, in the early days of his career when he'd learned to operate in the dope world or how to investigate homicides. But that was all about other people's bodies, not his own—except the time he was shot. That was simply a race against death. Rough emergency room medicine. Stop the bleeding and wait. There was nothing for him to learn, it was just a struggle against the darkness.

"At this point, we have a very clear picture of the disease and its progression. The bad news is that you're already at stage three. The good news is that the bone marrow biopsy was negative."

Faith slipped her hand inside Gage's under the table and squeezed it.

"The extent of the disease accounts for some of the symptoms, the nausea for example."

"And the dizziness?" Faith asked, and then held her breath.

"The MRI showed that the cancer hasn't spread into his brain."

Faith exhaled.

"We suspect, however, that one or more of the enlarged lymph nodes are putting pressure on one of his arteries, which in turn reduces oxygen supply, causing the dizziness."

"Then why isn't it constant?" Graham asked. "It's happening less lately."

"In the short term, moving about repositions the point of contact and may reduce the pressure. In the long term, lymphoma can wax and wane. That is, shrink enough to stop interfering with blood flow."

Stern slid over two blood test summaries, one based on blood drawn earlier that day and one taken at the time of his biopsy.

"I've highlighted the tumor markers, ones that tell us about the course of the disease. The changes confirm that the lymphoma has mutated very recently, maybe just in the last month or so, and has become aggressive."

"Which means?" Gage asked.

"That we should begin treatment before it turns into a wild-fire."

Gage caught the motion of the resident nodding.

"During the first few weeks you'll be able to carry on normally, but after that you'll start to experience some of what appear to be worsening symptoms, nausea for example, and you'll be at increased risk of infection as the chemotherapy depresses your immune system. You'll need to take some time off and you'll need to make sure you are no more than twenty minutes from an emergency room. It's a good idea to plan for it now. It will be a rough regimen, but we need to match the aggressiveness of the treatment to the aggressiveness of the disease."

Gage noticed he was facing a wall of medical books and journals behind Stern. He scanned the alphabet: *American Journal of Clinical Oncology. British Journal of Cancer. Bulletin du Cancer. Leukemia and Lymphoma.*

What's it come down to?

"Are you ready to give us the bottom line?" Gage asked.

The resident stirred in her chair. The researcher stared ahead.

Stern's eyes remained fixed on Gage, and then said, "We know that, at least, we can shrink the tumors."

"But the cancer will still be there," Gage said. It wasn't a question.

"Unless there's a revolution in the treatment of your type of lymphoma, it won't go away."

"And the tumors will start growing again."

"Yes."

"How many times can you stop it?"

"Maybe twice. Maybe three times."

"For how long?"

"I don't know. As little as one month. As long as eighteen months, maybe even longer."

"So basically what you're saying is that one way or another, later or sooner, it's going to kill me."

Gage winced as he said the words. He knew he was pushing too hard and Faith wasn't ready. He held her hand under the table in apology.

"You're healthy in every other way, so yes, in the end."

"What about clinical trials?" Faith cut in. "I've been reading where . . ."

"Right now we're trying two variations on the best available treatments to see which is most successful in extending the time to recurrence."

"So I'll play guinea pig?"

"Sort of."

Gage scanned further down the alphabet: *Medical Oncology. Pathology and Oncology Research. Radiotherapy and Oncology.*

His eyes drifted back to *Pathology.*

Gage pushed it to the end. They both needed to know.

"Assuming I don't get run over crossing the street, what exactly will I die of?"

"Pneumonia. Your immune system will eventually fail."

Gage heard Faith take in a breath. He remembered her father dying, suffocated by fluid collecting in his lungs. He reached his arm around her as tears formed in her eyes.

Stern, Faith, and the others stood up to leave. Gage remained seated. He looked up at Stern. There was a question left.

"You said there's such a thing as a complete response," Gage said.

Stern nodded.

"What are my chances?"

"I can't answer that with any precision. It's one of the things we're trying to find out by doing this comparison. But whatever response you have will be time limited since we can't eliminate the cancer at the DNA level."

e're going to have to pass on the Sheridan case," Gage told Alex Z and Sylvia when he stepped into her second-floor office. "I need you to write up what you've done so far. I'll forward everything on to Joe Casey. The FBI can take over."

Seeing them standing close together, Gage had the feeling they had been waiting for him.

Alex Z peered up at him. "What's going on, boss?"

"I'll need to take a little time off, so it's time to phase out."

"You're talking about chemotherapy, aren't you?" Sylvia asked. "I'm so sorry. What can I . . ."

"Just carry on with your work."

"Have you told the rest of the staff? I've heard people talking, wondering why you haven't been checking in with them. I even got a call from Derrell in London asking if something is wrong."

"I'll do it later today." Gage looked at Alex Z. "Set up a conference call so people out of the country can listen in."

"Can't we take a break, let things lie for a while, and finish after your treatment?" Sylvia asked.

"By the time I'm done and able to work again, the chips will have made it to wherever they're going and will have disappeared into new computers. It'll be as if it never happened. The case is out of our hands, whether we sit on what we know or give it to Casey."

"But there's no way Casey can do it." Sylvia's tone was flat, no sign of the frustration he knew she felt. "And I figured out what you were going to do. You weren't going to hand this case off to the FBI. If it weren't for the diagnosis, you would've gone to China and worked backward to Ah Ming yourself."

Gage smiled. "I knew hiring you was a brilliant move."

Sylvia didn't smile back.

"You think the Chinese are going to cooperate with the FBI? Their economy is built on theft, and their police are infiltrated with gangsters. Everything we've done will just end up in a file box somewhere."

"I'm not sending any of our people over there." Gage spread his hands to encompass the three floors of investigators. "No one else in the office has the kind of connections I have in China, and without them it's too dangerous. And remember, that file box is called intelligence. Someday the FBI will get another chance at Ah Ming and our stuff will help." He looked back and forth between them. "That's how it has to be, so let's wrap this up."

Gage returned to his office to call Burch in order to arrange a final meeting with Lucy. He also needed to begin following his own orders by preparing an investigative memo for Casey to accompany the data and reports.

As he sat down at his computer and opened a new document, he felt a kind of finality, like he'd come to accept the reality of the possibility he'd presented to Burch: that it was time to hand the firm over to his staff and follow Faith around the world. And now, staring at the blank screen and reaching for the keyboard, he felt like he was about to write his professional last will and testament. He'd always told his staff that investigators were only as good as their last case, and this was his.

CHAPTER 26

Faith paused at Gage's office door carrying a binder of her lymphoma research. She observed him in profile as he focused on his screen. She watched him type a few words, then glance to his left, reaching for some papers near the windowsill. He looked up as though something outside had caught his attention and paused. After a few moments, he shook his head, then moved a sheet closer to his keyboard.

A quarter of a century, Faith thought to herself. *A quarter of a century. Where did it go? If only I could stop time, get some of those years back.*

She knew that they hadn't been wasted; they were just gone, lost in the infinity of the past.

What is it about time? she asked herself. *It marches, grinds, skips, flees, stops. What does that mean, time stops? It doesn't stop. It just seems to when the mind can't deal with the present.*

Time doesn't stop, the mind just freezes.

Time.

What is time?

I know. I know exactly. It's an acid that eats away at life.

GAGE TURNED AND LOOKED AT FAITH, but now she didn't see him.

"I was just there myself," Gage said to her.

Faith blinked. "Where?"

He pointed to the side of his head. "In here."

He got up from his chair, walked to her, and folded his arms around her.

"I'm sorry," Gage said. "You don't deserve this."

"No, Graham. I wouldn't trade a minute, not a second . . ."

They held each other in silence, in their private universe, then Gage took her hand, interwove their fingers, and they walked back into the world.

THE GLARE OF THE NOONDAY SUN, ricocheting off glass and steel of nearby buildings gave the street a clarity, a distinctness of color and shape that was rare in the city. Even the surface of the windless bay seemed as flat and shiny as a sheet of gray-blue steel.

They walked a few blocks inland to Wushan Garden and entered through what used to be the driveway of the converted auto repair shop. The owner waved at them, and then hurried through the crowded restaurant toward them.

"Graham, why you not call?" Danny Tang said in his restaurant English. "I got no table."

"We'll wait. I wasn't sure what our plans would be. I didn't want to leave you with empty seats."

"Come to kitchen. I show you something."

"I'd like to, but Faith and I have some things we need to talk through."

"Go ahead." Faith smiled and tilted her head toward the back of the restaurant. "We have time."

Danny led Gage through the dining room toward the steaming, rattling, banging, sizzling sounds of his kitchen. They ducked though swinging doors, past the flaming woks, and into the walk-in refrigerator-freezer.

"Look at this one." Danny pointed at a forty-pound halibut

hanging from a hook. "I caught early morning outside Golden Gate. How much you like? I drop off this afternoon."

"That's a beauty, but I couldn't."

"You better say. I bring anyway."

"Okay, but only enough for Faith and me for dinner tonight."

When Gage returned to the dining room, Faith was sitting in a booth sipping tea with the clinical trial literature lying unopened on the table.

"What poor, unsuspecting creature did Danny yank from its watery home this time?"

"Halibut."

"I thought he was a salmon guy."

Gage shrugged and smiled. "I guess it got away." He picked up his menu. "You know what you want?"

"It's not in my hands. Danny's wife told me she wants to try a new dish on us. Something vegetarian she said even you would like."

Gage shook his head. "Why does everyone suddenly want to turn me into a guinea pig?"

"It must be your soft fur," Faith said, running her hand down the back of his head.

He glanced back toward the kitchen. "I hope it isn't something with eggplant."

"I was looking out for you. She promised. No eggplant."

Gage pointed at her binder. "So what does the Internet have to say about my chemical dip?"

"Everything confirms what Stern said. All the first-line treatments are pretty much the same, chemotherapy plus an antibody to target the fast-growing cells."

"So it's kind of a crapshoot which one we go with."

"That's not the recommended language. Apparently the proper medical phrase is equally efficacious."

"I'm thinking that maybe I should do it at UC San Francisco,"

Gage said. "That way we won't have to drive down to Stanford for every infusion. Maybe they can send her the progress reports and I can still get my checkups with her."

"Stern figured you might want to do that and also get a second opinion before you start, so she e-mailed me a list of doctors." Faith took a sheet from the binder and passed it to him. "These are the lymphoma people."

"Sounds like a horror movie."

"Sorry, lymphoma specialists."

"Stern is all right," Gage said, looking down the list. "I like a doctor who's not afraid of being second-guessed. I'll make some calls this afternoon."

Danny approached the table gripping a steaming plate of mushrooms and broccoli in one hand and a bowl of noodles in the other. He served them a little of each, then stood back.

"I am thinking of this for the menu. It's up to you. You two like it, it's on. You not like it, it's off."

Faith picked up a sauce-covered piece of broccoli with her chopsticks, placed it in her mouth, closed her eyes.

"Absolute heaven," she said. "You don't even need to listen to him. A second opinion isn't necessary."

Danny looked down at Gage and grinned. "It's even better with eggplant."

urch and Lucy arrived at Gage's office late in the afternoon. He asked her to wait in the lobby while he spoke to Burch in the conference room.

"I don't want to put you in a difficult position with your client," Gage said, sitting down across from Burch, "but I prefer she doesn't know why I'm giving up the case."

"Where do things stand now?"

"There's no question about it. Ah Ming was behind the robbery."

"Not that. I mean with you."

Gage hesitated.

"The bottom line." Burch said the words with a tentativeness telegraphing that he hoped he was ready for the answer.

Gage watched Burch's hands grip the table edge.

"They can shrink it back a few times, but they can't stop it. At least I'll be able to see the end coming."

"That's a cheery thought."

"It's a lot better than being blindsided."

"Actually, it isn't." Burch's voice hardened. "And that's how you're different from me and everyone else I know. The rest of us just want to die in our sleep. No one wants to look it in the face, except you."

Burch paused and his face reddened as if he'd grasped that he'd misdirected his anger, then asked, "How much time?"

Gage shrugged. "A few years, guaranteed."

"Is Faith doing okay?"

"It's hard because we never play let's pretend, but she's getting by."

Gage glanced in the direction of the lobby. "I don't want to keep Lucy waiting too long."

Burch didn't respond, as if unwilling to let go of the moment, then nodded.

"I'm pretty sure the chips are on their way to China," Gage said. "The problem is that the direct link between Ah Ming and the crime got cut."

"Cut?"

"Murdered."

Burch's eyes widened, then narrowed. "Let's tell the Sheridans that this is now something for the FBI or ICE to take over," Burch said. "You agreed to stay with it only as long as it took to find out whether Ah Ming is responsible for Peter's death. You've done that."

"But I don't want Sheridan doing something foolish. Ah Ming won't even let him crawl away if he shows up there again."

Burch paused, his active eyes seeming to watch an idea work itself out. Then he asked, "Don't they have the right to the information? They hired me and I hired you. That means they own it."

"Send the retainer back."

Burch thought for a moment, then nodded. "That'll do, but since Sheridan is my client, I'll cover your costs, too."

"It's not your problem," Gage said. "It's an investment in my peace of mind." He rose to his feet. "I'll finesse it with Lucy."

CHAPTER 28

Hold my calls," Gage said to the receptionist when he arrived at the office the following morning. "I need to finish something before I head out for a meeting."

Gage poured himself coffee in the kitchen, then began to review the reports prepared by Alex Z and Sylvia. Ten minutes into it, an intercom beep jabbed though the envelope of his concentration.

"I'm sorry, Graham," his receptionist said, almost whispering. "But there's a woman here. She says she has to speak to you and won't take no for an answer."

"Who is she?"

"Peter Sheridan's mother."

Gage sighed. He didn't look forward to lying to a grieving mother, particularly since he didn't know whether it was for her benefit or for his own. To tell himself that it was both felt too much like a self-serving accommodation.

As he slid aside the reports, he wondered why she'd chosen this moment to come out of hiding, but then decided he didn't care about the answer.

She wasn't his problem.

He glanced at his watch. He had to leave in twenty minutes if he was going to have time to pick up Faith at the Embarcadero BART station and make it to UC San Francisco for his appointment.

"Put her in the conference room. Get her some coffee or tea or whatever she wants. Tell her I don't have much time."

Gage printed out the list of questions he and Faith had prepared for the oncologist, folded it, and stuffed it into the inside pocket of his suit jacket. He then walked down the hallway strategizing about how to get rid of Linda Sheridan. He had nothing to say to her that he hadn't already said to her daughter, and he'd moved on, not to another case, but to another life, or what was left of it.

Linda Sheridan sat facing away from the door, a cup of tea sitting in front of her on the table. Her black hair concealed all but a glimpse of her gold earrings.

"I'm Graham Gage," he said, as he took the last step toward her and reached out his hand.

Linda slid back her chair, then struggled to her feet and turned to face him. Soft eyes looked up at him. She didn't offer her hand. She just stood there, unmoving, like a memorial to some ancient time. A tremor shuddered through him as he was wrenched backward from mature, reflective thoughts of death, to a youthful terror, looking up from the oil-stained pavement of a narrow Chinatown alley at those same eyes staring down from an apartment window.

"Ling?"

"Yes."

"How . . ."

Gage gestured for her to sit down and took a chair next to hers. He leaned forward and took her hands in his.

"Where have you been? Casey told me you left witness protection."

"I couldn't take the isolation. They gave me a new name and dropped me in a small town in Iowa where every Chinese person worked in a restaurant or a dry cleaner. That wasn't what I wanted for myself, so I went back to Hong Kong."

"You shouldn't be in San Francisco. What if someone recognizes you?"

"I needed to see you." Her face was heavy with sadness. "About Peter."

The name jerked Gage back into the present.

"Linda Sheridan . . ." Gage felt racked by the vertigo of two worlds crashing together.

"I met my husband in Hong Kong. I went to college there and got a job as an account manager at the bank he used. He insisted the children and I move back to the U.S. when he started to have doubts about how the mainlanders were managing the takeover."

"Why didn't you come see me before? Why didn't you come with Lucy?"

She shrugged. "Partly because I wanted to escape from the reality of what Peter had become. Partly because Peter was a creature of my isolation. And partly because I crossed a bridge to get away from the world I met you in." She looked down at their hands. "Maybe it was because I lived so many years in fear of exposure it became a way of life."

"Why now?"

She looked back up. "Lucy told me you decided not to continue."

"There's nothing more I can do."

Gage hated himself for lying. Shame, and then anguish welled up in him. He felt like begging for her forgiveness. He was about to respond to her truth, the truth that saved his life and his career, with a lie.

He looked away. "I've taken it as far as I can."

Linda waited until Gage looked at her again, then stared into his eyes, searching for something.

Gage let her find it.

"Thank you, Graham," she said, wrapping her hands around his. "I understand."

Linda rose again and walked from the room, her limp tearing into the fabric of time.

What could she possibly understand? Gage asked himself in the hollowness she left behind. *That she risked everything for me and I bailed on her the only time I'll ever have a chance to repay her?*

What's life for, if not to spend on something decent?

Isn't that the real question?

Isn't that what she did?

CHAPTER 29

I need to postpone my treatment." Gage told Dr. Stern after he and Faith sat down in her office at Stanford. "There's something I need to do. It'll take two weeks, maybe three."

"Unless you're planning to discover a cure for lymphoma during those weeks, I'm not sure you have the time. You're not that far from stage four. Suppose it invades your kidneys, or liver, or stomach, or brain? The chances of stopping it plummet. Even if that doesn't happen, what good are you going to be doubled up in some hotel bathroom?"

Stern glanced down at Gage's open medical file, then shook her head. "Where, exactly, do you intend to go if I can't stop you?"

"China. I don't know where else."

"Acupuncture, fish eyes, and elk penis aren't going to stop the disease or even help with the symptoms."

Stern turned to Faith. "What do you think?"

"I don't want him to go, but I understand why." Faith paused and bit her lip, then said, "If you agree, then I can accept it."

Stern turned back to Gage. "Tell me."

"It's a personal thing," Gage said, touching his chest.

"Does it have anything to do with that scar?" Stern pointed at him. "It looked like a .357 or a 9mm. I worked in the emergency room at SF Medical before going into oncology. I handled four or five gunshot victims a night."

"I can't answer that."

"There's such a thing as a doctor-patient privilege. Spill it."

Gage paused and looked at Faith. She nodded.

"You don't repeat any of this and all you put in my file is that the patient decided to delay treatment. No explanation."

"You've got a deal."

Gage nodded. "A long time ago I was a homicide detective in San Francisco."

"I know."

"How do you know?"

"When I am not forcing patients to get the treatment they need, I read the papers, I watch the news. It's an odd thing. A psychologist"—she glanced at Faith—"or maybe an anthropologist, needs to look into it. When people get cancer and show up here, somehow they start to think they're anonymous, maybe because cancer shuts them off from the world, maybe it's because people who spent their lives caring about others are forced to focus on themselves. It's very human. In fact, it's more than a matter of anonymity, it's like they feel invisible. But they aren't. And you aren't. So, years ago . . ."

"My partner and I caught one of three overnight homicides. Ours was typical for Chinatown in those days. Execution style. No known witnesses. But then an old informant named Snake Eyes paged me as I was leaving the victim's autopsy late the next afternoon. He put in 911, meaning urgent, and our code for where to meet.

"We'd done a lot of big cases. Sometimes he informed for money, sometimes to get out of jail. We did a lot of damage to the tongs and triads.

"By the time I drove up, Snake Eyes was already at his spot by Portsmouth Square, leaning against a restaurant wall across from where the old men play mah-jongg. I grabbed a city map and walked up to him, playing tourist. He glanced at it as if helping me with directions then pointed toward Spofford Lane and whispered to me that he knew where the killer in my case was hiding."

"Was he after money again?" Stern asked.

"And to get his brother out from under a federal gun case. Twenty-year minimum. I was willing to make the deal because I was close to nailing his brother on an extortion case anyway, so it didn't make a difference. He'd do at least ten."

Gage spread his hands. "Spofford Lane is like a box canyon. Six-story buildings framing the end of the street, like an echo chamber."

He thought back on the cascading clicks of mah-jongg tiles from the second-floor gambling parlors and the thud of cleavers dismembering chickens and splitting pork ribs, the sizzle of fat hitting wok oil, kitchen workers yelling and laughing.

"It's odd that after all those years the sounds I heard there are as real as my cell-phone ring is now."

"Were you scared to go in there?"

"A little edgy. I didn't intend to walk in too far. About a third of the way down, Snake Eyes stops and turns toward me; the expression on his face wasn't like we were finally getting to the heart of what he had to say, but like resignation."

Gage shook his head.

"I can't say I even heard the gunshot. Just felt the slug punch into my chest. Actually it was less than a punch, more like somebody poked me with their finger. I turned to run, but my legs went out from under me.

"I spotted a dead-eyed Chinese guy step around from behind

a Dumpster, then I looked up at Snake Eyes. All he said was, 'Sorry, man; they got my sister.'

"I heard footsteps and grabbed for the Beretta in my holster, but hands locked onto me and held me down. A Vietnamese guy yanked it out. I was as scared as I've ever been. I figured they were going to finish me off with my own gun.

"The guy stood over me, rolling the gun over his hand. Then he fired. Not at me. At Snake Eyes. At first Snake Eyes didn't get it. He just stood there, with his hands wrapped across his stomach, blood oozing through his fingers. He dropped to his knees and his expression changed when he grasped that he'd been set up just like he'd set me up. The shooter kicked him in the ribs, knocked him over, and slammed the side of his face into the blacktop."

Gage paused, now remembering the silence in the alley, the shots snuffing out the kitchen sounds, freezing the gamblers and cooks in their places.

"Remember, they still had me pinned down. The shooter wiped off the Beretta and forced it into my hand. He pressed the barrel against the back of Snake Eyes's head and used my finger to pull the trigger.

"I was sure I was next. A two-for-one. But then they backed away. I'm trying to stay conscious. Hoping I could ID somebody, but they evaporated. I looked up and searched the apartment windows. They were as dead as blank television screens. Except one. There were these two eyes staring down at me. And that was the last thing I saw before I passed out."

Gage shook his head as he thought about what happened next.

"I had already been suspended by the time I woke up in the recovery room. The only reason I was alive was because somebody called 911. There was lots of bad publicity. Headlines about a rogue cop executing a gangster. I figured it would blow over. But six weeks later, the case was at the grand jury."

Stern raised her hand. "But how could—"

"The FBI took over the investigation and turned up three eyewitnesses who claimed I shot Snake Eyes first, then Snake Eyes shot me back in self-defense, and then I finished him off before I collapsed.

"But a couple of weeks later, people in the department were telling me an FBI agent named Joe Casey had refused to close the case even though the DA was a few days away from indicting me. So I called him up."

"Didn't you have an attorney fighting for you?"

Gage nodded. "Hired by the Police Officers Association. The kind that yells in court about how his clients are innocent, then cuts deals. And he was pushing me to take a manslaughter offer from the DA. If I pled out, they wouldn't charge me with murder. Instead of twenty-five to life, I'd do a flat fifteen, and the department would avoid a long trial with bad publicity.

"Casey only agreed to meet me if I brought a letter saying I was representing myself and signed a Miranda waiver. We met at the alley an hour later.

"Based on the evidence he'd been looking at, I guessed what had been bothering him. The first thing he'd done was examine Snake Eyes's shirt. A guy in the property room showed it to me after Casey had looked at it. What had troubled him was the footprint, the ball of somebody's shoe—"

"Which meant that somebody had kicked him over and—"

"The tread mark didn't match mine."

Gage held up two fingers.

"The second thing was the gunshot residue pattern. It was on my fingers and my windbreaker. Not the back of my hand or my palm.

"As we were standing out there, Casey was getting annoyed because I was reading his mind."

Gage pointed down.

"He had his briefcase in his hand and I guessed what was in it. I told him to show me the photos. One showed the blood spatter pattern on the pavement. I traced it out. It meant that Snake Eyes's head had to have been in contact with the blacktop, left side down, but the witnesses claimed I was standing over him when I shot him.

"He gave me some lame excuse about witnesses not being computers, but I knew what he was really saying. The DA couldn't ignore eyewitness testimony in a high-profile case and still get reelected."

"But there was another witness."

Gage nodded. "A terrified one. Her uncle denied it was her and claimed she was in school at the time of the shooting. And she'd said the same thing to the detectives when they caught up with her."

"What about the record of the 911 call?"

"It was local and it came from a phone booth. But I was sure it was her. Her voice. She was the only one out there who did anything to save my life and I figured that meant that she wanted it saved for something more than me serving fifteen years in prison."

"Why didn't you go over . . ."

"And see her myself? I was afraid of being accused of witness tampering.

"A long week later, Casey called. His first words were, 'I talked to her today. Her name is Ling and she remembered something. Something she couldn't have gotten from television reports." Gage gripped his biceps. "It was the bruises on my arms and shoulders where they'd held me down. They showed in the photos that were taken in the hospital. Everybody thought they were from the paramedics.

"He also told me that an hour after he left her apartment, some gangster sprayed it with about fifteen rounds. Ling caught one in the hip and one just above her knee."

Stern covered her mouth.

"Her uncle lucked out and was at a doctor's appointment. One went straight through the back of the chair he always sat in. Despite all that, she was still willing to testify."

"But could she identify the men who shot you?"

"She knew them all. She worked in a massage parlor in Chinatown. Her boss had to pay for protection and the women—"

"You mean she was a prostitute?"

Gage nodded. "But she'd been saving her money and going to community college during the day."

"What about the three witnesses?"

"They confessed in a heartbeat when Casey threatened to prosecute them as accessories after the fact. The gang paid them ten grand up front and they were supposed to get another ten after I was convicted."

Stern seemed transfixed as Gage came to the end of the story, lost in a final image of Ling, now Linda Sheridan, emerging from hiding to testify against those who'd shot Gage and murdered Snake Eyes, then fading away. Cut off from family and friends, alone and isolated by a secret defining her adult identity.

"Did they let you see her?"

"After her last day of testimony. Casey set up a meeting at the DA's office in the Hall of Justice."

"What did you say? I mean what could you say?"

Gage stiffened. "I'd rather not talk about that. Let's just say I thanked her and hadn't seen her since, until yesterday. Her son got involved with gangsters like those ones who shot me. He was killed. He was only sixteen years old. A confused and angry sixteen."

"Can't anyone else . . . ?"

"No."

Stern looked at Gage, weighing something in her mind.

"Excuse me a moment," Stern rose and left the room.

Faith rose also, then crossed her arms across her chest and shivered. "Why do they keep these places so cold?"

Stern returned a few minutes later carrying a prescription pad.

"I still think you're dead wrong to do this, but I looked at the CT scans and your blood work. You're still under the thresholds we talked about."

She sat down at the desk and began writing.

"Take your own syringes if you have any doubt about safety, particularly in China." She tore off the prescription and handed it to him. "Use them to get some blood drawn and get it tested every week."

Stern looked down, thought for a moment, then wrote again.

"This is for nausea. I'm not sure how much it'll help, but it may a little. As for the dizziness, you're going to have to live with it." She slid over the prescription and started on another. "And if any of these symptoms interfere with your sleep, take one of these."

"What do you want me to do with the blood results?"

"I'll e-mail you a list of values and the range of increases or decreases for each one that we can accept. If the results exceed those parameters, I need you to come home. You understand?"

"Yes," Faith said, looking over at Gage. "He understands."

"I want to hear my patient say it."

Gage nodded. "I understand."

Then he felt Faith's eyes on him. They both knew something Stern couldn't know: that when he came home—or even whether he'd come home alive—wasn't entirely in his hands.

CHAPTER 30

J oe," Gage said walking up to Joe Casey in a booth in Denny's in San Jose, "this is Sylvia Washington."

"Nice to meet you." Casey stood and shook her hand. "I saw the news coverage when you went down." He smiled. "At least you got the bad guy. How's the shoulder?"

"Good as new."

Gage knew it wasn't, but that's all she'd ever say about it.

After the waitress poured them coffee, Gage laid out his theory about Ah Ming shipping the computer chips to China.

"Tell me what you need," Casey said, "and I'll tell you if I can give it to you."

Gage slid over a list of the company names Alex Z had abstracted from the documents in Ah Tien's briefcase and the papers Lester Hardiman had taken off his body.

"The most important thing I need to know is whether there's any criminal intelligence information on these companies."

Casey read down the list and set it aside. He then took a sip of coffee as he ordered his thoughts.

"First, I know what you're going to do next." Casey raised his palms toward Gage. "But don't tell me. I don't want to end up in the middle of a diplomatic explosion if you get caught and are seen as a proxy for the FBI.

"Second, since whatever I find may involve active cases and informants, all I'll be able to tell you is whether or not the names of these companies have come up in other investigations and whether you're on the right track. I won't be able to give you details.

"And third, if anyone asks, you're just a guy I knew a very long time ago."

"How soon can you find out whether any of the local companies just shipped out a container?" Gage pointed at the list. "Especially Sunny Glory. It's coded in Ah Tien's address book. It has offices here and in Taiwan and shows up in some shipping documents."

"I'll call ICE this afternoon. The rest will take a couple of days." Casey paused for a moment, then said, "And there's one more thing. Ah Ming's been a crook for thirty years, maybe more. No one has even gotten close to getting him, and this may be the only chance for the next thirty years. Like my wife would say, it's like the planets are aligned. You're the only one I know who has the connections and savvy to maybe pull this off. But be careful; there are too many bad ways this can end."

GAGE'S CELL RANG as he and Sylvia drove out of the Denny's parking lot. It was Casey.

"Hey, man, is Sylvia okay? She said nothing during the whole lunch. I heard she was a pit bull when she was a cop, but today she was more like a lapdog."

"It's nothing." Gage glanced over at her in the passenger seat. "Just a complicated case and she's new to the international angles. That's all."

Gage disconnected, then pulled to the curb in front of a car lot and looked over.

"What is it?" he said.

"I don't think you should be doing this."

"The other day you told me you really wanted to get this guy."

"That was the other day. This is now. I did some research. If they're telling you to get treatment, you should do it, instead of—"

"I got a note from the doctor and a hall pass, too."

"I'm being serious."

"So am I. I made a deal with one of the best oncologists in the country. If things start to go bad, I'll come back."

"I still don't like it." Sylvia stared ahead at the cars driving by. "I never told you this because I thought you'd think I was a wimp, but when the department dumped me after I got shot, I went into a tailspin. They had guys over there who were too fat to get in and out of a patrol car without greasing up, and they dump me because my shoulder couldn't do a 360. Being a cop was my whole life. If you hadn't shown up . . . I mean, when you walked into my room in the physical therapy department, it was like I had something to hold on to, like I was worth something again."

"So you figure you owe me something?"

"Exactly."

"And if I needed you to take a risk, you'd do it?"

"In a heartbeat."

"And I owe Peter's mother something. She went to the limit for me and I'm doing the same for her."

CHAPTER 31

G age got another call from Casey as he was parking his car behind his building. He was surprised he had gotten back to him so soon.

"I need to see you," Casey said. "I'm at First and Market. I'll swing by and pick you up. Three minutes."

"What's up?"

"I'll tell you when I get there."

Gage walked out to the sidewalk. Casey drove up a few minutes later and Gage got in.

Casey gripped the wheel with both hands. He didn't look at Gage. He hit the accelerator, pushing them back hard against the seats. He sped along the bay for two blocks, then stopped in a red zone in front of a pier.

Only then did he turn to face Gage. "What the fuck do you think you're doing?"

"What do you mean?"

"There was something hinky about what happened at Denny's. I just called Faith and told her I was worried about you and made her think I knew what was going on. And she spilled the diagnosis."

Gage felt his face flush. "You mean you tricked her."

"It was for your own good."

"It was not for my own good and it's nothing to worry about."

"That's not how I hear it."

"A little chemical dip. Not a big deal."

"And exactly when is that going to be? You're asking me to help, but all you're doing is making me a coconspirator in your suicide."

"It's not suicide. It's a risk, but it's not any different than if they found it a month from now."

"The fact is that they didn't find it a month from now and a month from now it could be a whole lot worse." Casey threw up his hands. "I've never known you to deceive yourself like this."

"I'm not deceiving myself. The oncologist will monitor it the whole time."

"What, from half a world away?

"The world's gotten smaller. She's a text message away."

"Yeah. Right. How long have you known?"

"Not long."

"And when were you thinking of telling me? You didn't tell me you had cancer, you didn't tell me how bad it was, you recruited me to help you, and now you're going out of the country despite what the doctors say. Did I miss anything?"

"You said this is going to be the only chance to get this guy and I'm the only one who can do it. That hasn't changed."

"I said chance and maybe. I never said one hundred percent. And you bet it's changed. Tell me. You're dying, aren't you? Faith wouldn't say it, but I could tell it in her voice."

"They can fix it, not permanently, but they can stop it for a while."

"Bullshit. Any stopping of it will be temporary. I called my own doctor and asked him."

"Temporary will have to do."

"So then take the dip. Don't go running off. Ah Ming is just a crook. You don't owe anybody anything." Casey shot out his arguments as if from an automatic weapon. "So he gets away. That's life. What's so important about him?"

"Ling."

Casey rolled his eyes. "Ling? What does she have to do with it? Are you into some kind of cosmic payback? Like you gotta balance the scales before you check out?"

"There's nothing cosmic about it. Now she calls herself Linda. Peter Sheridan was her son."

Casey stared at Gage. "But how . . ."

"It's a long story. I owe her. You know I do."

"But she can't expect—"

"She doesn't know and she doesn't need to know."

"What about Faith?"

"There's nothing more important to me than Faith, you know that. But if there hadn't been Ling, there wouldn't have been Faith. I would've bled out on the pavement. And if Faith can handle it, then you can, too."

"But—"

"But what? If you don't want to help, that's up to you. I'm going. If all goes well, I'll be back in a few weeks." Gage reached for the door handle. "You don't need to drive me back."

Gage stepped out onto the sidewalk, closed the door, and then walked away. He heard the passenger window lower and glanced back to see Casey rolling up toward him.

"Get in."

They drove back to Gage's office in silence. As Gage turned to get out, Casey reached over and gripped Gage's shoulder.

Gage looked back.

"You always win these things," Casey said. "Always. It started the first day we met. Damn you. I lost sleep worrying about you then, and I'm just about to start again."

"It's just something I have to do."

"I know." Casey lowered his gaze and shook his head. "I hope I'd do the same."

He then reached into his suit pocket and handed Gage an ICE database printout.

Gage read it over.

Sunny Glory had shipped a container from Oakland to the southern Taiwanese port of Kaohsiung twenty-four hours after the robbery.

CHAPTER 32

G age was finished packing and was on the deck barbecu-
ing salmon and vegetables when Faith arrived home from
UC Berkeley. She spread place settings on the table, then
shifted the canvas umbrella to block the setting sun. They gazed
out over the oaks and through the pines and redwoods toward the
San Francisco Bay as they ate. A young red-tailed hawk cruised
the currents rising in the canyon below. A container ship sailed
in under the Golden Gate Bridge, the wake rocking flocks of
returning fishing boats before breaking against both anchorages.
Along the near shoreline, Gage spotted the great white cranes
lining the Oakland port that lifted a million containers a year
and only days before might have lifted the stolen chips that had
cost a boy his life.

"What fake e-mail account did you set up for the trip?" Faith
asked.

"Doris Day."

She smiled. "That had to have been Alex Z's idea. He loves
those old movies." She tapped her chin with her forefinger. "The
question is, which one?" She thought for a moment, then smiles.
"I got it. *The Man Who Knew Too Much.*"

"Exactly."

Faith joined Gage in laughing, a little too long and a little too hard, which made the following silence all the more painful. They then felt an awkwardness that they'd never experienced together. They both sensed an emptiness in the still air surrounding them as they watched the soundless motion of ships moving on the bay and of traffic crossing the bridges. A breeze rustled oak leaves above them and broke the spell.

"Graham," Faith said, examining his uneaten salmon, "you need to eat a little more."

"Actually, I was just going to . . ." He shrugged. "Well, maybe I wasn't."

Faith looked at him with loving disapproval.

"But I will."

Gage picked up a mushroom with his fork and shook it free onto his plate.

"You promise to come back right away if Dr. Stern says so?"

Gage held out his left hand, and then tapped on his wedding ring.

"I do."

CHAPTER 33

F lying over the South China Sea toward Hong Kong, Gage remembered the old days when landing at Kai Tak Airport turned airline passengers into voyeurs. As the planes touched the runway, travelers gazing out of their windows would find themselves peeping into offices and apartments. They'd see televisions in crowded living rooms flickering with music videos, Chinese opera, or reruns of *Baywatch;* T-shirted men sitting in tiny kitchens, rice bowls poised at their lips, chopsticks digging and scooping.

But that wasn't what Gage saw as his plane swooped down over Lantau Island to land at Chek Lap Kok. The airport, which he knew old-timers and China hands would call new long into its fourth decade, was an architectural phenomenon of which any city in Asia or Europe or the Americas would be proud. In Gage's mind, that was the problem. There was nothing Hong Kong about it.

The plane jolted against the tarmac, and in that moment Gage realized what had prompted that thought. It wasn't Hong Kong that had changed, it was him.

"YOU DIDN'T NEED TO COME all the way out here," Gage said to Jong Arng as he stepped into the arrivals hall. "I could've met you at the hotel."

Jong Arng, Thai for "Cobra," had been waiting for Gage after he passed through Immigration and Customs.

"Mai pen rai."

The Thai expression meaning "no problem" was Cobra's response to just about everything: monsoons, flat tires, gunshot wounds, or an unexpected request to fly from Bangkok to Hong Kong.

As Cobra drove them toward Kowloon, it struck Gage that throughout the years Cobra had retained the solid build he'd had in the 1980s as a young Taiwanese intelligence officer managing the heroin trade in the Golden Triangle. If Alan Lim had quick eyes that revealed an agile mind, Cobra had slow, steady ones that concealed it.

It sometimes bothered Gage that Cobra played such a huge role in what was even then a dead fantasy: that the Nationalist Chinese Army could overthrow the mainland government. Cobra's youth had made him prone to an unthinking patriotism, not all that different from the CIA agents who transported Golden Triangle heroin to fund its covert actions in Vietnam in the early 1960s before the United States acknowledged its involvement in the war.

By the time Gage met him, Cobra had come to acknowledge to himself that it was all a fantasy. He realized that the Nationalist Third Army was never going back to China and that its heroin traffic had devolved from a political necessity into a matter of guns and money. He resigned his commission in the Taiwan Ministry of Justice Intelligence Bureau, married a Thai-Chinese teacher of English literature, and remained in Thailand.

While Cobra abandoned the ideology and the lost cause, he took with him his connections from the lowest *nak laeng* tough guys on the streets and in the karaoke bars to the *jao phor* mafia godfathers in their office towers and armed and fortified compounds, from the chemists in the field to the heroin brokers playing mah-jongg at the Krung Thep Palace Hotel, and from the Royal Thai police officers and soldiers who drove the heroin south, to the generals and admirals who provided protection to the poppy fields, the labs, and the ports.

It was that background that led Gage to ask him to fly to Hong Kong. Not only could Cobra help identify Ah Ming's sources for Double UO Globe, 555, and Triple K heroin, but Sunny Glory's link to Ah Ming meant that if the chips were in the container the company had sent out after the robbery, it would pass through the jurisdiction of his former colleagues at the MJIB.

"If I'm right," Gage told him, as the office towers of Central Hong Kong came into view, "the container carrying the chips is on its way to Kaohsiung."

"*Mai pen rai.*"

"No problem? Not so fast. We—you—will have to hide a tracking device on it."

"*Mei kuan hsi.*"

"What's *mei kuan hsi?*"

Cobra glanced over, smiling. "Taiwanese for *mai pen rai.*"

"I should've guessed."

"You know when the container will arrive?"

"According to the shipping schedule, three days."

Cobra nodded. "As long as you have the cash, I'll find people to do what we need."

"I'll see Sheridan this afternoon. His headquarters is in Central. Thirty-ninth floor. Apparently he's a major shareholder in the company that owns the building."

"So I guess he has the money."

"More than enough. But I don't know whether he's got the heart."

Cobra lowered his head a fraction to see the skyline.

"People up in those skyscrapers rarely do."

"In the meantime, go see Andrew Tang at the Royal Hong Kong Yacht Club. He set aside one of the GPS units the club uses to track members' sailboats during races of the high seas. Once you've placed it on the container, he'll link it to our cell phones and make sure somebody's monitoring it twenty-four hours a day."

"What if I can't recover the device afterward?"

"I'll cover the loss. Then let's meet for dinner at Jimmy's Kitchen at six o'clock. I want you to meet Sheridan so if something happens to me, he'll know he can trust you."

Cobra looked over, eyes intent on Gage. "What do you mean, if something happens to you?"

Gage shrugged. "Nothing. Just a precaution."

CHAPTER 34

After checking in, Gage caught a taxi from the Renaissance Kowloon Hotel overlooking Victoria Harbour to the China Travel Service to fill out a visa application and to drop off an Irish passport he'd begun using when he became too well known in Asia. He then caught another cab toward Sheridan's office, located a block above the commercial Queen's Road in the heart of Central Hong Kong.

Halfway there, he caught a wave of jet lag and decided to take Dr. Stern's advice to get some exercise. He told the driver to pull over near a restaurant on Ice House Street, then hoofed it the rest of the way. And after a moment of dizziness as he hiked up the final hill, the walk cleared his head and he felt steadier when he met with Sheridan.

From the moment they'd shaken hands in the lobby, Sheridan impressed him as one of a type: a Brit of deceptive outer reticence and inner overconfidence who had gained Britain an empire with a velvet glove, but forced them to keep it with an iron fist. And the London School of Economics diploma hanging on the wall of his office told Gage that Sheridan didn't want anyone to forget that he was a foreign financial conqueror.

"I think the chips are on their way to China," Gage said as he sat down across from Sheridan.

"Nothing new there," Sheridan said, dismissing the hard-fought particular fact with an easily won general statement. "The business section of the *South China Morning Post* reported yesterday that representatives from Intel and Microsoft are in Beijing right now demanding stronger enforcement." He glanced at a copy of *The Economist* lying on his glass-topped desk and offered a diplomatic smile. "When one has a business in Hong Kong, one has to keep up, you know." He looked back at Gage. "Where exactly are these chips going?"

"It's better if you don't know the details. There's nothing you can do to help, and there's a risk you'll do something foolish like running headlong at Ah Ming again."

Sheridan straightened in his chair and squared his shoulders.

"You seem to have forgotten that I'm the one who discovered Ah Ming was the man my son was allied with and I'm the reason you're sitting here."

Gage was stunned, not by the silliness of Sheridan's claim to heroism, but by the fact that the man had no idea why Gage was in his office or who his own wife really was. And he now understood why Sheridan had made Linda return to the San Francisco area against her will, forcing her into a seclusion that had abandoned her son to the world. But he also understood it wasn't entirely Sheridan's fault. It was likely she'd lied at the beginning of their relationship about how she was wounded and about her underground life in San Francisco.

Maybe she'd done it for his good, to protect him by wrapping him in ignorance. But as Sheridan rose in the business world, hers became an unacceptable past. And looking across the desk at Sheridan now, the man wearing an expression of oblivious entitlement, Gage wondered whether she ever trusted him at all.

"That's not quite true." Gage modulated his voice, then increased its intensity. "Your son told you about Ah Ming before you went over there. Getting your head cracked open just gave you an additional reason to go after him."

Gage glanced around at the staged antique Chinese artifacts on the counters and shelves and then pointed at the Lucite-encased integrated circuit sitting on his desk.

"It would be better if you stick with what you are good at."

"You don't seem to understand. I'm Peter's father and I—"

"Never having lost a child I wouldn't presume to understand. And I don't need to. All I need to understand is how to do what needs to be done. Anything that interferes or puts me and others at risk isn't acceptable. If you can live with that, fine. If not, I can still make an evening flight back to San Francisco."

Sheridan's face reddened and he tried to stare down Gage, but in his inability to speak, they both understood that he'd have to resign himself to the logic of real life. Ah Ming had let him crawl away for the same reason Gage wouldn't let him back in: he wasn't up to whatever would come next.

Sheridan took a deep breath, his cheeks puffing out as he exhaled, displaying the resignation of a businessman forced to cut his losses.

"Okay. You win this one. Jack Burch told me that you're the best and I trust Jack." Sheridan leaned forward and rested his forearms on his desk as if in surrender. "What do you need?"

"I'm putting together a team in Taiwan. I'll need some money to pay them and to buy the equipment they'll use. I would've brought cash from the States, but didn't want to take a chance of being questioned about it if I got searched going through customs."

"What are the odds you'll succeed?"

"Fifty-fifty. No better."

"Fifty-fifty isn't that good in business, particularly when it seems to be all or nothing."

"It is."

"And this isn't business. How much do you need?"

"Fifty thousand US. Five thousand of it Hong Kong dollars and the rest in Taiwanese NT."

Sheridan picked up his phone and directed his secretary to make the arrangements.

"I'll have it this afternoon."

"Let's make it six P.M. at Jimmy's Kitchen. I'm having dinner with someone I need you to meet."

Sheridan smiled. "Just about every deal I've made in this town has taken place at one of those tables. I think I may start to like you after all."

As Gage rose to his feet he realized he could both warn Sheridan off and include him at the same time.

"One more thing. Lucy and your wife don't need to know what we're doing. There's no reason to risk them making an off-hand comment the wrong person might hear. It's a much smaller world than you might think."

GAGE'S CELL PHONE RANG as his taxi emerged from the Victoria Harbour Tunnel from Hong Kong to Kowloon.

It was Sylvia.

"Casey called with more information about the container. The bill of lading says it's filled with soybeans and it's still headed to the Sunny Glory branch in Taiwan. He has security people at the shipping lines checking every day to see whether they transfer ownership to another company before the ship docks at Kaohsiung."

"That would be a shrewd maneuver on Ah Ming's part, but he may not have a way to do it now that Ah Tien has been cut out."

"And I got a call from Lucy. She was grateful you stayed with the case, but sounded frustrated when I couldn't tell her what you're up to."

"I think it's more than just frustration, it's anger. Ah Ming is close by—she can feel his presence like he's radiating heat—and I'm thousands of miles away, seemingly too far away to damp out the fire. And she's young and naïve enough to believe a straight line is always the shortest distance between two points. Sometimes it's an arc."

CHAPTER 35

J ack told me you were at Berkeley the same time I was," Sheridan said to Gage as the waiter delivered drinks to Gage and Cobra at the table in Jimmy's Kitchen. The lights bearing down from the steakhouse's coffered ceiling and reflecting off the white tablecloth and polished silverware felt as though they were attacking Gage's eyes as he looked across at Sheridan.

"I went to graduate school after I left police work."

"Criminal justice or sociology or something like that?"

"Philosophy."

Sheridan's face assumed an expression of feigned incredulity. "Jack told me that, but I didn't think he was serious. I can't imagine there is much opportunity for 'All men are mortal, Socrates is a man, therefore Socrates is mortal' in your line of work." Sheridan offered a snide laugh. "Or maybe it's Bernie Madoff is mortal."

Gage watched Sheridan sip his bourbon, smirking like a man who understood bottom lines, but nothing about humanity. His rigidity made Gage wonder whether Peter had been a possession that Ah Ming had taken away, not a troubled son who had needed a father.

"It's not about syllogisms." Gage fixed his eyes on Sheridan. "It's thinking about what we're doing."

"There certainly is nothing wrong with that."

Sheridan signaled to the waiter to bring three more drinks. Gage caught the waiter's eye, a wave of nausea causing him to shake off the one intended for him.

"And you," Sheridan said, looking toward Cobra, "where did you study?"

"The National Central Police University in Taipei and then at the Military College."

"And what is it you do for a living now?"

"I'm like a private investigator."

"In Taiwan?"

"No, Thailand. Mostly business intelligence."

"Thailand. Interesting. I'd thought about building a factory south of Bangkok, but the corruption was so far beyond what I found in China, I didn't have the stomach for it."

Cobra and Sheridan then began trading tales of Thai and Chinese corruption as they drank. But while finishing his second drink in the collegial atmosphere that developed between them, Cobra slipped and called Gage by his nickname among people he worked with in Thailand, Santisuk.

"Santisuk? What's Santisuk?"

"It means peaceful," Cobra answered. "And it's more the how than the what."

Sheridan looked at Gage. "What did you do to get a name like that?"

"He didn't kill a thief he could have," Cobra said, "or maybe he should—"

Gage glared at Cobra and shook his head.

"Don't stop there. Tell me."

"We don't know you well enough," Gage said.

Sheridan looked hurt and puzzled, again excluded from

something about which he really only wanted to be a voyeur. He picked up his menu and stared at it.

Gage felt a flush of annoyance at Cobra, who never should've said the name in front of Sheridan any more than Lew would ever call Cheung by the name "Ah Ming" around strangers. But then a fragment of a question dug at Gage as he stared down into his empty glass. It was one he'd asked himself at various times in his life. But now was the wrong place and the wrong time to try to answer it and he tried to fight it, but it kept digging at him.

Who were these people really? Ah Ming and Ah Tien and Cobra, beyond the parts they played in the world and the names that served as disguises—even Santisuk.

Especially Santisuk.

Or maybe the question wasn't who they were, but what they were. A separate self? A second self? A fictional self that wasn't real, but only in the consequences of its actions?

He tried to push it away, but the thoughts drove on, gouging through him.

And did that second self die with the first, or did it live on even more tangibly than the natural one in the chains of causes and effects it had initiated in the world?

He didn't know the answers to any of those questions. But he did know that they weren't the kind a manicured deal maker in Hong Kong like Sheridan would ever ask himself.

Gage looked again at Sheridan. "Did you bring the money?"

Sheridan nodded.

"Give it to Cobra."

Gage watched Sheridan survey the linen-covered tables, the hardwood paneling, the highball glasses, and the platinum-carded, black-suited businesspeople around them who'd never be seen handling cash in public, and then Gage saw the ruffle of his suit jacket as Sheridan passed an envelope under the table.

CHAPTER 36

C obra remained silent as they drove to Gage's hotel. Both of them knew it wasn't necessary for him to lose more face by apologizing. The slip wasn't a mistake he would've made on the job in Bangkok or Taipei, but it was an easy one to make during casual conversation at a steakhouse in Hong Kong.

Gage directed Cobra into his room and continued on into the bathroom to take some of the antinausea medication prescribed by Dr. Stern. He then sat down at the table, activated the encrypted e-mail app on his cell phone and checked for messages.

He decrypted the first one, from Sylvia. "It looks like Casey found intelligence information that there may be a connection between Sunny Glory and United Bamboo." Gage smiled. "And here's one from Faith with a p.s. to you. She says she's relying on you to protect me from the *pi pawb.*"

"Since when does Faith believe in evil spirits?"

"She doesn't. It's just her way of saying that whatever is against me is evil."

Gage set his phone aside. "What time is your flight to Taipei?"

"Ten. I'll stop by the yacht club on the way and pick up the GPS. Andrew was excited about having a chance to help you."

"His older brother owns a restaurant a few blocks from my office. Some junior gangsters tried to lean on him for protection money, but he was afraid to go to the police. I asked a real gangster to tell the kids to lay off. He introduced me to Andrew at his granddaughter's wedding. He told me to call him if I ever needed anything in Hong Kong."

"Andrew said they're sponsoring an ocean race for the next ten days. They're expecting a storm to pass through so there won't be anything unusual in him paying extra attention to their monitor in order to keep an eye on the container."

Gage looked through the window at the lights of the slow-moving oceangoing ships in the distance.

"I'm really counting on you. You lose that container and we're dead in the water."

"My men understand if they mess up, they'll have to swim behind it until it gets wherever it's going."

Gage turned back to Cobra, finding him with a half smile on his face.

"Have you talked with Kai about helping you out until I can get to Bangkok?" Cobra asked.

"She'll meet me at the airport. Her heart really went out to Peter's mother. She plays the tough guy, but she has a lot more *nam jai* than she'd like to admit."

"It's not just her heart going out to Linda Sheridan." A glint in Cobra's eyes joined his smile. "You realize she's still hoping you and Faith will break up."

Gage shook his head. "Kai knows that won't happen." He shrugged. "Anyway, we have an understanding."

"Maybe she's thinking that if she succeeds in helping you figure out Ah Ming's heroin connections, your heart will grow fonder, especially if things get a little dangerous."

"Then I'll try to make sure we don't end up in the same foxhole."

Cobra cocked his head and raised his eyebrows. "I've never known her not to accomplish what she sets out to do."

"As I said, we have an understanding."

"We'll see how well she honors it."

Cobra reached into his shirt pocket and withdrew a slip of paper. He unfolded it and held it out toward Gage.

"This is the name of the medical clinic in Bangkok where you're supposed to go for the blood tests."

"How . . ."

"Faith called my wife, my wife called the doctor, the doctor called my wife, and my wife called me."

"Did Faith tell her why?"

Cobra shook his head. "She just said some confusing things about a tail wagging the dog, or the other way around, and me keeping you on a short leash or us both ending up in a doghouse." He grinned. "I'm really not sure how all these American idioms fit together, but I still caught the meaning."

"You didn't tell Kai about any of this, did you?"

"No." Cobra's grin faded. "It wasn't my place."

CHAPTER 37

L ying in bed after Cobra left, Gage wondered whether it had been a mistake asking for Kai's help. While few in Thai society moved more easily between the aboveground and the underground, none had the history they had together, one that left him with a doubled view of her: as a woman and as a DEA dossier.

> **Thai name:** Sukanda
> **Chinese name:** Chen Mei-li
> **B.A. from the University of California, Los Angeles**
> **M.B.A. from Chulalongkorn University, Bangkok**
> **Owner:** Siri Construction
> **Retired:** marijuana—ganja—trafficker
> **Marital status:** *mia noi,* minor wife of the former marijuana exporter and current minister of the interior, in charge of the police and domestic intelligence

Gage hadn't been sure what Kai had seen in him when he'd come to Thailand on that trip fifteen years earlier: the rescuer of her father's investments in the United States that were almost lost in a real estate scam, a way out of a failed marriage, or love at first sight.

It turned out to be a little of each.

Exhausted when he'd left Bangkok, Gage had missed all of Kai's cues, ones that had been formed in a society that had a named smile for every occasion, no matter how painful. And like Chinese culture, where face was the currency of life, well-read Thai signals saved face, and Gage had missed them altogether. He hadn't realized the nature of Kai's feelings until he returned to Thailand on a money laundering investigation a few months later, one on which the fate of a London private bank's future rested. He'd called ahead and asked her to introduce him to Li Chung-yun, a heroin trafficker known as Eight Iron—and not because he played golf, but because he'd used the club to beat an informant to death who'd betrayed him to the United Bamboo. Kai knew him well since her construction company had built shopping centers and office buildings for him in northern Thailand.

When Gage had entered the arrivals area of the Suvarnabhumi Airport on this second trip, Kai's driver intercepted him and took him to an executive suite at the Emerald Hotel, then handed him a key card and walked away. As Gage looked through the darkened room toward the window overlooking the lights of downtown Bangkok, he saw a candlelit dining table. And as he emerged from the hallway into the room, Kai rose from the couch and glided toward his jet-lagged body and pressed up against him before he could form a face-saving sentence that would back her off without humiliating her. Only then did Gage realize that Kai thought she, and not the case he'd been working on, was the real reason he'd returned to Bangkok. He'd pulled away and held her by the shoulders at arm's length.

"Who will know but us?" Kai had asked.

"Isn't that enough? Your husband's collection of wives and mistresses may be a model over here, but it isn't for me and Faith."

Kai stepped back toward the couch and drew on a silk robe. She didn't camouflage her disappointment in either anger or in a juvenile pout.

Instead, she'd asked, "Can we still have dinner?"

"As long as you stay on your side of the table."

Kai put on a face of disappointment, real, but exaggerated. "Is that where I have to spend the rest of my life?"

Gage nodded.

Kai shrugged. "Then I guess we have an understanding."

CHAPTER 38

Because Kai's husband was the minister of interior and in command of the airport security, Kai was able to meet Gage at the gate when he arrived in Bangkok from Hong Kong.

As they walked toward the arrivals hall, she wearing an embroidered Cheongsam silk dress and he in a suit, they knew other travelers were examining them through the lens of stereotype, assuming that he was a *farang*, a foreigner, there to meet what the Thais called a chick, a sex toy rented for the week or the month, or perhaps an Internet-ordered bride to take home.

Nausea surged through Gage as they stepped into the exhaust-fouled air outside of the airport. He gritted his teeth and tensed his stomach in a failed attempt to fight it off as he climbed into her Mercedes parked at the curb.

"I spoke to Eight Iron," Kai said, as her driver pulled into traffic. "He'll meet us tonight. I promised him if he gives you what you want, you'll give him a way to hurt United Bamboo."

Gage held his breath for a moment. The nausea lessened. He breathed again.

"Will he object to you translating?"

"He trusts me. And like they say on American TV, he knows where I live."

"What time?"

"Not till seven o'clock." Kai smiled and glanced at her watch. "It's too bad we have an understanding,"

Gage forced a smile back. "I feel safer because we have one."

As they drove south on Rachadapisek Road toward downtown, Gage saw the residue of the second Asian economic collapse, the first caused by the Thai devaluation of the baht in the 1990s and the more recent by the U.S. mortgage crisis. The recovery had been weak. During his last trip, at the bottom of the collapse, he recalled thinking that the two names for the city, Bangkok, meaning plum orchard, and Krung Thep, meaning City of Angels, had seemed either indictments or satire. Then, the skyline, marked by half-empty office buildings, jagged and towering concrete monsters, had seemed both hopeless and foreboding in the polluted air of Bangkok. Even now, many of the stores that had once drawn up-country teenagers to the city for work were still dusty hulks, the windows plastered with frayed and yellowed signs advertising Versace, Rolex, and Armani, luxuries that remained beyond the reach of those who didn't work in the resurging underground economy. And the used car lots on either side of the street still overflowed with repossessed or surrendered Mercedes, BMWs, and Volvos, the onetime status symbols of those who'd ridden high.

"How has Siri Construction been surviving?" Gage asked as they passed an abandoned high-rise.

"A few projects were canceled, but having a husband who's a cabinet minister guarantees that we kept most of our government contracts."

"The prime minister should've put Somchai in charge of finance instead of interior. His ganja dealing did more for the economy than globalization and all the free trade agreements combined."

"The prime minister offered it, but he wanted interior, and he put two hundred million baht into the prime minister's campaign to get it. He needed to be in charge of the police so they couldn't cooperate with the DEA and extradite him to the U.S." She grinned. "Of course, I wouldn't mind visiting him there, especially if they kept him near San Francisco."

Gage gave her a sour look and shook his head.

She winked at him. "A girl's got to try."

GAGE LAY DOWN IN BED after Kai dropped him off at his hotel. Night sweats were keeping him awake, but he hadn't taken the sleeping pills prescribed by Dr. Stern, fearing a chemically induced grogginess when he met Eight Iron.

A ringing sent him reaching for his cell phone on the side table. It was Sylvia.

"Lucy's disappeared."

Gage swung his legs over the edge of the bed and sat up.

"I tried to reach her on her cell and home phones, but she didn't return my calls."

"Did you go to her apartment?"

"Her neighbors haven't seen her for days. I drove right from there to her mother's house. Linda hasn't heard from her either. She called her husband. He wanted to fly over, but she convinced him to let us look into it first." Sylvia paused. "I hate even to say the words, but do you think Ah Ming picked up the drumbeats and grabbed her?"

"A hostage is no good unless you use it. And he's not using it."

Gage thought back on Sylvia's comment about Lucy's anger and her comment about the shortest distance between two points.

"Have Linda e-mail you photos of her, then send people to

scout around East Wind. I'll bet she's playing surveillance cop and sitting on a rooftop or at an office window watching with a pair of binoculars and making cell-phone videos, thinking Ah Ming will commit a crime in the middle of his parking lot and all she has to do is call it in to the police. Grab her before his guys spot her."

CHAPTER 39

As Gage walked down the hallway of the hotel's small private banquet rooms, he spotted Eight Iron's lead bodyguard standing in front of a closed door.

Even though Gage had known him for years, Kasa didn't greet him, just cast dead eyes on his approach. Gage knew Kasa came doubly armed: with a semiautomatic under his loose shirt and with Shan tattoos, a body-length forest of real and mythological creatures, gods and demons, and scripts and sacred mantras to protect him from evil, from sickness, and from harm at the hands of others.

Gage wasn't convinced that Kasa believed in the efficacy of the colored ink, because the last time he'd stepped up to protect Eight Iron, he led with his gun, not with his chest.

Eight Iron and Kai were standing together when Gage entered the rosewood-paneled banquet room.

"Thanks for meeting me," Gage said to Eight Iron through Kai, who translated his greeting into Chaozhou Chinese.

Eight Iron looked him over. "You've lost a few pounds."

Gage wasn't interested in engaging in small talk with Eight Iron. This was a meeting of necessity, not choice. But he knew he had to play along.

"Just been working out a little more than usual." Gage let his gaze fall from Eight Iron's round face down to the blue golf shirt stretched tight over his stomach. "Looks like you put on a few."

Eight Iron patted his belly. "But unlike in the States, over here it's a sign of wealth and contentment."

Gage tilted his head toward the door. "I didn't see any signs like that on Kasa."

"I should've called you last year when I thought I saw him smile. It could've just been him passing gas. I was upwind, so I couldn't tell."

Kai turned so that only Gage could see her face and her rolling eyes.

Gage directed Eight Iron to sit between Kai and himself at the circular table, then waitresses wearing side-slit dresses served wine followed by a series of Chaozhou and Cantonese dishes. A mix of background nausea and worry over Lucy left Gage without an appetite. He made a pretense of eating, more moving bits of food around his plate than bringing any of them to his mouth. Eight Iron, on the other hand ate with the lack of inhibition of a predator devouring a kill.

It was only after the waitress cleared the last plate and Eight Iron instructed Kasa to block anyone from entering that they turned to business.

Gage wasn't sure whether Eight Iron was still an enemy of United Bamboo, for alliances shift over time and, where there is profit to be made, enemies become friends, or whether Casey's intelligence connecting Ah Ming and United Bamboo was correct. He figured he'd try to prompt a reaction from Eight Iron by which he could judge before revealing too much.

"I was hired to investigate a deal involving a man who used to live in Thailand. He's known as Ah Ming."

Eight Iron's eyes widened a fraction. "Has this deal happened already?"

"Let's talk a little bit more before I answer that."

Eight Iron smiled. "You want to know if I'll try to grab something for myself."

"Basically."

"The answer is no."

"Retired?"

Eight shook his head. "A few years ago, one of my people was extradited to the States. He met a Hell's Angel in jail while he was waiting for his trial. The Hell's Angel came to visit me after he was released."

"And now you're sending methamphetamines to the U.S."

Eight Iron smiled. "You're as quick as ever. Yaba pills are much simpler to make and sell than heroin." He held up a forefinger. "First, there are no seasons to worry about like with poppies. Production is year-round." He held up another finger. "Second, there are fewer transportation risks in yaba. No more moving opium resin from the fields and then the finished heroin to the port, so there are fewer police and military officers to pay off." He held up another. "Third, it's cheap and easy to get *ma huang,* what you call ephedrine, and the other chemicals from China. That's the reason the Hell's Angels wanted to outsource their manufacturing. They'd only have to import one thing, the pills, instead of all the precursors." He lowered his hand. "And since there's no smell, we're undetectable in the city. There's no reason anymore to fight snakes and malaria in the forests. Any industrial lab will do."

"Why'd you trust him?"

"Because he went to trial and won. He would've pleaded guilty or his case would've been dismissed if he'd cooperated with the DEA."

Kai interjected her own comment in Chinese and then in English: "I guess you could say that the DEA put together a drug deal."

"They did better than that. Since we started last year we've worked up to a hundred kilos a month. It costs us less than eight hundred dollars a kilo to make and we sell it to the Angels for eight thousand a kilo, delivered to the East Coast of the U.S."

"But not as good as heroin."

Eight Iron shrugged and said, "The profit in heroin was falling anyway. Afghans flooded the market after your government overthrew the Taliban. Our quality has always been better—even now our China White is ninety-nine percent pure—but we can't match their quantity."

"So the answer to my question is that you're making too much money to complicate your life?"

"Exactly." Eight Iron looked back and forth between Kai and Gage. "And now that you know something dangerous to me, we can trust each other."

Gage found nothing dangerous about it. Eight Iron hadn't admitted anything more than what Cobra could've found out at any of the narcotics traffickers' karaoke bars or mah-jongg clubs. Without names, places, and routes, no one could attack Eight Iron. He was no more at risk now than he had been five minutes earlier.

Gage decided to ignore the lie and push on. "I take it you know Ah Ming."

"You suspected I did. That's why you wanted to meet with me." Eight Iron cast what the Thais called *yim mee lessanai*, the wicked smile, then looked at Kai. "At least Kai did. I'm sure she told you about my fifty kilos."

"You ever go after him?"

"About a week later, I spotted him playing mah-jongg with other United Bamboo members at the Krung Thep Palace Hotel, but it wasn't a good place to go to war. We tracked down some underlings and Kasa used them to send a message, but I never got to Ah Ming himself. Next I heard, he'd left for the States. I have good connections, but I didn't think it was safe to reach out quite that far."

Eight Iron paused, and his eyes went vacant for a moment, then he said, "He's a brilliant man, Ah Ming. An entrepreneur. He came here after he killed a gambler in Taiwan. In less than six months he reorganized the underground lottery and unified it under his control. That's where he developed his signature, the severed head with a one baht note stuffed in the mouth. He only had to do it a few times before all the competing groups got into line. That moved him up from just a *nak laeng* to a godfather, and a couple of years later he took control of the United Bamboo heroin operation."

"I assume he made other enemies besides you."

"Back then it was mainly Big Circle. Lots of Chinese fugitives gathered in Bangkok in the nineties and the organization grew like a fungus."

"Is that why he moved to the States?"

Eight Iron shook his head. "United Bamboo won that war and Ah Ming was rewarded for his part with the West Coast of the U.S." He smiled again. "He decided to experiment with what the financial people call vertical integration. He wanted to control the heroin supply chain all the way from the poppy fields to the sellers in the States just above street level.

"It used to be"—Eight Iron glanced at Kai as though she were the repository of Thai drug trafficking history—"that United Bamboo would buy a kilo over here for five thousand and sell it for fifty when it arrived in the U.S. Ah Ming's idea was to follow it down one or two more steps and net three or four hundred thousand a kilo with very little additional risk."

Gage now understood the deeper meaning of the intercepted call that Alex Z had located in which dealers had complained that Ah Ming had flooded the streets with Triple K and 555.

"I don't know whether he succeeded with that," Gage said,

"but he succeeded in adding a second kind of crime to his enterprise."

Gage paused to let the implication appear in Eight Iron's mind, that there may be another way to strike at Ah Ming, and then said, "You still want to get even with him?"

"Of course." Eight Iron's eyebrows narrowed as he looked at Gage. "But what's in it for you?"

"The son of my client was killed in a robbery in California. Ah Ming was behind it."

"You mean he ripped off someone else's heroin?"

"No. Something different."

Eight Iron rocked his head side to side as though sorting through the risks, then asked, "Who do you have helping you over here?"

"Kai and Cobra."

Eight Iron nodded, and then said, "The beauty and the beast."

Kai smiled as she translated the compliment, then asked Gage whether he had an understanding of what Eight Iron said. Gage didn't smile back for fear that it might be source of distrust since Eight Iron wouldn't grasp the meaning, and Gage didn't want to explain.

"I take it you came to see me because Ah Ming's new enterprise has a connection to Thailand."

Gage shook his head.

Eight Iron paused, biting his lower lip. His gaze moved from the table to the Chinese paintings on the walls, to the side cart bearing wine bottles and flowers.

"I see what you're aiming at." Eight Iron smiled. "You want to tie him to a heroin deal here since you can't tie him to the robbery over there."

Gage nodded. "If you can find out whether he's got a deal working right now, I can put an end to it."

"And him?"

"And him in the States."

Eight Iron put on a deliberative expression, even though he and Gage both knew he'd already come to a decision.

"I'll try to find out, but not for your sake, for mine. I lost money and face, and things between me and Ah Ming need to be rebalanced."

They stood and walked toward the door. Eight Iron stopped and turned toward Gage.

"You do realize," Eight Iron said, "that at the end of this, it will be you against him. Man to man. That's the way he is and the way he'll want it to be and that's the only way you'll take him. That is, which is far more likely, if he doesn't take you first."

GAGE RETURNED TO HIS ROOM while Kai escorted Eight Iron to the lobby. She telephoned Gage as she drove away.

"Did you see that?" Kai asked. "He started to drool like one of those big red dogs with the floppy ears . . . I don't remember the English name."

"Bloodhound?"

"That's it. A bloodhound."

"The problem is that bloodhounds are hard to control," Gage said. "And I'm not sure we have a leash strong enough to restrain him."

"Is that why you didn't tell him you were tracking the chips?" Kai paused for a moment. Gage could hear the rumble of traffic on the road. She then answered her own question. "I get it. You want him to believe that this is all or nothing and it all depends on him."

"Exactly."

CHAPTER 40

Gage lay awake, worried about Lucy, feeling the failure of having misread her, of not having anticipated that the urge to act would overtake her. He imagined her lying on a rooftop overlooking East Wind, peering down or slumped in her car peeking through the windows and Ah Ming's people scanning their surroundings, checking for surveillance, any movement, any change from the ordinary, any vehicle parked too long, whether occupied by a cop looking to take them down or by a crook looking to take them over. And, compounding all that, Sylvia trying to search without appearing to be searching, trying to avoid giving herself or Lucy away.

His cell phone rang. It was Sylvia.

"We found her."

"You mean she really was surveilling East Wind?"

"Worse than that. Remember what you said about the shortest distance between two points? She went in. I had Viz spotting on the entrance while I watched the back. He saw her walk inside."

"What's she doing there?"

"I don't know yet. I sent Annie Ma to look around inside, but she didn't see her."

Gage thought for moment, trying to work his mind past both his anger at her and his fear for her.

"Let's hope she went in pretending to be a potential customer."

"But what if she confronted him?

"Then it's already too late. They would've stuffed her into a car trunk and taken her to a safe house to interrogate her."

"You want me to call the police and report it as a kidnapping?"

"No. They wouldn't find her and it would prove to Ah Ming she knows something. It would only make it worse for her—I'll call you back."

Gage telephoned Cobra who was staking out the Sunny Glory branch in Taichung, a few hours' drive north of the Kaohsiung Port, waiting for the container to arrive.

"Whatever is happening over there hasn't changed anything over here," Cobra said.

"Call me if you pick up countersurveillance. If so, we'll abort this thing and I'll send people in to shake up East Wind."

After Gage disconnected, he allowed himself to feel the annoyance engendered by Lucy interjecting herself into what he was doing. It was something of an emotional high-wire act because he was angry at a person, a young person of intelligence and potential, who might have already been tortured and murdered.

Gage's cell phone rang. It was Sylvia.

"She just walked out of East Wind." Instead of relief, Sylvia's voice vibrated with worry, even fear. "And we're in big trouble. Viz is sending me live video. Guys are on either side of her. Suits. They're heading toward a van parked in front."

"Are they holding her?"

"One had his hand on her elbow . . . still walking . . . they're stopped . . . she's looking around . . ." Sylvia blew out a breath. "She's walking away."

"Anyone following her?"

"Doesn't look like it. The two guys got into the van."

"Stay with her, but don't get close until you're sure no one is watching her."

Gage allowed himself to enjoy the feeling of annoyance. It's easier to be angry at the living.

Twenty minutes later Sylvia called.

"We lost her going into an apartment complex in South San Francisco. She was out of sight by the time we snuck through the gate behind another resident. We're looking for her car . . . Hold on a second . . . I think Viz found it . . . He's got it . . . I'll call when we figure out which apartment she's in."

A few minutes later Sylvia called back.

"I'm with Lucy. She got herself hired using her Chinese name. Part-time. Working mornings."

"Put her on."

The next voice was Lucy's, and angry. "I just couldn't sit around and wait."

"You should've talked to me first. Ah Ming is dangerous and smart and has near-perfect instincts. If he reads tension on your face, he'll act on it."

Lucy didn't respond. Gage could hear her breathing.

"Did he hire you himself?"

"No. The head of the shipping department."

"Has he noticed you?"

"I don't think so. He can't see my cubicle from his office in a far corner and it's not along the aisles he walks down either from the back lot or from the front door. I can just not show up anymore. I don't think they could find me."

"Quitting so soon may raise suspicions. I'm not saying this to scare you, but they certainly would be able to find you. You're an amateur and amateurs always leave a trail. Let me talk to Sylvia."

Gage heard Lucy pass the phone.

"Do you think she could deal with staying on at East Wind?" Gage asked.

"Let me go into another room." After a few moments of shuffling, Sylvia said, "We caught her by surprise, but she didn't fall apart. And she was able to forge past employment records and was cool enough in the interview to get herself hired."

"It would help us if we had an inside person even if all she does is watch. But we'll need a plan to get her out if things blow up. And don't tell Casey about her being in there. It would compromise the criminal case against Ah Ming if a defense lawyer figured out that there was someone in East Wind who Casey knew about and had some control over, even if only through us. It could be construed as an illegal search."

"Got it."

"Put her back on."

Gage heard more shuffling as Sylvia walked back to where Lucy was waiting.

"We want you to stay at East Wind," Gage told her, "but don't play detective on your own. Just watch and report to Sylvia."

"I'm sorry for not asking you, but I'm grateful you're letting me help out."

"I'm just trying to make the best of a bad situation. And don't make it worse by telling anyone. Call your parents. Say that you've been distraught about your brother and went to a therapist who suggested you take some time off so your academic future wouldn't be compromised. You decided on your own to change apartments. Be apologetic. And call them every day."

After repeating the plan to Sylvia, Gage hung up and called

Cobra. "We've got it straightened out. What about the container?"

"It's due into port tomorrow. A classmate of mine from MJIB training days manages security for Hanjin Lines down at Kaohsiung. He confirmed it's still owned by Sunny Glory, but he can't be certain it will actually be hauled there. It could get diverted and sent directly to Sunny Glory's customer. Whoever that is."

"Then make sure we don't lose it."

CHAPTER 41

K ai telephoned Gage at sunrise, unaware that Lucy had cost him most of a night's sleep. He made up an excuse about catching up with some work and put her off until noon. Over a lunch in the hotel café, she reported on her conversations with Eight Iron.

"Last night he went to a casino in the Khao San district, near the river. He talked to some *jao phor* godfathers. He didn't get any specific information about dates and routes, but he found out Ah Ming has been getting a regular supply of Triple K and 555 from the Wa State Army through a syndicate set up by United Bamboo."

"How far do you think Eight Iron is willing to go?"

"It's a little complicated. If he asks about the heroin, then a load is captured right away, everyone will think he was behind it. And if it gets captured by U.S. agents, he'll look like a DEA informant, particularly since everyone knows he isn't in heroin anymore. People will assume he cut a deal to avoid prosecution for yaba."

"Does that mean you think he'll bail on us?"

Kai shook her head. "He wants this too much. He put the

word out that he has an old customer who wants a big load. He made it sound urgent and implied that the customer is already in Thailand. He flew up to Chiang Rai early this morning. He may need you to go up there and pretend to be his buyer. He wants someone to blame if things blow up."

"You mean me?"

"No, he means you," Kai said, flashing grin. "I've got other things to blame you for."

"Get in line."

"Behind who?"

"Maybe the DEA. The last thing I need is to have my name show up in a DEA intelligence report negotiating for heroin. But the more serious problem is that I might know some of the people he's dealing with from the old days."

"No one would wonder about Cobra."

Gage shook his head. "If someone has to face off with the Wa State Army, then I'd rather do it myself. I've got less to lose."

Kai's brows furrowed and she peered at him. "What do you mean, less to lose?"

Gage shrugged, then came up with a reason different from the one he was thinking, but no less true.

"Only that Cobra's got to live here after this is over. As long as he's in the shadows and the Wa don't know about him, he'll be okay. If we can't guarantee that, I'm not sure I want you involved in this either."

Kai looked down and picked at her rice, then looked up with raised eyebrows and said, "Well . . ."

"Well what?"

"If this is going to be our last day together, maybe we should go up to your room and . . ."

Gage smiled at Kai as if at a persistent child. "You're what the kids in the States used to call scandalous."

"That settles it. If I'm getting the blame, why shouldn't I at least get to commit the crime?"

"Because you'd have to make me a coconspirator to do it."

"I promise I won't . . . what's the American word?"

"Snitch, you won't snitch."

"Right, I won't snitch on my coconspirator."

Gage leaned back in his chair and shook his head. "Would you explain to me how come wherever our conversation starts, it always ends up here?"

"I'm from an old and mysterious culture. We've learned to flow with the inexplicable current of events." Kai smiled. "I think it would be better if the white ghost surrendered to the flow."

"There's nothing inexplicable about the current. It's just you paddling."

Kai released a fake sigh. "Apparently I have lost my subtlety."

"And I take it that's somehow another reason we have to sleep together before I leave?"

"Of course, everything is a reason why we have to sleep together. I thought you understood that."

CHAPTER 42

The container arrived at Kaohsiung," Cobra told Gage in a call from Taiwan. Kai was driving them toward Eight Iron's compound in northern Bangkok. They'd just passed the trunk of the flat-topped Elephant Tower office building. "Sunny Glory's was one of the first off the ship. It's in customs now. We're set up to follow it when it gets released."

"What about security at their warehouse?"

"Nothing more than before."

"Doesn't that suggest the chips might not be in there?"

"Maybe, maybe not. Adding extra security could raise questions. The workers might not know that there is something hidden in the container and it's better not to give them a reason to ask. If they don't know something worth protecting is on its way, they can't set up Sunny Glory from the inside to be ripped off."

"Kai and I are in the middle of something, and I may need your help down here a little sooner than I expected."

"Just let me know. My people are all ex–Ministry of Justice Intelligence agents, most with backgrounds in electronic intelligence. They'll follow through if I have to leave."

Kai honked her car horn as they rolled to a stop in front of a razor-wired metal gate, the only opening in the ten-foot-high walls surrounding Eight Iron's mansion. An eye appeared on the other side of a peephole. When the gate slid open, they discovered that the eye belonged to a guard cradling an AK–47 across his chest. A second guard stood at the bottom of the stairs and others at each corner of the house.

The interior that met Gage when they crossed the threshold into the living area was far different from the array of utilitarian chairs and couches that he'd encountered the last time. Mirrors, pieces of jade, and furniture whose placement seemed determined more by superstition than function told him that someone had made serious efforts to ensure that no good luck would ooze out of the house and no bad luck would flow in, feng shui and AK–47s willing.

Eight Iron met them in his teak-paneled office on the ground floor. He directed them to one of two facing couches. The low table between them and Eight Iron seemed to divide them into teams, voiding Gage's hope that he could generate a feeling of working together.

"Welcome to my modest home," Eight Iron said as he sat down. Gage watched him rub the dragon head carved into the armrest as though it was a rabbit's foot.

"It's far from modest," Gage said.

"My most recent minor wife is an interior decorator."

Kai's voice hardened as she translated the words "*mia noi*," minor wife.

Eight Iron made a regal gesture with his hand. "She suggested a few things and I allowed her to do them." His hand swooped down and he poured white tea into small red clay cups, then handed one to each of them.

"I didn't expect to hear from you so soon," Gage said.

"And I didn't expect things to move so fast."

Gage tensed at the delight in Eight Iron's voice.

"There's a big load of 555 in production up there." Eight Iron pointed northeast, toward the Golden Triangle. "And there's a lot of worry among the Wa about the financing. How the syndicate will pay for it and even whether they ever will. They don't like what they view as the novelty of it. And given the demand for China White these days, they aren't sure they should've bothered with it."

"What did they mean by novelty?"

"They didn't say directly, but I got the idea that no money would actually change hands."

"You mean the Wa is fronting the whole load?"

"They wouldn't do that. It's something else."

Kai glanced over at Gage. He didn't look back, but guessed she was thinking the same thing he was. If it was Ah Ming's deal, the novelty would be that it would be barter, not cash: chips for heroin. Heroin into the bodies of American drug users, chips into Thai-made electronics. It was brilliant and exactly the kind of mutation in crime he'd talked about in his speech to the International Fraud Investigators Association. And it made him feel both insightful and stupid at the same time. Ah Ming had combined robbery and drug trafficking in a way Gage hadn't anticipated, but now knew he should have.

It was almost as if Gage hadn't been listening to his own speech.

Not only had Ah Ming figured out how to do a drug deal without money and without a money trail, but he'd obtain the heroin almost for free: just the cost of the robbery plus a few thousand dollars in shipping fees.

"Why were people willing to talk to you about it?"

Eight Iron smiled like an actor knowing he'd delivered the perfectly spoken line. "Because they thought I was approaching them about buying yaba pills. Apparently the Wa laboratory producing the heroin is also used for making yaba. They've gathered all the ephedrine and other precursors to make a huge batch in the next few weeks. They want it sold in advance, so they're on the hunt for buyers."

"Sounds like they're under pressure to finish the heroin first."

"From what I gather, it's almost done. At a lab inside Thailand. It used to be in Burma, but the skirmishes between the Wa and Shan forced it to move across the border."

Not only had the Wa and Shan been fighting to free themselves from China and Burma, but had been fighting each other over the heroin trade by which they financed their armies.

Eight Iron sipped his tea, then said, "But you're not really interested in those details as much as in the big news. Which is that United Bamboo is the buyer and the broker is one Ah Ming has used in the past." He took another sip of tea and smacked his lips. "I've already sent Kasa to Mae Sai."

"Hold on." Gage locked on Eight Iron's eyes. "I don't want anyone grabbing the heroin. We don't even know for certain it's for Ah Ming, and we don't want to start a war."

Gage then remembered Eight Iron had said he needed a fake foreign buyer and Kasa didn't qualify, both because he was well known in the Golden Triangle as Eight Iron's enforcer and because he was a Shan. The Wa would never sell to a Shan even through a broker they trusted.

"Why'd you send Kasa up there? You told Kai you just needed someone to play the part of a customer, and that's a part he can't play."

"I only sent him up there to find the lab and arrange to follow the 555."

Gage remembered Kai's image of Eight Iron as a bloodhound and decided that he needed a leash.

"I'll send Cobra up there to work with him."

Eight Iron smiled again. "If you'd like. We can always use someone with his skills."

As THEY WERE driving away, Kai glanced over at Gage. "He plans to intercept the heroin. That's why he rushed Kasa up there. Has to be."

"It's possible. I don't see Eight Iron spending his own time and money unless he expects to get something concrete in return. A warm feeling of having gotten revenge isn't enough. He wants to feel either white powder or someone's blood between his fingertips. And another thing. First he wanted someone to play customer and go meet the broker and now he doesn't. That tells me something else. He's trying to keep us from finding out what's really going on."

"And whatever that is might account for his enthusiasm."

Gage looked toward the crowded road ahead. His mind felt fogged like the gray haze enveloping the city. In the distance he spotted a northbound Skytrain rocketing along the elevated track, the smiling faces in the advertisements on the side mocking the economic disaster the city had become. His eyes lost focus as he stared at the red, white, and blue paint streaking the sides of the cars.

And the movement led him to an answer.

Gage held up his right hand. "The chips are over here in Taiwan." He held out his other hand, lower and to the left. "The heroin is down here."

"And they have to meet," Kai said.

Gage lowered his hands and nodded. "That suggests the heroin probably won't be traveling the usual route south to the Bangkok port and then to the U.S. And even without understanding the financing, that might be what he's figured out."

He pictured a Southeast Asian map, the three-hundred-plus degrees that would exclude Bangkok: Burma, Cambodia, Southern China, Vietnam, even Malaysia.

"That's why he needs Kasa up there, starting at the lab. And why we need Cobra right next to him."

CHAPTER 43

Ah Ming sat alone in his office, remembering his escape from Taiwan after he killed the gambler, being passed from one United Bamboo member to another, a chain that led from Taipei, to Hong Kong, to Singapore, to Bangkok. A trunk of a car, a fake passport, a night flight, an unlit tarmac, a dark SUV. And he recognized why these thoughts came to him now. He had broken the links between himself and the robbery, but with the cost that there was a broken link in his organization.

By limiting those who knew of his own role, he'd ensured that only two men would be in a position to inform against him: Lew and Ah Tien. But because of Lew's age and reticence to travel, over time Ah Tien had become too central to everything, especially the offshore operation, and now too dead.

He needed someone to send east and it could only be himself or Lew, and it couldn't be himself.

Ah Ming stepped to his door, spotted Lew standing by a near cubicle, and signaled to him to come to his office. As he waited, he noticed a new employee standing at the copy machine, a young Eurasian woman, poised and attractive. Her facial features, her nose and cheeks and skin tone, seemed familiar, but he shook off the thought, deciding that he must've seen her before as he skirted the cubicles making his way to and from the warehouse entrance.

He followed Lew into the office, directed him to a chair, and then shut the door.

"Without Ah Tien, I need to make other arrangements." Ah Ming sat down behind his desk and rested his forearms on the blotter. "I need you to manage the exchange."

Lew didn't react and Ah Ming hadn't expected him to. He knew the old man had suffered too much in his life to react to words alone.

"But if you do it, all parts of the operation will connect to you. We need to make sure you don't leave a trail back to me."

Ah Ming let the notion linger, then said, "My first thought had been that after the deal was done, you'd simply follow Ah Tien's practice and stay overseas until it's time for a new cycle. But then I realized I'd been taking you for granted in recent years and perhaps you've already been thinking ahead, toward retirement."

Lew still didn't respond.

"I've relied on you as though you were my own uncle. The decision is yours, but to make your choice easier and to reward you for your service, I'll give you a percentage of this deal."

Lew shook his head. "That's not necessary. I've saved enough and my needs are simple."

"In any case, I owe you this." Ah Ming rose. "The money will be waiting for you on your return. Do with it what you will."

Ah Ming walked Lew back to his office, then returned to his own.

LEW SAT DOWN AT HIS DESK surprised that Ah Ming had divined his desire to retire. He wondered whether Ah Ming had sensed what he had just discovered himself: a longing to return to his home village. He gazed up at a charcoal drawing of steep karsh mountains along the Lijiang River that he'd cut from a calendar he'd bought on his single trip back to China since his escape in the 1970s. He thought of his university colleagues who had tried to convince him during the visit that the Cultural Revolution that had destroyed his career as a history professor now existed in the Chinese imagination only as an embarrassment. But he'd felt a bitterness and a distrust that hadn't abated during the weeks he spent there. Indeed, standing outside of his ancestral home and looking down at the graves of his parents whose funerals he missed during his exile, he'd felt a hot rage he'd feared would never cool.

Through his open door, Lew caught the motion of Ah Ming walking from his office and through the back exit of the warehouse. He then imagined himself taking that same route and never coming back.

AH MING DROVE to a Walmart five miles away where he bought a prepaid phone, then on to Coyote Point along San Francisco Bay and walked to the water's edge. He punched in a series of digits.

"*Yes?*" a man answered.

"I'm sending Lew to the northern place."

"When?"

"Tomorrow."

"What do you want me to do?"

"Observe."

"Should I call you if he's detected?"

"No."

"Then what should I do?"

"Eliminate him."

He then dropped the phone into the dirt, stomped it, and threw it far into the bay.

CHAPTER 44

Cobra came to Gage's Bangkok hotel room after flying in from Taiwan. He took a chair at the dining table, poured him a cup of tea, and also sat down.

"The container is at Sunny Glory," Cobra said. "But probably not for long. In the old days, we never let anything stop moving, and they won't either. They'll just add whatever goods they want to send on to the next stop and then haul it back to the port."

Cobra's cell phone rang. He listened, snapped orders in Taiwanese, then hung up and looked at Gage.

"The container just left."

"You were right."

"Not exactly. It was empty."

The flowchart in Gage's mind of the possible routes the chips could follow and how the deal might be structured went fuzzy.

"Are they on to us?" Gage said. "Or was this the plan all along?"

Gage felt his fists clench and then a flash of panic that he'd wasted the last weeks, foolishly gambling with his health and his life. Time now felt like a vise. The past completed, fixed in place, and the time moving at him, closing the gap between the present and the future, squeezing him.

He pushed past the thought. "Or worse. Maybe the chips weren't in it in the first place."

Gage heard a knock on the door. He opened it for Kai and filled her in. They could do nothing but wait for more information from Taiwan, so he turned to the problem of Eight Iron.

"Kai and I both think Eight Iron is up to something," Gage told Cobra. "If he grabs the heroin, all our work was for nothing. Ah Ming will freeze everything in place until he sorts it out."

"I'm willing to head up there, but I'll be outnumbered. The area is crawling with Shans connected to Kasa."

"And I'm not sure I want you guarding a heroin shipment, or worse, going to war over it, either against the Wa or against Eight Iron."

Cobra smiled. "I don't think my wife would forgive me if I ended up with new holes in my body."

And Gage knew he wouldn't forgive himself.

"What's stopping Eight Iron from just grabbing it on the trail from the lab?" Kai asked.

"It would make it too obvious that he's behind the theft," Gage said. "A guy shows up who's been out of the business for a long time, then a huge load gets snatched."

"So it's a matter of timing," Cobra said. "He needs to make his move in a way that will disguise that it's him doing it."

"As soon as the heroin leaves the lab," Gage said, "assuming we can catch up to it, we'll make a decision on how to play it. Which means you'll have to hook up with Kasa and stick with him until the heroin shows up."

"Which means I'm not sleeping at home tonight."

"At least you'll have some company."

"What company?"

"Kai. Kasa won't make a move against you if she's around. He knows her husband would use the police and army to crush his whole organization."

"And not because of love." Kai smirked. "He just needs me to manage the harem."

"I'm glad you still have your sense of humor," Gage said, "and of adventure. I'll have to stay here. A white ghost hanging around this deal would be taken for DEA."

Cobra nodded. "*Mai pen rai.*"

"I wouldn't say 'no problem' so fast. We still don't know where they'll be moving the heroin."

Cobra's cell phone rang. He answered, listened, then disconnected. "A truck backed up to the loading dock. It could be they're transferring the chips into it."

Gage pictured his map again, this time from the perspective of southern Taiwan and the South and East China Seas. "I wonder if their plan is to slip them into another company's container in Kaohsiung to give them an additional layer of insulation."

"But if it's going by container anyway," Kai said, "why not make the exchange here in Bangkok. Haul the container to a local warehouse, take out the chips, substitute in the heroin, and send it on to the U.S."

Gage thought for a moment. "No. That couldn't be it. Too risky. The last thing they'd want to do is ship the heroin directly from a source country. That's like asking for it to be searched by customs."

They all fell silent. They knew they were just floating, drifting from speculation to speculation, hypothetical to hypothetical, and there was only one way to find solid ground.

Kai and Cobra rose and headed for the door.

fter Kai and Cobra left, Gage took a cab to the Jira Medical Center on the first floor of a high-rise in central Bangkok. It was the office of the doctor Cobra's wife had chosen. The few steps across the sidewalk felt to him like he was fighting through dirty, gray cotton. Crossing the threshold and into the air-conditioning was like breaking free.

"My name is Gage," he told the receptionist. "I have an appointment with Dr. Mana."

She smiled. "Yes, of course."

She gestured toward the bank of chairs on the opposite wall of the empty waiting room, then reached for her intercom.

A few minutes later Mana entered through the door next to the reception counter. He brightened when he spotted Gage, then extended his hand, Western fashion.

"Khun Malee told me to expect you."

"I appreciate you taking the time to see me."

Mana signaled a nurse to follow, then escorted Gage into an examination room.

"Just sit up there," Mana said, directing him to the exam table. "And I'd like you to remove your shirt."

"I can just roll up my sleeve. I only need blood drawn."

"How about I'll be the doctor and you be the patient," Mana said in an I-won't-take-no-for-an-answer tone and matching Thai smile.

Gage gave Mana a look of surrender, then removed his shirt and pulled himself up onto the end of the table.

Mana extracted two vials of blood from Gage's arm, then handed him an e-mail. It was addressed to Gage.

> Dear Graham:
>
> I met Dr. Mana at a conference at the Mayo Clinic a few years ago. He attended the best university and medical school in Hong Kong and teaches oncology at the Chulalongkorn Medical Faculty.
> He is also following my instructions.
> Do what he says.
> By the way, Faith and I had lunch. She tried to explain you to me. I'm not sure I got it. She promised to try again.
> Please be careful.
>
> Louisa Stern

Gage smiled and laid the e-mail on the table behind him.

Mana performed the same examination of his neck and arms that Stern had done.

"Nausea?" Mana asked.

"A little."

"More or less?"

"Less."

"Dizziness?"

"None since Hong Kong a couple of days ago."

"Appetite?"

"*Rad na gai* for lunch." Gage smiled again. "You can tell Dr. Stern I ate the whole thing."

Mana smiled back. "I will. She decided to cut out the middleman and she asked me to send your blood results directly to her." He raised his eyebrows. "Any objection?"

Gage shook his head.

Mana passed Gage his shirt. "If you're here in a week, please come back. Otherwise, good luck to you."

As Gage stepped back onto the sidewalk, he decided to walk at least partway back to the hotel. He needed to think outside the confinement of a cab creeping through traffic. He paid off the waiting driver, then started toward his hotel, winding through lottery ticket sellers, fruit vendors, and noodle carts. Workers heading toward buses and Skytrains jostled him, and businesspeople elbowed him aside as they fought for taxis.

His nausea ratcheted up in the exhaust blasts from tuk-tuks and motorcycles, and as it faded, the chaos of sounds, smells, and movements provoked an inner anarchy of images: Faith, Ling, Kai, Casey, Stern, Sheridan. And that morphed into anger, a molten heat that spread inside his chest, not directed outward toward the world jarring him, but at himself, or at least at that part of himself that was killing him.

Questions rose like street signs in front of him: *Why not earlier? Why not on the day of the diagnosis? Or on the day of the bone marrow biopsy? Those would've been good days for rage.*

Walk down to the basement of his house, pound the heavy bag until he was drained.

Gage answered the question as soon as he asked it. The fury had now emerged because he had become a bystander, his work not yet completed, but out of his hands, and his mind was now loosed to wander uncontrolled. A frightening image came to him of a flashlight rolling down a hillside from a dead man's hand

Whether or not he'd fulfill his obligation to Linda Sheridan and whether or not Ah Ming would win in the end would be answered solely by Kai and—

Fingers reached into his back pocket. He grabbed the wrist and twisted the arm it was attached to. He took back his wallet. He found himself gripping a skinny street kid with up-country tribal features, wearing a dirty T-shirt and shorts. He searched the boy's pockets and found no other stolen wallets or money, only a gold candy wrapper folded like a keepsake. He released his grip, but the boy didn't run. He just stood there with his shoulders hunched, head down, waiting to be beaten or handed over to the police.

Gage turned and walked away. He didn't look back.

At least it hadn't been a knife held at my throat or a gun barrel pointed at my chest.

He continued into Lumpini Park, passing old women engaged in tai chi and aged men playing *makrook thai* and finally a vendor selling fresh snake blood drained from disemboweled cobras lying in a bucket next to his wooden cart.

Gage thought about his conversations with Stern and the research he and Faith had done and now admitted to himself a truth that had only been inert words before. There was no secret about the course the disease would follow or how it would end and when: give or take a margin of error, he knew how long he would live.

He paused in front of a pagoda clock tower housing an old Swiss Heuer and looked up at its rusting face.

It's not a knife or a bullet that I have to fear. It's a ticking clock.

Gage wondered why death hadn't been constantly on his mind, why even the nausea and dizziness hadn't distracted him from what he had set out to do.

But no answer came.

He left the park and found himself in front of a small Theravada Buddhist temple, its triangular red roof sweeping down toward gold, birdlike chofas at the corners. A disabled man with twisted arms and legs loped along the sidewalk like a dog. He stopped in front of the temple and offered small garlands of white flowers for sale. Gage bought one, sniffed the scent of *malik* and *dok ruk,* and then gave it to a hunched woman shuffling toward the entrance. She draped it over withered hands formed into an arthritic *wai,* then bowed and hobbled inside.

An indistinct thought began forming in Gage's mind, then evaporated. It was something about the work he did and the reasons he did it. He grasped for the wisp as it dissipated, then looked up at the *phra chedi,* the domed pagoda housing images of the Buddha and photographs of revered teachers. Then came a bitter thought that didn't escape his grasp: even the devout, those who prayed, lived, and finally died for nirvana, couldn't accept the oblivion that was its aim and essence. No different from those European Catholics who venerated fragments of saints' bones, they needed their idols, their photos, and their images to bow to.

What am I ready to accept? Gage asked himself as he turned away. *And how will I know it?*

And when?

IT WAS AFTER DARK by the time Gage got back to his hotel room. An e-mail from Faith arrived as he lay down on the bed. It was about her teaching day and about the estimates for the new retaining wall below the house, and about her not being able to find the juicer they'd received as a Christmas gift from her mother ten years earlier. He smiled as he read it. Somehow she knew when it was all going to hit him, and why, and how to pull him out of it. He imagined her sitting on the couch in front of the fire place sipping wine—

His cell phone rang, wrenching his mind back to Bangkok.

It was Cobra. Gage could hear the rumble of car tires on pavement. They were heading north. He'd learned from his agents in Taiwan that Sunny Glory had loaded unmarked boxes on a junk-style coastal fishing vessel at the port of Taichung. It then broke for the open water of the Formosa Strait and the East China Sea.

"We got a partial hull number, but there was no way we could install the tracking device."

Gage felt his body tense and then a feeling of floating, almost of disassociation, of having broken free of what had anchored him and his plan in place.

"That's the bad news," Cobra said.

"And the . . ."

But Gage didn't need to finish his question and Cobra didn't need to answer it. The only reason Sunny Glory used a smuggling boat was because they had something to smuggle.

They'd found and lost the chips in the same instant.

CHAPTER 46

After collecting a change of clothes, a driver, and a body-guard, Kai and Cobra had headed toward the Thai-Burmese border, aiming for Mae Sai, east of the lab Eight Iron had described. They'd swung by a branch of Siri Construction at the north end of Bangkok and picked up shortwave radios as backups to their cell phones. Assuming they could locate and follow the heroin, there was no way to guarantee the entire route would have cell service. They might even end up on the open sea. They'd slept on and off during the ten-hour drive and arrived midmorning at an empty roadside café on the outskirts of Mae Sai where Kasa was waiting.

As Kai introduced Cobra to Kasa, they squared their shoulders as men who knew each other by reputation, then sat down and leaned over the worn teak table.

"We followed the heroin all night," Kasa told them, in Thai. "The mule train is no more than two hours from town. At this point, we don't know which warehouse they'll take it to or where it will go from there."

"How will we follow it?" Cobra asked.

"A truck of our own. Drivers on the highway treat each other like comrades. We'll fit in."

Cobra cast a glance toward Kai. The reason to use a truck was so that Eight Iron could transport the heroin back once he grabbed it.

"And if ours breaks down?" Kai asked.

"That's a risk we'll have to take."

"Why not carry motorcycles in the bed?" Cobra said.

"I'll call Eight Iron." Kasa rose to his feet. "It's up to him."

He returned a few minutes later.

"Eight Iron says you can send one motorcycle rider and we'll send one."

"I'll do it myself," Cobra said, "and Kai will ride with the driver in the cab."

Kasa shook his head. "Eight Iron won't allow it." He looked at Kai, but spoke to Cobra. "Her husband will blame Eight Iron if something happens to you and he doesn't need that kind of trouble."

Cobra and Kai knew they couldn't force the issue, so they let it go.

Kasa directed them to his Land Cruiser parked in front of the café and got in behind the wheel. After Cobra took the front passenger seat, Kai signaled her driver and bodyguard to follow in her car, then climbed in behind Cobra. As Kasa drove them toward the outskirts of Mae Sai, Kai called Gage, speaking in English, knowing Kasa couldn't understand.

"I have two things for you," Kai said. "First, Cobra's people are working their sources in Taiwan. The only thing they're certain of is that the boat turned north instead of south. They're trying to find out exactly where it's headed, but for security reasons sometimes the captains of these boats don't even know where they're supposed to land until they're already way out on the water."

"Ah Tien's address books suggests he had connections all along the coast," Gage said, "from Bangkok all the way up to Shanghai."

"That means we have less than three days to find the boat in a hundred thousand square miles of ocean."

"More if it the storm my yacht guy in Hong Kong warned Cobra about forces them to take a wide route."

"And second, Eight Iron won't let me go along."

"Then we'll have to come up with a way to protect ourselves that he will accept." Gage thought for a moment, and an idea to apply an old method to a new situation came to him. "Do you have people who can hold Kasa for a few days?"

"My driver and bodyguard. They won't like it, but they'll do it. They can hide him in the Siri Construction warehouse near Chiang Rai."

"Then pull over. Give Cobra your phone and Eight Iron's number. Tell him to walk far enough away so that Kasa can't overhear. He can call Eight Iron on his own phone and translate for me."

Once Cobra had walked twenty yards from the cars, he put both his own and Kai's cell phones to his ears.

"I've got Eight Iron on the other line," Cobra told Gage.

"Tell him we have some security concerns and we need to be businesslike about it."

Cobra translated for Eight Iron.

"He understands."

"Tell him that you'll be riding in the surveillance truck and that Kasa refused to allow Kai to go along."

"Okay . . . He says he doesn't want to take the risk."

"I'm not going to argue with him. I want Kai with me anyway. Tell him we need a guarantee he won't steal the heroin."

"Okay . . . he understands."

"Now tell him we want to hold Kasa as security, but we'll

release him when we're satisfied that the heroin is out of his reach."

Cobra translated. "He agrees."

"Why'd he give in so easily? He must know how much the deal is for and that the load will be worth at least sixty million dollars wholesale when it arrives in the U.S."

Gage heard Cobra speak a few words in the background.

"He says he trusts you when you say you'll bring down Ah Ming."

"That's not a very good reason to pass on that much money. Tell him we want Kasa to surrender to us before the heroin leaves Mae Sai."

"He says okay and wants me to put Kasa on the phone."

"Listen in and then take Kasa's phone away from him."

A few minutes later, Kai called Gage with the news that everything was settled.

"Eight Iron was way too agreeable," Kai said.

"Which only means we don't understand what he's up to. Make sure your people take seriously the kind of guy they're dealing with. Regardless of how Kasa is acting now, he can strike any time. Remember what happened when Ah Ming ripped off Eight Iron. There was lots of blood in Bangkok and most of it was on Kasa's hands."

"What about the fishing boat?"

"I'm working on an angle. Have Cobra call his people in Taiwan and get the names and hull numbers of all the boats that sailed out of that port around the same time as the one carrying the chips."

"That's assuming that they don't repaint or renumber the one with the chips while it's on the water."

"If they do, then I guess we'll be looking for the one with fresh paint."

obra looked over at Kasa, who was driving with what seemed to him to be the casual anticipation of a man leaving on a vacation, not on a journey that would leave him jailed in a makeshift cell in the industrial district of Chiang Rai. He skirted a valley carpeted with paddies and furnished with thatched-roof shelters for those who tended the rice, and then came to a stop at the base of a hill. He led them on a climb of a humid, sweaty six hundred feet, then pointed out one of his men sitting on a bicycle at the west end of the valley and another reclining, pretending to be asleep in the bed of a pickup truck parked at the east end. Forty-five minutes later, they spotted a twenty-mule train walking a path along the opposite hill, appearing and disappearing as it wound through the low rain forest.

Cobra scanned the sky looking for Thai police air surveillance. The most vulnerable time was when the heroin emerged from the jungle. But nothing marked the blue above them except some high clouds and birds in flight.

They watched the drivers transfer heavy burlap packs from

the backs of the mules into the beds of two pickup trucks, then watched them roll east.

As soon as they returned to the Land Cruiser, Shan voices emerged from the staticky background of Kasa's CB radio.

"My people are both behind and in front of the pickups," Kasa told Kai and Cobra. "They're moving slowly and checking for surveillance."

Cobra knew the Wa wouldn't take a direct route to get where they were going. They might travel a complicated thirty kilometers to reach a destination a short ten kilometers away.

"They'll signal us when the heroin gets to its destination." Kasa smiled and patted his stomach. "It may be a while before we have a chance to eat again. We'll stop on the way."

Kai cast Cobra a watch-out-for-an-ambush glance.

Kasa drove to a shacklike café next to a four-story guest house fronting the river. As they walked to a table near the window facing the street, Kai telephoned her driver and bodyguard to tell them their location, then ordered food to be taken to them in the parking lot when they arrived.

Over bowls of spicy Thai rice noodles and Lao sausages, Cobra asked Kasa about his seeming lack of concern about his coming imprisonment.

"I have been through this before, except usually I'm the one doing the guarding. In a few days all this will seem foolish. Eight Iron doesn't want your heroin. He has his own way of making money."

Kai noticed two men enter the restaurant and then take a table at the opposite side. They had hill tribe features, but their slacks and shirts and neat haircuts put them a generation away from their home village.

"It's really interesting," Kasa said. "This is the first time anyone has been held hostage to guarantee a load owned by neither party."

"Unusual circumstances," Kai said, keeping her eyes on the men, "require unusual methods."

She looked back at Kasa. He shook his head.

"Those two aren't mine." Kasa smiled. "I thought they were yours."

They ate in silence until Kasa's cell phone rang. He listened for a moment, then disconnected.

"The truck and the motorcycles are ready."

Kasa drove to an auto repair shop where a wood-railed flatbed truck was waiting, its back covered with a green canvas. Two dark-skinned men rode up on battered Honda motorcycles. They looked over at Kai, then dusted off their worn T-shirts and khaki shorts and walked over.

Cobra felt an edge of unease as Kasa introduced them as Moby and Luck. Their names told him they were Kasa's tribesmen and would be loyal to him over Eight Iron.

As if to emphasize that point, Moby spoke in Shan and Kasa translated.

"The pickups are at a warehouse on the east side of the town."

"I'll stand by with the truck," Cobra said to Kasa. "You and Kai go take a look."

Cobra walked with Kai to her car to retrieve the shortwave gear, then whispered, "Make sure your people are ready to grab Kasa if he tries to make a run for it."

Kai nodded, and then reached under a rear passenger seat and slipped him a small 9mm.

They returned to the truck, agreed on frequencies, tested the equipment, and then Cobra, Moby, and Luck climbed into the cab.

Kai directed Kasa to get into the front passenger seat of the Land Cruiser and gestured for her bodyguard to sit behind him. She sat behind the driver.

Kasa guided them through the dirt backstreets of Mae Sai,

past itinerant laborers and the food carts where they ate, flop-house hotels where they slept, and warehouses where they worked loading and unloading trucks.

After the third turn, Kasa glanced back at Kai's bodyguard.

"What have you got pointed between my shoulders?" Kasa asked. "A Beretta, a Glock, maybe something Chinese?"

"Nothing you need to be concerned about," Kai said. "We're all friends, and we'll stay friends as long as you cooperate."

Cobra called to say he was stationed on a side street a hundred meters west of the warehouse.

Kasa signaled the driver to pull over just before an intersection. An old man squatting by the side of the road rose, approached his window, and whispered in Shan.

Kasa gestured toward the corner, making a curving motion with his hand. "He says the trucks they're using are parked behind the warehouse."

Kai pointed at the old man, "*Koon poot passa Thai dai mai?*" Do you speak Thai?

He nodded.

"Then we'll go together to take a look."

Kai glanced sideways at her bodyguard, then nodded toward Kasa. The bodyguard tilted the barrel upward, pointing it at the base of Kasa's skull. She then walked with the old man around the corner and down an alleyway. He stopped at the back of a dried fish store, then led her inside. From a rear window they watched laborers loading two trucks with sacks of Swatow (Thailand) Fifth Flavor Brand cassava powder that bore the name printed in both English and Chinese.

She called Cobra. "They're two older, dark green, heavy-duty Isuzu cargo carriers. Wood-framed beds. Blue canvas. The sides of the trucks say Thailand Transport, painted in yellow. The license plates are O5782 with the truck code 71 and S7231 with a truck code of 78. I'll send you a photo. Looks like they're hiding the heroin in cassava powder."

Kai raised her phone toward the trucks, snapped the picture, and sent it.

The old man then led her to the corner of the alleyway where they waited to see whether the trucks would head south toward the Bangkok port, east toward Cambodia, Laos, or Vietnam, or north toward Burma.

The trucks crept to the end of the alley and turned north.

Kai called Cobra as she walked back to the Land Cruiser. The driver looped around the block and cut in ahead of the trucks, slowing them down long enough for Cobra to reach the border before they did.

After a drive of three kilometers, Kai spotted the crossing. Her cell phone rang. It was Cobra calling from the other side.

"I can see you. Look up toward the first turn in the road. I'm just past the temple."

"We'll lead the trucks through," Kai said, "then drop off."

Kai took the semiautomatic from her bodyguard's hand, racked back the slide to chamber a round, and then said to Kasa: "Let's try to stay friends just a little bit longer."

CHAPTER 48

G age spotted Kai walking toward him where he stood at the China Eastern Airlines check-in counter at Bangkok's Suvarnabhumi Airport. It was four hours after she'd chained Kasa to a lathe in the Siri Construction warehouse in Chiang Rai. And five hours after that they were approaching a passport control booth at the Hongqiao Airport on the western outskirts of Shanghai.

Zhang Xianzi, a Chinese People's Liberation Army general, stood waiting on the other side. Gage knew no one who understood the coast of the East China Sea better than Zhang and how to exploit that knowledge for personal gain. With the frame of a middleweight boxer, Zhang was dressed in a business suit and accompanied by a uniformed soldier. Gage noticed that his face had softened over the years, but he didn't doubt that concealed behind it remained the calculating and mercenary mind that not only had advanced his career and made him wealthy, but had now drawn Gage back to him.

Zhang glanced at Gage, then fixed his eyes on Kai as the two of them retrieved their passports and approached him.

"And who is this lovely person?" Zhang said, smiling at Kai.

Gage introduced Kai by her Chinese name, Chen Mei-li, then added, "But everyone calls her Kai."

"Kai," Zhang said. "I don't know the name Kai. Where's your home village?"

"A few miles outside Jieyang in Guangdong Province," Kai said, "but I was born in Isaan, in northern Thailand."

Zhang raised a forefinger and said in Mandarin:

So bright a gleam at the foot of my bed,
Could there have been a frost already?
Lifting myself to look, I see that it is moonlight.
Lowering my head, I dream that I am home.

Gage knew that if he hadn't already been feeling queasy, Zhang's histrionic performance would have brought it on. He felt Kai stiffen next to him, but knew she'd play along. He also knew that Zhang would drop the act once he understood that Kai wouldn't be sleeping with him.

"Li Po," Kai said, giving Zhang a soft smile, and then translated the poem into English. "My father read that poem to me and my sister at bedtime. I haven't heard it since she recited it at his funeral."

"Then let me welcome you to your homeland." Zhang turned to Gage. "Where are you staying?"

"The Cypress Hotel," Gage said. "It's close to one of the companies . . ."

Gage paused and looked at the soldier.

"It's okay," Zhang said. "This is Technical Officer Shiu. He can be trusted. You can call him Ferrari." Zhang smiled. "You'll soon find out why."

Gage nodded to Ferrari, then looked back at Zhang.

"The hotel is close to a company whose name came up in connection with the smuggling operation."

Ferrari took their bags and led them toward a Yukon with the boxy license frame of the type used in the States, rather than long narrow frame made to fit Chinese plates. Gage had no doubt that it had been stolen in the United States and smuggled into China, and he suspected Zhang had intercepted it and kept it for himself. It was a natural conclusion. Gage had first met Zhang in connection with an auto smuggling case. Car carriers bearing Mercedes SUVs had been hijacked on their way from the factory to the Port of Bremerhaven in Germany. The vehicles were then loaded into containers and shipped to Shanghai. Gage suspected Zhang had appropriated a few for himself and other officers as a kind of tax imposed on the conspiracy by the PLA.

While Ferrari loaded their luggage into the back, Kai and Gage settled into the rear passenger seats and Zhang climbed into the front.

The Hongqiao Special Economic Zone came into view as they left the airport. Gage spotted a sign for ChinaCom among dozens of other high-tech companies along the highway just before they turned into the grass-covered and tree-bordered hotel grounds. Gage had decided not to tell Zhang that China-Com might be the ultimate recipient of the microchips. It wasn't worth the risk that Zhang might make a preemptive move. Gage had always known Zhang to be in a hot rage for profit and figured it would be wise to take his temperature first.

After they checked in and Zhang went to make dinner arrangements, Kai came to Gage's suite to wait to hear from Cobra. They didn't know whether he was in an area where he had cell service or would have to use the shortwave. Gage examined the scratched and battered radio as she got it ready on the desk in the bedroom. He suspected that years earlier she'd used it to contact mother ships anchored off the coast of Vietnam, waiting to on-load bales of Thai marijuana for the voyage to the western United States, Canada, and Europe.

On the half hour, Cobra's voice chirped in from the receiver's speaker.

"Isaan one, Isaan one, over."

"Isaan one, over," Kai answered.

"We're with our friends. All is well. Over."

"Is the weather good? Over."

"Just what we expected. Over."

"Isaan one, out."

"Isaan one, out."

"Why the weather report?" Gage asked.

"Just to make sure he's all right. If things were looking like they were going wrong or they had overpowered him, he would have said it was warmer than expected."

"Sometimes when I look at you it's hard to imagine you in the dope trade. But right now it's not hard at all."

Kai smiled. "Those were wild days. I'm not sure I've felt this much alive since then." Her smile died and she looked out the window at the green hotel grounds and the distant gray high-rises and factories. "Somehow the years between then and now have just evaporated. It makes me wonder what I've really been doing all this time and how I've gotten to where I am." She shook her head. "But now is the wrong time to think about this." She smiled again. "I think I'll wait to have my crisis after this one is over."

Gage smiled back. "Anytime you're ready."

Kai packed up the shortwave gear and slid it under the bed.

"You ready to clue in the general about what's going on?" Kai asked.

Gage imagined the fishing boats sailing the East China Sea and the trucks traveling the Burma Road.

"I'm not sure; something doesn't feel right, but I don't know what it is."

Gage knew that nausea and weakness were graying his mind,

but he couldn't shake free from it to see the whole of what was generating his unease. Part of it was that he had neither a guarantee the chips really were on the East China Sea or the heroin really was in those bags of cassava powder. That wasn't all, but he didn't know what else.

"We'll have to feel him out before we disclose anything important."

They rode the elevator down to where Zhang was waiting for them in the bar. Walking toward him where he sat at a low table by the window, Gage examined him against the backdrop of the flowering gardens where old women in straw hats were bent over tending the plants. The women seemed oblivious not only to the hotel guests talking business and drinking, but to those like Gage who were wondering where these women had come from and how it was that life had led them to work into old age just a pane of glass away from the kind of crime and corruption represented by men like Zhang.

Zhang waited until their drinks were served, then asked, "Time for business?"

Gage nodded. "But let me start with a hypothetical." He leaned forward and lowered his voice. "Suppose there was a smuggling transaction involving the coast of China. On one side are stolen items. On the other, contraband."

"What contraband?"

"I'll get to that later."

"By container or by fishing boat?"

Given the thousands of fishing boats in the straits between Taiwan and China, Gage didn't think there was a risk in answering.

"Fishing boat."

"And you're thinking . . ."

"Border trade."

"And that's why you called me."

"Exactly."

When Gage first met Zhang, he commanded a PLA-controlled port on the North China Sea, used by the military to circumvent official government trade barriers with South Korea and Taiwan and to earn income by taxing goods passing through. Only half the PLA's budget came from the central government; the rest they earned in business and managing illegal trade.

"It is likely that neither side has disclosed to the border trade commander the nature of the goods that will be passing through his jurisdiction."

"What makes you think that?"

"Risk and the high value of the goods."

"That would mean the contraband is doubly smuggled," Zhang said, "into China and also past the commander. They want the protection without paying the full price the amount of risk demands."

"That's what I'm thinking. The question is whether, with full knowledge, the commander would allow the transaction to occur in exchange for adequate compensation."

Zhang shrugged. "It depends on what that is."

"The stolen items."

"What are they worth?"

"At least a few million dollars."

"And the contraband has the same value."

"Probably the same, or very close."

"So it's a barter of some kind."

"It seems that way."

Zhang took a sip of his drink and looked out at the elderly gardeners. Finally, he said, "The commander would want deniability."

"Which would at least mean he wouldn't interfere."

Zhang opened his palms on the table before him. "He can't act on what he doesn't know about."

"How would you suggest we approach such a commander?"

Zhang grinned. "You know how and you just did, at least indirectly. And that tells me you think the port they're using is along the East China Sea."

Gage nodded. "At least the stolen goods on one side of the transaction."

"And the other?"

"I don't know yet."

"And when do you expect this hypothetical to become real?"

"It left port within the last twelve hours and we think it will arrive within the next three days. Maybe sooner."

The maître d' arrived to escort them to the dining room. Gage let Kai walk ahead with Zhang. They spoke quietly in Chinese. Gage hoped Kai was continuing to display warm feelings toward Zhang's poetry and gestures. He believed that he had a better chance to judge the depth of the general's thinking if his attention was divided and he was a little off balance.

Gage found that Zhang had arranged for flowers matching the red and purple bougainvillea theme of the garden and for a centerpiece of sculpted fruits and vegetables. Silver-clad chopsticks were laid next to flowered China place settings in front of the three tall-backed upholstered chairs.

The investment Zhang had made in the dinner communicated to Gage that he expected a big payoff.

Waitresses bought crab and egg-drop soup, followed by a series of northern Chinese dishes.

Gage saw actual delight in Kai's face and a bit of the shark in Zhang's as southern Chinese Chaozhou steamed fish was carried in last.

"I ordered this especially for you," Zhang said, serving Kai the first piece.

It was pure Zhang, Gage thought. Either he knew already or

did the research to discover that her family's ancestral village was in a Chaozhou-speaking area.

Kai closed her eyes as she tasted it and set down her chopsticks.

"Wonderful," she finally said, opening her eyes again and smiling at Zhang. "You're very thoughtful."

Gage knew that there was a single word in Chinese that meant both opportunity and danger and wondered if there was also one that meant both thoughtful and devious to describe Zhang and another that meant grateful and suspicious to describe Kai.

"Are we ready to move from fantasy to reality?" Zhang asked, then looked from Kai to Gage.

"Let's first take the hypothetical a step further," Gage said. "Would our commander know how to dispose of microprocessors?"

Zhang stared down at the plate of steamed fish as he answered. "The question isn't what a commander would do, but"—he now looked up at Gage—"and this is only a hypothetical . . . it's what a general would do."

"Well, what would a general do?"

"A general would prove to his superiors he's taking vigorous action to suppress software and hardware piracy so the Central Committee can satisfy the Americans that China is a good citizen of the world economic community."

Gage smiled to himself. Zhang had mastered political craft in the years since they had last worked together. Back then his first impulse would've been to grab the chips and sell them on the black market, not giving a thought to how he could leverage the seizure into personal power. But Gage didn't fool himself. Deception was also part of political craft and he had no reason to think Zhang was telling the truth.

"What would our hypothetical general expect in compensation for his patriotism?"

Zhang bit his lip for a moment, then said, "I think he'd need to hear a proposal."

The pause told Gage they were now out of Zhang's territory and into Gage's.

"How about a confidential reward from the company that insured the chips. It could be paid into a Hong Kong bank account?"

Zhang shook his head. "A general couldn't have his name associated with that or he'd soon find his head lying on the ground next to him."

"Suppose it was deposited into an account in the name of a Hong Kong company. Let's call it, hypothetically, K-A-I Investments Limited."

Kai smiled. "Very good. I like that name."

"Why K-A-I?" Zhang smiled. "Oh. I see. I like that, too."

"How much money would it take?"

Zhang rocked his head side to side, then said, "The general wouldn't be greedy. Enough to ensure he could travel in comfort outside of China, perhaps to fund his children's college education in the States."

"I suspect the insurance carrier would pay around a quarter of what the chips are worth." Gage then estimated a low total so Zhang wouldn't feel betrayed later if the value fell short of what the victim company claimed. "That would make it twenty-five percent of about one point five million dollars."

Zhang's eyebrows rose even higher than Gage expected, then he asked, "When could the general find out whether the insurance company will agree, at least in principle?"

"Maybe late tonight."

Gage rose from his chair. He reached into his pocket and handed Zhang a list of thirty boat names and hull numbers.

"The microchips are on one of these. How about find out where along the coast they're expected." Like other ports, border trade ports required shippers to identify ships and cargos before arrival, in the official ports to assess duties, in the PLA ports to assess fees and bribes. "Once we have a deal, I tell you which one is carrying them."

"Careful as ever, aren't you?"

Gage knew Zhang wasn't expecting an answer, so he didn't give one. Instead, he said, "Why don't I leave you two to enjoy the rest of the evening while I go make some calls?"

The look of the shark once again crossed Zhang's face.

Gage winked at Kai as he passed by her and headed out the door.

CHAPTER 49

There's a chance we can recover the chips without jeopardizing what I'm trying to do," Gage told Jack Burch in a call from his room. "But it'll cost something."

"I'll work that part out, just tell me who gets the money."

"A company in Hong Kong."

"Which one?"

"Whatever one you set up."

Burch laughed. "So it's that way."

"It's always that way over here. Talk to you later."

"Hold up a second. Isn't there something you're supposed to tell me?"

"I'm fine. Following doctor's orders."

"Thanks. I needed to hear that."

Gage disconnected, then called Sylvia.

"Get a hold of Joe Casey and find out the name of the company that insured the chips. Just say the parties want to deal directly with the carrier and to leave the FBI out of it. I talked to someone who might be able to recover them. He's the biggest fish in these waters and needs to be fed."

Gage's cell rang a few minutes later.

"It's called Industrial Insurance," Sylvia said. "Out of the Bahamas. Casey gave me the name of the adjuster in the States and threw in a little tidbit he said might interest you. Get this. He got a message from the Ministry of Justice Intelligence Bureau in Taiwan that they intercepted a call from an unknown person in the San Francisco area to a known United Bamboo enforcer containing a threat against someone named Lew who was supposed to be on his way north. The order was to kill Lew if anything goes wrong. Casey doesn't know if he's the same Lew as the one at East Wind, but he wanted you to know."

"What did MJIB want from the FBI?"

"Help in stopping a homicide. They think north means Taipei since it's on the north end of the island."

"Maybe Ah Ming is sending Lew over here to do the deal. If ICE confirms that Lew is heading this way, then Casey has a legitimate basis to tell the Taiwanese that north is outside of Taiwan altogether and that he'll track the matter himself."

"Don't you want to talk to Casey yourself? I know he wants to talk to you. He said something about his losing sleep."

"There's no reason to leave a cell-phone trail from me to him. Tell him I'm sleeping like a baby and he should, too."

Gage called Burch and gave him the name of the insurer.

"They'll need to make a quick decision," Gage said.

"I'll give them until midnight Pacific Time. Eight A.M. tomorrow where you are."

Gage heard a knock just after hanging up. He figured Zhang was too anxious to wait until morning for an update. He opened the door to find Kai displaying the Thai *yim cheua-cheuan*, the you-can't-outfox-me smile.

"Nice try," she said.

"I thought you were interested." Gage grinned at her. "The poetry, the food from home."

"The guy's just a . . . how do you say . . . just a fucking car thief.

Sorry, a general fucking car thief. I'll bet he didn't even pay for that suit he was wearing."

"I hope you didn't hurt his feelings."

"I just slipped in that my husband is the minister of the interior, you know, head of the police and intelligence."

"How'd he react?"

"His moment of profound disappointment was quickly surpassed by the pull of *guanxi* and right away he said he'd like to meet Somchai to do a little networking."

Gage reached for the doorknob. "And now you're going to your room?"

Kai shrugged and then gave him an up-from-under look.

"I don't know. The poetry and all kind of put me in the mood for . . ."

Gage shook his head as he started to ease the door closed. "There's nothing that doesn't put you in the mood. I'll see you in the morning."

AT 6 A.M. Kai returned to Gage's room to await both Burch's call and an update from Cobra. It had been a hard night; Gage had woken up three times in a heavy sweat.

Kai sat down on the edge of the bed and leaned back against the headboard, resting her hands on the sheet, then jumped up.

"Did you spill something?" she asked, wiping her hands on a dry sheet corner.

Gage glanced back from where he sat at the desk and lied. "No, I dropped a wet towel there after I took a shower. Just toss the bedspread over it."

Gage answered his cell phone on the first ring. It was Burch.

"Industrial Insurance has accepted our terms and e-mailed a draft agreement. I added a confidentiality clause with respect to the award, the amount, and the name of the recipient company, and they agreed to it."

Gage nodded at Kai.

"How do they want to handle the condition of the chips and the quantity?"

"That is a little complicated. Off the record they told me they suspect the victim of the robbery is inflating his losses, maybe by thirty percent. The insurance company has the serial numbers of all the chips Intel sold to him in the last six months, but they don't know how many he had left in stock."

"Which means we won't know the total number and type until we recover them . . . if we recover them."

It struck Gage that he needed a hostage of a different kind to make this work.

"Suggest they put money in your trust account based on the claim as it stands, even if they believe it's inflated. When the time comes, they can send over a technician to examine and inventory the chips. But don't tell them yet where we think the chips will be. Make them think they're in the States. Things are going to get messy enough and I don't want them trying to go around us thinking they can save a few bucks. The last thing we want is to have the guy helping us here feel betrayed. It might get people killed."

"You mean you."

"Among others."

CHAPTER 50

S unrise found Cobra staring at the tarp covering the back of the second of the two heroin trucks heading north on the Old Burma Road in Southern China. He let his eyes take in the passing bamboo, palm, and pine trees of the surrounding hillsides just emerging from the darkness, but still ghosted by the low clouds of the high forest. He felt Luck stir as he slept in the cab between him and Moby in the driver's seat.

Moby downshifted as he approached a tight turn. The gears ground and the truck bucked. He looked over at Cobra and shrugged, his eyes glinting red in the taillights shining back at them.

Cobra had found Moby and Luck to be no different than other Shan tribesmen he'd met over the years, men who were instrumental in the drug trade, but who never saw any of the real money, never even seemed willing to let themselves think about it. They were soldiers in a war of all against all, members of tribes that had fought each other and foreign invaders for two thousand years. For them, heroin was merely a commodity, no different than the rice or soybeans the Thais and Burmese sold on the world market to purchase arms from China to use against them.

And they knew how to handle themselves.

Cobra looked at his watch and then his cell phone, but there was no service in the canyon through which they were passing. He switched on the shortwave knowing Gage and Kai would be standing by.

"Isaan one, Isaan one. Over."

"Isaan one here. Over," Kai answered.

"We are still with our friends, over."

"Where are you? Over."

"North of Pu'er, south of Kunming."

"And the weather? Over."

"Still good. Over."

"Isaan one, out."

"Isaan one, out."

"WHY DON'T YOU GO DOWN and collect your friend Zhang," Gage told Kai, as they once again packed up the radio. "We can have breakfast up here."

Gage ordered room service and it had been laid out on the dining table in the living room, overlooking the hotel gardens by the time Kai and Zhang arrived.

Zhang reached into his shirt pocket and pulled out Gage's list of boat names and numbers. He held it up long enough for them to see that names of ports had been written next to each, then put it away.

"Do you trust this man Burch?" Zhang asked.

Gage nodded.

"What about the people in Hong Kong who'll handle the company and the bank account?"

"Jack didn't tell me who he's using, but it'll be a firm he's done a lot of business with."

"And that puzzles me. I checked on Burch. He's big. Huge. He's Global 500 not Formosa Strait smuggling. Why would he risk involving himself in something like this?"

Gage found the question irrelevant. Zhang was using his temporary leverage from Gage, needing his help to mine for information about Burch in order to exploit it, and maybe Burch, later. But Gage wasn't going to give him the opportunity.

"He doesn't know what this is all about."

Zhang smiled. "Deniability."

Gage shook his head, not returning the smile. "Not even that."

Zhang seemed to realize that his move had been blocked and resigned himself to now having to make a decision. Holding his teacup in his hand, he gazed out of the window and down toward the gardens below like a high diver on a windy day.

And then jumped: "We've got a deal."

Gage called Burch from the bedroom while Kai and Zhang ate breakfast.

"The insurance carrier agreed to the escrow idea," Burch said. "They figure they can recover part of their loss by discounting and reselling the chips. And I bought a company from a friend in Hong Kong. He was with Arthur Andersen before it evaporated. He set up a number of shelf companies about two years ago and has been selling them off over time. An older one is more expensive, but I figured it would draw less attention than a new one. I don't know if the person you're dealing with understands any of this, but if he does, he'll find it reassuring."

"He won't, but I do. This is his first time he's dealt offshore at this level. And don't use the phrases shelf company or shell company when you talk to him, he'll just get confused. Just say ready-made."

Gage wrote down the name of the company and the location of the bank and the account number, then disconnected and walked back into the living room.

"The company is called Calico Limited."

Zhang smiled. "I was hoping for K-A-I."

Gage shrugged. "Not everything is possible."

"It does seem that way, doesn't it," Zhang said, then reached again for the list of boats and handed it to Kai.

From her pocket, Kai pulled out a slip of paper showing the partial hull number of the smuggling boat, then scanned down numbers and looked up at Gage.

"It's on its way to Qidong."

Gage turned toward Zhang. "Which is where?"

"North along the Yangtze. Jiangsu Province. Just a few hours' drive from here."

After Zhang left to make arrangements for the trip, Gage brought up a map of the Qidong area on his cell phone and displayed it for Kai.

Gage then texted Alex Z asking him to search Ah Tien's address book for names and companies in that area.

When he looked up from his phone, Kai said, "I'm worried that with Zhang we could have another Eight Iron on our hands. This is his world, not ours, and he could cut us out and steal the chips. He's a snake. Two PLA officers got executed for being involved in the car smuggling case from when you first met him. He was up to his neck in it, and all he got was promoted."

"I don't think he'll be that shortsighted about this. He's getting at least half a million dollars and an offshore company and a bank account. He's spent his whole career landlocked and we're giving him the tools to go international. It's something he'd never be able to do on his own, or at least without having to share with others in the PLA. And the only reason he's getting any of this is because Burch told his people in Hong Kong that this is a legitimately acquired insurance reward."

Kai pulled back and looked at Gage. "Legitimately?" Her voice whined with sarcasm. "Did you say legitimately?"

"Apparently you didn't study cultural relativity in college in the States."

"I didn't need to. I practiced it."

CHAPTER 51

When Gage and Kai walked out the hotel exit, they spotted Ferrari dressed in civilian clothes standing at the curb next to a five-year-old Toyota van with tinted windows. He pulled open the sliding door as they approached and took their bags around to the back. They found Zhang sitting on one of two rear bench seats facing a table on which lay maps, note paper, cell phones, and thermoses of tea.

Soon after leaving the hotel grounds, they passed hundreds of taxis in a line extending from the airport, each driver leaning against his car, waiting his turn to grab a fare for the long ride into the commercial center of Shanghai or to the Nanjing Road shopping district. Gage felt anger rumble inside him when he noticed that most of them were smoking, killing themselves, embracing the cancer that he was fighting, wasting their bodies and their lives.

He forced himself to look away as Ferrari cut north.

Ferrari took them along the far western edge of the city of twenty-three million, skirting the center gasping for the ocean air sweeping the gray-brown haze of diesel fumes and coal ash inland. The pollution didn't bother Gage as much as the cab drivers' cigarette smoke, for when hundreds of millions live in poverty, pollution can be seen as a sign of progress, even of hope.

Gage studied Zhang talking on his cell phone, a man he knew to be content in that unpredictable nexus where power and greed conjoined in state-authorized corruption. He then realized that Zhang was so focused on the money he never asked who Gage was working for and what he stood to gain. At the same time, he doubted Zhang would ask what was being exchanged for the chips. He'd likely figure it out on his own and surely keep it to himself.

As they drove farther north and west, Ferrari slowed next to Anting Automobile City. Zhang looked out of the window and pointed at a billboard displaying a Formula One race car, blurred by its two-hundred-mile-an-hour velocity.

"The Shanghai Grand Prix," Zhang said, glancing over his shoulder at Ferrari. "Maybe someday . . ."

In the rearview mirror Gage could see a smile emerge on Ferrari's face.

"But not now."

Ferrari hit the accelerator and they merged back into traffic.

Gage glanced down at Zhang's cell phone lying on the desk. "You have any leads about when the chips will come to shore?"

"Not yet, but it won't make any difference. My people will be watching for it."

"Maybe this will help them."

Gage handed Zhang a list of the names and decoded numbers they recovered from Ah Tien.

"My staff located two companies that might be involved. They were listed in an address book belonging to a man named Ah Tien in San Francisco. Tongming Tiger and Efficiency Trading. Both are in a city called Nantong."

Zhang nodded. "I know the place. Commercial and agricultural. About a million people. It's west of the port and next to a Special Economic Zone."

"And someone at the local trade bureau may be helping them."

Zhang looked from the sheet to Gage. "What did this Ah Tien have to say about them?"

"He's not talking anymore."

Zhang drew back, then said, "Oh, I see." He then scanned the company names and read one aloud: "Chao Yang. That's Chaozhou for Sunny Glory." He looked up. "Are all these people Chaozhou?"

"I think the ones in Thailand and Taiwan are."

"Dangerous people," Zhang said, then smiled at Kai. "Except you, of course."

"Thank you, that's very generous." Kai pinched Gage's thigh under the table as punishment for Zhang's crime.

Gage knew once Zhang made the Chaozhou connection, he'd assume that the contraband was heroin, for they controlled the major trafficking syndicates and had managed the trade routes for more than three generations. There was no reason now not to specify the origin of the heroin.

"The contraband I mentioned is being trucked north from Thailand. And there may be a man named Lew Fung-hao on his way from the States to meet it."

Gage decided not to tell Zhang about the enforcer traveling from Taiwan that Casey had learned about. He didn't want Zhang to think U.S. law enforcement was paying attention.

Zhang punched a number into his cell phone, then passed on Lew's name and the names and telephone numbers from the list.

"I need to have what you would call a hypothetical discussion with the commander of the Qidong port," Zhang said. "We'll have to come to an agreement about the contraband. We have capital punishment in China, a great deal of it and enforced rather capriciously, so this could be a little tricky."

They drove on through the rice, wheat, and cotton fields of Jiangsu Province toward the dock where the ferry crossed the Yangtze River, then waited in a long line of cars and trucks. They were among the last to make it on.

Gage and Kai left the car and took the stairs to the upper deck. As he looked out over the Yangtze, it seemed more like the East China Sea into which it fed. The opposite bank was not only lost in fog, but was too far away to be seen even on a fogless day, and the river was populated mostly by oceangoing ships. Only the barges reminded Gage that they were on a river.

After they left the ferry behind on the northern bank, they drove to the crossroads between the Qidong port in the east and Nantong City in the west.

A car was waiting to take Zhang to meet the commander.

As Gage and Kai rode with Ferrari toward Nantong, Gage felt just as he often had at homicide scenes so many years ago in San Francisco. He'd walk into a house or an apartment or a basement and see a corpse splayed out. Then he'd smell food cooking next door and overhear the sounds of laughter, of everyday conversation, of people oblivious to a violent death that had been inflicted on the other side of their wall. He'd think of the victim's relatives a thousand miles away, equally oblivious, laughing at a crude joke at the moment of death—

Then a call, a knock, a chill, a new world.

Everyone is oblivious to almost everything, Gage thought to himself as he looked out at the countryside, imagining the tough little farmers far inland carrying their oranges a thousand feet down to the Yangtze, workers hunched over in wheat fields and rice paddies, all of them knowing nothing of microprocessors, or of offshore corporations, or of stolen SUVs. But they didn't need to know, at least about these microprocessors or this offshore corporation or Zhang's SUV.

On the other hand, Gage knew that if he kept his strength and had his way, in the next few days men in Nantong, and even Lew himself, would hear the knock and feel the chill and face a new world because of the death of a confused teenage boy a couple of weeks earlier on a warehouse floor an ocean away.

CHAPTER 52

C obra sat on his motorcycle in the shadow of a tree a hundred yards from a gasoline station in Southern China where the two heroin trucks had stopped to repair a flat tire. They were just a few miles from Kunming. Cobra had starting using the bike to follow them because it reduced his chances of losing them in the chaotic traffic in the city of a million and a half people. But he was tired. He'd stayed awake all night, fearing that if he fell asleep, he'd wake up when his body hit the pavement a second after Moby and Luck tossed him from the truck.

His mind began to drift as he gazed down the dusty, oil-spotted road. He shook his head and the trucks once again became clear. He needed to concentrate, control himself, if for no other reason than he didn't want to be seen staring. He knew nothing would give him away more easily than glazed eyes, seen from a distance, fixed toward something no longer in focus.

He edged forward to stay in the tree's shadow, moving with the transit of the sun.

A grease-covered mechanic bent low and rubbed a rag on the side of the tire and squinted at the printing. He then hopped into a battered pickup truck and raced off, leaving a spray of dust and gravel behind.

Cobra's mind again began to drift, now back in time to just after he'd resigned from the MJIB and he'd married Malee, trying to find a way to make a living, and to stay alive doing it. He saw himself in Bangkok, standing just inside the door to an underground casino, the eight baccarat tables populated by Thai-Chinese *nak laeng* tough guys and *jao phor* godfathers, the walls lined with their bodyguards. He'd felt motion in the threshold and the room went silent. He looked over to see a *gwai lo*, a white ghost, standing next to him surveying the crowd.

Cobra shifted his weight and blinked hard at the truck in the distance. He pushed the bike forward again, then took off his cap so the sun edging the tree's shadow would keep him alert. But his mind wouldn't stay focused; it had to do something while he waited and his eyes watched. A mind can't be blank.

Cobra followed Gage's gaze and saw the questions forming in the minds behind the gamblers' faces: *Who is this crazy white ghost?* Some asking: *Is it about me?* Guards drew their semiautomatics, but Gage ignored them, scanning the tables until he fixed a stare on a man calling himself Henry Hong, a gangster just arrived from the States who's bought his way into the game with two hundred thousand dollars. A couple of the casino guards started to advance on Gage, but the owner, Thanom Suanmali, waved them off. He wanted to see what Gage was up to, how tough he was, how Gage would stand up against the hardest men in Bangkok. They all watched Gage walk up to the table at which Hong was gambling. The other players backed away. He pointed at the stacks of cash in front of Hong.

"Is that yours?" Gage asked.

Hong stared back, trying to break Gage's gaze, but then lowered his eyes and said, "It's all mine." But his voice was so weak that he forfeited whatever loyalty he might've expected from the others.

Gage picked up the bills and then looked at Thanom, now a referee in a game with higher stakes. "You speak English?"

"Some." Thanom smiled. "Michigan State, 1986." He nodded at the cash in Gage's hand. "I take it that's not his money."

Gage shook his head. "Stolen from my client in the States. His name is Ho."

"That's odd. He said his name was Hong." He pointed at a guard who patted Ho down and withdrew a passport and brought it to him. Thanom glanced inside, then tossed it on the floor. "I believe you. As weak as he is, you should just kill him. No one will mind. You'll be doing us a favor."

Ho's eyes turned wild, jerking side to side, looking from guard to guard, from gun to gun.

Gage shook his head again. "This is only about money."

"Since you're now our guest, it's up to you." Thanom grinned. "How'd you get in here? It costs me a lot of money to keep people out."

Gage shrugged. "I think I'll keep that to myself. I may need to come back."

"You won't need to. I'll have whatever money he has left by tomorrow."

Thanom pointed at Cobra. "Make arrangements to collect it all and deliver it to our friend." He then looked again at Gage. "What's your name?"

"Graham Gage."

Thanom nodded and smiled. "I think we'll call you Santisuk if you come this way again. Thanks for the very interesting evening."

Cobra and Gage walked out together.

"What's Santisuk?" Gage asked.

"A nickname. It means peaceful."

I still don't know if he was right, Cobra thought as he watched the heroin trucks. But the name caught on with people in Thailand because it seemed to ring true, but . . . but Gage's force of will was the nearest substitute for violence Cobra had ever seen.

Maybe, Cobra now wondered, Thanom had meant the name as irony.

Cobra's heart thumped harder as he watched the small pickup truck return, its tail pressed low to the ground by the weight of the tire in the bed.

In a few more minutes it would be mounted, and it would be time for the truck to move on, and for him to make some decisions.

age and Kai checked into the Nantong Center Hotel in the financial heart of the city an hour after Zhang separated from them at the crossroads. Gage chose it from those suggested by Zhang because it catered to foreigners and Chinese who came to meet with traders and manufacturers in the Special Economic Zone, an onshore haven with offshore tax benefits. It was also at a low-enough end of the trade that it was unlikely he'd encounter anyone who might know him.

Gage found that his suite was just clean enough: well-swept concrete floors discolored by ground-in grime, traces of bathroom mildew, a teacup-ringed, child-size cherry wooden desk, and double beds with stiff sheets and hard pillows.

"Commander Ren is considering our proposition," Zhang said, when he and Kai arrived in Gage's room an hour later. "I suggested a private financial arrangement between him and me. His only requirement is that he doesn't want to be in Qidong if any contraband passes through the port."

"Will we need him at that point?"

Zhang shook his head. "Not once we learn how the deal is structured, and we've made progress on that end. Ren says that Efficiency Trading is a China-Taiwan joint venture, set up through the local trade bureau. The domestic shareholder is called Lao Wu, Old Wu."

"How old is old?"

"Early seventies. And the foreign shareholder is a Taiwanese company on Ah Tien's list. Sunny Glory, in Taichung."

"And in San Francisco."

Kai looked at Gage. "And that closes the circle."

"Maybe. Maybe not. It could be one that closed around a prior deal, not this one. The killing of the kid during the chip robbery may have reverberated through their operation, forcing them out of their routine."

But they all knew it was all they had to go on.

"Have Sunny Glory and Efficiency Trading done much business during the last few years?"

Zhang reached into his jacket pocket and pulled out his notes. "The port's paperwork shows mushrooms, ginger, and cashews coming in and processed garlic going out."

"What about the other company Ah Tien had coded, Tongming Tiger. Any shipments between it and Sunny Glory, in either direction?"

"None. Tongming Tiger is a domestic dealer in pharmaceuticals, medicinal herbs, and grains. As far as we can tell, it has no connection either with Sunny Glory or Efficiency Trading."

Gage had been hoping to find a pattern or something he could imagine on a flowchart, but he hadn't found it. And he didn't want to assume that since all three weren't connected aboveground they must be connected underground.

He looped back through the conversation, arriving at Commander Ren's mention of the trade bureau. "Who at the trade bureau was involved in setting up the Efficiency Trading joint venture?"

"A man whose name was also in Ah Tien's little book. Mao Zhou-li."

Gage walked to the window overlooking the street. He needed time to think about how to approach the trade bureau, knowing the wrong move might reverberate all the way back to Ah Ming. Day laborers were crowded around a pushcart below him on the sidewalk, flame and steam rising from a wok on top. Next to it a woman was selling dumplings and fish.

"What did you put down for us on the hotel registration form?" Gage asked Zhang, turning back.

"That you're an American businessman and Kai is your translator. I told the clerk you're here to look into setting up a joint venture with a Chinese state enterprise to process ginger for export."

"And you?"

"I represent the state enterprise."

"And what do we know about ginger?" Gage asked.

"There can't be that much to it," Zhang said, answering like a person who knew nothing about farming, who thought money was complicated and nature was simple.

Gage saw Kai clench her jaws at Zhang's arrogance and ignorance. She knew otherwise, for her father had been an agricultural trader in northeastern Thailand.

"My father worked with ginger farmers and processors before he started his own business. I know enough to bluff anyone who might ask."

WHEN THEY LEFT THE HOTEL to walk to the restaurant down the block to meet the port commander, Ren, for lunch, they stopped to watch a group of farmers arguing with a city official. One was waving a heavy cotton bag as if it could speak for him.

"He's saying that he and his family were moved here by the government from an area flooded by the Three Gorges Dam," Kai told Gage. "Just downstream of Chongqing. He has orange seeds in his bag. The government promised him land to replace the orchard he was forced to abandon."

"I take it he didn't get any."

"No," Zhang said. "And it's the same all along the lower Yangtze. All these farmers want to live near the river, but there's not enough land. And there hasn't been for a thousand years. It's time they accepted that fact."

The restaurant owner was also watching the scene. He broke away to invite them inside the heavy, wood-framed building.

Gage had seen many like them in China, nineteenth-century teahouses wrested away at the beginning of the twentieth century from country folk and converted into Shanghai-style social clubs, with bourbon replacing tea, and jazz replacing Chinese *zheng*. They were seized by the Communist Party for communal use in the 1950s and finally privatized in the 1990s after it became glorious for the few to be rich.

The owner led them past chickens and ducks pacing in cages, turtles and frogs resting in plastic tubs of shallow water, and snakes sleeping in glass tanks. Crabs, shrimp, lobsters, and salt and fresh water fish inspected them from aerated commercial aquariums as they walked by.

Gage observed a thief's pride of ownership on the man's face, an expression revealing that the restaurant was his, but that he hadn't earned it. Gage suspected he'd been the manager during communist times and grabbed it for himself during the first, chaotic capitalist years.

Commander Ren was waiting in a private dining room. At first sight, he seemed to Gage to possess the manner of a young Zhang, except that he was taller and darker. As he rose, he displayed more military bearing than Zhang had ever shown, but his eyes, darting from Gage to Kai and back, seemed at least as calculating

Ren's attire, particularly his cheap watch and mass-produced shoes, suggested to Gage that he hadn't gotten to the big money yet, maybe because he was unwilling to take the kinds of risks Zhang had always been willing to take, ones that now might lead to a bullet in the back of the head instead of a Hong Kong bank account.

As Gage walked across the room to shake Ren's hand, he noticed that in business banquet fashion, bottles of beer and cognac were lined up on a side table next to the window. And he knew then what Zhang hoped to accomplish with the meal and how it would end.

By the time they'd moved past the shark fin soup and the sautéed prawns in garlic, Ren and Zhang had gone from beer to cognac. By the time they consumed the steamed freshwater fish, the goose tongues, and the chicken feet, the two were red-faced. By the time they'd finished the roasted snake, the fried scorpion, and the *tungpo* pork fat, the two soldiers had toasted Kai, Gage, each other, the weather, the cook, the Yangtze, and each day of the week.

Neither Zhang nor Ren seemed to have noticed that Kai and Gage had nursed the same beers throughout the meal. She and he understood the dance in which Ren and Zhang were engaged and their participation wasn't required.

Afterward, Gage guided Zhang and Ren to the hotel where he rented them a double room to sleep off their lunch.

Gage and Kai then walked in silence along the river while they waited for Cobra to check in, both understanding that his day wasn't being spent as harmlessly as theirs.

fter the tire had been changed, Cobra and Luck had ridden their motorcycles behind the Thai heroin trucks into the commercial center of Kunming. They'd left Moby and their own truck near the shop where the tire had been repaired. He'd remain there until Luck called him. The two traded the lead position, switching when the traffic was thick or when they were stopped at an intersection. The mass of trucks, scooters, bicycles, pedestrians, fruit sellers, and food stalls crowded with customers spilling into the street made for a slow-going pursuit.

They trailed the heroin into an industrial district bordering a residential area of three-story commercial town houses with small groceries, pharmacies, hardware stores, or video rental shops on the first floor and living units above. The two trucks then made a final turn into a large alleyway and swung in behind the loading dock of a warehouse.

As the drivers reviewed the bills of lading with a clerk, Cobra and Luck parked their motorbikes sixty yards away, near a food cart. They bought noodles and took their bowls and sat down in metal chairs at a folding table in the midst of a dozen others crowded with workers eating, talking, and laughing. From there, Cobra surveyed the dozen laborers seated on the ground at the back of the warehouse. Most wore the traditional Shan, Hakka, or Meo *longyi*, ankle-length shirts knotted at the waist, while others had adapted to the Chinese laborer's uniform of shorts and T-shirts. Cobra guessed they were tribesmen who'd made an after-harvest trek down from their plots in the hills to earn cash in the city.

Ten minutes later, two Chinese trucks drove in from the opposite direction, then backed to the rear of the Thai trucks. Cobra couldn't make out the license plates or the company names, but he could see logos of lions painted in red against the gray background of the doors.

"I'll walk around the block," Cobra told Luck as he got up from the table, "and come up from the other side so I can get the license plate numbers. You watch from here."

Cobra slipped around the near corner and headed along a row of first-floor shops. He next walked the length of the block turning left and left again. By the time he'd gotten into a position twenty yards away, laborers had begun transferring the sacks of cassava powder with the heroin concealed inside from the Thai to the Chinese trucks. He stood facing an empty storefront that was advertised for rent and tried to make it appear that he was inspecting it and noting down rental information as he wrote down the license numbers and the company names that were printed on sides of the trucks. As he snapped a photo with his phone, he spotted Luck walking back to the table from the direction of the warehouse.

Cobra retraced his steps, this time stopping at a small grocery store to buy two Cokes, opening them as he walked back. He found Luck sitting again at the table, sweating in the midday sun, acting as though he'd never left. The previously empty tables around theirs were now filled with workers, talking and laughing and slurping their noodles.

Cobra handed Luck one of the sodas as he sat down. Luck sipped his Coke, never taking his eyes from the trucks in the distance. Finally, Luck caught Cobra's eye, then nodded toward an alley running between the buildings behind them, indicating that they needed to get away from those around them in order to talk. He rose and Cobra led him between the tables and past the cart, then down ten yards to the opening.

"It looks like they're about ten minutes from transferring everything into the Chinese ones," Luck said. "I think we—"

Luck looked past Cobra and his eyes widened as he drew back.

Cobra crouched and started a turn as if to defend himself, then spun back and drove his fist into Luck's stomach. Luck bucked forward and Cobra dropped him with punch to the fleshy part of his cheek.

When he looked down, Cobra spotted a knife lying on the dirt next Luck's body.

Only then did Cobra glance back at the alley behind him. He'd guessed right. It was empty. The only person who could have set a trap in that spot was Luck, but instead he had trapped himself.

Cobra confirmed that Luck still had a pulse, then dragged him in among the garbage cans and propped him against the wall. He walked back to Luck's motorcycle and searched his knapsack. Inside he found three meters of rope, a syringe, heroin, and a strip of cloth for a blindfold.

Cobra cooked up the heroin in the alley and injected Luck, then ripped out the electrical wires of Luck's motorcycle and broke off the top of the spark plug with a rock. He then sat down at the table and drank his Coke and watched the last of the bags loaded into the Chinese trucks.

He followed the Chinese trucks the rest of the way through Kunming and fifty kilometers up the highway until he was satisfied both that they were continuing north and that he was the only one trailing them. There was no reason to continue following them since there was no way he could stay awake much longer. He turned back south, hoping Gage would find a way to track the heroin from the other end.

Cobra tossed Kai's gun and Luck's cell phone into the Panlong River, rode to the railway station, and abandoned the motorcycle among a collection of others in the employee parking area. He broke off the spark plug in this one also, then caught a taxi to the airport, all the time wishing the flight to Shanghai was six hours, rather than three. He needed the sleep.

CHAPTER 55

L ew Fung-hao's back felt like a rusted hinge as he pried himself out of the economy seat he'd occupied on the flight from San Francisco. Even though he stood to earn hundreds of thousands of dollars in the next few days, he couldn't find it in himself to spend any of it for business or first class. And he found it confusing, wondering, as always, how much of himself was composed of character and how much of mere habit.

As he approached Passport Control, Lew was thankful he'd obtained American citizenship and traveled on a U.S. passport, for the immigration officer scanned it and stamped it without glancing at either his name or his face and waved him through.

Memories began to press in on him as he looked at the uniformed soldiers and at the place names on the arrival and departure boards. He knew the grip of the past would've hurt worse if he'd landed in the south, in Guangdong or Shantou, where the Red Guards humiliated him and drove him from his professorship. Nonetheless, he had to fight off those and other images and remind himself that he had survived, and that he would survive, for the stiffness that plagued his joints hadn't yet impaired his mind.

Lew approached a money exchange booth and traded a thousand dollars for yuan. It offended him that he should have to carry pictures of Mao and the other gangsters, even if only on currency, so he stuffed the bills into his wallet without counting them.

Morning sunlight reflecting off the pavement and wing-shaped steel of the Shanghai Pudong Airport greeted him as he stepped from the terminal and merged with the mass of travelers. He shielded his eyes as he walked along the sidewalk to the taxi queue.

A few minutes later, he leaned down toward the passenger window of the taxi that came to a stop in from of him and asked the driver, "How much to Nantong?"

"Just you?"

"Only me."

"Twelve hundred."

"Eight hundred."

"A thousand."

Lew counted out the yuan from his wallet, showed it to the driver, then slid it into his shirt pocket. The driver got out of the cab and looked for Lew's luggage to put in the trunk. Lew held up a zippered canvas bag to indicate that was all he had, then climbed into the backseat. And as soon as the taxi left the airport grounds, Lew pushed the duffel against a rear passenger door, rested his head on it, and curled up on the seat.

Lew didn't sleep as much as descend into a jet-lagged, gray daze of jumbled images and road vibrations. Later, he drew in a breath of the sea air and guessed that he was near the mouth of the Yangtze or, perhaps, was only dreaming he was.

In the early afternoon, Lew heard the taxi driver's voice calling to him.

"We're near Nantong. Where do you want to go?"

Lew pushed himself up, withdrew a notebook from his bag, and read out "36 Yang Lao Lane."

The driver continued on for another ten minutes, until he was at the edge of the city. He pulled over next to an old man sitting on a mat on the sidewalk, repairing shoes.

"*Shifu*. Do you know Yang Lao Lane?"

The old man smiled. He seemed pleased that he'd been called master in the old, respectful way. He pointed east, toward a commercial district.

"How far?"

"About a kilometer. If you come to the bridge over the Haohe River, you've missed it."

The taxi driver continued, slowing to read street signs until he finally turned right. He crept along while he and Lew peered at house numbers until the driver stopped at number 36. Lew handed the cash to the driver, then picked up his bag and stepped onto a narrow sidewalk. He found himself standing in front of a high wall behind which he could see the upper floor of a modern, stucco two-story house.

He pressed the buzzer and waited until an elderly housekeeper opened the gate.

"*Amah*," he said. "I'm Lew Fung-hao."

The *amah* nodded. "Please come in. Mr. Wu is at the Efficiency Trading office."

From inside the gate, Lew could see a generic house that he knew he could've found anywhere the Chinese diaspora had settled: in Taiwan, in Thailand, in Vancouver, or in Monterey Park, California. Oversize, salmon colored, with a front courtyard, large double-paned windows, and a garage for two cars. Although he had no particular interest in the meaning of architecture, it seemed to him for a moment as though the Pacific Rim had become a single country with a unified culture and it gave him an apprehensive feeling that he didn't understand.

As he entered the anonymous house, he saw the interior was true Chinese in the late-nineteenth-century Shanghai style.

Dark solid wood furniture, simple in form and elegant in style. He glanced toward the dining room and was stunned by a thirty-foot-long fine-grained wood table made from a single slice of what must have been an ancient hardwood tree. Each chair was nothing but a two-foot stump cut from a thick branch and stood on end.

Lew couldn't imagine its cost, but he could guess its route: cut down by poachers in Laos or Cambodia, forestry officials paid off, sold to Thai traffickers, trucked through Thailand to a shop where it was smoothed and polished, then smuggled into China by truck or boat.

How much? Lew wondered. Fifty thousand dollars? A hundred thousand? Maybe more. From that piece of furniture alone Lew concluded that Old Wu wasn't a modest man.

Just after the *amah* escorted Lew into a sitting room and had served him tea, Wu charged in. Lew looked up to see a man a few years older than himself wearing a white shirt, dark tie, and black, creaseless slacks. He wasn't sure he liked Wu's looks. Chubby faced, broad nosed, with a full head of hair in disarray. Gripped between his index and middle fingers were the remains of a still-smoldering American cigarette and under his arm, a worn leather briefcase. To Lew, he seemed rushed and undisciplined and, therefore, unpredictable.

Lew rose and reached out his hand.

Wu accepted it saying, "Good to meet you. I'd been expecting Ah Tien again. I hope he's well."

"He's fine." Lew let his face fall. "There was a death in his family so he couldn't travel."

Wu gestured for Lew to sit and took a chair across from him. "I know you're anxious to know where we stand."

Lew nodded.

"We expect the chips to arrive the day after tomorrow. We've received regular communications from the captain since he left Taiwan. Everything is normal."

"And the white powder from the south?"

"That, too, is on its way."

Ten minutes later, Wu delivered Lew to the front steps of a small hotel. Lew walked across the worn marble floor to the reception desk, surrendered his passport to the clerk, and filled out the registration form. Key in hand, he walked to the tiny elevator, then found his third-floor room where he lay down. As he drifted his way toward sleep, he thought again of the disheveled man and his rare wood table. Its presence in the house would prompt every visitor to ask where he got the money, and any answer Wu gave would raise suspicions. Wu now struck him as a man who invited scrutiny for the pleasure of deflecting it, and he knew that such a man could neither be trusted nor relied upon.

CHAPTER 56

Gage's cell phone rang with a call from Cobra as he and Kai waited in his room for General Zhang and Commander Ren to wake up from their naps. In the reflection of the mirror above the desk where he sat, Gage could see Kai sitting on the edge of the couch, her attention seemingly turned inward, perhaps occupied by thoughts that had come to her as they walked along the river.

"It looks like Eight Iron was planning to make a move on the heroin," Cobra said. "The rider he sent along was ready to put me out, but I got him first."

"Dead?"

Cobra laughed. "Only to the world for a while."

"Hold on." Gage made a scribbling motion with his hand and Kai retrieved a notepad and a pen.

"How is it traveling?"

"In two First Auto Works heavy transport trucks. Old-style, snub-nosed cabs. Double wheels in the back. Gray, with painted red lions on the cab doors. The beds are framed by wooden stakes and covered by a green canvas. Yunan Province plates. I'll send you photos and bring the numbers with me."

"When's that?"

"Late tonight, maybe early tomorrow morning."

"We're at the Nantong Center Hotel. I'll book you a room. Let's meet downstairs for breakfast at eight o'clock."

"What about Kasa? Should Kai let him go?"

Gage thought for a moment, then said, "That's as good a way as any to clue Eight Iron in that he's lost his link to the heroin."

"I just hope he trusts you to do the damage to Ah Ming you promised and stays out of it."

"How about have someone keep an eye on him just in case. Let Kai know when you've got it set up and she then can have her people cut him loose."

"Has she been honoring your understanding?'

"I'd say she's been very well behaved."

"Maybe not for long," Kai said. "Tell him you tried to deflect me to a car thief."

"Maybe not so well behaved after all. I'll see you in the morning."

After Gage disconnected, he realized Kai's last line didn't have its usual snap, and when he looked up, she was staring at him in the mirror. Then her eyes lost focus like she was looking past him at something in the far beyond. He had the feeling she was near a moment of insight, poised at some kind of threshold. He watched her. A minute passed, then Kai's eyes came awake again and her face reddened like she'd arrived with great anticipation at a party a day too early or a day too late. It lasted only an instant, then a somber expression replaced it.

"Silence," she finally said. "My mind just went silent." She looked at Gage. "For years it seems my thoughts have raced from one thing to another. Nonstop. Especially around men. Like a gambler or maybe like a prospector, except I never win and never find the gold." She paused, then took in a long breath and exhaled. "Silence. Who would have thought? Maybe that's what

I've been looking for all my life. A silent moment like that with a man, in a room or walking along a river."

Kai turned toward the window overlooking the city. "That could be the real reason I came along with you. Until now I thought it was just sex or adventure or something forbidden or out of reach that got me here." She looked back at Gage. "It was just the opposite. I needed a safe place to feel that unmoving moment, where I could stop trying to justify myself."

"If you stay with Somchai, you might not ever have one again."

"I know." She sighed. "Our life has been about money and politics and business, and getting more and more. But I ended up with too much of everything and none of what I really needed." She sat down in the desk chair and looked at herself in the mirror. Finally, she shook her head and said, "I can't believe I actually said that out loud." She glanced up at Gage. "I think the twisted rope that has tied me to him all these years may have just come unwound."

CHAPTER 57

Kasa lay on a cot in the eight-by-eight storage room attached by a chain running from his ankle to an industrial lathe bolted to the warehouse floor. He was watching the third to the last video of the twelve-volume *San Kuo, The Three Kingdoms,* a tale of the ancient struggle among the Wei, Shu, and Wu warlords for control of China.

Kai's bodyguard appeared at the door and pointed a semiautomatic at him.

"It's time to leave."

"Right now?" Kasa said, without looking over. "I have two episodes left. Maybe you can come back later."

The bodyguard stiffened, recognizing that Kasa's gesture was a feint, but not sure what his next move would be.

"Kneel down on the floor and put your hands behind your back."

The bodyguard had tried to sound casual and businesslike, but he knew that Kasa could hear the strain in his voice.

Kasa complied and the driver stepped into the room and handcuffed him.

After taking two steps toward the threshold, Kasa stopped and looked back at the television. He smiled as one of the warlords said, "I will kill him while I live, or die doing it," then walked out.

They urged Kasa through the warehouse and out to the car where the driver was waiting. They drove him into central Chiang Rai and released him next to a crowd of Japanese tourists in front of the Monkey Wat. The driver reported in to Kai as they sped to a bar where they bought each other whiskeys to soothe their fears. Once calmed by alcohol, they surveyed the prostitutes sitting together around a table in the corner. They chose two sixteen-year-olds, paid the bar owner his buy-out fee, bought two bottles of cognac, and walked with the girls to their upstairs room.

The driver first handed the girls a hundred baht each for an hour, then looked at the bodyguard and gave the girls a thousand each for the night.

Kasa would surely be gone by morning.

TEN MINUTES AFTER HE WAS DROPPED OFF AT THE TEMPLE, Kasa arrived at Eight Iron's Chiang Rai office on the bank of the Mae Kok River. He met with the manager, and then called Eight Iron in Bangkok.

"I need you to go meet our people in Kunming," Eight Iron said. "There's a problem. We've lost the trucks, and the police found Luck overdosed in an alley with a syringe in his pocket. He's under guard in the government hospital. Moby is waiting for you."

Kasa took a company van from behind the building and drove to a nearby service station, filled the tank, and checked the oil and tires. The manager was waiting with a stack of yuan when Kasa returned. He took the money, collected three mobile phones, a semiautomatic pistol and a box of bullets, then raced north toward Mae Sai, Burma, and China in the far beyond.

For the entire first hour of the drive, as he pushed through the dust and exhaust and swerved around slow trucks and on-coming traffic, he fingered the tip of the bullet that he hoped would soon blast a hole in the back of Cobra's head.

CHAPTER 58

Kai and Gage walked down a floor in the Nantong Center Hotel and knocked on the door to Zhang's room, hoping he and Ren had woken from their alcohol-induced afternoon nap. Zhang opened it on the second knock. They could see Ren in the bathroom combing wet hair away from his puffy face. The steam from shower and the scents of soap and shampoo clouded the doorway, then Zhang's stale cognac and pork breath broke through, and bile rose in Gage's throat.

Gage swallowed hard and then said, "The trucks from the south are on their way. They'll be here in a day or two."

Zhang nodded. "We'll have time to arrange everything." His tone was crisp, not the rough voice of someone who'd just awakened from an alcohol-induced stupor.

"We?"

Zhang glanced at Ren and nodded. He then pointed downward and said, "We'll meet you in a few minutes. He wants to show you how the people and companies are distributed around the city."

Kai and Gage went down to the lobby where Gage made a room reservation for Cobra.

ZHANG SNAPPED HIS CELL PHONE SHUT as he and Ren left the elevator and moments later Ferrari pulled the mobile office to a stop in front of the hotel. The evening air was still and the streetlights were coming on as they entered the van. Ferrari reached back and handed each of them a map of Nantong in both English and Chinese, with all the businesses marked that had appeared in Ah Tien's address book.

Gage felt an uncanniness looking at the annotated map. It somehow reminded him of the CAT scan he'd done, a picture that would reveal a disease or, perhaps, a projection of a diagnosis onto a picture. It made him feel as though the next hour of inspecting the places shown on the map would be like an exercise in pathology, an examination of the social tumors, or at least their outer shape, that had led to the death of Peter Sheridan.

Ferrari first drove northeast to Lao Wu's Efficiency Trading, composed of a metal building, part office and part warehouse, the size of an American auto parts store. Its green paint had long faded, and cardboard covered a couple of broken second-floor windows. It had a single loading bay, its roll-up door closed, trash collected along the wall, and used cardboard boxes folded and piled by the rear fence. An old cargo van was parked on the street with the company name painted on the side with two laborers asleep in the front seat.

The mood of neglect suggested to Gage that Lao Wu was either irresponsible or a man at the end of his career, or both. And as he scanned the street, he noticed that the rest of the businesses were also small and old, suggesting that economic development in the area had started there twenty or thirty years earlier and had moved on.

Ferrari's next stop confirmed it.

Tongming Tiger stood along a four-lane road lined with factories and cold storage facilities on the western edge of town. Most of the businesses had luxury cars and SUVs parked in front.

A dozen loading docks gaped from the football-field-size Tongming Tiger warehouse, with laborers swarming from truck to truck, loading and unloading, while supervisors stood by marking off deliveries on bills of lading. Semis were lined up at the gate and extended thirty yards down the street, their exhaust seeming to create their own gray microclimate of clouds and fog.

Kai reached for Zhang's binoculars and read off the printing on the bags and boxes that workers were moving by hand or forklift: rice, wheat, dried corn, food preservatives, components for traditional Chinese medicines, including dried reptiles and insects and roots, mushrooms, and bark.

If the key to successful drug trafficking was to conceal it within normal business activities, Gage thought, *then Tongming Tiger was ideal.* Millions of dollars in chips or hundreds of kilos of heroin could slip in and out unnoticed by the workers who bore it from truck to warehouse, even less by the fluorescent-lit clerks on the second- and third-floor offices.

Ferrari pointed to a middle-aged balding man walking from the entrance toward a Nissan sedan, then spoke a few words to Zhang in Chinese.

"That's Dong," Zhang said. "The owner. A very modest person. He's worth millions, but he and his wife live like mice in a little house by the river. His only vice is a little gambling in Macao every few months."

"Hold that thought," Gage said. "In the next few days we'll find out whether modesty is just the part he plays."

As they drove in silence back through Nantong, Ren and Zhang slid down in their seats and closed their eyes.

Ferrari turned left a few blocks before reaching the Nantong Center Hotel and pulled to the curb.

"Why are we stopping here?" Kai asked Ferrari.

"Tian Nan ... Hotel," Ferrari said in broken English, pointing at the sign over the entrance.

"And?" Kai asked.

Zhang stirred, then stretched over to peer out through the van side window, and said, "Ah yes, the Tian Nan Hotel." He looked at Kai, then at Gage, and smiled. "A person by the name of Lew Fung-hao checked in here this afternoon."

CHAPTER 59

Wu and Lew sat together at a small table in the Tian Nan Hotel restaurant. Even though the rooms above were small and crowded with single beds, Wu had chosen it because it catered to Chinese, rather than foreign businesspeople, and the menu accommodated tastes from almost anywhere in China.

One of Ren's plainclothes soldiers secured a table next to them. She grasped at their words and at the sentence fragments that emerged out of the surrounding chaos of clacking dishes, murmured conversations and bursts of laughter, but the only ones that reached her seemed unrelated to smuggling.

"I can tell by your accent you're from the southern coastal area," Wu said, as the waiter delivered plates of Lucky Fish and steamed vegetables and bowls of rice.

"I was born near Shantou and lived there until 1971 when I . . ." Lew stiffened and his voice trailed off.

Wu wasn't surprised by Lew's difficulty in speaking of the past. He'd met many like Lew. Diaspora Chinese who'd returned to do business, but who were unable to adjust to the political reality of a modern China that had ripped through the seams of its communist past.

"You can speak freely," Wu said, glancing around the restaurant. "Things have changed. There's no need to worry. Even those who suffered the worst and fled to America and Hong Kong are now coming back to live here." He pointed up at a television hanging from a bracket in the far corner of the room. "There are no secrets anymore. The state television shows documentaries about Red Guards harassing and beating people and about the famine."

"My memories of those days have become a filter against the present," Lew said. "I'm not sure I can see China very clearly." He shrugged. "Maybe I never will."

Wu slid a piece of fish into Lew's rice bowl, then said, "In some ways it was easier for those who stayed to adjust to the changes because we could watch them happening."

Wu chose not to speak of the dead who hadn't survived to watch anything: those executed or murdered and the thirty million who starved to death.

"I was in my late twenties when the Cultural Revolution began," Wu said. "I was working as a clerk at a collective farm just west of here. I was considered a necessary evil because I could read and write. Then the Red Guards came along. They didn't see me as necessary, only as evil, and sent me into the fields as a laborer. Two years later, everyone who depended on the farm was starving because there was no one left with management skills."

Lew set down his chopsticks. "I was a history professor." He shook his head as if to say that if he'd understood more, he might have suffered less. "The Party let me come back to the university after six years of hard labor and reeducation, but then everything turned upside down again when the students turned against us."

Wu didn't expect Lew to describe what had happened to him—that generation never did—but the memories returned:

intellectuals dressed like clowns and paraded through the streets, to be beat and spit upon.

"Other professors committed suicide, but somehow I found the strength to resist and then to escape to Hong Kong."

"A survivor."

Lew nodded. "And you, too."

"As it turned out, the communist leaders were right in their analysis of the danger the former capitalist classes held for the revolution." Wu smiled. "Capitalism does seem to be genetic. I saw a chance to open a business and somehow knew how to run it. It grew over time into Efficiency Trading."

"Maybe if I'd held out longer . . ."

Wu shook his head. "It's better to have left." He smiled again. "America is a wonderful place. I've seen it. My son was a student at Columbia and I stayed with him for a month last year." His smile turned into a grin. "And Las Vegas? Fantastic." His excitement pushed him forward in his chair. "Have you been?"

"No, I've lived a quiet life."

Lew picked up his chopsticks and poked at the fish, but he didn't pick up a piece.

In the silence, Wu inspected Lew's eyes. They were deadened by what Wu knew had to have been an unquiet life, or maybe a quiet one ruthlessly lived. The big boss in San Francisco never would've trusted a weak man with the mission that had brought Lew to Nantong.

Wu stared down at Lew's now idle chopsticks.

Was there blood on those hands? Wu asked himself. *Maybe. Maybe not.*

Wu settled on maybe, for the American end of the heroin trade was much more violent than in China where it's like any other kind of commodity. At the same time, organizations like Ah Ming's also needed people with fingers clean enough to handle the money without drawing suspicion. In any case, Wu decided, it wasn't a topic to be raised at this table, for here they were just two old men whose lives by chance had converged.

"And what about the future?" Wu finally asked.

"I'm thinking about retiring."

"Here?"

Lew shrugged. "Maybe. Though I find the thought surprising."

CHAPTER 60

Cobra nodded toward Gage and Kai as he entered the Nantong Center Hotel restaurant and then walked to the breakfast buffet table and served himself a bowl of *da mi zhou*, steaming rice porridge, and sprinkled *pao cai*, pickled vegetables, on top.

"What have I missed?" Cobra asked as he sat down.

Gage filled him in.

Cobra looked at Kai. "I had to leave your shortwave transmitter in Kunming. The airport security people wouldn't have let me take it on the plane. It's illegal to bring that kind of gear into China without a license. And your gun is at the bottom of the Panlong River."

"No problem. I've got more."

"We'll have to divide up," Gage said. "Eight Iron might try to catch up with the heroin and make a grab for it, and Zhang might give up on the offshore account and double-cross us."

"And Ren could double-cross Zhang," Kai said.

They looked up to see Zhang heading toward them. Gage introduced Cobra using his Thai nickname.

"Jong Arng . . . Jong Arng. Sounds like a nickname. What's it mean?"

"Cobra," Gage answered. "It means Cobra."

Zhang's eyebrows rose a fraction. "Years ago, when I supervised a border trade land crossing in the south, I attended an intelligence briefing at the Chinese embassy in Bangkok. There was discussion of a troublesome Taiwanese MJIB agent known as Cobra." Zhang smiled. "I was told it was an accurate name. You wouldn't be him, would you?"

"No," Cobra said in even voice. "It must've been someone else."

Gage didn't want Zhang to think about it further so he issued assignments.

"I'll work with Zhang on Lew. Kai will take Tongming Tiger. And Cobra, Efficiency Trading."

As they walked to the vehicles waiting outside, Zhang made a call to share Gage's plan with Ren and his people.

Gage got into Zhang's van.

"There seems to be a certain toughness about Kai," Zhang said, as Ferrari drove them toward Lew's hotel.

"She knows how to handle herself."

"That's not quite what I meant. On the surface she can be very charming, but underneath she's like us. I'll bet she's really something in bed." Zhang looked over and grinned. "You wouldn't happen to have any personal knowledge?"

"We've been friends for a long time. That's all there is between us."

"I sense there's even less between her and her husband."

"He's a little man in a big job. And he won't last. Even if his party forms the next government, he'll be dropped from the cabinet. It's embarrassing for Thailand to have a cabinet minister who can't get a visa to the United States because of a history of drug trafficking."

Zhang already had plainclothes soldiers surveilling Lew's hotel, so he directed Ferrari to park around the corner. Ferrari pulled down a black curtain to conceal the rear of the van, then moved over into the passenger seat so it would seem to passersby that he was waiting for the driver to return from one of the shops along the street.

Ten minutes later, Zhang's phone rang.

"A taxi just picked up Lew," Zhang told Gage. "My people are behind it."

Zhang stayed in communication with the surveillance team following Lew as he wound through Nantong.

Ferrari skirted Lew's route for ten minutes, then pulled over.

"We don't need to show ourselves," Zhang said. "It looks like Lew is heading for Tongming Tiger."

Gage called Kai, already there.

"You remember the guy from the trade bureau whose name was coded in Ah Tien's address book?"

"Mao," Kai said. "Like Chairman Mao. Who'd have thought that someone with that family name would be responsible for making capitalism flourish."

"I'm thinking you should try to pry some information out of him. I'll ask Zhang to work it out with Ren."

Ferrari started up again. He drove around a corner and came to a stop a block away from where Kai was parked with a view of the entrance to Tongming Tiger.

Zhang called Ren and reported back to Gage. "Ren can meet Kai at the trade bureau and introduce her to Mao. He'll say she wants to move ginger through the port and needs to register a Thai-Chinese joint venture to handle it."

"Are you sure Mao will meet her?"

"Don't worry. He'll meet with her whenever she wants. All these guys are greedy bureaucrats looking for their cut. And he knows that anyone referred by a port commander is for real and is ready to spend money."

Gage called Kai. "Zhang will hook you up with Ren. Set the meeting around lunchtime so you can get him drinking."

"You mean get his brain fuzzy?" Kai said, laughing.

"I don't get it."

"Mao-Mao means fuzzy in Mandarin."

"I've got one for you, too. Tell Mao-Mao you're with New Life Trading."

"I like the sound of that one. Maybe I'll open a Bangkok branch for real."

AFTER AN HOUR OF INACTIVITY, both Zhang's and Gage's cell phones rang.

"Lew just walked out of Tongming Tiger," Kai told Gage. "He's alone."

"We'll follow him. Stay there and keep an eye on the company until your meeting with Mao gets set up."

Gage tapped Ferrari on the shoulder and pointed toward the driver's seat. Ferrari slid over and eased the van forward as Lew entered a red taxi. They followed the cab through town to an L-shaped compound located in the far eastern part of the city. Four or five businesses occupied each arm of the building.

Lew slipped from the cab, spoke briefly with the guard at the gate, then walked inside.

Ferrari stopped fifteen yards past the entrance, then Zhang walked back, but arrived too late to see which business Lew had entered. He used his phone to take a photo of the company names posted near the entrance, then returned to the van, and read them off: "Eastrade Electronics, Jinqiao Fish Wholesale, Qingdao Trading, Huang Medical, and Golden Export."

"Can you find out if Eastrade Electronics or Huang Medical deal in computer processors or just in already manufactured products?"

Zhang made calls to obtain the information as they waited for Lew to reappear.

Gage checked in with Kai.

"We followed Dong in a big circle starting from Tongming Tiger," Kai said. "He started at an herb trader, then went to a fertilizer factory, and finally to a huge pharmaceutical company. It has a guarded gate, so we couldn't follow him in and lost sight of him. It looked to me like they were just regular sales calls."

As Gage and Zhang waited outside the business compound Lew had entered, Cobra called to say there was regular but slow-paced activity at Old Wu's Efficiency Trading, but no signs of Wu himself. There were two clerks working in the building and a few laborers resting outside after unloading bags of what appeared to be processed garlic from delivery trucks.

An hour later, Lew walked back out through the compound gate and caught a cab that took him to the Enterprise Tower at the far south end of the city. Zhang followed him inside and watched him enter an elevator at the same time as a delivery boy. Zhang watched the numbers light up as the elevator rose through the floors. It stopped on the eighth and eleventh. He checked the business directory framed on a wall and photographed them all, then focused in on the names of the companies on those floors. He identified two more that might use computer chips and called his staff to research them.

AFTER ANOTHER HOUR, they trailed Lew back to the Tian Nan Hotel, and Ferrari followed him into the restaurant. He returned after a few minutes and reported that Lew was eating alone.

"What do you think?" Zhang asked Gage.

Gage thought back over Lew's route.

"My guess is that he's confirmed all the links, but I think we're still about five steps behind him."

A young man in a short-sleeved shirt and matching green

slacks walked up to Ferrari's window. He handed over an oversize envelope through the driver's window, then started to raise his hand in a salute. Ferrari stopped him with a shake of his head.

Ferrari handed the envelope back to Zhang, who tore it open and paged through what Gage could see were over a hundred bills of lading. His face reddened as he got to the last one and tossed them on the table.

"These are the shipping documents for all the boats due into Qidong tomorrow. There's nothing coming from Sunny Glory and nothing going to Tongming Tiger or Efficiency Trading or any of the companies we saw today."

Gage felt a return of the same feeling of panic, fearing that he had wasted days of his life and had risked others, chasing a mistake about Ah Ming's plan, the same desperation he'd fought back when he learned that Sunny Glory had sent away an empty container. An image of the coast of China Sea came into his mind, then it expanded south to include Vietnam and Thailand—a thousand other ports and inlets toward which the chips might be headed.

Zhang glared at Gage and his voice hardened. "Is this what you Americans call a wild goose chase?"

CHAPTER *61*

Ms. Chen represents a firm that wants to export ginger to Taiwan," Commander Ren told Mao, after he and Kai sat down in his trade bureau office. He gestured toward the map of the Nantong Special Economic Zone displayed on the wall behind him. "She's already looked into renting office space."

Kai suppressed a smile as Mao scooted forward and perched himself on the front edge of his oversize desk chair like a vulture on a low limb.

"My job with the trade bureau is to encourage economic development through the creation of trading relationships between local and foreign companies."

Ren raised a palm and smiled. "No need for the welcoming speech. She's already committed to the project. It's just a matter of how she goes about it."

"How about a joint venture with a local company?" Mao said.

"What would that cost to set up?" Kai asked.

"Nothing."

"How could that be?"

"The government has instituted incentives to encourage foreign investment. A joint venture designation, in tax breaks alone, can result in a twenty percent increase in profits."

"And a joint venture opens a local company to the world," Ren said. "If they have a foreign partner, they can obtain import and export licenses."

"What kind of investment are you talking about?"

"The government will expect nothing less than two and a half million yuan, and you'd have to send it in dollars. That's about three hundred thousand."

Kai drew back, feigning surprise. "That's a little steep for the small operation I have in mind."

Mao looked at Ren with a raised eyebrow. Ren nodded.

"There's a trick. You make a wire transfer to the joint venture in that amount and we label it as the foreign investment." He cast a coconspirator's smile toward both Kai and Ren. "Then we wire it out again and call it a purchase of goods or equipment. It almost zeros out."

"Almost?"

Mao held his smile. "There are certain small fees along the way."

By fees, they all understood Mao meant bribes, and Kai had no reason to think they would be small.

"Why are you telling me all this?" Kai asked. "An outsider."

"Commander Ren vouched for you. That's all I need."

"And if you succeed," Ren said, "so do we."

"Businesses in this area, far as they are from the major ports, have a hard time finding foreign partners. And unless you're part of a state enterprise, you need a foreign partner in order to make contacts overseas, but you can't get a foreign partner unless you already have the contacts."

Kai glanced at Ren, then back at Mao. "How much does the foreign partner need to know about my business? I don't want them going around me to my sources and cutting me out."

"All they need to know are the dates and times the goods will be received or delivered, and their destinations. They don't ask and don't want to know what is being shipped or where it comes from. And if you import the ginger through Qidong, there are no customs officials around to ask either."

Ren looked at his watch. "Maybe we should finish this conversation over lunch."

Mao took Ren's suggestion as an order and escorted them from the trade bureau building toward a restaurant a few doors away. As they walked, Ren and Kai scanned the cars and trucks parked on the street, the shoppers gazing into store windows, and suited businessmen and -women conversing on the sidewalk, checking for countersurveillance.

They noticed none.

A waitress led them through a chaos of greens and pinks multiplied by the mirrored walls and into a small dining room where Mao ordered lunch without looking at the menu.

Kai declined Mao's drink offers, saving face by claiming that she was taking a medication that advised against alcohol. He ordered beer and cognac for himself and Ren.

Toward the end of the meal, when Kai was sure that Mao had become fuzzy enough to feel as though she'd become his confidante, she picked up the trail of the conversation where they had left it.

"Three hundred thousand dollars is a lot of money to put into the hands of someone we don't know."

Mao's eyes sharpened through the alcohol-induced haze.

"But they'll know Commander Ren. And the deal would be structured so that no one"—Mao spread his hands as if to take in not just the trade bureau, but others beyond—"gets a cut until the money is sent out again. We've done it dozens of times."

Mao leaned forward, gripping his drink with both hands,

resting his forearms on the table. He looked at Ren as though seeking permission, but then pushed on without waiting for it.

"How about Mr. Zeng? He took over a state enterprise and formed a joint venture with his cousin in Taiwan. In the money came, and out it went."

"But they're relatives," Kai said. "They trust each other. I have none here."

Mao glanced at Ren again.

"What about the old man?" Ren said to Mao. "I think his name is Wu. He took the same kind of risk."

"Of course, Lao Wu. His Efficiency Trading was nothing more than a pushcart with a fruit topping until he got his partner in Sunny Glory. And the same with Guan at North China Produce and Hsu at Garden Trading and Gu at New Dawn."

"Would any of these people talk to me?"

Mao leaned even further onto the table and put his finger to his lips. "Never. It's one of these things we know but cannot discuss except among partners such as ourselves."

Kai reached for the cognac bottle and poured for Ren, Mao, and then herself. She knew that the symbolism of her taking a drink despite the perceived risk would play on him. She rose to her feet. The others stood and raised their glasses.

"To partners."

They echoed the toast, gulped the cognac, then sat again.

"Have you ever dealt with companies in San Francisco?" Kai asked, knowing that she might be pushing Mao further than he would want to go without her having money in hand. "I'm thinking of opening a branch over there, too."

"Yes, of course."

"Is there anyone you could refer me to? Someone you trust."

Mao nodded. "A young man . . . but he's now . . ."

"Now . . . ?"

Mao paused, his face sagging as he looked back and forth between Kai and Ren. "He's now unavailable."

Ren caught her eye and shook his head. They'd gone far enough and there was no reason to risk going too far. They might need Mao later.

After a few moments of silence, Kai poured Mao another drink and then turned the conversation away from business. Once their conversation was safely bracketed with food on one end and casual chat on the other, Kai brought it to an end.

"HE CONFIRMED THE LINK between Sunny Glory and Efficiency Trading," Kai told Gage, calling from the restaurant bathroom. She'd sent Ren and Mao ahead. "I'm pretty sure either the chips or the heroin are going through Efficiency Trading, and the man he referred to in San Francisco was Ah Tien. There was actual sadness on his face when he talked about the man being unavailable."

Gage passed on the information to Zhang.

"Zhang checked the bills of lading for incoming shipments," Gage said to Kai. "There's nothing coming from Sunny Glory and nothing going to Efficiency Trading. That tells me they must be using another one of the fake joint ventures for insulation."

Gage paused, then nodded for Zhang's benefit, suggesting that Kai had filled a gap in their knowledge. He didn't want to provoke another wild-goose-chase outburst, so he composed a story to match the facts confronting them.

"Ah Tien himself must've set one up to receive the chips. That way ownership of the cargo would stay in his hands until he was sure the exchange for the heroin would happen. If no one except him knew which boat the chips were coming in on, then it would be hard for Old Wu or Dong or even Mao to double-cross him."

"The problem is that we may not know which company it

is until Zhang does. Which means he'll be in a position to grab them."

"Let's meet up at the hotel and leave Ren's people to take care of the surveillance. We'll put together a list of all the company names we've collected and pass them on to my office to see if they can mine anything out of them and maybe . . . Is it worth taking another shot at Mao to see what else you can get?"

"Probably not. It turned out that Mao wasn't so Mao-Mao after all. He's a cagy little snap pea who drank his weight in cognac."

CHAPTER 62

Zhang paced the carpet in Gage's room. Gage knew what was on his mind. The general was about to allow heroin to pass through a port under his control, a capital offense if discovered. But if he missed the chips, he'd have nothing. No Hong Kong company. No bank account. No money.

"We won't be able to seize the chips if they pass through Tongming Tiger," Zhang said, turning toward Gage, Kai, and Cobra sitting at the table. "There are too many trucks coming and going."

"That depends," Gage said. "Did you find out whether any of the companies in the places Lew visited deal in chips?"

Zhang shook his head. "My people are still searching the tax and license records. So it takes time. And who knows? Maybe he went to those places to throw us off."

Cobra caught Gage's eye and gave him a look that said, *If Zhang doesn't find the chips, he's going to grab the heroin.*

"That's unlikely," Gage said, answering Zhang. "Lew probably hasn't been here before, and it takes a lot of familiarity to mislead someone."

Zhang stopped and bore down on Gage. "But we're running out of time to find out."

GAGE HATED SURVEILLANCE. It's best when things happen. It's worst when nothing happens. It's just nerve-racking when almost nothing happens.

At the end of the day, Dong left Tongming Tiger, but only went home.

Wu finally left his house, but only to meet Lew at his hotel for dinner.

Almost nothing happened.

At midnight, Gage turned everything over to Zhang's people and returned to the hotel to try to sleep. He called Alex Z before lying down.

"Nothing, boss. I even had Annie go over Ah Tien's address book again, just in case any of the company names were coded. Nothing."

"I'll need you to stay at the office this evening. Things should start to happen here tomorrow morning. Call me if anything breaks on your end."

"You feeling okay, boss?"

"I'm fine, Alex. Thanks for asking."

Gage called Faith, expecting to leave a message. She answered on the fourth ring.

"I'm so glad you called."

"Don't you have a no cell-phone rule in class?"

"I'm the only one in the room with the letters Ph.D. after her name, so I get to make the rules. Anyway, I didn't answer it until I got out to the hallway."

Gage heard footsteps as she walked.

"Dr. Stern e-mailed me your blood results. Everything is no worse than stable, and your red blood count is up."

"So Mother Stern says I can stay?"

"But I miss you, and I'm trying to get her to change her mind."

"I miss you, too. Another thirty-six hours and I'll be out of here and on my way home."

At least he hoped he would.

CHAPTER 63

Zhang and Ren arrived at Gage's room before sunrise dressed in civilian clothes. Both were carrying handguns. Gage didn't express his concern about them arming themselves, but knew Kai and Cobra shared it. Zhang and Ren only needed their military titles to carry off their parts since no one in Nantong would go to war against the People's Liberation Army. He wondered whether this was the reason Ah Tien had chosen Nantong, a city so dominated by the military that the Ministry of Public Security's Department of Narcotics Control would leave it alone.

Zhang laid out a series of satellite photos of the Formosa Strait and the East China Sea, then looked up at Gage.

"You never really believed it was a wild goose chase," Gage said.

"It still may be, but I thought it wise to keep track of the geese." Zhang pointed at a group of dark slivers circled on each photograph. "We've been tracking these. They started from Taichung and have been moving together up the coast. They're now a couple of hours out of Qidong."

A crack of thunder broke into their conversation.

Gage pointed out of his hotel window at the dark clouds and distant rain. "The storm might make it difficult. More for us than for them since we still don't know who's supposed to pick up the chips."

"But we know this," Ren said, laying a list on top of the photos. "Eastrade uses chips in its robotics factory, Huang Medical for hospital equipment, Hong Kong Micro for the military, and East China Electrosupply for security systems."

"But none of them are scheduled to pick up a load at Qidong." Gage looked at Cobra. "We'll have to do this the hard way. You and Ren go to the port." Then at Kai. "You watch Old Wu."

Gage needed to keep Zhang away from the chips. He decided to gamble that since Tongming Tiger didn't have an import license, the chips wouldn't be heading directly there.

"Zhang, you take Dong. Start at Tongming Tiger. I'll take Lew."

Even as he gave the orders he worried that Zhang and Ren knew more than they'd just disclosed.

WU ARRIVED AT LEW'S HOTEL AT 7 A.M. While they ate breakfast in the restaurant Gage checked in with Alex Z and Annie.

Nothing new.

Cobra called an hour later from the military installation that overlooked the Qidong port.

"The storm has turned the sky black in the east. The boats are moving in from the Yangtze and they're getting pounded. Everyone on the water is racing toward Qidong. Fishing craft. Smuggling junks. Barges. They'll be jammed together when they arrive. Ren says that there won't be enough room at the dock, so some will have to ground themselves in the mud. Makes me even sorrier about not getting the GPS on the thing."

"Where are you now?"

"In Ren's office. I can see all the way from the bridge at the top of the inlet, down along the port and out to the river. And trucks are lining up. Lots of them."

Gage looked over and saw Wu driving up to Lew's hotel. In the distance he saw Kai pulling to the curb. He disconnected and called her.

"If Lew and Wu leave together, I'll stay with them and you stay back and check whether they have anyone doing any countersurveillance."

AS THE GRAY HAZE of watching and waiting was returning, Zhang called, his voice dry with excitement. "The trucks from Kunming are at Tongming Tiger."

Gage clenched his fist. The heroin had made it. Cobra really had broken the trail between it and Kasa.

"We checked the license plates. They match. The trucks are gray with red lions painted on the doors."

Gage imagined Zhang's heart pounding as he overproved the point.

"Are they unloading?"

"Not yet. The drivers seem to be waiting for something. Dong hasn't even come out to look. But there's a whole lot of activity otherwise. Trucks are coming in from the companies Dong visited yesterday and some others, too. They're lined up down the street for a block."

Gage watched Lew and Wu emerge from the hotel together and get into a pale green van. The driver merged into traffic.

"The old guys must have heard the news," Gage told Zhang. "They're on the move. I'll stay with them."

Gage followed Wu and Lew to the Efficiency Trading warehouse. They walked inside. Moments later a truck with neither license plates nor a company name backed up to the loading dock.

Ferrari snuck along the side of the building, then returned.

"*Suan*," Ferrari said, pointing at the truck. "You say . . ." He hesitated, searching his memory.

"Like *suan ni bai rou*? Pork with garlic?"

Ferrari smiled and nodded.

They watched as Wu's laborers unloaded the truck and as it drove away.

GAGE'S PHONE RANG. It was Cobra, his voice panicky. "The boat's not coming in. It's not even in the group."

Gage could hear rain pounding Ren's office and window. Only a heavy mist was falling outside his van.

"How do you know?"

"Ren sent cutters out to tow one that had broken down and to stand by in case others have problems. They called in the ID numbers of all the junks."

"How many boats do we have to deal with?"

"Maybe forty already in the port, and a couple of dozen more are still heading in, riding the incoming tide. But it's hard to tell. The rain is murderous. The front edge is just hitting us."

"How much time until they reach shore?"

"Ten minutes. Maybe fifteen."

Gage guessed that Ren had also told Zhang. The chips had to be coming in. He closed his eyes. He remembered the heroin being transferred from Thai to Chinese trucks in Kunming. It gave him an idea for a story to tell Zhang.

"They must've shifted the chips to another boat during the trip up the coast. Tell Ren I'm not surprised. Since they changed trucks in China, we suspected that they might also change boats. He'll pass it on to Zhang, and maybe that'll cool him down for a little while."

GAGE CALLED ALEX Z. "A truck at Efficiency Trading has just unloaded a lot of garlic. That tell you anything?"

"Garlic . . . garlic . . . That's it, boss." He heard Alex Z slap his desk. "The bill of lading in Ah Tien's briefcase, the one from Sunny Glory in Taiwan to Sunny Glory in the U.S., it was for processed garlic."

"But that only tells us how the heroin could be hidden leaving here. Wasn't there another bill of lading?"

Gage heard Alex Z shuffling papers on his desk.

"Yeah. Rare mushrooms from one unnamed company to another."

Gage disconnected, then called Cobra. "Are any of the boats bringing in mushrooms?"

Gage heard Cobra working his way through the PLA paperwork.

"Two. One is for China Food Resources and the other for North China Produce—hold on."

Gage heard Ren speaking in Chinese in the background, then Cobra again.

"And North China Produce is one of Mao's joint ventures."

"How many trucks are out there?"

"About a hundred. Hold on. We're scanning with binoculars, but with the rain it's like looking through fog . . . Wait . . . wait . . . wait . . . Got it. A North China Produce truck is loading up. Dark blue. Yellow lettering."

Gage called Zhang and passed on the news.

"Dong finally came out to the Kunming trucks," Zhang said, "but didn't even look inside. He just scanned the street and went back inside his office. I wonder if that means he suspects something."

FOR THE NEXT HALF HOUR there was no movement around Wu's building, except for the storm front charging inland, wind-ripped rain swirling around them and pounding the pavement, each drop seeming to burst upward on impact.

Gage's cell phone rang, faint against the thudding on roof and the spray splashing across the windows. But the noise couldn't blunt the edge in Cobra's voice.

"We're following the North China Produce truck back toward town. And we're not the only one."

"Zhang's people?"

"No way to tell."

A rumble of anger started to build in Gage as he put Zhang's number on his cell-phone screen.

If this guy goes for the chips, Gage told himself, *I'll bury him with the heroin. Bury him.* He took a long breath, tried to steady himself, and then pressed "send."

"There's a car following the North China Produce truck," Gage said, aware that a twinge of accusation was latent in his voice.

"It's not my people," Zhang said. "If I intended to break our agreement, there were better ways to start than that."

"What about Ren?"

"No, he's just leaving for Shanghai. He told me he didn't want to be here when the heroin arrived. I put him on leave until after the boat is out of Chinese waters again. His men are now under my control. In any case, he's too new to take a big risk like stealing the chips from me."

Gage called Kai. "I need you to head east toward the Qidong port. Cobra's following a North China Produce truck carrying the chips. We may have bumped into countersurveillance, and Cobra will need to break off before he gets made."

"I'm on the way. I'll call him to set up the switch. We can probably do it at the crossroads where the highway from Shanghai meets the one between Nantong and the port."

Gage disconnected and looked at the map of Nantong Ferrari had given him. The chips were traveling east toward the city, but he still didn't know how the deal was structured, who was going to do it, where it was going to take place, or, given Dong's behavior, whether it would take place at all. Even more, a chill told him that he could still lose track of both the chips and the heroin, and he'd lose his grip on both ends of the noose he'd hoped to slip around Ah Ming's neck.

GAGE'S PHONE RANG.

"Dong came to his office door and waved to his crew and they started unloading the bags of cassava powder from the Kunming trucks," Zhang said, "but slowly, like they don't want to uncover the heroin until they're sure the deal is really going to happen."

"They must've gotten the go-ahead when the chips left the port."

"And what about my chips?"

Gage didn't like Zhang's claim of possession. The insurance money would be his at the end, but the chips, never.

Gage kept his worry to himself.

"Cobra is behind them. Kai will trade off with him at the Shanghai turnoff so he doesn't get made."

ANOTHER TWENTY-FIVE MINUTES PASSED, then Lew and Wu came into Gage's view at the side door of Efficiency Trading. They squinted up at the rain, then strode to their waiting van and drove east through town with Gage behind them. He could see both Lew and Wu talking on their cell phones and Wu pointing and directing the driver. They moved without urgency, but he could see the driver checking his mirrors: rear-right-left, rear-right-left, rear-right-left.

Wu's driver slowed at a stoplight, then floored it, blowing through the red. Ferrari backed up to shoot around the cars blocking him, but Gage grabbed his shoulder to stop him. In just a few gut-turning moments Wu and Lew shrank into the distance and disappeared into the smoke-gray storm.

Gage called Kai. "I lost Lew. His driver jumped a stoplight and took off."

"Did he see you?"

Ferrari pulled his cell phone out of his pocket. Gage held a palm up toward him. Ferrari cast him a questioning look, but put it back.

"I don't know. I would've done the same thing at some point whether I spotted someone following me or not. Where's the North China truck?"

"It's parked in an alley next to a huge indoor produce market. The driver just walked back out to the street. He's standing there under an umbrella like he's waiting for a bus. We're at a service station, but I have a little bit of a view down the alley."

"Where's the car that was following it?"

"It stopped, too. It's not hiding, so it must be with them. I'm not sure how long we can stay here without attracting attention. We can only check the oil so many times."

"I'll put Ferrari on the line. Give him directions to where you are."

After handing the phone back to Gage, Ferrari wound through backstreets, emerging on the boulevard west of Kai.

"I'm heading east on . . ." Gage said. "There you are."

Ferrari stopped a hundred and fifty yards from the alley.

Lew and Wu drove up five minutes later. Gage didn't show the relief he felt, or the fatigue that was creeping through him; he just looked at Ferrari and pointed at his cell phone. Ferrari nodded and called Zhang.

"It's a good thing you were able to stay with the North China truck," Gage told Kai. "Zhang would've tossed us into the East China Sea."

"And it's a hell of a lot of backstrokes to Bangkok."

"Even more to San Francisco. Can you see anything?"

"The truck driver has opened the rear doors. Wu and Lew

are looking inside at some boxes stacked at the back . . . Wu's driver is now moving them into the back of their van."

"What's the other car doing?"

"Nothing. There's a guy in the driver's seat watching. It must be their security . . . Wu just put in the last box."

Gage saw Wu emerge from the alley and make a low wave.

"Did you get burned?"

"No, he's signaling to the car that was following him. It's moving up."

"You stay with the North China Produce truck and we'll stay with Wu and Lew."

Gage and Ferrari fell in a good distance behind Wu and Lew and the car following them. Gage watched Kai pulling out into traffic to follow the truck. He knew an observant eye would have seen a loose caravan, but because of the crush of traffic the links connecting them were invisible to everyone else.

Wu and Lew led them west through the center of town.

The North China Produce truck turned off, heading north, with Kai following it. A few minutes later she called Gage to report that it had arrived at the Efficiency Trading dock where workers were unloading the boxes of mushrooms.

The rain had let up. Now no more than a heavy fog.

Gage followed Wu's van farther west. It pulled up next to the Tongming Tiger warehouse.

The car following them drove off, its job done.

Wu and Lew got out of the van and walked inside.

Ferrari swung around the block and parked twenty yards behind Zhang on the street along the loading dock side of the warehouse.

"The boxes from the North China truck are in the back of a pale green van Wu and Lew drove up in," Gage said in a call to Zhang.

"I see it."

"Is Cobra with you?"

"He just climbed in."

"I'm sure you'll want to follow the chips. I'll stay with the heroin."

A new light-duty Volvo-China truck without license plates drove up to Tongming Tiger. Two men in black suits got out. One was slight, quick, and businesslike. The other was a giant: a bulbous body, with a huge round face and carrying an over-size briefcase. Gage used his cell phone to take photos as both hustled toward the warehouse.

Ten minutes later, Wu, Lew, and the two new arrivals re-emerged. Now Lew held the briefcase, the weight inside causing him to limp as he walked.

The giant moved the boxes from Wu's van to the Volvo truck. As soon as the rear truck doors closed, the two drove it away. They didn't look back.

"I'll stay here until the heroin leaves," Gage said, as Zhang pulled away to follow the Volvo. "Let me know as soon as you figure out the boxes' destination."

Wu and Lew reentered the Tongming Tiger warehouse, and within a minute laborers moved to finish unloading the heroin trucks.

Kai called to say that the North China Produce truck had left Wu's Efficiency Trading and was now driving toward them at Tongming Tiger.

Forklifts emerged from the Tongming Tiger warehouse bearing pallets of bags labeled "Jiangsu Compound Fertilizer" and slid them into the empty Chinese trucks.

The North China Produce truck passed by Gage ten minutes later and rolled to a stop next to a pile of cassava bags containing the heroin. Laborers began stacking them inside.

The Chinese trucks headed south toward the highway.

The North China Produce truck headed east toward Qidong and Ferrari fell in seventy yards behind it.

Gage's phone rang.

"We lost the chips," Cobra said, his voice tense and hard. "We got cut off at an intersection and the Volvo got away. Zhang is going crazy."

"Can he hear you?"

"No, he's pounding the table and yelling at people on the phone to spread out and look for it."

"In about two minutes he's going to decide to forget the chips altogether and just make a move on the heroin. As soon as you think he's made his decision, you know what to do."

"I can take him, but what do we do after that?"

"If we find the chips, no problem. If we don't, I'll hold him while you and Kai get out of China."

"No way. We're not leaving you behind."

"Then I guess we'll have to take him with us."

"What should I tell him?"

"Say we think the chips will end up at one of the companies his people identified. We have no proof, but at least it may buy you some time."

Cobra rode along listening to Zhang yelling directions to his driver and working his phone. They raced first toward the business compound Lew had visited, then to the Enterprise Tower.

No Volvo. No chips.

At the second disappointment, Zhang fell silent. He leaned over the table and stared at the map. Cobra watched his eyes scan from the city in the west to the port in the east, and then pause.

Cobra reached into his pocket and turned off his cell phone, then pulled it out.

"My battery is dead. Let me use yours to call Gage."

When Zhang reached out with his phone. Cobra yanked on his forearm and lapel and pulled him out of his seat and onto the top of the table. He then grabbed the back of Zhang's jacket, yanked it up over his head, and ripped the 9mm out of his shoulder holster.

The driver slammed on the brakes and reached over the seat to grab at Cobra, but missed.

Cobra threw the coat back over Zhang's head and stuck the gun barrel in his ear. The hard steel of the muzzle froze Zhang in place, splayed on the table.

The driver raised his hands.

"If you lift up, it'll be the last thing you do," Cobra said, then reached for his own phone and turned it back on.

"Graham, I had to take him."

"As long as we find the chips he won't care. Remind him he'll get five hundred thousand dollars at the end of this. Maybe that'll keep him quiet, at least for a while."

"We checked the business compound and Enterprise Tower. The Volvo wasn't at either one."

"Stand by. I'll work on it."

Gage called Alex Z.

"Annie has got an idea. I'll put her on."

"No guarantee, but it might be Huang Medical," she said. "What threw me off was that Ah Tien wrote W-O-N-G next to the coded number, assuming that was how the company spelled its name in English. It's the same Chinese character for Huang, H-U-A-N-G. Wong is Cantonese and Huang is Mandarin. Remember? Ah Tien's parents wanted him to marry someone who spoke Cantonese, like them. Same character, different pronunciation, and different spelling in English."

"Can't be. Zhang already checked the Huang Medical office. The Volvo we were following wasn't there."

"There were two coded telephone numbers for Huang Medical in Ah Tien's book. One is the office. The other is the factory. I called that number. It's in the Nantong Special Economic Zone."

Gage visualized the positions of the SEZ, Nantong, and the port. An offset triangle: north, south, east. He couldn't use Cobra because he had to control Zhang, and Ren was gone. It had to be Kai.

"Call Huang Medical back," Gage told Annie. "Have Alex Z run the call through a Nantong exchange. Tell them you're in the city. Say you're leaving town tonight and want to visit their plant. Tell them Mao at the trade bureau recommended them. Give your name as Chen Mei-li, that's Kai's Chinese name. Try to find out as much as you can about what they do and how they do it. Give whatever you learn to Alex Z."

Gage called Kai and told her to start driving to the Special Economic Zone, then sent her the photos he'd taken outside of Tongming Tiger of the Volvo and the two men.

Gage called Cobra back. "We have a lead. Huang Medical has a plant in the SEZ. Kai is headed that way. Is Zhang behaving?"

"So far."

"He knows all he has to do is make a phone call to grab the heroin. It would take all of ten seconds, so be careful."

"Mai pen rai."

Gage followed the North China Produce truck back to the Efficiency Trading warehouse. Bags of garlic were added. The heroin was now buried again. The truck then pulled away, heading farther east toward the port.

Annie called with the results of her contact with Huang Medical. "They said they have visitors all the time. The whole point of the SEZ is to generate foreign business. They'll leave my—her—name at the main gate. I told them I'd be there within the next forty minutes. Apparently it's a long drive to the SEZ, then to their factory inside."

"Let me talk to Alex Z."

"What can I do?"

"Play professor," Gage told him, "Make Kai sound like she knows what she's talking about. A wrong word and . . ."

BY THE TIME KAI ARRIVED AT THE SEZ GATE, Alex Z had trained her in the role of a medical equipment retailer from Bangkok looking to create a Thai brand name using equipment manufactured by Huang in Nantong. The guard directed her driver to the plant. She examined all of the vehicles as she drove through the lot to park, but didn't see the Volvo.

A young account manager greeted her. He seemed to her geeky enough to be believed on technical matters, but not so much as to be unable to cut a deal.

"What we sell," Kai said, repeating the speech Alex Z had given her, "are computer workstations for hospitals and medical clinics."

He nodded, then she saw his eyes holding on her like he was a hunter and she was the prey.

"We'll handle the software development in-house, but we're looking to outsource the manufacturing."

He nodded again. "Of course."

Nothing more.

His eyes moved from her and he gazed down the hallway. She could hear a low hum coming from the factory floor.

"Would you mind if—"

He shook his head. "I'm sorry, we can't let visitors in there." He pointed upward. "But we have an observation area. It has a good view of the production line."

He guided her to an elevator and up what counted as two floors but felt like six. They stepped out into another hallway leading to a glassed-in booth, overlooking acres of workers, equipment, and assembly stations. He gestured toward an area almost below them. "In this section we assemble control panels for x-ray machines. In the distance, you can see where we build workstations. That's where your work will be done." He turned toward her. "We build them for Chinese companies like Lenovo, Interon, NetForce, ChinaCom, and CompEast and for foreign companies as far away as Germany and Russia. The entire range of bandwidth and processor speed. What are you aiming for?"

Kai's heart raced at ChinaCom, but crashed at speed. She remembered that Alex Z said something about bandwidth, but she thought that was only a network concept.

She evaded the question by answering: "The fastest you can handle." And then changed the subject. "You mind if I take a look at your shipping and receiving facilities? We have something of a bottleneck."

"We have no bottleneck here."

The self-satisfaction in his voice combined with his predatory glare made her want to deck him.

They rode the elevator back down and he led her on an angular route, pausing over and over at windows and glass doors along the way to point out various elements of the shipping process. Kai could feel her nerves vibrating with urgency. Finally, he opened an exit door and she found herself at the loading dock overlooking dozens of trucks and trailers. She walked to an open roll-up door. The rain had subsided, but the air was thick and humid. She scanned the yard, beginning to her left and working in and out. She caught movement to her right. A hand bringing a cigarette upward toward a face so huge and bizarre that she almost failed to notice the Volvo truck he was leaning against.

Almost.

Kai reached for her cell phone as she backed up into the loading area and gave the appearance of refocusing her attention on the account manager.

"This is a tremendous operation," she told him. "Would you mind if I made a call to my partner at the hotel?"

He nodded, but he held his place as Kai rested her thumb on the "send" button, his eyes once again locked on her. She held the phone to her ear and stared at him until he turned and walked away.

"Graham," Kai whispered, "they're here. The Volvo is in back and they do work for ChinaCom. And the giant is next to the truck. He's huge. The biggest Chinese guy I've ever seen and even bigger than he looks in the photo. A body like a Sumo wrestler and a head like a watermelon."

"So I've heard. Now get away. I'm not sure Alex Z taught you enough to bluff for very long."

"Right now, I'm trapped between a giant and a prick, I think that's the word, but I'll talk my way out of here."

"Let Cobra know when you're past the gate, then he'll tell Zhang the name of the company."

Gage called Cobra. "Tell Zhang we've found the Volvo and to get someone moving toward the SEZ."

"What if he starts to say anything else?"

"Tell him you'll blow a hole in his head, then remind him that he's forty-five minutes away from cashing in. And don't let him go until the heroin is beyond the area patrolled by the PLA station at Qidong. Zhang isn't crazy enough to bring in PLA units outside this area. He'd lose control of it."

"How will he figure out which of the chips at Huang are the stolen ones?"

"Tell him I'll have the serial numbers tomorrow. Which means he'll need to keep the company locked down overnight."

Gage and Ferrari followed the North China Produce heroin truck back to the fishing boat at the Qidong port. The tide was going out. Gage knew that if the boat was going to make it, they'd have to load fast. And he was certain they wouldn't miss it.

As Gage watched the furious loading of the cargo, Kai called to say she was out of the SEZ.

Gage then gave Cobra the name and location of Huang Medical to pass on to Zhang

Thirty minutes later, Cobra called back to say that Zhang was satisfied that the men he'd sent to Huang Medical had found the Volvo and were now searching the warehouse.

"But don't give him back his gun," Gage said, watching the boat sail into the fog-shrouded Yangtze, "until I tell you to."

CHAPTER 64

L ew and Wu drove back to Wu's house. They sat on facing couches and drank to each other. They didn't have to say the words aloud, but they knew they shared the feeling: it was a young man's game, but they'd played it and played it well.

Maybe I was wrong about Wu, Lew thought. *Maybe he could be a friend.*

It had been many years since he had someone he could trust. When he was young, everyone betrayed him, and after he fled, he slipped into work he could never talk about.

But with Wu it was different. They could talk. They were in it together. Lew was in it with Ah Ming, too, but that was different. Ah Ming was his boss, and Ah Ming was no one's friend.

They finished their bourbon and drove to a pay phone from which Lew called Ah Ming.

"All is well," Lew told him, "but I'll take a short vacation," then hung up.

Wu took Lew back to his home and led him into the dining room where the two sat down to a meal intertwined with glasses of wine. They were two businessmen who just finished a deal.

This, Lew thought to himself, wasn't the China he'd left.

As Ferrari drove them back from the port, Gage woke up Sylvia at her home in South San Francisco.

There was groggy expectation in her voice. "What's going on?"

"We're getting close to the end and it looks like we'll recover the chips."

"Thanks. My police-trained mind hates to see anyone get away with anything."

"Ask Casey to e-mail you a list of the serial numbers, then forward one to Jack Burch for his records and one to me on the Doris Day e-mail account."

"Does that mean you're coming home?"

"I'll head back to Shanghai tomorrow morning and catch a flight."

Gage disconnected and began making plans to tie things up. Cobra and Kai would want him to come back to Bangkok to celebrate their success, but it wasn't possible. He had to get back for his chemical dip. He noticed he'd been feeling better for the last forty-eight hours and wasn't sure why. Maybe it was just because he was doing something, no longer the bystander he'd been in Bangkok. Maybe because that's just the way cancer is: there are good days and bad.

His cell phone rang.

It was Kai.

"I am at Wu's house and I'm not the only one watching."

"You think it's the enforcer from Taiwan?"

"Must be. He showed up a few minutes ago."

"The deal's done. What's he hanging around for?"

"I don't know."

"Unless something went wrong and we don't know about it." Gage felt a tightness in his stomach. He still didn't know for certain whether the chips really had been delivered to Huang at the SEZ. "I'll tell Cobra to head your way. I'll do the same."

As Ferrari drove, Gage realized the irony of what he'd been

doing. From the start, he'd been trying to protect drugs and stolen chips and now he'd moved on to trying to protect the criminals themselves.

Kai interrupted Gage's musings.

"We've got trouble. Big trouble. Taiwan just grabbed Lew."

Gage overheard Kai snap an order in Chinese to her driver.

"What happened?"

"Lew left the house like he was going to catch a taxi. The guy put a gun to his head and pushed him into a car."

"What direction are they going?"

"East toward you."

"How fast?"

"Not too. I think he could be looking for a place to try to lose anybody who might be following him, but he can't make any slick driving moves and still keep his gun on Lew. If he gets stuck in traffic, Lew might escape."

"Has he spotted you?"

"Could be. Maybe. I don't know. He keeps checking his mirrors, but he'd be doing that anyway."

"Have your driver call mine. Tell them to work together. But you can't stay with him too long before he notices you. Cobra and I will have to replace you."

"Where are you now?"

"Still heading in from the port. Maybe fifteen or twenty minutes from the city."

Gage called Cobra. "Lew's been kidnapped. Has to be Ah Ming's guy from Taiwan. Kai is behind him, but I'll need you to take over for her."

"Where are they?"

"Heading east through town."

"I'm south-central. We can intersect her in a few minutes. What should I do about Zhang?"

"The boat is probably still in the Yangtze and he could send out a cutter to grab it. And he still hasn't gotten proof—we still haven't gotten proof—that the chips are at Huang Medical. He'll have to stay with you for the ride. Call Kai. Have her guide you to her. We'll decide what to do about Zhang later."

"What should I tell him?"

"That we're after Lew. We need to find out what went wrong."

Kai called back a few minutes later to report that Lew and his kidnapper were still on the main road east out of Nantong, but hadn't yet tried to lose her.

Within a few minutes Cobra spotted her.

"I'm about twenty meters behind Kai," Cobra told Gage. "I can see the car Lew is in."

"What's the road ahead look like?"

"It's turning into highway. Scattered businesses and undeveloped property."

"Look for a wide place in the road and ease on past Kai, she'll slow for you."

As soon as Cobra's and Taiwan's cars had passed her and were out of sight, Kai accelerated again.

Cobra followed as Taiwan crossed the eastern city limit, still on the road toward the Qidong port.

"I'm at the crossroads between Nantong and Qidong," Gage told Cobra. "I don't think he'll keep going east. My guess is he'll turn off, and head south to Shanghai or north to Rudong. He'll want to dump Lew some place where no one will connect the body with either Nantong or the port. Can you get ahead of him?"

"Sure. He's still moving carefully."

"Pass him just before the north-south turnoff, then head north a few hundred yards. If he follows, stay in front of him and I'll come up from behind. If he heads south toward Shanghai, I'll get ahead of him and you catch up from behind."

"I'm about five minutes away."

"I'll call Kai and tell her to go straight through toward Qidong in case he doesn't turn off either way."

Gage had Ferrari turn south from the crossroads, drive for a hundred yards and then pull off by the side of the road.

Cobra called to give his position.

"I'm making my move to pass him. We're pulling away . . . more . . . more . . . He's maintaining his speed . . . Okay. Can you see us? We are making the turn north."

"I have you. I don't see him yet. The fruit trees along the side of the road don't give me much of a view . . . There he is. He's waiting for traffic to clear . . . Get going before he sees you've slowed . . . He's turning your way."

Gage grabbed Ferrari's shoulder and made a circular movement with his right index finger. Ferrari made a U-turn and drove north. He blew the stop sign at the crossroad and shot through the intersection. Tires squealed behind them. They were a half-mile behind Cobra, the two-lane road shouldered on each side by rain-soaked rice fields. He called Kai to tell her they were heading north and to follow them, then called Cobra when Ferrari had gotten him and Gage up to about thirty yards behind Taiwan's car.

"Let's get this over with. The farther we go, the more of a chance he has to get away."

"How do you want to do it?"

"You think he likes rice?"

"What?" Cobra laughed. "I got it."

Cobra slowed as Ferrari sped up, bracketing Taiwan. Gage signaled to Ferrari, pointed at the car's left rear bumper and made a pushing motion with his palm. Ferrari looked over and smiled, then gripped the steering wheel with both hands and eased up closer.

Taiwan looked wide-eyed in his rearview mirror and tried to

pass Cobra, but Cobra's car moved to the left to block him. He tried to dive along the right shoulder but Cobra slipped back, blocking him again.

Ferrari then made his move. The differential between his speed and Taiwan was no more than five miles an hour, but the tap was just enough to send Taiwan's car spinning. It spun right, skidding and sliding on the mud until his wheels planted themselves ten yards into the rice paddy.

Ferrari locked up his brakes and skidded to a stop at the edge of the road, just past where Taiwan's car had run off.

Cobra's driver turned his van around and headed back.

Stuck in the mud thirty feet from the pavement, the doors blocked by mud, Taiwan rolled down his window and fired a handgun toward Gage's van, the slugs punching through glass and metal. Gage threw open his door and he and Ferrari dove through it, hitting the ground rolling, then used the van for cover.

Taiwan squirmed out, then fought his way through the mud to the front of the car and began firing at Cobra's van bearing in.

Holes appeared in the windshield.

The wheels locked as Cobra's driver hit the brakes.

Cobra jumped out just before it came to a skidding stop nose to nose against the front of Gage's car. He crawled forward, dropped down next to Gage, Zhang's 9mm in his hand, his eyes wide, and oblivious to the blood oozing from a bullet hole in his shoulder.

"Let me have him," Cobra said, sliding himself farther toward the rear of the car to get a shot, his back leaving a blood smear on the paint.

Gage reached for him. "Stop. You've been shot."

Cobra reacted in anger, rather than in fear. "*Ta ma de.*" Motherfucker.

Gage took the gun from Cobra's hand and sat him against a

tire, then gestured to Ferrari to apply pressure to the entrance and exit wounds.

Gage then looked toward the van. He couldn't see the driver, but he caught a glance of Zhang crawling out of the sliding door left open by Cobra.

"Are you okay?"

Zhang nodded.

"Can you divert the guy so I can get a shot off?"

"I'll do better than that."

Zhang reached down toward his ankle and pulled out a tiny semiautomatic from its holster.

Gage pointed the 9mm at Zhang's face.

Zhang froze, the gun still by his shin.

"Let's deal with one thing at a time," Zhang said. "By my calculation, the heroin is out to sea anyway."

Gage glanced at his watch, then lowered the 9mm.

Zhang worked his way toward the back of his van. Taiwan took a few shots at Zhang's feet, then stopped when Zhang paused behind the rear wheel. Zhang caught Gage's eye, then waved his gun to signal he was going to take some shots.

At the first pop, Gage dove for the back of the van. At the second, Gage peeked around toward Taiwan's car. He couldn't see him, but heard him yelling.

Then a hand and gun appeared, firing not at Gage or at Zhang, but into his own car. And not as though he was trying to hit Lew, as much as trying to force him out of the car to serve as a shield for his escape.

Taiwan reached over again and fired into the car a second time, aiming lower, and Lew struggled with the door until it opened wide enough for him to crawl out. He reached out with his hands and forearms. They sank into the muck, sucking him out of the car.

Taiwan fought the mud as he slid along the car to get to Lew, trying to use the open door for cover. But as he pulled himself around the car, he exposed his side and Gage dropped a slug into his upper thigh.

Taiwan crumpled into the mud, his gun hand buried.

Kai's car skidded up. She jumped out and followed Gage and Zhang to where Taiwan and Lew were trapped.

Lew's wide eyes, framed by grime, looked up at the white ghost pointing a semiautomatic pistol at his kidnapper.

After Zhang collected the wounded man's gun, Gage turned to Lew.

"Are you hurt, Mr. Lew?"

"Who are you?"

"Someone who got here just in time." Gage gestured with his gun. "Do you know why he grabbed you?"

"He wouldn't say."

"Why are you in China?"

Lew shrugged.

Zhang shook his head in an exaggerated expression of disappointment, then hiked through the mud to where Taiwan was lying on his side. Zhang rested his crusted boot against the side of the man's face.

Gage didn't need a translation of what Zhang said to him to understand its meaning.

Taiwan didn't answer. Zhang pushed harder and half the man's face sank into the oozing mud. His expression transformed from agony to panic.

"You'll have to make a choice in the next five seconds," Zhang said to Taiwan. Kai whispered a translation to Gage. "Do you want to cooperate and live or suffocate right here?"

Taiwan twitched.

"Die?"

Taiwan struggled against the weight of Zhang's boot and shook his head.

"Live?" Zhang asked, removing his boot.

He nodded.

Zhang slogged over to Lew.

"Now, what do you want to do?"

Lew lowered his head, and nodded.

ZHANG CALLED AHEAD to a retired military doctor in Nantong as Gage and Ferrari helped Cobra into Kai's car. After it sped away, they returned their attention to Taiwan. Ferrari bandaged his wound, and then emptied his pockets and handed the contents to Gage.

While Ferrari took control of Lew, the other drivers carried Taiwan to the van where the table had been taken down and they laid him on the floor.

Gage examined the man's possessions: a Taiwanese passport, notes and telephone numbers, a hotel key, Chinese yuan and New Taiwanese dollars, and a photograph of Lew that looked to Gage like it might have been taken inside the East Wind warehouse in San Francisco.

Zhang gestured to the driver to bring Lew to the van door and handed him the photo.

Kai stood close to Gage in order to translate.

"This is how things stand," Zhang said to him. "If you cooperate, you'll be allowed to go home in a few weeks, longer if you can't travel. Until then you'll be under my protection and supervision."

Zhang took out his PLA identification card and held it out so Taiwan could read it.

Taiwan nodded.

"We only have a few questions before we start driving to the doctor."

Taiwan grunted.

"Answer carefully. You only have one chance to make things right. You understand?"

Taiwan nodded.

"Why did you kidnap Lew?"

Taiwan hesitated, glancing between Zhang and Gage. He winced against the pain, then said, "I was told if anything went wrong with the deal to kill him."

"What went wrong?"

"Nothing. The deal went as planned."

"But?" Zhang said.

"But I spotted people watching Wu's house. My instructions were to break the link to the United States if the deal was compromised."

"What did you think was happening?"

"I thought it was Chinese police getting ready to grab Lew. I needed to keep them from questioning him."

"Have you told anyone about the problem?"

Taiwan shook his head. "I was told to act on my own."

"When do you have to report in?"

"Within the next two hours. After that, there'll be questions."

Zhang and Gage stepped away from the van.

"Can we trust him to make the call now?" Gage asked Zhang. "I can't tell how sincere he is. I mostly see pain on his face."

Zhang displayed his gun. "The man wants to live, and this will purchase some sincerity."

They walked back.

"We want to you make the call now," Zhang told Taiwan. "What are you supposed to say?"

"Either that everything is fine or that the problem has been solved, and then hang up."

Zhang smirked. "And how is everything?"

Taiwan swallowed and glanced back and forth between Gage and Zhang. "Everything is fine."

"What's the telephone number?"

On hearing the number, Lew's shoulders sank. He buried his face in his muddy hands.

"Ask him whose number it is," Gage asked.

As Zhang translated, a look of panic swept Taiwan's face.

"Tell him it's a test," Gage said, "and he better not get it wrong."

Taiwan looked as if he was struggling to overcome great internal resistance, perhaps even violate a vow of loyalty he'd once taken during a secret brotherhood initiation in an incense-infused room.

"It is a mobile phone in California."

"And?"

"It is a man named Ah Ming."

"You passed the test," Gage told Taiwan. "You'll live to kill again."

Zhang pulled out his cell phone, punched in the number, pressed "send," waited for the first ring, then handed the phone to Taiwan.

"Everything is fine."

malee will kill me ... and she'll never forgive you," Cobra said, looking up at Gage from the dining room table where he had been laid in the doctor's house in Nan-tong. His voice was groggy from the painkiller that was now taking effect. "She might not let us play together again."

"She'll be so happy to see you she won't notice either the en-trance or exit holes."

"I'm lucky there was an exit hole." Cobra winced. "Did you hear Taiwan yelling when the doctor dug out the slug?"

Retired colonel Dr. Yin entered the dining room to check on his patient. Even in his seventies, Yin hadn't seemed discon-certed by the appearance on his doorstep of two gunshot vic-tims, a PLA general, a Thai-Chinese woman, an old man, and a white ghost. The wry expression on Yin's face told Gage that for him it was just another day in modern China.

Yin checked Cobra's bandages, verified that the bleeding had stopped, and announced that he was free to leave. He said he wanted to keep Taiwan for a few days because Gage's slug had punched through his hip and he needed to stabilize it.

Zhang assigned two soldiers to guard Taiwan and handed Yin

all the money he'd taken from the wounded man's pockets, an amount equal to $2,900 US, more than a year's pay for a doctor.

Kai and Gage helped Cobra off the table and draped a blanket around him, then guided him to Kai's car and eased him into the rear passenger seat.

Zhang followed them outside. "There's still the matter of my chips."

"I'll have the serial numbers as soon as I get to the hotel."

"What if they're not there?"

"They'll be there. Ask Taiwan."

"I already did." Zhang smiled. "Not all that screaming was medical. He said 'everything is fine,' I just wanted to make sure how fine."

"You have to learn to lay off," Gage said. "That guy was ours."

Gage glanced into the car. Cobra was asleep in the front passenger seat.

Ferrari brought Lew outside and Gage positioned him in the back between himself and Kai. Then Ferrari drove them to the hotel. And while Ferrari took Lew to Kai's room, Gage and Kai helped Cobra to his own where she arranged him in bed.

Gage checked his phone and found the list of serial numbers Sylvia had sent and forwarded it onto Zhang. Gage and Kai found Zhang waiting at his door when they arrived. The tension and expectation in Zhang's walk as they entered the room reminded Gage of a lion looking forward to his next kill.

"When do you want to make the announcement of the seizure?"

Zhang's question suggested to Gage that the general was now in pursuit not of financial, but of political gain and it was too soon to make that move.

"Not until the heroin is on its way from Taiwan to the States. That way there's no turning back for Ah Ming."

Gage felt a wave of exhaustion shudder through him. He

looked toward the window so Zhang and Kai wouldn't see it on his face. His mind went gray for a moment. He knew he wasn't seeing something. Some complication. He could feel the pressure of Zhang's gaze. A thought came to him: Ah Ming would hear on the news about the PLA raid and the chip seizure and might conclude that his operation was compromised and abandon the heroin at the U.S. port.

Gage looked back at Zhang. "When the time comes, have Huang Medical turn itself in. That way you won't have to explain how you got involved in this, and Ah Ming will think the seizure isn't related to him. The company can say that they were suspicious about the origin of the chips. And have Huang make up a purchase order for a fake company and a fake invoice to give themselves a paper trail. Make the payment terms sixty days from now. That way they won't have to answer any questions about how they paid for the chips."

Zhang smiled. "You think like a criminal. Maybe you made a bad career choice." His smile faded, then he adopted a sage's smile. "Your idea is perfect as far as my government is concerned. It'll be a way for China to assure corporations in the West that it's complying with their demands for enforcement in technology crimes, but we won't have to punish a successful company."

And, Gage thought to himself, *Huang Medical's continuing success will necessitate regular kickbacks to Zhang to keep his mouth shut, probably paid into his offshore Calico bank account.*

And Gage wanted something, too. "I need to reward someone for his help. Any objection to an FBI agent coming over and collecting the chips? Maybe make a show of it. He works out of Silicon Valley."

"I can deal with him directly if you want. I'll look better that way."

"And I need you to hold Lew for about thirty days."

Zhang squinted up toward the ceiling. "What would Cobra say?"

Kai answered. "*Mai pen rai.*"

"That's it." He smiled again. "*Mai pen rai.*"

"One other thing," Gage said. "Find out where Taiwan was staying—gently—and have someone search his and Lew's rooms."

"I'll have my people bring everything to you. Neither one will need a hotel anymore."

Gage locked his eyes on Zhang. "Don't you mean, they won't need rooms for the next couple of weeks?"

"Yes, of course . . . that's exactly what I meant."

CHAPTER 66

Gage and Kai walked over to her room and sat down at the dining table with Lew. Ferrari checked the windows and confirmed that an attempted escape would only result in death ten floors below, then he stepped into the hallway.

Lew had adopted an impassive expression, seemingly strengthened by time and distance from the violence and blood, and from Zhang.

"Did Wu have anything to do with my kidnapping?" Lew asked Gage.

"As far as we know, Ah Ming ordered it directly from the States."

For reasons Gage didn't understand, Lew sighed as though grateful that it hadn't been Wu who'd set him up.

"We want Ah Ming. We know he was behind the robbery where that boy was killed."

"I had nothing to do with that."

"At this point we can't prove otherwise."

"I just handle paperwork."

"Somebody had to. How well did you know Ah Tien?"

"He managed some affairs for Ah Ming and I managed others. I was shocked to learn he was murdered. I wasn't involved. I don't approve of violence."

Gage felt a flush of anger at Lew's evasion and self-deception. "But you sure seem willing to overlook a hell of a lot of it." He bore down on him. "You know the American expression, what goes around, comes around?"

Lew drew back. "You won't let Zhang hurt me, will you?"

"This is his territory, not mine. But in exchange for the right answers, I'll try to dissuade him."

Lew sat in silence for a few moments, then said, "I realize I'm not in a strong position, and I don't know exactly what you've done today. I don't even know whether Zhang has seized the heroin and the chips. But do I know this. I won't do anything to harm anyone except Ah Ming."

Lew looked at Kai. "I think you might understand. I won't help General Zhang against anyone here. My life began in China and in a way I hadn't anticipated, it is my home again. And if this is where my life has to end, fine, it will end."

Gage pointed at Kai. "She and I need to talk."

Kai instructed Ferrari to order dinner for Lew, then she and Gage walked back to his room.

"I think he means it," Kai said, sitting down on the couch. "And he knows you won't let Zhang hurt him. He sized you up right. He's a survivor."

"I think he's lying about the robbery and I think he's lying about Ah Tien. Ah Ming wouldn't send him over here if he wasn't completely trustworthy, and if he's trustworthy in one thing, he's trustworthy in the other." Gage paced the floor, getting angrier with each step. "That little weasel is starting to tick me off. His self-deceiving melodramatic 'China is my home again' is sickening. All China needs are more Lews. He knows we can't make him on the robbery or Ah Tien's murder. He's also figured out we need him for something. And we do. We need to tie the heroin to Ah Ming and I doubt I can do it without him."

"There's another American expression I learned in the States," Kai said. "Take what you can get."

"You're right. Let's go make a deal."

Kai and Gage arrived back at her room just after the room service waiter set bowls of noodles on the table. Ferrari followed him back into the hallway and closed the door.

Lew laid his chopsticks across the bowl and looked up.

"What does Ah Ming think you're doing now?" Gage asked.

"We agreed—or at least I thought we had agreed—before I left that since I worked so closely with him, I had better stay away for a while. I wouldn't even contact him again at least until after the heroin had been distributed."

"When will that be?"

"The same day the container arrives."

"At Sunny Glory?"

"Sunny Glory?" Lew's voice rose. "You know about Chau?"

"I know a lot of things."

Uncertainty crossed Lew's face. Now he wasn't sure exactly what Gage knew.

"Chau has no idea what's really going on," Lew said. "He's willing to believe all of this is about avoiding trade restrictions going into China and customs duties in the U.S."

"You mean that's what he wanted to believe."

Lew shrugged. "We didn't care what he believed. He was convenient because he has branches both in the States and in Taiwan."

"And he's greedy."

Lew nodded.

"Isn't Chau in United Bamboo?"

Lew shook his head. "But I think his partner in Taiwan is. Chau isn't tough enough for that kind of life."

"Does Ah Ming deal with Chau directly?"

"Only Ah Tien and I dealt with him. Ah Ming would terrify him."

"You mean he wouldn't be able to believe what he wanted to believe."

"Yes, I guess you could say that."

"What about his customs broker, InterOcean?"

"Only me and Ah Tien. We picked them for the same reason we picked Sunny Glory. They have branches in both San Francisco and Taiwan."

"These people are all Chaozhou and involved in smuggling," Kai said. "Surely everyone must at least suspect the possibility that it's heroin they're moving."

"They have no idea the shipments coming out of China originate in Thailand. They're chiselers at heart. They don't think about things they don't want to think about."

"What about the Thai end?" Gage asked. "Who does Ah Ming deal with?"

Lew shook his head. "I can't answer that. It'll get you no closer to Ah Ming and it'll hurt others unnecessarily. If you want to widen your net, you'll have to cast it elsewhere."

Gage decided not to fight him. His more immediate need was local.

"What about ChinaCom?"

Lew nodded. He'd answer that question. "ChinaCom wanted some separation between themselves and the chips, so they brought in Huang Medical. If you know about ChinaCom, you must know it was a ChinaCom executive who brought the cash to pay for the chips. I've been thinking that he secretly owns Huang himself."

"And you used the money in the briefcase to pay for the heroin?"

"Yes."

"What currency?"

"Dollars. The supplier insisted on dollars."

"What route will the heroin follow to the States?"

"The reverse of the one the chips followed. Through Sunny Glory in Taiwan and back onto a container. Unless there are delays, it will go out on the Hanjin *Beijing* to the Port of Oakland and will be trucked to Sunny Glory in San Francisco."

Lew smiled. Gage saw in his eyes that he was drawing back to stab Ah Ming.

"East Wind makes pickups at Sunny Glory almost hourly. That's Ah Ming's secret. His heroin operation is invisible. After the heroin arrives, the trucks will collect boxes of processed garlic, like on any other day, but the ones with special numbering will contain the heroin. A dash and two ones after the product number. The drivers continue on their routes and make their deliveries. It's for much younger men than me to know who receives the heroin, cuts it, and delivers it to the distributors. Ah Tien knew and managed everything, but he's gone."

Gage looked at Kai; she shook her head. There was no reason to pressure him about who pulled the trigger that killed Ah Tien. Lew wasn't about to confess to participation in a conspiracy to commit murder.

KAI AND GAGE LEFT THE HOTEL for a walk along the river. Gage needed to think and needed distance and evening air. He felt his body starting to let him down, a kind of fatigue that seemed to radiate outward from his heart to his limbs.

Within a block they came upon an outdoor food market. Flames shot up from woks resting on gas burners, and the smell of garlic, ginger, and smoking peppers infused the breeze flowing in from the Yangtze. Workers were buying dinner on their way home, and after-school children with their heavy backpacks and little uniforms were chattering as they walked hand in hand.

It was a mundane place to make a tough decision.

They paused and leaned against a railing and stared down at the water. Rippling streaks of light reached toward them from the shops and office buildings on the opposite bank.

"If we let the heroin go to Sunny Glory and track it from there," Gage said, "we'll have a very complicated job of connecting it to Ah Ming. Chau will claim Ah Tien used Sunny Glory without Chau's knowledge, and Ah Tien's dead. And even if the U.S. attorney accepts our theory about what happened, Ah Ming will claim he knows nothing. He'll say East Wind was used by disloyal employees, Lew, in particular, who'll have appeared to have run away."

"What about sending Lew back to the States? Force him to testify about Ah Ming?"

"He'd tell the prosecutor about the connection between the heroin and the chips. That would expose Zhang and his cut, and us."

Gage noticed an old man sitting on a bench next to a food cart. He dug snuff out of a container etched with a drawing of a eucalyptus leaf and snorted it into each nostril.

"I know what I'll do." Gage straightened up, then looked over at Kai. The fatigue lifted for a moment. "I'm going to give Ah Ming a billion-dollar overdose."

CHAPTER 67

F ind out whether the FBI brass will allow Joe Casey to come to Shanghai to recover the chips for the United States," Gage told Sylvia over the phone when he and Kai arrived in his room. "The Chinese will want some political mileage out of the recovery. It would help if an FBI supervisor from Silicon Valley showed up. If he'll do it, I'll have the PLA general who made the seizure contact him either directly or through diplomatic channels."

"What's his name?"

"Zhang. General Zhang Xianzi."

Gage caught Burch while he was driving in to work.

"I was hoping to hear from you," Burch said. "Faith said the good blood test results mean the doctor is still giving you a long leash, assuming there aren't any new holes in that aging skin of yours."

"Not mine, but a couple of other people weren't so lucky."

"I hope that doesn't include the people who were helping you."

"One got a through-and-through and—"

"A what?"

"A slug went in one side and out the other."

Burch gasped. "Damn."

"That's kind of what he said, but in Fukienese."

"How about the chips? The insurance company has been filling up my voice mail."

"We've got them and we're ready to move to step two."

"Just say the word and Zhang's new company will jump down off the shelf."

"Tell the insurance company to send the reward to your trust account and book a flight for an Intel technician to arrive in Shanghai in the next couple of days. Zhang will let him examine the chips, but he won't relinquish control until he has verification that the money is in his company account."

"What kind of verification will he accept?"

"He's a suspicious and old-fashioned guy. He'll want actual hard-copy proof of everything. I'll get a secure fax number here, and we'll have your bank fax the confirmation that the funds have been sent from your trust account to Zhang's. We can then have his bank fax him the wire transfer receipt so he knows the money has arrived."

"What if he doesn't accept that?"

"Then he can fly to Hong Kong and go to the bank himself. But he won't. He doesn't want to be seen running off to Hong Kong right after a big seizure in his territory. It would look too much like somebody paid him off. You and I know that would never happen, but suspicious minds might draw other conclusions."

"And everything you've told me suggests he's not the sort of person who'd accept a private reward for fulfilling his official duties."

"That's why we can sleep at night."

KAI AND GAGE RETURNED TO KAI'S ROOM and sat down with Lew at the table. His noodles were untouched. An oily glaze had risen to the surface of the soup in which they sat.

"General Zhang will take you into protective custody. You won't be allowed to make any calls except those I direct. Understood?"

Lew nodded.

"That includes to your new friend, Mr. Wu."

"But he's expecting to see me tomorrow."

"That's been taken care of. The hotel will call Wu with your regrets. He'll believe you're on your way to Shanghai."

"I understand."

"You also better understand that if Ah Ming finds out what's going on, he'll come after you again."

"I understand that all too well."

Gage leaned forward, laying his forearms on the table and interweaving his fingers.

"I'll need you to do a few things in the next couple of weeks."

"What will I get out of it?"

"One, you'll stay alive, and two, you'll get a chance to disappear."

"That's not much for an old man."

"That's all there is. And if I find out you're trying to reach out to Ah Ming, you won't even get that. You're on thin ice already and if I could prove what you and I both know, I'd haul you back to the States and get you and Ah Ming tried for murder, so you better hope the ice doesn't melt before I leave here."

Gage waited until Lew nodded, then said, "You'll be making some calls. Kai will work out the scripts and Zhang will tell you when to make them." Gage pointed a forefinger between Lew's eyes. "And don't play any games."

Gage grabbed Lew's chopsticks, and jammed them into his noodles, leaving them propped up in the bowl like two incense sticks at a funeral.

Lew's eyes widened when he caught the meaning, and then he lowered his head. After a few moments, he looked up at Gage and said, "There will be no games."

CHAPTER 68

When Kai and Gage went to check on Cobra, they found Zhang had sent a nurse to sit with him. It didn't seem to Gage to be a Zhang-like thing to do. Gage wondered whether he had a bighearted moment after collecting his chips or whether he just wanted to make sure Cobra didn't die at a place and time that would require an explanation he couldn't provide without risking a bullet in the back of his head.

Gage closed Cobra's door, then invited Kai for a drink.

"How are you doing?" Gage asked after they sat down in the hotel bar. "It was a big day."

"I'm fine now, but I was terrified when I drove up to where you were stopped. I saw Cobra lying on the pavement. I knew he was hurt." Her eyes became moist. "I couldn't see you at first. I thought..."

"I'm sorry. I should've made sure you could see me."

Kai wiped her eyes as the waitress set down their drinks. She then looked at Gage.

"It was a terrifying moment. Death so close to us. It made me realize that half my life is over and I don't have a clue what I've been doing all these years. You don't have that problem. You've never had any doubts."

But she was wrong. It had been doubt and the need to think about what he had been doing with his life that had taken him away from police work and into graduate school. It was something that Faith had understood from the start. And he knew, and was grateful, it was something Faith understood now.

"And I want to feel alive all the time, not just when I'm on some adventure, not just when I'm on the edge." She looked down and shook her head. "My adventures have just been escapes from thinking about what's really important, what I really want out of life." Kai was half smiling when she looked up again. "All these Westerners come to Thailand to learn about Buddhism and about mindfulness and never seem to grasp that we're no better at any of this than anyone else." She blew out a breath. "It's time for me to start over."

"What does that mean, starting over?"

"I need to leave Somchai. Money and reflected glory from a politician aren't enough. I never needed him for the money anyway. I think I really only needed him because I was a dutiful daughter, and dutiful Chinese daughters get married and put up with anything. I won't deny Somchai was my choice, and my mistake. My father let me make it. He could've forced me to marry someone of his choosing, but he didn't, and I'll always be grateful for that."

Kai paused and her eyes went vacant as they stared into the past.

"When I was first in the States, I was offended and then amazed by American girls. By the end I thought I was becoming one. I couldn't imagine that I would spend my marriage as a minor wife. Even now there are times when I still can't believe it. That alone had a lot to do with the unthinking way I've chosen to go through life."

"Somchai will fight back if you try to divorce him."

Kai blinked and refocused on Gage. "I know. Hard. The first

thing he'll do is call his accountant to see what properties he can take from me. After that, he'll try to figure out how to prevent me from keeping anything at all. But I don't care. I've always had my own money. While he gambled away most of his, I invested mine. I have land in the names of male relatives he can't touch. And I have Siri Construction. He had nothing to do with that."

Kai thumped the table between them with her forefinger.

"And I'll tell you this—"

Gage raised his palm toward her and glanced around the bar. "Not so loud."

She lowered her voice and leaned toward him. "I'm going to keep half of what we made from ganja. That was hard work and I did at least half of it. No, I did more than half of it. I'm the one who hiked to those plantations in Laos and Cambodia, slogging through the jungle, attacked by bandits. I was the toughest twenty-year-old any of those people ever dealt with. I'm the one who went to the warehouses, argued over prices, not him. I'm the one who smuggled in the cash to pay off the police and the military. He was too busy drinking with the American buyers and playing baccarat and mah-jongg. He would've been nothing without ganja, and without me."

Gage inspected her face with its intensity, its anger, its pride. He took a sip of his drink to delay having to respond. He felt Kai gazing at him. When he looked up, Kai's eyes had lost focus again. Then her head fell and her body slumped.

"I just did it again," she said. "Defined my life with respect to him."

"And with respect to money."

Kai looked up. "What's wrong with me?"

CHAPTER 69

When Gage woke up in the early morning, and even with the drapes still closed, he knew the storm had moved past them and up the Yangtze, maybe even to where the orange trees once grew before the construction of the Three Gorges Dam. He rose and looked outside. The wincing light revealed a partly cloudy sky and a translucent curtain of rain to the west and a mass of buildings. Huge blocks of concrete and stucco in shades of gray studded the land. And in that moment he discovered the trick of relevance his mind had been playing on him since his arrival: the city wasn't composed only of two houses and two hotels, a couple of offices and warehouses, a few roads and a rice paddy. It was a city of hundreds of thousands of people whose economy had risen by a multimillion-dollar flood tide of chips and heroin that had ebbed, then flowed, with the moon and the sea.

And he wondered whether he'd been as invisible to the city as it had been to him.

After showering and dressing, he walked down the hall to Cobra's room. The nurse assigned by Zhang came to the door and eased it open. Cobra was sleeping, oblivious to the slug that had gouged his flesh.

Gage left him in the womb of his sleep and rode the elevator downstairs to the dining room for breakfast. Kai joined him a few minutes later.

"Make sure Lew doesn't try to do anything in code or trick you with some double meaning. Remind him about Zhang if he needs it."

"I know Zhang will be pleased to have been remembered."

"I'll give him a call to find out what story he's decided Huang will use."

But Gage didn't need to phone. Zhang invited himself to breakfast. He helped himself to *da mi zhou* and *pao cai* from the buffet, then signaled the waiter to deliver tea as he walked toward them.

"A beautiful day." Zhang said, sitting down at their table. "We recovered eleven thousand six hundred and eighty-nine chips, exactly. I had a clerk check the Internet for wholesale prices in the United States, and they ranged from two hundred to four hundred dollars each."

"I'm glad it worked out," Gage said. "And I'm sorry about that incident with Cobra."

"It's all right," Zhang said, smirking. "I could've taken him anytime."

Kai snorted.

"I'm sure you could have," Gage said, bumping Kai with his knee under the table. They weren't done with Zhang yet.

Zhang poured himself tea, then said, "Lew was right. The little fellow who came with the giant to pick up the chips from Tongming Tiger is a director of ChinaCom. He's also the owner of Huang Medical. I have him sitting in a small room wondering whether I'm going to tell ChinaCom he was working his own side deals or whether we'll have him harvested for body parts." Zhang took a sip. "Of course, I'll do neither. He's much more useful to me alive and in place."

"What about the giant?" Kai asked.

"He's a powerfully built man but has a very low tolerance for pain. He also lacks loyalty. He's the one who confirmed our suspicions about the director."

Ferrari arrived to take Kai out to Qidong where Zhang had delivered Lew overnight.

"I didn't get a chance to thank you for your help yesterday," Gage told him. "You were brilliant." Kai translated. Ferrari smiled and shook Gage's hand. "I hope someday you'll get a chance to drive on the grand prix track."

Gage and Ferrari both looked down at Zhang, who glanced back and forth between them, then nodded and said, "Soon, very soon."

After they left, Gage led Zhang to his room and called Burch at his home in San Francisco.

"I'm here with Zhang."

"The insurer is ready to send seven hundred and fifty thousand dollars to my trust account," Burch said. "I hired a chartered accountant in Hong Kong to serve as the acting director of Calico. Zhang will need to sign a power of attorney instructing him to enter into an agreement with the insurance carrier for the return of the chips. If I can get it by tomorrow morning my time, Intel can have a technician on a plane by noon."

"Hold on." Gage lowered the phone and relayed the plan to Zhang.

"I don't want to sign anything. I can't have my name connected with this."

"Just sign it Zhang. How many million Zhangs are there in the world? Twenty, thirty, forty?"

"About seventy-five. What about the bank account?"

"The only identifying information on the opening form will be the names of Calico Limited and the chartered accountant as its director. He'll show the bank manager another power of attorney directing the bank to accept instructions from him and a letter explaining that the funds represent a professional fee. That's it."

Zhang bit his lower lip for a moment. "I'm still a little uneasy about this."

"If you want, you can close the company in a couple of days. Have the accountant set up a new company, run the money through an underground bank, and use a different front person. That way the money can't be traced back to this deal."

"Would this accountant do that for me?"

"He knows it's an insurance company reward and not drug proceeds, so he'll do whatever you want with it."

"Then let's go ahead."

Gage raised the phone to his ear. "Jack?"

"Still here."

"He agrees."

"What about Joe Casey?"

"Sylvia is in contact with him. She'll have him call you, but don't tell Casey who owns Calico."

"I'm not sure I even know," Burch said laughing. "How many Zhangs did I hear you say there were in the world?"

CHAPTER 70

Kasa arrived at the Sichuan Provincial People's Hospital in central Kunming to find two Chinese narcotics officers waiting for him outside of Luck's room. After driving overnight, he'd spent hours working through intermediaries to bribe their supervisor into releasing Luck into his custody.

"What happened?" Kasa asked Luck, as they walked past ambulances lined up by the emergency entrance.

"I tried to set up Cobra in an alley near the warehouse, but he caught on. When I came to, the police were all over me."

Luck stopped, then looked around and rolled up his sleeve to expose his forearm. He pointed at the license plate numbers written in ink, then rolled it back down.

"There were both old gray FAWs with canvas-covered beds. Red lions painted on the cab doors. I had photos, but Cobra took my phone."

"Moby bought a couple more motorcycles. Take one and lead him to where they transferred the heroin. We'll relieve him tomorrow."

KASA SHOOK HIMSELF AWAKE at the sound of his cell phone ringing on his hotel room nightstand. He checked the screen. It was Moby calling from outside the warehouse.

"The two Thai trucks we followed from Mae Sai to Kunming just arrived."

"What about the Chinese ones that picked up the heroin from them?"

"Not here."

"I'll send Luck over so you can get some rest."

Kasa poked at Luck to wake him and then gave him his orders.

After Luck left, Kasa bought clean clothes, changed, and reserved two more rooms at the hotel. He then drove to the Kunming Railway Station where five men carrying heavy packs waited near the curb.

To Kasa, their wary Shan expressions made them look rough not only on the edges, but all the way through. To those passing by on the sidewalk, they appeared to be nothing more than farmers come down from the hills to labor in the city.

The men piled themselves and their packs into Kasa's van. He drove them to the hotel and ordered them to remain in their rooms until Moby came to pick them up. He gave them a mobile phone and paid the hotel clerk for two days.

Kasa called Luck and followed his directions north through Kunming to the alley behind Yunan Agricultural Transport. As he watched the warehouse from the truck cab, Kasa tried to calculate when the Chinese trucks would arrive, knowing that would at least partly depend on how far they had traveled. While it was likely the heroin had been hauled to Hong Kong or Guangzhou to be hidden in a container, it was also possible it could've gone east to a port on the southern coast of Vietnam, though that would be risky. There was a lot of drug enforcement there because the Americans were putting pressure on the Vietnamese government both in regard to heroin and methamphetamines traffickers were smuggling into the United States and Europe. Even so, the odds were that it was at least a hard, nonstop, two-day drive up and two days back from wherever the heroin went, unless the destination had been a place he couldn't yet imagine.

All he could do was wait and think through his next steps and imagine the revenge he would take on Cobra.

Kasa left the truck and walked through the commercial district. He bought headache powder, a toothbrush, and some sodas. He took some of the powder to relieve a light throbbing at his temples. It wasn't just the pressure coming from Eight Iron to finish the job, but also internal pressure to avenge the loss of too many friends in the Shan wars against the Wa for control of the opium trade and for the creation of a state independent of both Burma and its Wa proxies. His aim throughout his adult life had been to do both, and Eight Iron knew and accepted it, and in doing so, leave a few dead Wa by the roadside.

I n the downtown Nantong office of Ren's uncle, Zhang and Gage stood by the fax machine to ensure no one else caught a look at the incriminating powers of attorney. Gage had tried to convince Zhang that an e-mailed document would be as authentic as a fax, but as Gage expected, Zhang wouldn't accept it. He wanted to watch the hard copy emerge from the printer. Zhang signed his family name, and Gage faxed them to Burch, to the accountant, and to the bank. They then drove to the PLA compound at the Qidong port.

"We're done," Kai told Gage as they entered the sparse and guarded conference room where she and Lew had been working on scripts.

Ferrari took Lew into the hallway.

While Zhang read them over to himself, Kai translated them into English for Gage.

"They're fine," Zhang said. "I don't see any ambiguities Lew might exploit."

Gage called Lew back into the room.

"When can I be released?" Lew asked.

"It'll be up to Zhang to decide."

"I need to get money from my bank account to live on. I don't have much family here, and they hardly know me."

"Depending on the timing, you may have a few days to transfer your money out before the U.S. authorities freeze accounts. They'll make you a target as soon as they can compare the employee personnel files with ICE travel records and notice the date you left the States and where you went." Gage shrugged. "On the other hand, they might focus only on Ah Ming and East Wind and leave you alone."

"That's not much to hope for."

"The alternative is that after everything is over you make a deal with the FBI to cooperate. Help them identify Ah Ming's assets and give them the names of the guys who did the robbery and the ones who killed Ah Tien. It's up to you. But they won't give you a complete walk."

Lew shook his head. "Prison would be a death sentence. You don't know Ah Ming. He can get to anyone."

"In other words, you don't want to end up like Ah Tien?"

Lew flinched.

Gage stared at Lew for a few seconds, then said, "It all looks a lot different from this side, doesn't it?"

After they returned Lew to his cell, Kai asked, "Will you really let him get his money?"

"Not . . . a . . . chance."

Gage then led her into an empty office in the compound where he called Burch.

"Did you talk to Casey?"

"He's waiting to hear from Zhang. He checked with the State Department. The Office of International Affairs suggested that Casey deal directly with a responsible party in China. They also gave him a contact at the U.S. Consulate in Shanghai."

"When can he travel?"

"The FBI in Washington authorized him to leave anytime.

It just depends on when Zhang is satisfied the funds are in his control. The money will be wired into my account later this morning. And the technician will be at the Shanghai-Pudong Intercontinental Hotel tomorrow. He wants to be on the Pudong side so he can use some testing equipment in Intel's affiliate company over there."

Gage kept Burch on the line and looked at Zhang.

"Let's make sure we all understand what's going to happen. Zhang and I have had some discussions since we talked last time."

"Okay."

"Today you'll fax Zhang confirmation that the insurance money is in your account."

"Right."

"Tomorrow we'll take the chips to Pudong. Zhang will give the technician one-quarter of the chips to examine. When that's done, Zhang will take those back and give him another quarter and so on."

"Right."

"The technician will return the final quarter to Zhang, then inform the insurer of the condition and value of all the chips. Based on that valuation the insurer will authorize forwarding an amount equal to twenty-one percent of the total from your trust account."

"Right."

"You'll fax Zhang a confirmation that the money has been sent, and the accountant will have the bank send a confirmation the money has been received into the Calico Limited account."

"Right."

"And Zhang releases the chips to Casey."

"And Zhang releases the chips to Casey."

"That means we're talking about approximately four days until this is done."

"I think that's right."

"Call Casey and tell him to expect a call from Zhang today and to be ready to travel to Shanghai tomorrow. He'll lose a day getting here. But first, you should have a talk with your new client."

Gage handed the cell phone to Zhang.

"This is Zhang Xianzi."

"I need to tell you a few things before we go any further," Burch said. "Under the American legal system, anything we discuss and anything I do on your behalf is covered by what's called the attorney-client privilege, but I need to hear from you that you understand what exactly we've decided to do."

"I heard him recount our agreement just now."

"So you understand that in exchange for the receipt by Calico of the insurance proceeds, you will release the chips to the FBI."

"Yes. That is my understanding and what I will do."

Gage disconnected, sent Zhang on his way, made himself a cup of tea, and then propped some pillows against the headboard and reclined on the bed. It was time to think about going home. He called Faith.

"I'm done."

"I'm so glad. I had a terrible nightmare. Just like the time you were in Pakistan. The night of the bombing at your hotel. Are you okay?"

"Everything worked out. Not exactly as I planned. Cobra got hurt, but he'll be okay."

"Has he told Malee?"

"He's afraid to call her. I'll make him do it soon."

"When are you coming home?"

"In a couple of days. I'll take Cobra and Kai to Bangkok, then fly back from there."

"Are you going in for another blood test?"

"I'll wait. I'll be home before we'd get the results."

"You want something special your first night back?"

"Of course. You."

CHAPTER 72

G age felt helpless as he watched Cobra suffer a long bumpy ride from Nantong to Shanghai. Even with the pain medication provided by Dr. Yin, every pothole wrenched his wounds and tore at his stitches. Because Zhang's van had been shot up, he drove them in his Yukon he'd had delivered overnight. The chips followed behind in the Volvo light duty truck he'd confiscated from Huang Medical.

After they drove onto the Yangtze ferry, Kai and Gage left Cobra sleeping in the SUV and Zhang standing by the driver's door working his cell phone. The cool air flowing in from the East China Sea chilled the passengers who'd left their cars to walk to the interior lounge or to the protected starboard side of the boat. They chose to stand at the bow railing. Kai's eyes teared as she faced toward Shanghai and looked farther south toward Bangkok. He knew the tears weren't solely the product of the buffeting wind, for he knew she had left part of her life, and most of her evasions, behind in Nantong.

They returned to the car as the ferry was about to dock. Cobra awoke to the sounds of motors revving and to the clanging and grating of metal as the ramp lowered to permit the vehicles to roll toward land, then he fell asleep again.

Zhang returned them to the Cypress Hotel on the outskirts of Shanghai, and from Gage's room, Zhang made his first call to Casey.

"It would be better if you didn't mention my name," Gage told Zhang.

"Why not?"

"He'll have to put it in a report, and if it's in a report, lots of people would be in a position to ask questions."

"Why doesn't he just leave it out?"

"Because he is old-school FBI, what we call by the book."

"I have met people like that." Zhang smirked. "They don't make the big money."

Gage took Zhang's phone, punched in Casey's number, put it on speaker, and then set it on the table between them.

After Casey answered, Zhang said, "Special Agent Casey, this is General Zhang Xianzi of the People's Liberation Army in Shanghai."

"How can I assist you?"

"I wish to report that the People's Liberation Army has seized more than eleven thousand microprocessors that I have reason to believe were stolen in California."

"And I've been instructed by the State Department of the United States and the Federal Bureau of Investigation to extend their thanks and congratulations."

"The People's Liberation Army and Foreign Ministry of the People's Republic of China invite you to travel to Shanghai to share in the announcement of the recovery."

"And I've been granted permission by the Department of Justice and the State Department to travel to Shanghai for that purpose and look forward to meeting with you then."

"I'm planning a press conference and would like you to attend."

"I'll be pleased to accept your invitation as will the members of the U.S. Consulate in Shanghai and our trade representatives who have worked with your government in these matters."

"I'll advise your consulate of the time and place. They will inform you upon your arrival."

"I look forward to seeing you then."

"I also."

Zhang disconnected and smiled at Gage.

"Very interesting. He's quite good. I couldn't tell what he knew and what he didn't know about all of this. He does the diplomatic dance very well."

"As I told you," Gage said. "He's old-school."

Zhang turned away from Gage and walked to the door. He paused and then looked back

"Casey is a man who can be trusted?"

As Gage nodded, a memory presented itself. "With my life."

ZHANG CALLED LATE IN THE DAY. By then he'd released the second batch of chips to the technician who'd assured him that the examination would likely move swiftly since none of the packaging in the first group had been disturbed.

Gage walked down the hall to Cobra's room. Kai was sitting with him.

"I replaced the bandages," she said. "And there don't seem to be infections in either wound. Dr. Yin did a good job."

"Are you ready to call Malee?" Gage asked Cobra, smiling and raising his eyebrows.

Cobra shrugged, winced from the pain, and extended his hand for the phone.

Cobra called Malee and began describing what happened. He jerked the phone away from his ear and turned it toward Kai and Gage.

Kai whispered to Gage, "She's saying . . ."

"You don't need to translate. I think I know."

Gage heard his name, and then Cobra handed him the phone.

"He's fine, really he is. He's smiling at me right now."

"The father of my children almost gets himself killed and he's smiling. I want you to hit him with the phone."

Gage covered the mike. "She says I have to hit you."

"I think it would be better if you just said you did."

"I hit him," Gage said to Malee. "He's not smiling anymore."

"I didn't hear anything. Do it again."

Gage slapped the speaker end of the telephone on his palm. "Okay, I did it."

"I don't believe you. There better be a bruise on him when he gets home. I want to speak to Kai."

"*Sawadi ka,*" Kai said. "*Sabai di ka.*"

Then a long silence.

"*Ka.*"

Another silence.

"*Ka.*"

Another silence.

"*Ka.*"

Gage leaned close and whispered to Cobra, "There've been too many yeses in a row, and Kai isn't going to rescue us."

Another silence.

"*Sawadi ka.*"

Kai disconnected from the call.

"You guys are in big . . . I mean big, big trouble."

CHAPTER 73

Kasa and Moby surveilled the Yunan Agricultural Transport warehouse in Kunming, waiting for the Chinese trucks to return from the north. Luck's watchful night earned him some rest. It was his turn to sleep in the back of the truck.

Kasa signaled to Moby as two dusty gray trucks drove toward them, stopping together at the warehouse. He held his breath as the cab doors opened, then blew it out in relief when he spotted red-painted lions.

Moby turned to climb down from the cab to awaken Luck, but Kasa grabbed his arm and pulled him back.

"Let's wait until they start making the transfer to the Thai trucks."

Kasa watched the drivers deliver shipping documents to a warehouse clerk, who marked them with a pen and stamped them with a chop drawn from a belt holster. The clerk then woke up the Thai drivers napping in the shade after lunch. They swung their trucks around and were guided backward until the folded-down gates of theirs and the Chinese trucks almost touched.

"Now wake up Luck," Kasa told Moby, "and give him one of the phones."

As Luck rolled his motorbike down a wooden ramp from the truck bed to the ground, laborers began transferring the heavy bags marked fertilizer from the Chinese to the Thai trucks. He pushed the ramp back and closed the gate. Moby drove with Kasa to the hotel where the team was waiting in front with their gear bagged up and piled on the sidewalk. They tossed them up onto the bed and climbed in.

Kasa walked down the street to the van he had driven up from Thailand, waited for a break in traffic, and pulled into the street. And after Moby closed in behind him, Kasa led them south through Kunming and back down the Old Burma Road. He pulled to the side ten kilometers outside the city and waved Moby ahead, who drove the truck another five kilometers before he, too, pulled over.

A half hour later, Kasa's mobile phone rang. It was Luck.

"I'm on my way, heading south with our friends."

A few minutes later, Kasa saw the Thai trucks appear in his side mirror. He waited until they were a hundred meters ahead of him, then he drove back onto the road. After matching the trucks' speed for five minutes, he called ahead to Moby.

"I think we're about a kilometer away from you."

As soon as Moby saw the trucks approaching, he eased out into the road in front to lead them, he hoped, all the way into Burma.

CHAPTER 74

Cobra had an uncomfortable flight from Shanghai to Bangkok, both because of the throbbing wounds in his shoulder and because he knew the conclusion Malee would draw from his age and his injury: it was time to settle down, open a business, and become a shopkeeper, a mouse. But he also knew this wounded Cobra wasn't ready to retreat into a hole.

Kai's trip was no less distressing for she understood there was a more than just a river to cross in traveling from a resolution made along the Yangtze to a confrontation with her husband along Bangkok's Chao Phraya.

As for Gage, he found that he'd arrived at the contemplative state that years ago replaced celebrations of success, for he'd learned success was a matter for the future to decide, not the present. He spent the weeks peering into black boxes, catching not their totality, but only glimpses of East Wind, Sunny Glory, Ah Ming, Lew, Ah Tien, Wu, Zhang, and Eight Iron, and from those glimpses he had drawn conclusions based on experience, on patterns he had discovered in a career as a traveler in the world of crime. Nonetheless, they were black boxes, with thick walls and dark recesses.

And something was different and new and disconcerting.

He'd always been reflective, but that had never separated him from the immediacy of the world. Now that had changed. It seemed to him as though he was seeing the world not from his eyes, but from just behind them, and he was troubled about the consequences. His relationship with Faith for all these years had been nothing if not immediate and unfiltered, and he wondered, even feared, that under the force of his disease, that was about to change.

MALEE STOOD WITH KAI'S DRIVER as Gage, Kai, and Cobra passed through customs and immigration, then entered the arrival hall of Suvarnabhumi Airport. Her eyes teared up when she spotted them. Only the restraint of Thai custom kept her from embracing Cobra after he worked his way through the crowd.

Kai and Gage waited a few moments before approaching the reunion.

"You," Malee said, looking at Gage and wiping her eyes. "I called Faith. She promised to put you in the doghouse and that's a bad thing in America."

"It's a very bad thing. But by the time she lets me out, I'm sure I'll have learned my lesson."

"That is just what she said." Malee pursed her lips and shook her head. "And in your condition. What did you think you were doing?"

Kai turned toward Gage. "What condition?"

"It's nothing. I'll explain what she meant later."

Malee's face reddened. "It looks like you better make room in the doghouse for me, too."

"It's okay, I was going to tell her before I left."

Malee pushed through the awkward moment. "I'm going to take my husband to Dr. Mana to have him examined." She looked at Gage. "Is there anything else you want to tell me before I find out myself?"

Gage shook his head. "I think Cobra told you everything."

"And stop calling him Cobra. His Cobra days are *over*."

"Then what'll we call him?"

"That will depend on how he behaves," Malee said. "There are lots of creatures in the animal kingdom, some with very un-flattering names."

WHILE MALEE DROVE COBRA TO THE DOCTOR, Kai's driver took her and Gage back to the Emerald Hotel. Gage checked in and Kai went with him to his room.

"What is it?" Kai asked, leaning back against the desk.

"I have a kind of cancer."

Kai's eyes widened.

"It's treatable. In fact, the doctor didn't mind me coming over here before I started chemotherapy. It's called lymphoma and it's—"

"Why didn't you tell me before?"

"Because I thought you needed to think things through without being any more confused about what you thought of me or felt about me. And I think I was right."

"I think you were right, too." She sighed. "But it hurts my feelings that you didn't trust me."

"You know I trust you. You've had my life in your hands this whole trip."

Gage walked over to her and put his arms around her. She leaned her head against his chest.

"I'm sorry I tried to take you away from Faith. Especially now. She must be so worried about you. I thought all this time I wanted to take her place, but what I really needed was a place of my own."

"That's what everyone needs. Unfortunately, you live in a society that allows little room for that."

Kai drew back and looked up at him. "It's just going to have to begin making a little more."

Kai walked toward the door, then looked back and smiled.

"The next time you talk to that fucking car thief tell him I miss him. Desperately."

"He would expect nothing less."

After Kai left, Gage did, in fact, call Zhang.

"The technician will be done by tomorrow afternoon and inform the insurers," Zhang said.

"What about Lew and Taiwan?"

"Taiwan is recovering and Lew has been quiet."

"If any problems develop, give me a call; otherwise, I'm out of it."

"Good luck on your end. Perhaps we'll meet again?"

"Perhaps."

CHAPTER 75

As morning fog was lifting along the border, the Thai trucks carrying the payment for the heroin crossed from China into Burma. The drivers had found nothing suspicious in the unremarkable trucks, motorcycles, and vans surrounding them as they traveled south. There were even times when they felt a sense of connection with the others on Old Burma Road, the comfort of a convoy.

Hours later, as the lead driver approached the Wan Pai turn-off, forty miles north of the Thai border, he noticed the truck in front of him slowing. When its speed dropped to five kilometers an hour, he moved to pass, but the truck bore to the left and skidded to a stop, blocking both lanes of traffic. Five gunmen jumped down into the rising dust and raced toward the Thai trucks. Before the drivers could pull weapons from under their seats, they found gun barrels pressed against their temples.

The fifth member of the team tossed his assault rifle into the bed of the truck that had blocked the road, then ran ahead to guide oncoming traffic around what appeared to other drivers to be nothing more than a minor accident.

MOBY STRAIGHTENED OUT HIS TRUCK and let the fifth man climb aboard. He led the caravan south to the Wan Pai turnoff, then east toward the Mekong River. Before reaching the village, Kasa passed them and led them onto a one-lane dirt road ascending into the mountains. As the rain forest thickened, Kasa looked for a clearing large enough to park the three trucks. He pulled past a break in the trees, signaled the two Thai trucks to enter, then backed in behind them. Kasa and Luck parked close to the road and walked toward the trucks. The Thai drivers were standing together under guard.

"Where is it?" Kasa asked the two of them.

"We only have fertilizer," the older of the two drivers said, transfixed by the tattoos exposed by Kasa's short-sleeved shirt.

Kasa directed his tribesmen to unload the bags.

"We were only hired to drive the trucks," the younger one said. "We have no idea what's inside and we don't care."

Kasa looked hard at both of them, then said, "Whoever tells me where it is will leave here alive."

The older driver looked over at the younger. "They'll kill us anyway. There's nothing to gain by telling them anything."

"Yes, there is," Kasa said. "A painless death."

The younger driver broke free and ran toward the cover of the forest. Kasa pulled his handgun and fired one shot, hitting him in the middle of his back. He fell forward, arms flailing, clawing at the ground, trying to pull himself forward. But the loose forest floor gave way, and his grasping dirt-filled hands slid back toward his chest.

Kasa walked up to the man, now sobbing.

"I still may let you live. Which bags contain the payment?"

"Please, please, I'm just a driver."

Kasa fired a slug into the ground next to his head.

"Lot 56. It's in bags marked Lot 56."

Kasa walked back and ordered the other driver bound.

When one of the trucks was half empty, Moby called out that he found one marked Lot 56. Kasa watched him cut into the bag, then wave and nod that what he hoped to find was there. They separated out twenty Lot 56 bags, piled them in the back of Moby's truck, then filled the rest of the space with bags of fertilizer to conceal the load, leaving just enough room for one of the motorcycles.

Satisfied that he'd accomplished his mission, Kasa walked back to the young driver and shot him in the back of the head.

The older driver made no attempt to flee.

Kasa admired his courage, but he was on the wrong side. The tribesmen holding the man eased away and Kasa dropped him where he stood.

His men removed the spare tires from the Thai trucks, rolled them into a small clearing, and returned to collect the bodies. They lifted them onto the top of the tires and splashed on gasoline.

Kasa left a motorcycle with one member of the team and instructed him to set the bodies and trucks ablaze four hours later, then to make his way home.

Kasa led the caravan back to the Old Burma Road and turned south toward Thailand. He dropped off the rest of team at their home village, while Moby and Luck continued on to the border, across to Mae Sai and south to Chiang Rai. They all met up again at Eight Iron's shopping center. Kasa took some satisfaction in the irony that it had been built by Kai's Siri Construction. They hid the truck in an outbuilding and transferred the load to one of a different make and style.

Kasa dropped off the van at Eight Iron's office and rode overnight with the others to a tire manufacturing company in the industrial district of Samut Prakan, south of Bangkok. Workers at the company unloaded the truck, stacking the Lot 56 bags in a secure and guarded storage room, and returned the fertilizer to the truck for the trip to an agricultural supply warehouse.

Kasa decided to leave Moby and Luck in the resort town of Pattaya. The farther they were from Chiang Rai the better. He gave them money for rooms, food, and prostitutes, left them at a beachfront hotel, then drove back north to where Eight Iron waited.

CHAPTER 76

I n late afternoon, Kai picked Gage up from the Emerald Hotel and drove over to Cobra's house.

Malee greeted Gage and Kai at the door and directed Gage to the outdoor veranda where Cobra rested in a rattan recliner flanked by three chairs and facing out toward the orchid garden.

Gage sat down, opened two beer bottles on the side table, and handed one to Cobra.

"I wonder whether Eight Iron and Kasa are ever going to get what they deserve. People call me Cobra, or if Malee has her way, used to call me Cobra, but those two are cobras with double sets of fangs." Cobra took a sip of his beer and gazed out toward the garden. "But not into my flesh. Kai told Malee she needed a security director for Siri Construction. Malee is supposed to tell her whether I'm interested. Kai was afraid to ask me directly. She thought I would be insulted and lose face if I felt she was viewing me as a has-been."

"You think you'll do it?"

"I'll wait until the hurt from these two holes goes away before I decide. Pain isn't always the best career counselor."

They fell silent and listened to the Zebra doves cooing in a cage behind them.

Gage felt it was all coming to an end. It was time to settle up.

"How much do you have left from what Sheridan gave you?" Gage asked.

"I think about eight thousand."

"Keep that, and I'll send over another fifty. And let me know what the medical bills are."

"They're too small to worry about. Dr. Mana just changed the bandages, checked for infections, and gave me an injection. He never even asked how I got shot."

"Let me know anyway."

"Maybe. When are you flying back to the States?"

"Tomorrow. The press conference in Shanghai is set for ten A.M. There's nothing keeping me here."

"What about Kai? You two still have an understanding?"

"One that will last this time. She's finally starting to figure out what she really wants in life. And the first step in getting it is to divorce Somchai."

Cobra shook his head. "This is a bad country for that. If the husband doesn't agree, there'll be no divorce. And even if he does agree, the terms can be ruinous for the woman."

"Maybe that's why she wants you as her security director. Somchai will think twice before he leans on her if he has to do it through you."

Gage heard Kai's and Malee's voices coming toward them. He leaned in toward Cobra.

"One last thing. Make sure your people get a tracking device on the container before it leaves Taiwan."

Cobra smiled. "*Mai pen rai.*"

Kai picked a couple of orchid blossoms, then walked over to the teak spirit house perched on a post in the garden. She reached inside and placed a small piece of mango on a dish in front of the smiling Buddha and scattered the blossoms around his feet.

She then turned around, spread her arms, smiled, and said, "Can't hurt."

After dinner, Kai drove Gage back to the hotel.

She didn't ask to come in.

CHAPTER 77

age caught a flight from Bangkok to Hong Kong, then
another to San Francisco, a route he had taken so many
times it had the feel of a routine. Even though the last leg
took thirteen hours, it had always been shortened by thoughts of
Faith and home. But this time seemed different, for home had a
puzzling sense of unreality about it. It made him wonder where
he would be in his life, even who he would be and what his life
would be, when he got there.

As the plane headed east from Chek Lap Kok Airport, Gage
caught a parting view of Hong Kong and Victoria Island. And as
the plane turned over the Pacific, Gage looked north toward the
Formosa Strait knowing that among those many boats cutting
through the water, one concealed in its hold many, many millions of dollars of China White heroin.

And the others? What about the others? What was concealed
in them?

And who had died for it? Or had killed for it?

But that would be for another day and for someone else.

GAGE PASSED THROUGH IMMIGRATION AT SFO, then slipped
through the crowd in the arrivals hall and walked out to the

curb. He looked up the ramp for Faith, then for a place to sit. He found a concrete bench on which the front section of the *San Francisco Chronicle* had been abandoned. The top half announced a construction bid rigging investigation. An old client had been the victim. He didn't bother reading the article, for when the call came into his firm, he knew he'd be handing it off to someone else. He then flipped over the paper and caught sight of Casey's face looking back at him from below the fold.

HISTORIC CHIP SEIZURE IN ASIA
John Beuttler
Shanghai, China
Associated Press

The Chinese Ministry of Public Security and the United States Federal Bureau of Investigation announced in Shanghai today the largest seizure of stolen microprocessors in Chinese history. The Intel chips were discovered at a northern China medical equipment manufacturer when an employee suspected that the shipping documents accompanying the chips were fraudulent.

General Zhang Xianzi of the People's Liberation Army unit that made the seizure said the confiscation was the result of China's intensive campaign to comply with trade and intellectual property agreements entered into with Western countries in recent years.

Senior Special Agent Joe Casey of the San Jose, California, office of the FBI said the chips had been stolen in a daring daylight robbery of a California computer manufacturer. One suspect was killed in the robbery and two were arrested. Casey does not know the route the chips traveled to China and the mastermind is thus far unidentified.

Casey said the seizure of the chips represents a significant step in the development of cooperation in commercial matters between the United States and China. Casey promised General Zhang whatever assistance and cooperation he might require in the investigation.

Zhang said that due to the sophistication of the perpetrators, the chance of making an arrest was small, but that the recovery was a significant step in itself. According to Zhang, the seller of the chips was described only as a large Chinese male, 30 years old, who fled China immediately after the chips were seized.

Gage looked up and saw Faith driving toward him. His heart filled with warmth and longing. He then knew that whatever had changed in him in China had left one thing the same.

ong felt his throat tighten as he walked into the reception area of Tongming Tiger and spotted the men who'd asked to see him. They'd been described by his secretary as Mongolian looking, but with odd accents. One glance and he knew they hadn't come from the north, and sweat moistened his palms when he heard the taller of the two men speak.

It was Colonel Thaw of the Wa State Army. He was a man with a hard and unforgiving voice that until this moment Dong had only heard on the telephone.

Thaw directed Dong outside and walked him to the far perimeter fence, across the parking lot.

"The return trucks were captured," Thaw said. "The payment was stolen, and two of our people were killed."

"I had nothing to do with it." The truth gave Dong confidence. "My uncle fought with the Kuomintang in Burma and led Wa troops. That's how I was introduced. I'd never jeopardize our relationship, and my uncle would never accept that kind of betrayal."

"Who knew what was in the fertilizer bags?"

"Only me. I did the packaging myself. Wu didn't even know. He'd gone off with a man named Lew from the States, I think San Francisco, but he's gone now."

"Did either Lew or Wu see the trucks that went south to Kunming?"

Dong nodded. "They brought the computer chips here after the heroin arrived."

"Are you telling me that the heroin, the chips, and the money were all in the same place at the same time?"

Dong watched Thaw's face harden, and he raised his hands in self-defense. "I didn't set it up this way, Old Wu did. And he was following orders from the States."

"Where is he?"

"Probably at home," Dong said, pointing east. "He doesn't go to his office very much anymore. But be careful until you know Lew's part in this. I think they may have gotten close."

Dong drove to Wu's house in his own car. Thaw and his bodyguard followed in another. The housekeeper opened the gate and guided him and Thaw into Wu's study where he sat behind his desk.

"There was a theft in Burma," Dong said. "The colonel needs to know where the heroin went."

Wu's face flushed. "He needs to know what?"

"You heard him," Thaw said.

Wu kept his eyes focused on Dong.

"What protection do I have from Lew's people?"

"I've been in business with the Wa for a long time." Dong glanced toward Thaw. "And my uncle has worked with them even longer. They'll protect you. They just want to know what happened and who did it."

Wu folded his arms across his chest. "Then your uncle will have to vouch for them."

Dong searched his cell-phone memory and read out the

number. Wu dialed. After a few moments, Wu said that Dong's uncle wasn't answering.

"Let's meet later this evening. Between now and then I'll keep trying to get through." Wu looked at Thaw. "Don't worry, as you can see I'm too old to run away."

Thaw nodded. "We'll be back here in two hours."

Dong drove back to his office. He fidgeted and paced for an hour and a half as he waited, then returned to Wu's house fifteen minutes early, wanting to make sure the old man would cooperate.

As Dong stepped through the gate, the *amah* told him Wu had left a half hour earlier with the two men. Dong's hands shook as his imagination lit up, and he felt dread, actual dread, for the first time in his life . Until that moment, he'd never allowed himself to wonder whether dealing in heroin was different from any other business. After all, it was a commodity like fertilizer and cassava and ginger and ginseng, a matter of supply and demand. Just capitalism. But now he realized it was capitalism out of the barrel of a gun. Suddenly his years of self-deception now appeared before him with the face of terror.

Dong fumbled with his ignition key when he tried to start his car, then called his uncle as he raced toward Efficiency Trading.

"Uncle, I need your help."

Dong heard his voice breaking and felt his eyes welling up.

He started to describe what happened, but his uncle cut him off. "They've already called. You're not in danger. Wu's the problem. He should've told them what they wanted to know right when they asked."

Dong disconnected and pulled to the side of the road. He sat for a few minutes, the car idling. The dread began to ease. It was replaced first by puzzlement, then by anxious reflection, and soon he found the answer, or at least an answer that would do until he had time to think things through.

What happened has happened, Dong told himself. *And life will go on.*

He eased out into the road and drove toward Efficiency Trading. There was no more urgency, no reason to risk attracting attention. He didn't see cars when he arrived. Light leaked from under the roll-up door of the loading dock. He walked around to the entrance, then wound through the building until he reached the warehouse. He stepped inside, frozen in place by a moment of suppressed terror, and then pulled his cell phone from his belt clip and punched in a number.

Forgive me, Lao Wu, Dong said to himself as he stared at the old man's body, his gaping mouth and glazed eyes. *I'll remember you on the Feast of the Hungry Ghosts.*

"Public Security," the dispatcher said.

"There has been an accident."

"Where are you?"

"Efficiency Trading on Wenshai Road."

"Do you need an ambulance?"

"No. It's too late."

"What happened?"

"The owner was crushed by bags of rice powder. The stack became unbalanced and fell."

"Did you see it happen?"

"I was just ten meters away. It was a terrible accident. A terrible, terrible accident."

CHAPTER 79

G age found that Dr. Stern and Faith greeted each other like pals when Stern entered the examining room in the Stanford Cancer Center an hour after he underwent a scan.

"I looked at the new images. There doesn't appear to have been much growth, except for the lymph nodes along your lower spine. Any pain along there?"

Gage shrugged.

"What about nausea?"

"Not bad."

"Dizziness?"

"Only when I saw Faith driving up to me at the airport."

Stern smiled. "How romantic. But that's not what I had in mind."

"It's okay."

"Slide up on the table and unbutton your shirt."

Gage did as he was told and then Stern worked the cold end of a stethoscope around his chest and back, listening for breathing obstructions. Stern then pulled out the extension on the exam table, and Gage lay back and stretched out his legs.

"Breathe in." Stern pressed the tips of her fingers under his left rib cage. "Your spleen is more enlarged than before you left." She then felt along his lower legs for any protruding lymph nodes. "Okay down here."

Gage sat up. "How did this morning's blood test look?"

"It shows an increased tumor burden. I wouldn't have wanted you to stay away any longer. It's time to start treatment."

Gage took in a breath. He realized that until that moment he had been deceiving himself. He'd been thinking and acting as if the inevitable was just one of a number of possibilities. But it wasn't. All the while the clock had been ticking, and the big hand was about to knock him flat.

"Then let's get it going. Except one thing—"

Stern and Faith cut him off together. "No way."

"Not that." Gage smiled at them. "I'm not going anywhere."

"You bet you're not," Stern said.

"I'd rather get the treatment down here. It's a longer drive, but I think you and I understand each other."

"I'd be more comfortable if I could monitor everything myself and wouldn't have to rely on secondhand information. We're heading down a hard road, and I'd like to be there each step of the way."

Gage pointed at file folder in Faith's hand. "We read the protocol for the clinical trial. The way I understand it is that both groups of patients get an antibody followed by chemotherapy, but each group gets a different antibody. The question we have is whether we get a choice about what group we're in."

"It's a double-blind study. I won't even know. I do know that the Phase I and Phase II trials have shown that both the antibodies are safe in targeting non-Hodgkin's lymphoma; the only remaining question is which one works the best. That's what this trial is meant to find out. But before we start, you need to know about side effects, both from the antibody and from the chemotherapy."

Faith reached into her purse and pulled out a pen and notepad.

Stern looked over at her. "Don't worry about getting all of this down. They'll be listed on the consent form." Then back at Gage. "Keep in mind not everyone gets all of them. They're likely to be some combination of fatigue, weight loss, infections, and hair loss. Nausea and vomiting used to be a more serious problem because chemotherapy activates certain nerves in the brain, but now we have medications that are usually effective against it.

"Fatigue will probably be your main hurdle. The chemotherapy will be in three-week cycles, so you'll have a series of ups and downs. The downs can be overwhelming. Simple things like climbing stairs can be daunting. So don't underestimate it.

"Patients react to chemotherapy differently. For some, the fatigue strikes right after the first infusion, for others two weeks later. For most, it increases as treatment continues; for a very few it peaks early, then decreases.

"Also watch out for dizziness. You'll need to move slowly at times, particularly when getting up or lying down.

"The last three side effects I want to mention are a reduction in red blood cells, which will result in fatigue; a lowered white blood count, which will reduce your resistance to infection; and excessive bleeding even from minor wounds. That means—"

Gage raised his hand.

"Get rest, avoid infections, and stay away from people who can hurt me."

"I'm not sure I would've phrased it exactly that way. But that's the general idea."

EVEN AS DR. STERN GUIDED GAGE AND FAITH to her office to sign the consent forms, he understood it would be a charade. The notion of consent was irony itself. He had no choice. If he didn't undergo treatment, he'd be dead in a couple of months.

After signing off, they walked upstairs to the infusion center reception area. He noticed the current week's *The Economist* on a side table and picked it up as they sat down. The name on the mailing label had been scraped off, but "Stanford University, Palo Alto, California" remained, suggesting to him that perhaps someone from Stanford's economics department was also a patient.

As he skimmed through the table of contents, he spotted a headline: "Chips Redux: They Went Thataway," and turned to it. The full-page article praised the Chinese government for the seizure and, at the same time, blamed it for the systemic cancer of lawlessness undermining world confidence in Chinese business.

Gage thought it was a reckless use of the term by a writer who obviously never had it.

The caption under the photo of Casey and Zhang standing behind a table displaying boxes of chips read: "Dream team stymies chip smugglers."

A nurse called his name and escorted them back to the infusion room. He inspected the faces of the half-dozen patients seated in recliners, IVs extending from pumps to their forearms, each displaying varying combinations and degrees of side effects: hair loss, fatigue; the fevered dressed for the beach, the chilled covered with microwaved blankets. Then there were those who were depressed into despondency, a blood test or scan away from failure. And there were some who displayed almost no symptoms at all.

Gage thought of Tex, his post-op nurse, and smiled to himself, thinking he'd like to join that group and wondering where was the sign-up sheet.

Two older male patients caught Gage's eye. They could tell he was new and welcomed him to the club with a thumbs-up.

The nurse directed Gage to take a seat and slid over a chair for Faith, then rolled up a small cart bearing IV supplies, a power infuser, and two IV bags, one containing saline, the other an antinausea medication. The nurse asked his name and birth date and handed him two acetaminophen tablets and an antihistamine capsule. She inserted the IV and started the flow. Thirty minutes later, the nurse brought over the antibody, once again confirmed his name and birth date, and connected it to the drip line.

Gage looked around the room as she walked away, wondering about what combination of side effects he would draw from the deck.

It didn't take long to find out: fever and chills.

The nurse reduced the infusion rate, and after a few minutes, the symptoms subsided.

Over the course of the next hour, the nurse edged the flow back to its initial level.

Three hours into the infusion, the antibody bag was empty.

Two hours after that, three chemo drugs had been pumped into him, and he was done for the day.

As Gage and Faith headed toward the exit, Gage spotted a familiar face, except drawn with only wisps of graying hair covering his scalp and with deadened eyes that stared down at a shadow blackening the carpet.

Gage walked over and sat down. "Tex?"

"Partner?"

"What happened?"

"My last six-month exam wasn't so good."

Gage wasn't surprised. He'd suspected from the way Tex had acted when they met in the cancer center a couple of weeks earlier that he already knew he was in trouble.

"More chemo?"

"My last round. Third time turned out not to be a charm. It doesn't seem to be working, and I can't do a bone marrow transplant again."

Gage found himself gritting his teeth, his eyes warming and wet.

"If my blood results aren't good enough today, the doctors are saying this might be it."

"Can I do anything?"

"Thanks, but no." He tilted his head toward the lobby. "My folks came out yesterday. They'll be with me at the hospice if it comes to that."

Tex sighed, lowering his eyes.

Gage reached over and put his arm around Tex's shoulders.

"Thanks for taking care of me in the recovery room, and for talking to me afterward. You made it a lot easier to face the diagnosis, and I know you did the same for lots of other people."

"That's why I stayed out here."

Gage nodded and forced a smile. "That, and the big mistake meeting."

"Yeah." Tex attempted to smile back. "That, and the big mistake meeting."

CHAPTER 80

General Kew Wai Su of the United Wa State Army stood before his senior staff in a meeting room at an encampment in the Loi Hpa-leng, a red cliff mountain range across the border from Thailand.

"According to our source in Nantong, the buyer of the heroin is Ah Ming in San Francisco," Kew said as he leaned forward and folded his hands together on the rough wood table. "He owns a company called East Wind. Lew Fung-hao is his right hand. He arranged for the heroin to be shipped to a Sunny Glory in Taiwan. We've spoken to the Chinese who drove from Nantong down to Kunming. They're certain they weren't followed. I can only conclude that someone was waiting at the Kunming warehouse to follow the Thai trucks south.

"Who could it be? And how did they know?" Kew paused, then scanned the faces of the four men sitting around him. "Two possibilities have come to mind. The first is Ah Ming. His man Lew may have seen the trucks leave Nantong for Kunming. The second is Eight Iron. After years out of the trade, he showed up claiming he had an American buyer. He asked a lot of questions and might have learned we had a big load heading north."

Kew's eyes settled on his second in command.

"I want to speak to Eight Iron in Chiang Mai. I need to know the name of his customer. Tell him anything. If he refuses to come, do whatever is necessary to bring him. Tomorrow. And I want to you to find out where the heroin is. Get someone started toward Sunny Glory in Taiwan tonight."

Heads nodded around the table.

Kew climbed aboard a waiting helicopter and flew to the western Thai border near the village of Mae Hong Son. He slipped into Thailand on foot and met with Wa soldiers operating on Thai soil. They drove down into a valley, then past the rice paddies, housing developments, shopping malls, and finally into the heart of the Chiang Mai.

To Kew the city always seemed a waste, a waste of billions of dollars of heroin profits that had been used to build things, rather than to pursue ideas. He thought of the power Thailand would've wielded in Asia and how it could've insulated itself from the economic disasters of the West had it understood this a hundred years earlier. But he set those thoughts aside as they drove over the moat into the old town and to his hotel. For those were ends, and his concern at the moment were means.

ON THE FOLLOWING MORNING, the driver returned and took him to the home of the local Wa heroin representative where he found Eight Iron and Kasa seated at a dining table guarded by soldiers. He held up his palm as he entered, preventing them from rising and offering a greeting.

"I'm General Kew. Something of ours has been stolen in Burma. I've brought you here because you recently showed unusual interest in heroin we were manufacturing."

"I showed interest," Eight Iron said, keeping his tone even, "not unusual interest."

Eight Iron noticed Kew hadn't specified what had been stolen.

He recognized it was a trap to see if he would slip and reveal guilty knowledge. He guessed if Kew knew anything incriminating, he would've confronted them in a Wa encampment in the forest, not invited them for a discussion in a dining room in Chiang Mai.

"A month ago," Eight Iron said, "an old American customer came to see me. I told him I'd moved into yaba, but if the money was right, I'd see what I could do for him."

"But you didn't follow through."

"I found out he was secretly representing Ah Ming who stole fifty kilos of heroin from me years ago and I figured he was trying to set me up."

"It seems to me it would've been a chance to get even."

Eight Iron shook his head. "If I stole it myself, I'd have to warehouse it until I could find a buyer and that was too much of a risk. And if I let the police have it, they might've traced it back to the source, and I didn't want to put the Wa at risk."

"Did your buyer know we were the source?"

"In a certain way he directed me to you. He said he needed 555 to compete with what the Afghans were selling to his competitors in the States. I only told him what was common knowledge along the border. That the Wa State Army was finishing a large production of 555, that the lab had been moved back into Thailand, and that the heroin now travels through China to the sea. If I knew he represented Ah Ming, I wouldn't even have passed on that."

"What's Ah Ming's real name?"

"Cheung Kwok-ming. United Bamboo from Taiwan. He moved from Thailand to the United States right after he robbed me." Eight Iron jutted his chin toward Kew. "How much of your heroin did he steal?"

Kew waved off the question, and asked, "Do you know of a man named Lew Fung-hao?"

"I don't know that name." Eight Iron felt himself tense, afraid he'd misjudged the extent of Kew's knowledge and had somehow trapped himself.

"Or a company named Sunny Glory?"

Eight Iron shook his head. That was the truth. He didn't know it.

"Where's your buyer now?"

Eight Iron shrugged. "He could still be in Bangkok, or he could've gone back to New York."

Kew glanced at Kasa, focusing on the tattoos that showed above his shirt collar, then returned his attention to Eight Iron.

"The theft occurred in Shan-controlled territory. This man with you is Shan."

"He's not involved in politics. Never has been."

Kew stared down as Kasa, not believing that at all, then walked outside and signaled to one of the men who'd brought Eight Iron and Kasa to Chiang Mai. The soldier was leaning against a Jeep and smoking a cigarette. He ground it out and straightened himself as Kew approached.

"How difficult was it to find Eight Iron?"

"Not a problem. He's become a creature of habit, home in the day and gambling at night. We can take him any time we want."

"Watch him twenty-four hours a day until I order otherwise."

Kew returned into the house, told Eight Iron and Kasa they'd be driven back to Bangkok, then left again.

DURING HIS HOURLONG FLIGHT from Chiang Mai to Bangkok, Kew accommodated himself to what his strategy would have to be: cut his losses and save revenge for later.

A driver and bodyguard met him at the Suvarnabhumi Airport and took him to meet with the leader of the Thai branch of the Chinese Big Circle gang. Kew trusted Catfish because his history was as brutal as the Wa's had been. It was summed up in his nickname. He'd received it not because of his appearance, but because he proved he could survive anywhere. He was a former Red Guard member turned criminal who escaped first from a reeducation camp, then from a labor camp, and finally from prison in Guangzhou where he'd joined Big Circle. Kew had known Catfish since the mid-1980s, when he made his way to Thailand to run the gang's Southeast Asia operations.

Kew laid out the course of his investigation, showing how two independent trails led to Ah Ming.

"Take back what's mine and keep a share for yourself," Kew said, ending the meeting. "And as for Ah Ming himself, do whatever the situation allows."

CATFISH CALLED A DAY LATER.

"There was a problem. My people in Taiwan discovered that Sunny Glory was being watched. There was no chance to make a move on the heroin."

"Ministry of Justice Intelligence Bureau?"

"No. We intercept the MJIB communications, and we'd know if an operation was under way."

"Then who were they?"

"I don't know. But our people in Taiwan are angry. They suspect you also made a deal with someone else."

"There's no other deal and those weren't my people. It must be Ah Ming's countersurveillance. Did his people spot yours?"

"We have no reason to believe they did. We used young women selling DVDs at an open air market across the road and their men didn't avoid looking at them."

"Then we're fine. He's just being careful. Maybe he doesn't trust Sunny Glory. The kind of man who'd steal from a business partner can't trust anyone."

CHAPTER 81

Gage found Lucy in the reception area wearing Levi's and a plaid shirt, dressed like an office worker who'd been called in on a weekend to finish an assignment. They walked together to the conference room where Sylvia waited.

"You really gave me a scare when we found out you'd gone into East Wind," Gage told her after they sat down. "We weren't sure you would be walking out again."

Lucy reddened. "I'm sorry. I just—"

"I know. Let's see if it paid off."

"It didn't about the robbery, but maybe other things. Sylvia told me the Sunny Glory container would be handled by Inter-Ocean Customs Brokers, so I checked the computer records. East Wind has never used them. Everything has gone through that other customs broker, Alan Lim. I also checked for Sunny Glory. East Wind has never received goods directly from their Taiwan branch. Everything comes though Sunny Glory's San Francisco warehouse. East Wind trucks pick up from Sunny Glory as part of their regular route. Garlic, ginger, and ginseng."

"At least part of the heroin container may contain garlic," Gage said. "That's what was loaded in China."

"What's going to happen to it over here?"

Gage smiled. "That's up to you."

"What?" A shock wave of panic seemed to pass through her. Her hands clenched on the desk. "Me?"

"I want you to be in control of the container. I want to jam it down Ah Ming's throat. When it gets close, Lew will tell both Sunny Glory and InterOcean Customs Brokers to take instructions only from you. He'll also tell your supervisor to stay out of it."

"Why would Mr. Lew do that?"

"We gave him a very limited number of options, and he made the wisest choice among them."

Another wave passed through Lucy. Gage guessed she was imagining the circumstances under which Lew had made his choice, and it wasn't something they taught in business school.

"Don't worry. We treated him well."

"Is there a way to get rid of your supervisor for a couple of days?" Sylvia asked Lucy.

"Alan Lim came by one day to take him to a mah-jongg game at the Masonic Lodge in Chinatown. Maybe he could do it again."

"I'll talk to him." Gage rose and escorted Lucy to the lobby. He paused by the exit to the parking lot. "How's your mother?"

Lucy smiled. "Fine, even better than fine. She said she had a conversation with an old friend, and it made all the difference."

After Lucy left, Gage returned to the conference room.

"We need Lucy's personnel file from East Wind," Gage told Sylvia. "That file is all Ah Ming would need to track her down if things go bad. Fake identities created by amateurs always have some connection to the truth of who they really are. Lucy may not see it, but Ah Ming's people will."

Sylvia nodded.

"But don't scare her. She's handling herself well right now and I don't want to make her nervous."

Gage's cell phone rang as he walked upstairs to his office. It was Cobra speaking in a whisper.

"I take it Malee is listening."

Cobra laughed. "It's just pretend. Now that she knows the whole story, she wanted me to do the last thing."

"You mean you got the tracking device on the container?"

"Not me. Malee wouldn't let me out of her sight. My people did. I told them if they didn't, one of them would have to ride on top of the thing all the way to California."

CHAPTER 82

G age waited for Casey to recover from his Shanghai to SFO jet lag before arranging to meet him at Abe's Fly Shop.

"You look beat," Gage told him when he walked in the door. "Let's go in the back so you can sit down."

"I don't know how you do so much traveling." Casey stifled a yawn as they sat down at Abe's workbench. "It'll be a week before I feel normal again."

"It's mostly just practice."

"I could do without it. I've been pretty lucky my whole career, never more than four hours from a trout stream, never forced to travel much for work, and never flew through more than three time zones." He cast Gage a resigned smile. "And you know what my wife wants to do when we retire? Travel. With all the Buddhist stuff she's been doing in the last few years, I figured she'd just want to sit in a dark room and meditate. But no. Travel." He pointed at a fishes of the world poster tacked to the wall. "Like they have trout in Tibet?"

"How about Chile or New Zealand?"

"No way. She's been spending too much time in the New Age

sections of the bookstores. Travel means going someplace cosmic like Nepal or India or—what's that little place over there?—no cars, no television."

"Bhutan."

"Yeah, Bhutan."

Casey fell silent for a moment, then said, "When we met at the FBI Academy, it never crossed my mind that she'd go Berkeley on me one day." He took in a breath and exhaled. "I might have to reconsider retiring. I'm not quite ready for twenty-four hours a day of cosmic oneness."

Gage raised his eyebrows. "Maybe you can compromise and take her to China."

Casey shook his head. "The two days I spent in Shanghai was about long enough. That place just oozes with corruption. And Zhang. What a piece of work."

"Who?"

"Zhang."

"Was he the guy in the photos with you? I don't recall meeting him."

"Yeah. Right. If I didn't know the reward for the recovery of the chips was received by a Mr. Calico, I'd think Zhang got a kickback." Casey inspected Gage's face. "You're looking better than I expected. What's going on with the treatment?"

"Just started. So far so good. Pretty soon it's going to fall on me like a hammer." Gage smiled. "You wouldn't believe what they're shooting into me. If it wasn't medicine, it would be a felony."

"Let me know if you need anything. My wife does a great chicken soup."

"Thanks, but what I mostly need is to set some things up, then ease on out of this. I won't be in any shape to contribute anything by the time the heroin arrives."

"How much heroin do you think there'll be?"

"Even deducting what Ah Ming spent on transportation, I think it should be just under the value of the chips."

A gleam replaced the dull of Casey's jet-lagged eyes. "I knew it would be a lot, but that's huge. Huge. You must be talking about four hundred, maybe four hundred and fifty, kilos. That's eighty, maybe ninety million dollars wholesale and . . ." He shook his head, then his brows furrowed and he squinted at Gage. "It can't be . . . a billion on the street?"

"That's about right."

"Who sends a billion dollars of heroin in one shipment?"

"Somebody who thinks he can get away with anything."

"Not this time."

"We hope."

"Why don't I bring in ICE? Let them do a controlled delivery."

"Not a chance. You remember what happened the last time a load this big came into the States? ICE brought in NBC News before the seizure so the brass could get their faces on TV. The whole investigation was driven by news value and photo ops instead of what the case needed. Most of the defendants ended up walking on the case. Not this time. There's no way ICE won't screw it up, even if they don't bring in the press. If they do an intensive search on a container from a known foreign exporter with no record of violations, on its way to a known domestic importer, also with no violations, and the container can't be traced back to a known drug source country, then any kind of delay will look hinky to anyone paying attention. And trust me, Ah Ming will be paying attention."

"What do I tell them?"

"Tell them exactly that. And tell them we put a tracking device on it overseas—"

"What? How'd you—"

Gage waved off the question. "The how isn't important. We couldn't take a chance of delaying it or showing ourselves over here, so we needed a way to monitor it from a distance."

"I'll give it a try."

"The alternative is this. I won't tell you which container it is until it's left ICE's control. They'll be completely out of it. They won't even get to come to the press conference. That's something I know they'll understand."

"YOU WERE RIGHT," Casey said, when he called Gage the next morning. "ICE was less interested in method and more interested in credit."

"Let me guess, you argued from the press conference backward."

"They only tried to insist on following procedure because it gave them control and they only wanted control so it would put them in front of the cameras. Once I explained to them they could share the podium, they backed off. They'll run the surveillance starting at the port and they'll interface—I swear to God they said interface—where do those bureaucrats learn to talk like that?—interface with us at the warehouse."

"I take it part of their interfacing is they get to search the container at East Wind and seize the heroin?"

"Exactly."

"Does it make a difference to you?"

"No, but the special agent in charge in my office is a little peeved. I had to assure him he'd be on the podium during the press conference and that the seizure would be described as a result of a joint operation. I also told him each agency will be able to issue press releases under its own letterhead."

"Then we're set."

"Only one more thing. That heroin damn well better be

there. I don't want to lose all the brownie points I got in China because the container turns up dry."

"*Mai pen rai.* Your brownie points are always my primary concern."

"My pen what?"

"I'll explain it later."

CHAPTER 83

"D r. Stern? This is Faith. I hope you don't mind my calling you on your cell phone."

"It's fine. How's Graham?"

"It's been a few days since the chemo and he's really weak, so weak that he's having trouble even tying his shoes and buckling his belt. He just fumbles. And he's really tentative when he walks down the stairs. He says it'll pass and didn't want to bother you."

"It's called the tough guy syndrome, and I don't think that's going to pass."

"I don't either."

"What you describe isn't only fatigue. It may be what's called peripheral neuropathy. It very often starts right after the first infusion. It causes weakness and numbness in the hands and feet and interferes with coordination and balance. It's nerve damage caused by the chemotherapy."

"Should we come in?"

"Let's watch it until his next infusion. It may decrease on its own. If not, the only solution is to change the chemo combination, but I don't want to do that unless it becomes unavoidable. The protocol he's on has been carefully thought out. I wouldn't want to mess with it. Have him stop by a couple of hours before his infusion next Wednesday, I'll give him some tests then decide what to do. Any other symptoms he has chosen not to mention to me?"

"He's not eating as much as he should."

"Get him on a high-protein diet. I'll e-mail you some suggestions. Maybe if you make the meals yourself, he'll feel obligated to eat."

"Is there anything else I can do?"

"Is there any brandy in the house?"

"I think so, or maybe cognac. What should I do with it?"

"Make him come home early . . . pour one for each of you . . . and watch the sunset."

CHAPTER 84

T he Hanjin *Beijing* is still scheduled to arrive on Friday," Gage told Sylvia as she crossed the threshold into his office. "I'll work on rerouting it from Sunny Glory directly to East Wind. I expect the container itself will be released early in the afternoon and I want you inside East Wind with Lucy when it gets there. I'd do it myself, but I can't take a chance that fatigue will hit me and I won't be able to protect her if something goes wrong."

Sylvia nodded.

"Pretend to be a potential customer. And don't forget to get Lucy's personnel file. ICE and the FBI will be investigating everyone who worked at East Wind to identify who was involved in the heroin. We need her to evaporate, and I don't want anything traced back to her and her mother."

"Everything will be in my hands when I lead her out of there. I promise."

"One more thing. I want Ah Ming there." Gage pointed at the floors of investigators below. "Have a couple of our people make pretext appointments with him from one P.M. until five P.M. They don't need to show up, just keep Ah Ming tied down there."

"Either that or slash his tires."

Gage smiled. 'I'll leave that up to you."

After she left, Gage called Alan Lim to see if he could get Lucy's supervisor out of the office.

"Kung is a conscientious guy," Lim said. "You'll need to get him far enough away that he can't just toss in his mah-jongg tiles and race back to East Wind if someone calls."

"How about a long weekend at Lake Tahoe?"

"I'll have my wife pitch the idea to his wife. She's a blackjack addict. She'll make him go."

"Tell him you won the trip in a raffle. It comes with a limousine and a suite at Harrah's."

Lim laughed. "That'll work. He's the kind of guy who'd rearrange his day just for a free lunch."

TUESDAY AFTERNOON Gage received a text message from Alan Lim. He'd finalized his plans with Kung. The men and their wives would be chauffeured away on Thursday morning and wouldn't return until Sunday night, or until FBI agents knocked on his hotel room door.

Gage didn't want to risk his fatigue putting other drivers in jeopardy on road, so he worked his phone. He first called Casey to tell him the place and time the container would arrive. In the fog of chemotherapy, he didn't realize the impact the news would have on Casey.

"Are you telling me Ah Ming is having the heroin delivered right to his own business? No middleman? No cutout?"

He hated making Casey feel like an idiot. He wasn't one.

"That arrogant son of a bitch. All the while we were watching East Wind, tons of heroin was passing right by us? Under our noses? This is embarrassing."

"You can't know everything."

Casey and Gage made arrangements to talk on Thursday evening to finalize the plans for the Friday delivery.

He then called General Zhang.

"How is life as a national hero?"

"Just delightful. I'm going to Beijing next week to have a prized, but very cheap-looking medal hung around my neck."

"And your Hong Kong business?"

"As you Americans say, it's just like money in the bank."

"I take it Lew is still cooperative."

"Of course. What alternative does he have? A couple of heroin traffickers were executed over the weekend. I had someone slip the newspaper article under his cell door."

"I'll need him to make the calls about this time tomorrow."

"I'll let you know when they're done." Zhang chuckled. "How's our Thai friend?"

"The one with the hole in his shoulder or the other one?"

"I don't seem to recall anyone with a hole anywhere."

"She's fine. I'll be calling her soon. Is there a message you'd like me to pass on?"

"Not yet. I think I'll give her heart time to grow fonder."

"Good plan."

His final call was to Kai.

"Good morning," Gage said.

"Good evening." Kai's voice was throaty.

"Did I call too early? You sound like I woke you up."

"Not really. I was just lying here thinking."

"About what?"

"I met with Somchai yesterday to talk about the divorce. He's pathetic. He thought he could intimidate me. I think he held back a little because Cobra was waiting outside. The only way I kept my composure was by imagining him as a *katoey*—one of those transvestite dancers down in Pattaya—except not so cute."

"What's going to happen?"

"We'll have a short war, and I'll make a bunch of calls crying to you. There are a lot of things I could have said to him, but I decided not to. There was nothing to be gained. Maybe I'll write a thinly disguised novel someday. Humiliate the son of a bitch."

"Just leave my thinly disguised name out of it."

"I might throw in Eight Iron's. Cobra tells me that his life has become real exciting. The DEA and the Thai narcotics police raided one of his yaba labs. They were working out of a tire plant in Samut Prakan, south of Bangkok. They seized a million yaba tablets—a million—the biggest methamphetamine seizure ever."

"He's a lot bigger than I imagined. Is there any reason to think Eight Iron's problem will link to us?"

"Nothing either Cobra or I can see. He was brought down by an inside informant, a lab rat who got arrested for molesting a little girl and then rolled on him."

Gage heard the rustling of sheets as Kai got out of bed. "What are you doing? I don't think it's time to get up over there."

"My neck is sore. I think I slept funny, or maybe I pulled something when I reached for the phone—whatever makes it your fault." Kai yawned. "Any news about Lew and Taiwan?"

"I spoke to Zhang earlier—"

"You mean the car thief?"

"You sound less hostile."

"Sorry, I misspoke. The fucking car thief."

"It looks like things are okay on that end. I'll call you when everything is over, probably Saturday morning, your time."

"Have you started treatment?"

"The time had come."

"Please be careful on Friday."

"Don't worry. From now on I'm just a bystander."

CHAPTER 85

A t noon on the day before the container's arrival, Lucy walked out of East Wind and strolled two blocks south where Sylvia and Gage were waiting in a van to drive her to meet the owner at Sunny Glory. Lucy sat in the front passenger seat next to Sylvia who was driving. Gage remained out of sight in the back, sweat beads forming on his forehead, fatigue setting in, the chemo infusion still wracking his body.

Viz, Gage's surveillance chief, was already set up across the street from Sunny Glory in the back of a step-side cargo truck.

Gage gave Lucy a bill of sale forged by Alex Z for Chau to sign.

"Remember, he's already gotten his instructions from Lew, so he's got no choice but to transfer ownership of the container from Sunny Glory to East Wind."

Lucy's hands vibrated as she took it from his hands.

"What if he asks about Ah Ming or Ah Tien and why they aren't the ones contacting him?"

"He won't. As far as he is concerned you're just a clerk delivering papers. In any case, he was picked by Ah Ming because he's a guy who doesn't ask questions."

"It felt easier lying my way into East Wind."

"Maybe because you knew you could run away if things got difficult."

Lucy sighed and shook her head as she looked back and forth between Gage and Sylvia.

"I don't know how you two do this kind of thing all the time."

"The more you do it, the easier it gets. It's just acting."

"But the other people aren't actors. They're real."

Gage smiled at her. "They don't know you're not. That's why it works."

Sylvia parked the van in sight of the front door to Sunny Glory, then Lucy got out and walked inside. She emerged a few minutes later, trying to suppress a grin. She only succeeded when she looked up and noticed Sylvia glaring at her.

"I'm sorry," Lucy said, after getting back into the van. "I don't know whether I was smiling because I was nervous or because it was so easy." Her face fell, and she shook her head. "I could have ruined everything."

Gage called Viz. "Did you see it?"

"You mean the Miss America moment? It cracked me up, but I didn't see anybody paying attention."

"Stay around to see if anyone did and tries to follow her, then set up at InterOcean around three o'clock. We'll get there just before four."

"I'll call you when I'm in position."

"Now," Gage said, turning his attention back to Lucy, "tell me what happened."

"Mr. Chau invited me into his office and told me Mr. Lew called. I handed him the bill of sale and as he looked it over he asked me my name and how long I had been at East Wind. Then he signed it. He seemed relieved. He had the receptionist make a copy and gave me the original back."

Gage reached out and took it from her.

"He's a dirty old man." Lucy reddened. "He tried to look up my skirt when I sat down."

"That means when he thinks about it later, he'll focus on something other than the bill of sale and what your face looked like."

Lucy grinned. "Should I roll up the waist of my skirt and make it a little shorter when I go into InterOcean?"

"Let's not draw too many conclusions from one experience and overdo it. Is everything set up for you to get away from work this afternoon?"

"I told everybody Mr. Kung said I could leave early for a doctor's appointment. And since he's not around to contradict me, nobody will say anything."

They dropped off Lucy near East Wind and returned to Gage's building to wait for the run at InterOcean Customs Brokers.

Gage went to his office and, for the first time in his career, napped at his desk.

At 3:30 he and Sylvia arrived back at the spot near East Wind where they had earlier picked up Lucy.

At 3:45 Lucy walked up to the van and got in.

Gage handed her more shipping papers created by Alex Z and added the original and a copy of the bill of sale signed by Chau.

"Don't try too hard," Gage told her as they drove toward InterOcean. "Remember, you're a clerk delivering papers. That's the part you're playing. It's a little more complicated than last time, but don't play it larger than it is. The key documents are the bill of sale and the power of attorney. They've already seen other versions of the Taiwan agricultural clearance, the bill of lading, and the insurance form, so the background for what you need to do is set."

"Make sure she doesn't do that goofy grin thing again," Viz

told Gage when he called to confirm that he was in position outside of InterOcean. "I almost spilled my coffee."

Gage glanced toward Lucy. "I think she learned her lesson. I'll call you when we've cleared the area."

Sylvia and Gage dropped Lucy off in front of InterOcean, a one-story office building that covered most of the block, then found a parking space.

Ten minutes later, she still hadn't returned.

Gage called Viz.

"I can't tell what's going on," Viz said. "I don't see her in any of the office windows facing the street."

"If she doesn't come out in five minutes, make up some pretext and go in."

"I'll call you before I do it."

Sylvia's phone rang right after Viz disconnected.

"May I speak to Mr. Kung, please?" a woman's voice asked.

"You must have the wrong . . . Lucy?"

Sylvia handed Gage the phone.

"Yes, Mr. Kung. I'm at InterOcean. They're telling me they need a power of attorney from Sunny Glory in addition to the power of attorney from East Wind."

"That's wrong. Once East Wind has a bill of sale from Sunny Glory, they own the contents. They can do whatever they want with the container. Sunny Glory is out of it."

"Yes, Mr. Kung."

Gage overheard Lucy telling the InterOcean clerk, "Mr. Kung says all we need is the bill of sale. Once title is transferred, a power of attorney from Sunny Glory is useless. It's not their container anymore."

"Mr. Kung," Lucy then said to Gage, "the clerk is new and he isn't sure."

"Reach for paperwork and tell him that Mr. Kung wants you to take it to Alan Lim instead."

Gage heard shuffling papers, then Lucy passing on the message.

"Mr. Kung, he looked over the paperwork again and says it looks okay. He'll take care of everything."

"Tell him the big boss at East Wind is counting on him and will send more business his way. And make sure he sees the note telling them to hire Golden Mountain Transportation to haul the container. Insist they do it. Hint that the East Wind president chose them personally."

A few minutes later, Lucy emerged from InterOcean. She wasn't smiling. She walked to the van and got in.

"I'm glad that's over. The clerk was an idiot. I could see everything falling apart because he didn't know what he was doing."

"Maybe," Gage said, "maybe not. Maybe he was just frightened. Whether or not they know Ah Ming is a crook, they know he's big in their world and tough. That's the kind of thing that can make people panic."

CHAPTER 86

"E verything set up?" Ah Ming asked his nephew, sitting across the breakfast table in his Hillsborough mansion at daybreak.

Ah Ming viewed Clarence Tung, the oldest son of his sister in Taiwan, as a lesser evil. Time had been short to replace Ah Tien, and trust seemed more important than competence. Until this point, Tung's job had only been to manage East Wind's money, and Ah Ming had paid his nephew's way through the accounting program at San Francisco State to give him the skills he needed to do it. One skill he brought on his own: how not to ask where the enormous amounts of money Ah Ming made were coming from.

A day earlier, Ah Ming told him—and no look of surprise appeared on his nephew's face.

"I checked the Hanjin Global Tracking system," Tung said. "The container ship docked a few minutes earlier than scheduled. All the containers will be offloaded by this afternoon. Ours should be released between noon and two. We'll start picking up the garlic and heroin from Sunny Glory at about five thirty."

Ah Ming nodded.

"I'll be doing the surveillance myself, along with four others."

"I don't want them showing themselves for any reason unless someone makes a move on the container. If that means they have to shit in a pot in the back of the van, then that's what they'll have to do."

Clarence's face flushed, then he nodded.

"Text me a sixty-six code when the container arrives. Otherwise I don't want any communications with anyone—Sunny Glory, InterOcean, even with the Hanjin Web site—until everything is done."

After Clarence left, Ah Ming waited ten minutes before heading out to ensure that he arrived at East Wind at the normal time. There would be nothing in his actions this day that would distinguish it from any other. Everything would be ordinary and routine. That was why he was invisible to the white ghosts. It was the reason he'd never been caught. And why he'd never be caught.

CHAPTER 87

A t 9 A.M., Gage drove over to the FBI and ICE raid staging area in a warehouse near the San Francisco Airport, a faded metal building with peeling paint and a refuse-strewn sidewalk concealing a temporary armory. Parked inside he found three Ford Explorers and the van that would carry the ICE search team into East Wind. A communications desk stood in one corner and next to it a GPS monitor to track the device installed on the container. A drug-sniffing beagle lay on the floor with half-closed eyes.

"Hey, old fella," Gage said to Casey as he walked up, then pointed at the twenty young agents checking their weapons and adjusting their body armor. "I didn't realize these kids were allowed to bring their grandfather along."

Casey sighed. "And I feel like one."

"Don't underestimate yourself. I bet you can still bench-press any two of them."

"Or three of you," Casey said, surveying Gage's body. "You look even skinnier than last time."

"That's why I'm glad to be out of this thing."

"We've got everything covered. You can sit back and enjoy

the show." Casey pointed at the other agents. "They're like a machine; you'll be amazed at what they can do and how they do it."

"What are you calling it?"

"Operation Snow White."

Gage smiled. "I was hoping for the Fall of the Ah Ming Dynasty."

Casey laughed. "I like that better, but it's too late to change."

Gage gestured toward the monitor. "What's the latest?"

"ICE said the East Wind container arrived at the port early this morning. The agent told me the load was originally supposed to go to a company called Sunny Glory. It was only transferred to East Wind yesterday, while it was still on the water. The paperwork came in late in the afternoon."

"If Ah Ming suspected he was under investigation, he'd have let it go to Sunny Glory so there wouldn't be a direct link to him. He must be pretty confident in this load."

"Big mistake."

"What time will ICE release the container?"

"Between one and two. We didn't try to expedite it. It'll take its turn just as if no one was watching. We just made sure it wouldn't be selected for a random inspection."

"I hope they're not going to try to follow it. Ah Ming may have people watching, maybe even try to divert the thing en route to another warehouse."

"I didn't want them trailing it on the ground." Casey grinned. "So I let them use what they call a high-flying surveillance platform."

"What we civilians call a drone?"

"Yeah. Don't you just love these guys? It'll be hovering at about four thousand feet, invisible from the ground. ICE will just be watching, unless something goes wrong. If that happens, we'll"—Casey gestured with air quotes—"interface with them."

Casey glanced at his watch. "The only hang-up is the duty

judge. He's insisting on a hard copy of the search warrant before he authorizes the search. It's going to cost us some time we can't afford to lose. He got burned on a telephone warrant when the agent misplaced the recording. I've got an agent sitting outside his chambers and as soon as the container starts heading toward East Wind and we're sure the heroin is in it, he'll submit it."

"What did you use as probable cause in your affidavit?"

"You."

Gage pulled back. "Me? You weren't supposed—"

"As an anonymous informant. I just said someone called into the drug hotline with a tip."

"That's not entirely true."

"It is true, it just isn't factual."

Gage narrowed his eyebrows at Casey. "When did you start talking like that?"

"I was reading one of my wife's books. It's called *The Greater Truth in the Lesser World* by Dr. Heinrich Weisener. According to Heinrich, there are facts that are uncertain, fleeting, and relative, and then there's truth that is absolute. So I figure as long as there's dope in the container, the affidavit is absolutely true."

"I don't think that's what he meant."

"Doesn't have to be. The book said we each have our own truth. So I can believe whatever I want to believe and the judge can believe whatever he wants to believe."

"Just to be on the safe side, give me the drug hotline number. Somebody better make a call."

"1-800-Badboys. Ask for Skip."

"Is the same judge going to arraign Ah Ming?"

Casey shook his head. "Probably not. By the time we get him down to the federal building and booked and photographed, it will be too late. We'll either hold him over till tomorrow or see if we can get a magistrate to stay after hours."

"Let me know when; I'd hate to miss it."

"Bring some popcorn."

"I'll even bring Faith. She's ten minutes away, waiting at my office with Linda Sheridan."

"For now, why don't you go get set up with our surveillance people outside of East Wind. They're expecting you. It's in a fifth-floor office across the street. It used to be the headquarters for California Seismic Consulting. The nameplate is still on the door."

"Good choice. With any luck we're going to rock Ah Ming's world. Maybe I should have brought Linda along, I would've liked her to watch Ah Ming being led out in handcuffs. Even though his arrest won't be for the death of her son, at least she'll know the guy will never be getting out of prison."

Casey nodded. "One way or another, he's gonna die in a federal pen."

"That was the whole point. All this was set up so Ah Ming gets taken alive."

Even as he said the words, Gage knew he shouldn't have. Since the infusion he'd been worried the drugs and the weakness would lead him to say and do things that in stronger days he wouldn't have—and he just did.

Casey gave Gage a hard look. "What do you mean, set up?"

Gage waved off the implication. "I just mean how things are supposed to work today." He pushed the conversation back Casey's way. "Just be careful. Ah Ming isn't a guy who'll want to live in a little box for the rest of his life. And I'd hate to see you get hurt."

"I was thinking the same thing." Casey reached down and picked up a piece of body armor large enough to cover him from shoulders to knees. "There's nothing he's got that can break through this. But it was nice to hear your concern."

"It wasn't my idea," Gage said, now smiling. "Faith made me say it."

Casey laughed. "Screw you, too."

CHAPTER 88

At a little after 11:30 A.M. Gage walked through the front door of the International Trade Building northwest of East Wind. He took the elevator to the fifth floor and entered California Seismic Consulting. He knew one of the two FBI agents manning the post. They'd met at a money laundering conference a few years earlier. Felix Melendez had impressed him as a grunt with a good heart and a man with none of the annoying habits that made a small surveillance room seem smaller.

Even though he'd never seen him before, Gage had no trouble recognizing the other agent, for Casey had described Buddy Eng, a former Oakland Police officer, as looking like nothing so much as an unmade double bed.

"Hey, gumshoe," Buddy said. "Casey said you'd be coming by. What've you got to do with this?"

"Nothing. I signed up for the cop ride-along program and they sent me over here. They said I could watch you guys give out traffic tickets."

"No can do. I left my ticket book at OPD when I left."

"Damn. I always seem to arrive too late for the real action."

"Have a seat," Felix said. "Don't mind Buddy. He was hoping

to bust a head or two today, but Casey gave him surveillance instead." He pointed toward Eng's stomach. "I'll send out for an extra large, all meat and triple-cheese pizza. That'll put him in a better mood."

Gage looked across the street at East Wind. "What did I miss so far?"

"Ah Ming arrived at about nine." Felix pointed toward the parking lot. "That's his black Mercedes. He hasn't come out since. The GPS shows the container is still in the bonded warehouse at the port. The latest word is that it's not going to be released until about two."

"Look over there," Buddy said. "Ah Ming's on his way to his car."

"I'll call Casey," Felix said. "This may screw up the timing. We want Ah Ming there when we go in."

"You guys have a bathroom around here?" Gage asked, needing a place where he could call Lucy.

Felix made a curving motion with his arm and handed Gage a key. "Down the hall to the left."

Gage walked into the hallway and pulled out his cell phone. He felt a weary shudder pass through him and his legs weaken. He found that he couldn't target his thumb to search his directory. He leaned back against the wall to steady himself and skimmed down recent calls until he found Lucy's number.

"I just saw Ah Ming leave," Gage said. "Where's he going?"

"I think just for lunch. He told the receptionist he'd be back for some appointments this afternoon."

"If anything changes call me. The container's now supposed to arrive at about three, so Sylvia will get there at two thirty."

Gage thought for a moment; there was something else he was supposed to ask her.

Lucy's voice broke the silence. "Is there anything . . ."

Then it came to him.

"Did you get your personnel file?"

"It was easy. There's this law that companies have to show it to you." She giggled. "I can't believe they obey a little law like that and break the big ones."

"That's the key to their success. And the arrival notice from InterOcean?"

"I got it." She giggled again. "I hope I didn't look too much like I was guarding the fax machine."

Gage returned to the surveillance office in time to hear Felix ordering the pizza he'd promised Eng.

"You want something?"

"No thanks, just ate."

Two days ago.

CHAPTER 89

C hau sat at his desk at Sunny Glory, rubbing his thumbs against his fingers, his legs bouncing under his desk. On the one hand, he was relieved he didn't have to handle the container. He'd heard rumors over the years that the big boss at East Wind was connected with United Bamboo in Taiwan and Thailand. But drugs? No one actually said drugs. All that would happen was that a container would arrive at Sunny Glory and East Wind trucks would come pick up specially marked boxes a few at time. They were always gone in a few hours. It could have been anything hidden inside. And the money was good. In cash and tax free.

On the other hand, what did it mean that East Wind was taking the container directly? Were they cutting him out altogether? If so, he knew he'd have to live a more modest life. He glanced at the Rolex on his wrist and the Mont Blanc pen set on his desk. They reminded him it had been East Wind money that had raised him above the other Asian food importers and whole-salers on the West Coast. Without it . . .

Chau stared at his phone, wondering whether he should call

the president of East Wind. Feel him out about what was going on. No, better wait for Lew to come back. He and Ah Tien had warned him never to contact the boss. If he hadn't yet been cut out of the operation, contacting him now would do that, or worse.

CHAPTER 90

F elix Melendez pointed at the monitor showing views from
the cameras Casey had installed both inside and outside
the Golden Mountain Transportation truck.

"The undercover agent just hooked up the container."

They watched the truck pull out of the Hanjin terminal and
work its way toward the freeway. The driver pulled over just
before the on-ramp and hopped down.

Side cameras showed him checking the tires, working his way
clockwise around the truck and trailer, beating each one with a
tire iron and listening to its sound, gauging the tire pressure.

A young man and woman walked by with a leashed beagle
that leaped toward the container as it passed. The couple re-
strained the dog, apologized for its misbehavior, and walked on.

They didn't turn back until the truck drove out of sight.

THE WOMAN CALLED CASEY WITH THE RESULTS.

"Chief, we got it. The dog went nuts, almost snapped the
leash."

"Give it to me."

"At 2:06 P.M. at the intersection of Maritime and Alaska

Streets in Oakland, California, Drug Detector Dog Freddie D alerted on Hanjin container EISU5605394/455440 being hauled by Golden Mountain Transportation Services, California commercial license plate number 5J4687."

Casey radioed the agent standing by the duty judge's chambers and had him fill in the blanks in the search warrant affidavit. Four minutes later, the judge signed the search warrant and thirty seconds after that Casey's radio crackled.

"You're good to go."

Casey alerted the search team, then called Gage on his mobile.

"It's here, man. It's really here. The dog went berserk."

Gage stifled a sigh as relief merged with fatigue. No reason for Casey to catch on that the certainty Gage expressed hadn't been the uncertainty he felt, for it was a long, long way from the east coast of China, to the west coast of California, and lots of people were ready to go to any deadly length for heroin worth a billion dollars on the street.

"Then it's all in your hands."

CHAPTER 91

Clarence Tung and his men waiting outside Sunny Glory were groggy from the heat and humidity released from their bodies trapped in the closed vans. Uncomfortable though he was, it thrilled him to think about how the heroin's arrival at Sunny Glory and its smooth distribution would move him up in Ah Ming's organization.

He knew it was a test and he was determined to pass it.

From a tinted side window, Clarence watched a parade of express mail couriers and clerks come and go through the front doors of Sunny Glory. Cargo vans arrived empty and left riding low on their shocks. He saw businesspeople arrive for meetings and clerks and warehouse workers leave for lunch and return. All that interrupted the stillness inside his van were the sounds of passing traffic and commercial jets that vibrated the van as they swept down toward the San Francisco International Airport, a few miles south.

As the sound of an airplane engine faded, Clarence heard one of his men yawn. Clarence turned to prod him to keep him quiet.

The doors on the van swung open.

Clarence and his men stared up the barrels of Glock pistols brandished by Asian men who climbed in and disarmed them.

"Who are you?" a flat-nosed invader asked. His voice was low and hard, and his eyes moved from man to man, trying to identify who was in charge.

Clarence straightened up.

"None of your—"

The barrel of a Glock cracked down across the bridge of Clarence's nose. It made a crunch that reverberated to the back of his head. His eyes blurred with tears, blood flowed into his mouth.

"Let me try again."

"We're just waiting to pick up some goods. That's all."

Flat Nose raised his gun.

Clarence cringed, covering his head with his hands. He felt his fingers crack, then numbness, then nauseating pain.

"We were hired to watch for a container," Clarence said.

"And then what?"

"Call in."

"To who?"

Clarence couldn't think of an answer, knowing his uncle would murder even one of his own relatives for disloyalty.

Flat Iron ratcheted back the slide on his Glock.

Clarence broke. "His name is Ah Ming."

Clarence felt his whole body slump with relief when Flat Nose tucked his gun into his shoulder holster. Then fear again when Flat Nose issued orders to gag them.

FLAT NOSE LEFT ONE OF HIS CREW in each van and walked to the driver's side of a Taurus parked close by.

The driver lowered the window.

Flat Nose leaned down. "You're right. They're Ah Ming's security people."

"Let's go in."

The driver grabbed his suit jacket and a briefcase from the passenger seat and followed Flat Nose through Sunny Glory's swinging front doors. They walked up to the reception desk where Flat Nose asked to speak with Chau.

"Do you have an appointment?" the receptionist asked, glancing up at the sound of his voice.

One look at his face and she grasped that he was a man who didn't make appointments.

Flat Nose shook his head.

"May I give him your name?"

"No."

The receptionist buzzed Chau and told him he had visitors.

"Please sit down," the receptionist told them. "He'll be out in a minute."

The men were still standing when Chau appeared. He looked back and forth between the two, then swallowed hard and led them to his office. Chau sat behind his desk, and the suited man sat in a chair next to the door. Flat Nose stood facing Chau.

"We want the container," Flat Nose said.

"Which container?" Chau tried to hold his voice steady even as fear welled inside him. "Containers are arriving here all the time."

"The one for the guy who runs East Wind."

"For . . . for . . . who are you?"

Chau flinched as Flat Nose stepped forward.

"That's not important. There's something inside that belongs to us. We'll take what's ours, then leave. No one gets hurt unless you decide to fuck with us."

Chau's voice rose in panic. "But the container isn't coming here." He couldn't give what he didn't have. "I signed it over to East Wind yesterday."

Flat Nose drew his gun. "I told you. Don't fuck with us. If you fuck with us, you're dead."

"I have a copy of the bill of sale. I signed it myself."

Chau reached into his out-tray with shaking hands, dragging the whole stack of paper out onto his desk. He tore through them, finally locating the copy and handing it to Flat Nose.

Flat Nose scanned it.

"Shit." Flat Nose turned to his companion. "Stay here."

Flat Nose looked back to Chau, then balled up the bill of sale and threw it at him.

"If it isn't at East Wind, I'm coming back here to fuck you up and your whole motherfucking family."

As the door closed behind Flat Nose, the impassive man in the business suit extracted a handgun from his briefcase.

"Call the receptionist," the man said. "Tell her you don't want to be disturbed. And speak calmly."

Chau reached for the phone and passed on the message, then looked up at the man and asked, "All right?"

The man didn't respond. He just stared ahead.

Although Chau hardly noticed him when Flat Nose was in the room, he found this visitor far more unnerving and frightening than the one who had left.

The man stared and stared.

Chau finally lowered his eyes.

FLAT NOSE LEFT TWO MEN to guard Clarence's group and took the rest with him toward East Wind. He called his boss in Big Circle in Bangkok as he drove.

"The container isn't on its way to Sunny Glory. It's going straight to East Wind. Chau showed me the bill of sale. Signed yesterday."

"Do you believe him?" Catfish asked.

"He's too scared to lie. It looks like they were going to have the container stop first at East Wind, then take the white powder to Sunny Glory for distribution. That must be why they had security set up there."

Silence followed Flat Nose's analysis.

Finally, Catfish said, "It doesn't really change anything except now we can hit Ah Ming at the same time. How soon can you get there?"

"Fifteen minutes. We're on our way."

"Then do what you need to do. General Kew is here waiting."

CHAPTER 92

Just after 2:50, Gage listened in as Felix radioed to Casey that Ah Ming was in his office and that the GPS monitor now showed the container was about ten minutes away from East Wind.

Casey confirmed with the two other surveillance teams posted around East Wind that they'd heard the update.

Felix handed the radio to Buddy who read to Casey from his log.

14:03	Asian female arrived. Loft at 14:11.
14:16	Two white males in suits arrived. Left at 14:27.
14:32	UPS truck arrived and dollied boxes inside.
14:35	Black female entered.
14:36	UPS driver exited.
14:37	Delivery truck pulled away from the loading dock.
14:40	UPS truck returned and dropped off another package.
14:33	UPS driver exited again.
14:46	Asian male in overalls sweeping the sidewalk in front.

FROM INSIDE A VAN parked a few blocks from East Wind, Casey monitored the communications between the undercover driver of the container truck and the communications officer in the staging area.

The driver had noticed no one following him, and video from the drone showed no one.

The radio chatter that had previously been mere background noise now came in clearly, the voices crisp, distinct, and urgent.

Only two voices spoke: the driver and Casey as Control.

"Control, I'm just turning off Bay Shore."

"Control check."

"I can see East Wind."

"Control check."

FROM HIS PERCH, Gage watched the Golden Mountain truck pull into the East Wind loading area, then back up. A warehouse worker jumped down to the pavement and guided the driver until the rear of the truck bed came to rest against the tire-tread-covered edge of the dock.

For the first time Gage imagined himself standing outside an interrogation room in the federal building looking through a two-way mirror as a handcuffed Ah Ming was interrogated by Joe Casey.

INSIDE, LUCY PRETENDED to give Sylvia a tour of the ware-house. They paused and watched the driver lower himself from the cab and climb the outside stairs to the dock level. Lucy left Sylvia and walked up to him, asking for the shipping documents. He passed them to her attached to a battered aluminum clipboard, then she turned and walked back to where Sylvia was waiting.

The driver lowered himself from the dock and began to un-hitch the trailer.

Sylvia walked Lucy toward Ah Ming's corner office.

The aluminum clipboard turned leaden in Lucy's hands. For a moment she feared sweat would stain the delivery receipt. And not because she was nervous about the mechanics. She'd done fine at Sunny Glory and at InterOcean. No, the problem was that Ah Ming was the man responsible for her brother's death. Ah Ming was evil, and for the first time she was about to hear the voice of evil himself.

"Easy," Sylvia said. "Remember who you are. You're a clerk. That's all." She pointed at a spot along the warehouse wall ten feet from Ah Ming's office door. "I'll be right there."

"I can do this," Lucy whispered. "I know I can do this."

GAGE, FELIX, AND BUDDY WATCHED two cars pull to a stop outside East Wind. Six men jumped out and strode through the front door. The drivers remained outside.

"Who the devil are they?" Felix asked, grabbing his radio. "Casey, six Asian guys just marched into East Wind. Real businesslike. Can't tell what they're here for, but they have gangster written all over them. Maybe to pick up the dope. Over."

"Then we're going in. No reason to take any chances and maybe we'll grab more of the gang. Alpha Team?"

"Copy."

"Bravo."

"Copy."

"Charlie."

"Copy."

"Let's roll."

LUCY KNOCKED ON AH MING'S DOOR. In the weeks she'd worked at East Wind, she'd never even seen the inside of his office, never had been closer than fifty feet of him.

"Yes," Ah Ming said.

She walked inside. Like his dark suit, dark tie, and white shirt, the office was stark, nearly bare. A desk and two chairs. A phone. A fax. She saw his face in profile. He was leaning back in his seat, staring at a blank wall. He waved her to come forward without looking at her.

"Mr. Kung told me to give the shipping documents to you. A container just arrived."

"Just leave them on my desk."

Lucy laid them down but held the clipboard in her hands.

"The driver needs a signature on the receipt."

Lucy reached out with the clipboard. He sat up, turned his chair toward the desk, and took it from her hand.

She felt herself flush.

Ah Ming signed the receipt, tore off a copy, then held out the clipboard.

Lucy took it back. It felt weightless in her hands as she turned away.

Gotcha, she said to herself.

She walked back into the warehouse.

Gotcha, gotcha, gotcha.

As Sylvia stepped forward to intercept Lucy on her way to return the receipt to the undercover driver, she noticed six Asian men striding toward Ah Ming's office. She'd spent enough time on the street to recognize the walk. She grabbed Lucy's arm and pulled her close, taking her under control, forcing her to march toward the exit.

"Let's go."

"What about the receipt? I have to take it to the driver."

"Let me have it. Let's go. Don't look back."

"Where's my personnel file?"

"I've got it. Go, go, go. We've gotta get out of here."

But Sylvia wasn't sure they were going to make it.

As Ah Ming lifted his desk phone to make a call, he noticed the shipping papers Lucy had left on his desk. He reached to slip them into the tray at the corner. The words "InterOcean" and "Sunny Glory" glared out at him from the bill of lading. He dropped the phone back into its cradle. His heart raced. His throat closed.

The container was from InterOcean, from Sunny Glory.

Who did this?

Someone is forcing it into my hands.

Chau? Did Chau get caught and turn snitch?

Ah Ming's thoughts jumped from face to face and place to place.

Who is it? Lew? Clarence?

It made no difference.

Whoever did this knows everything.

Everything.

Ah Ming reached into his middle desk drawer, pulled out a 9mm pistol, and rose to his feet.

His doorjamb exploded as one of Flat Nose's men kicked it open.

Ah Ming fired once. A shot to the chest. The man dropped in the doorway.

Running footsteps told Ah Ming there were others.

"Control. Shots fired. Shots fired."

"Control check."

Gage forced himself to remain where he stood. He needed to hear what Casey was going to do and how he would do it, and then decide what he could do. The fear behind that thought was that with his slowed reflexes and fatigue he was more likely to endanger Sylvia and Lucy than protect them.

Buddy pushed himself to his feet to get a better view. "Somebody's trying to grab the load."

Felix put his radio to his lips.

"Casey."

"Check."

"It's a rip-off. It's gotta be those guys."

"Give me descriptions."

"We couldn't see them that well. Leather jackets. Dark pants. Generic gangster wear. That's all. Sorry."

AH MING EDGED HIS WAY along the wall toward his office door, then yanked the wounded gangster to his feet. Using the gasping, staggering man as a shield, Ah Ming pushed him out into the warehouse, then he backed through a heavy metal door leading to the employee parking lot. When the door swung shut, Ah Ming dropped the man in front of it.

A human doorstop.

FROM THE OFFICE WINDOW, Gage spotted Casey's teams racing toward the entrance and the loading area.

The two cars parked in front that had been waiting for the gangsters' return fled in opposite directions and the two other FBI SUVs broke off to chase them.

His cell phone rang. It was Sylvia.

"I've got Lucy. It's chaos in here."

"Casey's on his way in. No more than ten seconds. Just stay down until it's over."

Gage saw Ah Ming running down the steps into the parking lot and realized that Casey had no one left to cover the rear. Chasing Ah Ming would be a job for another day. For now, Casey's job was to save lives, capture the gangsters, and seize the heroin.

But Gage knew he had a promise to keep.

He started for the hallway.

FLAT NOSE RAN AT THE CLOSED REAR WAREHOUSE DOOR, then bounced off, swearing. He put his shoulder into it, slowly pushing the dying man aside, off the landing, and down onto the pavement eight feet below.

AH MING GLANCED BACK and saw Flat Nose emerging from the warehouse, eyes darting. He realized Flat Nose would have a clear shot if he got into his car, so he decided to run for it. He fired once at Flat Nose, who jumped off the landing and squeezed in next to the steps and fired back.

Ah Ming slid behind his Mercedes, fired, ducked behind another car, and fired again, finally running south through the back gate of the parking lot into the alley.

GAGE RAN TOWARD THE STAIRWELL. Dizziness overcame adrenaline as he reached the top step. He grabbed the handrail to steady himself, clenching his teeth to fight off a wave of nausea, then breathing deep to force oxygen into his bloodstream and clear his head. He started down, hand over hand on the railing, uncertain whether the dizziness would return, and uncertain whether his misfiring nerves would send him tumbling.

And they did. He missed the last step. Stumbling, then falling, his shoulder taking the hit, snapping the side of his head into concrete. He dropped to his knees, then forward onto his hands, his chest thudding and his mind whirling. He closed his eyes and slowed his breathing. It felt as though his heart was battling his lungs.

Gage reached for the banister. Up on one foot, then the other. Straightening up. Dizzy for a moment. The thought of Ah Ming fleeing turned him toward the door. He pushed through it and out onto the sidewalk.

An image of the grid of streets and alleys came to Gage and

with it the knowledge Ah Ming couldn't run down the long east-west routes without risking he'd get shot in the back. He had no choice but to cut through buildings and work his way through the blocks.

South was Ah Ming's only way out. Gage's only move was to head west to the first corner and then parallel Ah Ming's flight.

Gage turned too fast and stumbled. He caught his balance on a light pole, then started again, feeling as though he was dragging his legs behind him. He swung his arms trying to pull himself along and find a rhythm.

Two gunshots echoed, confirming to Gage he was heading in the right direction.

Gage crossed the street, then moved along the side of a two-story warehouse filling the block. He stopped at the next corner and peeked around, hoping to catch sight of Ah Ming crossing the alley. He saw workers crouched down behind cars and trucks, but couldn't spot Ah Ming.

He fumbled trying to pull his gun out of its holster; his hands were weak and his fingers stiff. The two-pound semiautomatic felt like a twelve-pound chunk of metal.

Gage spotted a heavy Asian with a wide flat face emerge from a back door, his gun hand tracking, his eyes scanning. Several workers saw him and pressed themselves hard onto the pavement as Gage stepped around the corner and dropped down behind a car. One of the workers waved at him, assuming he was a cop, and pointed toward a low office building across the alley.

Gage had guessed right. Ah Ming was cutting through the blocks. The problem was how to keep up.

The gunman scoured the street for Ah Ming. When he turned away to the east, Gage ran across the intersection, hoping to reach the next alley before Ah Ming did. He ran to the next corner, then edged his way around and spotted Ah Ming running from the back of a building halfway down the block. The gunman wasn't yet in sight.

Gage lifted the gun in his right hand, trying to hold it high next to his shoulder, but his arm was weak and his hand shook. He swung his left hand up and wrapped it around his right, then slipped around the corner, sliding along a wall until he was able to take cover behind a panel van.

Ah Ming started walking west toward Gage, glancing back every few steps, stopping to turn door handles, trying to find an unlocked one to get him through to the next block. In less than thirty seconds he was only twenty yards east of Gage.

Gage waited until Ah Ming turned back to look for the gunman, then took a half step outside of the protection of the van and aimed his barrel at Ah Ming's back.

"Drop the gun."

Ah Ming spun and fired as he ducked behind a car. The bullet grazed the side of the van and cut a path through the windshield of a parked car.

Gage ducked back.

"Give it up, Ah Ming. The FBI has your container. It's over."

Gage glanced around the edge of the van and down the alley. He saw the gunman peek from behind a pickup truck about twenty-five yards beyond Ah Ming and then begin to inch forward.

"Somebody's coming up behind you. Make a choice. Me or him."

"Who the fuck are you?"

"That's not important. What's important is that I'm not here to kill you. But that guy behind you sure is. I just came for you and the heroin, and I already have the heroin."

Ah Ming broke from the car he was hiding behind and cut in between two Dumpsters angled against a redbrick wall fifteen yards down and across the alley. He was protected on either side now, but he would have to take out either Gage or the gunman if he wanted to get away.

"You've got yourself boxed in," Gage called to him.

"Just until I catch my breath, *gwai lo*."

"Who is that guy?"

"I don't know."

"Maybe somebody should've told you the container was coming to East Wind instead of Sunny Glory."

"How the fuck did you know?"

"Just a guess. And I can guess at a few other things."

"Then who are they? And how did they know the container was coming to me?"

"That I don't know. Surrender to me and we can figure it out together."

Two shots cracked. One slug thudded against a doorjamb behind Ah Ming, the other pinged a Dumpster.

Gage fired toward where he last saw the gunman and then heard himself say to Ah Ming, "I need to keep you alive."

The words surprised him.

"What for?"

Gage wasn't sure, but said, "It would take too long to explain. Who do you think that guy is?"

"I don't know."

"He seems to want you dead."

"He wouldn't be the first."

"Whoever he is, he's got to be connected . . . somebody big enough to move that much dope."

"How do you know any of this, *gwai lo*?"

Gage left the question hanging, then closed in.

"I was in Thailand when the heroin went north through China."

Silence.

"I was in Nantong when Lew and Wu traded the chips for the heroin."

Silence.

"I gave the chips to the Chinese."

Silence.

"I followed the heroin from China to Taiwan to Oakland."

Silence.

"I have Lew locked up in China."

Silence.

"I have the Taiwanese guy you sent to kill Lew locked up, too."

Silence.

"You want more?"

"No, but you couldn't do it alone. Who betrayed me? Lew?"

"Only after you tried to kill him."

"You're lying."

Ah Ming laughed with a bravado that revealed his uncertainty.

"Have any enemies in Thailand?"

"Some."

"Maybe somebody with a long memory."

Ah Ming fell silent. Finally, he said, "Shit. It's Eight Iron. Eight Iron is behind these people. I should have killed him fifteen years ago."

"I don't think it's Eight Iron. Eight Iron is making yaba and he had no way to follow the heroin. He tried, but we blocked his people at Kunming."

Gage heard a scraping noise coming from the east, in the area where Gage last spotted the gunman.

"You better keep an eye out for that guy. He wants you bad."

"He can't show himself without running into a cross fire, that is, if you really want to keep me alive."

Gage heard Ah Ming remove the clip from his gun, checking to see how many bullets he had left, and then the racking of his jamming it back in.

"Tell me about Eight Iron. What did he get out of helping you? Money?"

"Just revenge."

"There had to be more. He's a greedy man."

Gage kneeled and looked under the van and between the wheels of the cars parked down the street. He could just make out the gunman's pant cuff next to a car tire thirty yards away. He fired a shot that ricocheted off the pavement and into the tire. The cuff disappeared. The tire flattened.

"Kunming?" Ah Ming asked.

"Yeah, Kunming."

"I know what Eight Iron was after. It was the *ma huang*, the ephedrine."

Ephedrine? "What ephedrine?"

Ah Ming laughed. "So you don't know everything, white ghost. Think. How did we get the heroin? You didn't figure that out, did you? You didn't even see it. And Lew, the little snake, didn't tell you. Now look where we are."

Gage's mind worked back upstream.

"You mean you traded the chips for ephedrine and the ephedrine for the heroin?"

That was the novel financing the Wa were worried about. It was mostly a barter deal. There was money involved, but it crossed no borders and left no trail.

"Close enough. Then Eight Iron stole the ephedrine coming down from Kunming in payment for the heroin. He needed it to make yaba."

"And somehow Eight Iron arranged to blame you."

"That's right. Eight Iron tricked you and blamed me."

"And these guys are stealing back the heroin they sold you, because they believe you stole their ephedrine."

Gage knew right then it had to be. Only the source of the heroin would know it had gone to Nantong and, more important, would know who'd come to pick it up. Then it was just a matter of busting heads in China to find out where it was shipped in the United States, then busting a few more in the States to take it back.

Now he understood why Eight Iron was so eager to join Gage's team, and why he gave them Kasa. But there was no reason to hold Kasa hostage. Eight Iron never wanted the heroin. He wanted the ephedrine. No—Eight Iron wanted more than just the ephedrine. He wanted Ah Ming dead, and he didn't care who died with him.

The gunman took a shot at Gage. The slug clipped the rear corner of the van, then cut into Gage's left shoulder. He stared at spreading blood. Only now fatigue seemed to be his friend, for it neutralized the shock.

Dr. Stern's words came back to him: *Watch out for excessive bleeding.*

Gage jammed his gun into the holster and pressed his hand over the wound. He could feel the lead lodged under his skin. Then the pain hit him. Gage gritted his teeth and pressed harder and rocked back and forth until the sharpness was dulled by his body's defenses and the coagulating blood began to seal the wound.

age's cell rang. It was Casey.

"Buddy said you went running after Ah Ming. We heard some shots. You okay?"

"Yeah. I'm two blocks south of East Wind. In an alley. You still in the warehouse?"

"Everything's secure. We burst in on some guys who came to rip off the dope. All but one gave up pretty easy. Where's Ah Ming?"

"Near me, but trapped."

"I just sent some SFPD backup that way."

"Call them off. There's no way they'll understand what's happening here."

Casey switched to his radio and ordered the officers to take positions at the ends of the alley, then returned to his cell. He called ICE to send over their drone.

"Tell me what is going on."

"I'm near the west end. Some Chinese guy is way east of me on the other side of Ah Ming. He's committed to killing Ah Ming, otherwise he would have bailed already."

"Must be with the Big Circle guys who came to rip off the dope."

"How do you know they're Big Circle?"

"Buddy came down and looked them over. He recognized the dead one. Some asshole named Red Fire. His fire is out now. How close are you to Ah Ming?"

"He's across the alley, down about fifteen yards. He's hidden between some Dumpsters and the back wall of an auto repair shop."

"I'll send over some snipers and take him out. And the BC, too."

"Hold off. There's no way out of here. We need to take them alive."

Gage had said it again, surprising himself, shocked that he'd used the word "need."

He heard a shot and a ricochet off a Dumpster, followed by the opening of a car door. In the silence that followed, he could make out the crunching noise of rolling tires, a car being pushed forward. He glanced around the van and saw it, a small Honda creeping down the alley toward both him and Ah Ming.

Ah Ming fired at the car. Glass shattered. The gunman yelped and swore. The car stopped rolling.

"I think Ah Ming may have hit the BC," Gage told Casey.

Gage looked under the cars again. The gunman lay on the pavement. He rolled to his side and curled up, holding his upper chest.

"Make sure your people have gotten into position at the east end of the alley so Ah Ming can't get out that way. And tell them to keep their fingers off their triggers. I don't want them trying to take him out and shooting me instead."

Casey gave the command, then said to Gage, "I'm sending others to the rooftops on the north side of the alley. I can't take a chance of Ah Ming getting out of there and taking a hostage or killing some innocent person."

"But let me try to talk to him."

"Okay, but the first time he points his gun at anybody, he's dead. And you tell him that. Dead. Dead. Dead."

CHAPTER 94

G age disconnected the call with Casey.

Everything was starting to have a sense of inevitability about it. Everybody was going to do what they were going to do. The gunman, Ah Ming, and himself. They all knew it. And that understanding brought a reflective silence into the alley.

Gage rose from his knees and propped himself on the edge of the panel van's step-up bumper.

Why am I trying to save this guy?

The question evoked an image of him standing in front of the Buddhist temple in Bangkok.

Karma. That's what they call it, that's what they claim it is. Karma.

Some necessary link, some rational connection, between how we live and how we die. Between who we are and what we deserve.

Ah Ming is death. Isn't that what Ah Ming deserves?

But cancer is death, too. Does that mean it's what I deserve?

Did the question even make sense?

Gage then began to think about the gunman and Ah Ming,

not only as men who placed no value on life, but as bodies, two healthy bodies their owners had put at risk.

Karma, explain this one.

HIDDEN BETWEEN DUMPSTERS, Ah Ming pressed his back against the sooty wall of the auto repair shop. The odors not only of recent garbage, but the residue of years of compacted refuse caking the walls of the Dumpsters, filled his nose. He could see the knees of his suit shining from the oil and grease coating the pavement under him. But what plagued him now wasn't disgust at the filth in which he might die, it was the thought that the white ghost across the alley had found him out. He felt exposed, like his clothing had been ripped from his body, like a night hunter wrenched from the darkness, dragged aboveground and into the midday sun.

And he felt shaken for the very first time.

Life had always been simply a matter of living, then not living. It had never entered his imagination that he would spend the last of it in a six-by-eight-foot cell or die like a trapped rat in a grimy alleyway.

However it was supposed to end, it wasn't supposed to end like this.

CHAPTER 95

Motion caught Ah Ming's eye. He looked up and spotted agents positioning themselves on the rooftops of the buildings in front of him, three stories above the alley.

"So, *gwai lo,* is this what you had in mind?"

"They aren't going to shoot unless you raise that gun."

"What about you?"

"That's not what I came for, but it's up to you."

"So we have a little more time."

"We have a little more time."

"Then tell me. Why are you here?"

"Peter Sheridan."

"Peter Sheridan? That name doesn't mean anything to me."

"How about Ah Pang? You remember Ah Pang. The kid who got killed at the chip robbery in San Jose. Thomas Sheridan is his father."

"A weakling."

"Maybe he just learned his limits. You're the guy squeezed like a rat behind a greasy Dumpster. Not him."

"You have nothing to connect me with the robbery."

"Ah Tien."

"You're lying. I know he didn't talk."

"He was afraid you'd kill him when he came back for his father's funeral so he left some shipping documents behind, a road map. When your people kidnapped him, they left his briefcase; and when they killed him, they left his address book: Sunny Glory, Lew, Efficiency Trading, Old Wu."

"Fucking Vietnamese."

Gage could see a spot of laser light bouncing around on the wall above Ah Ming's head, then another, and another.

Casey's voice emerged out of the silence. "This is the FBI. Throw down your weapon and step out."

Silence.

"Throw down your weapon and step out."

Silence.

Gage's cell phone rang.

"What's he been talking about?" Casey asked.

"Nothing. Just talk."

"Will he let us come in to get the wounded BC? This'll look real bad in the press if we let him bleed out."

"I don't think he'll let you. Life isn't something he seems to care about, and he sure as hell doesn't care about FBI public relations."

Gage called out to Ah Ming, "The police want to come and carry out the Big Circle."

"So what. It's his own fucking fault. He should've stayed out of my business."

"His answer is no," Gage told Casey. "Is Sylvia still in the warehouse?"

"No, some clerk collapsed and I let Sylvia take her to the hospital. I don't want to know what Sylvia was doing in there. In fact, I'm not even sure I saw her."

From a distance, Gage heard the thumping, whirling sound

of helicopter blades approaching from the south. Soon it would be above them.

"Is that yours?" Gage asked Casey.

"It's NBC. We're bringing the drone over. Hold on, let me get rid of it." Casey switched to his radio, leaving the cell line to Gage open.

"Control?"

"Check."

"Call Channel 3. Get that copter out of here. There are armed men on the ground. It's putting everyone in danger. Tell them to move it or the pilot will be spending the next year in federal prison for obstruction."

Gage heard the helicopter edging closer. It emerged high above the building behind Ah Ming, the afternoon sun glinting off its glass bubble and polishing its white body. It froze in position, then spun out of sight, later reappearing far to the west, steadying itself for a long live shot. It was far enough away that Gage couldn't hear the whirling blades, but he knew its camera was locked on the alley. It hung like a clock against a vast blue wall, marking time.

"Remain where you are." Casey's voice boomed over the loudspeaker, blasting through Gage's cell phone. The words echoed and faded. A dominating and expectant silence returned to the alley.

Gage peeked around the corner. He couldn't see Ah Ming. "What's going on? Who are you yelling at?"

"It's the BC. He's trying to crawl toward Ah Ming. He's like a wounded, rabid dog. Some mother's son turned into an animal . . . what a waste."

Both Ah Ming and Gage heard the clunking of the BC's gun butt on the pavement and the scraping of his shoes as he crawled toward Ah Ming.

"I'm gonna drop a stun grenade. That'll stop him." Through the phone Gage heard the rip of a Velcro strap, then Casey: "Counting down . . . five . . . four . . . three . . . two . . . one."

Gage dropped to his knees, shielding his head and covering his eyes and ears and pressing himself against the van. The explosion reverberated off the brick walls lining the alley. He felt the van rock back and forth, then shudder to a stop as dust, paper, and trash blew past.

The force of the stun grenade broke the gunman's will, but the billowing dust and debris gave Ah Ming a last chance to run.

He took it. And Gage knew why. The same inner will that had made him hard and tough in his teens, that made him a godfather in his thirties, that permitted him to kill without mercy, that allowed him to live radically alone, now drew him to his feet, lifted his gun hand toward the agents on the rooftop, pulled his finger hard on the trigger, then forced his legs into a sprint west down the alley amid bursting sniper fire.

Slugs that missed him or passed through his body bounced off the walls, skipped across the street, drilled into parked cars, even thudded into the van that gave Gage cover.

"Cease fire! Cease fire! Cease fire!" Casey yelled.

If the weapons followed Ah Ming any farther, the slugs would ricochet into Gage.

Gage caught sight of Ah Ming as he came parallel, his sprint devolving into a stagger, dragging his left leg behind him, his right arm limp. Bleeding from just below his shoulder. The right side of his suit jacket punctured in two places, shiny wet circles surrounding the holes. His gun was now in his left hand.

Gage couldn't tell whether Ah Ming even realized the shooting had stopped, so intense was his drive, so overwhelming was his will to stay on his feet, to keep moving. Gage drew his gun. He rose, his legs weak. He struggled to raise it, then braced himself against the back of the van, his shoulder throbbing.

Ah Ming turned toward him.

"Go down, just go down," Gage said. "Please. Just . . . go . . . down."

Gage could see in Ah Ming's eyes all the man's rage, fear, and ambition, now focused on Gage, his whole being reduced to one irrational thought: by killing Gage, the nightmare that had become his life would end and he could walk away.

Ah Ming raised his left arm and tried to steady the barrel in Gage's direction. Weakened by the slugs that had ripped through him, his arm shook, the gun wavered. Ah Ming willed his arm to fix on Gage. And it did.

Gage fired. The slug hit Ah Ming in the middle of his chest. His arm fell, but he didn't. He stared ahead, eyes glazed and unfocused. He didn't see Gage anymore. His eyes didn't register at all. Then his heart stopped, and his body surrendered.

CHAPTER 96

As Gage lowered his gun, he had only a vague sense of police rushing in. He gazed down at Ah Ming's crumpled form lying before him. Even though life had left his body, somehow death hadn't yet arrived, and Gage knew it wouldn't for another generation, for he understood that Ah Ming was more than just his life, his biography. He was a history, a violent, perverse history. A terrifying robbery, Peter bleeding out on a warehouse floor, Peter's grieving mother, desperate father, and courageous sister, Ah Tien's lonely execution, Eight Iron's manipulation, Lew's complicity, then abandonment . . . and finally a heart-stopping bullet in the chest.

All this was the history of Ah Ming, and Gage was a part of it—no, it was more than that. At the end, as Ah Ming willed his gun to lock on Gage, he knew he'd become all of it.

The last month welled up inside him. It resisted acknowledging what death brings even to the worst of mankind, resisted a final truth.

What did Casey say? A waste. It was all a waste.

Gage started to turn away, but a chill shot through him and he was lost in an image of himself standing over Ah Ming's body. The image contained an unformed idea, floating just out of reach.

He knew he had to grasp it at its origin and think it through to wherever it led. He once again saw himself standing in front of the Buddhist temple in Bangkok. Then his wedding day, looking into Faith's eyes. Then Linda Sheridan limping from his office. Finally, he saw the cancer that would kill him.

Ah Ming was death. Cancer was death. And since the day of his diagnosis Gage had them linked in his mind in a way he hadn't understood. Did he really think that he could prevail over his own death by saving Ah Ming's life? Slap away the hand of fate?

No, that's not right. This wasn't about sowing and reaping, the scales of justice balancing, or justice winning out, or karma, or just deserts. The world just doesn't work that way. There was nothing inevitable about Gage's cancer or Ah Ming's death. Gage knew, finally knew, that fate was no more or less than a series of chance events and human choices. Ah Ming was dead because Gage killed him, and Gage was going to die of cancer. Nothing would change either one.

A wave of weariness crested above him. It seemed to pause, as if waiting for him to finish his thought. He felt himself reaching out, grasping at images that dissolved in his hands. Then he was wrenched back inside himself as words captured the images warring in his mind.

It was an illusion of immortality.

As long as the hunt for Ah Ming continued, Gage wouldn't have to look cancer in the face. But now the hunt was over, and the wave crashed down.

Gage felt a hand grip his arm. He jerked it away.

"Graham, it's me."

Faith was standing beside him. She wrapped her arms around his chest.

"Sylvia called . . . I came . . . I heard the shot . . . I thought . . . Casey, he . . ."

Gage reached his arm around her and pressed her against him. Her tears soaked through his shirt, warm and wet against his skin.

Casey took the gun out of Gage's hand and passed it to a uniformed cop, then led Gage and Faith past the swarming police officers and through the news crews gathering at the end of the alley. Gage felt the peering eyes of secretaries and clerks who listened on the radio or watched the live feed on their office computers. A pouting street woman leaned against a wall, waiting for everyone to leave so she could return to her alley home. An ambulance passed them on its way to where Flat Nose lay in the alley. A coroner's wagon crept up and stopped, waiting for Ah Ming's body to be released. A warehouse supervisor gathered up his workers, herding them back to their jobs.

"The show's over. Time is money."

An SFPD homicide detective, black suited and red tied for television interviews, stepped into Casey's path as he led Gage and Faith away.

"This is a homicide. Nobody's gonna run off. I need a statement. I need to know what happened."

Casey grabbed the detective's shoulder, spun him around, and then yanked back on his collar. Casey pointed upward and jabbed his finger at the NBC helicopter hovering above.

"Get the video, you idiot. The whole world knows what happened."

Casey pushed past the detective, through the mass of patrol cars with their lights flashing and around the television news vans with their antennas raised toward the sky. He guided Gage to an ambulance parked at the corner. The EMT pulled open the rear doors and sat Gage down on the ledge where he cut off Gage's shirt, bandaged the wound, and stabilized the arm.

After the EMT left to report in, Casey glanced around,

making sure all the cops and news reporters were out of earshot. Then he leaned down toward Gage.

"To tell you the truth I don't really know what happened out here. For a while I thought I did, but I don't, not a clue. Maybe, someday, you'll explain it to me."

Gage looked up at Casey's face, now decades older than when they first met in that Chinatown alley. And he knew he owed Casey more than just an explanation. But it was a place to start.

Someday.

s I recall," Dr. Stern said two days later when she entered the examining room where Gage and Faith waited, "my orders, rephrased by you, were to get rest, avoid infections, and stay away from people who can hurt you. Is there anything about those orders you haven't violated?"

"No infection."

"Let me see, tough guy. Take off your shirt."

After Gage slipped it off, Stern unwrapped the bandaging that covered the stitches he received in the emergency room at SF Medical after the surgeon dug out the slug.

"Nice work. Faith, why don't you come look at this?"

Faith got up from her chair and looked over Stern's shoulder.

"I see a little redness there." Faith shook her head, feigning a kind of professional disapproval. "Just as we thought, a little infection."

"Can I still do chemo today?"

"Of course. The blood results show you're healthy enough. You'll just need some antibiotic ointment."

Stern applied cream from a tube she took from a cabinet and then rewrapped the wound. Both she and Faith sat down. Gage slipped down from the exam table, then pulled on his shirt.

"You mind if I ask you something?" Stern asked, crossing her legs, resting her folded hands on her knee.

"There's nothing you can't ask."

"I watched on television. Why'd you let the man point that gun at you for so long? I thought my heart would stop. And now that the media is reporting who he really was, I just . . . I just don't get it. He could have . . ."

"As it turns out, it's not that complicated. I'm really not a tough guy. Never was. The truth is I wasn't ready to face my own death."

Stern leaned back and studied Gage. For a few seconds she sat, lips compressed, eyes narrowed, gaze unfocused, then she sat up.

"I think I understand. I really think I do."

"I thought you would."

Stern turned toward Faith. "And you knew it all along, didn't you? You knew. That's why you let him go."

Faith nodded. "I knew."

"You have more courage than I have. I don't think I could have done that."

"Everyone has to approach death in their own way in order to remain who they are. And I married him for who he is."

Stern looked back at Gage, started to speak, then paused. He knew what she was thinking, the question she was asking, the question he was asking himself: Would he ever be ready?

Gage looked down at Faith gazing up at him. He'd learned something else in the alley. Faith was all death could take from him; everything else he could leave behind.

Note to the Reader

'm not a tough guy either. And that's just one of the similarities between Gage and me. Not only do he and I share the same sense of the world and walk the same moral landscape, but he knows the rough ground of crime and the hard people who make it so only because I traveled there and learned it all before him. And he knows how to live in the shadow of death only because that shadow fell over me first.

As I approached the fourth Gage novel, and my seventh overall, it seemed to me it was time to show some aspects of what that life is really like. And not for my sake, but for others who live, have lived, or will live—or who will die—in that shadow. And what I learned over the last fifteen years of biopsies and chemotherapy, of hospitals and examining rooms, of radiology labs and infusion centers is that—contrary to the mythology of panic and terror, collapse and paralysis, that surrounds cancer—we carry on.

Except for those who have been inflicted with forms that are too disabling or who survive only weeks or months—we carry on.

Mothers mother. Fathers father. Workers work. Sellers sell. Writers write. Doctors doctor. Liars lie. Cheaters cheat. Predators prey.

We are who we are, and we do what we do.

Regardless of what our initial reaction to the diagnosis might have been—rage, fear, resignation, self-estrangement, or self-pity—it fades. Regardless of the promises we might have made to ourselves—to be kind or generous or Zenlike in our equanimity—we return to whomever we've always been. Regardless of the ways in which we might have viewed ourselves—as patients, victims, sufferers, warriors, or survivors—in the end we rediscover who we've always been. Regardless of the ways we think the world has been changed and remade—brighter or dimmer, engaging or indifferent—in the end we find it's the same world and we are the same in it.

And we carry on.

All this should be obvious. And it certainly is, inside infusion rooms and radiation oncology departments and in all the other places where patients are diagnosed and treated. But outside, however, in fiction and in memoir, on talk shows and in film, and in the cottage industry of self-help and popular psychology, the mythology lives on.*

The adversity Gage faces in *White Ghost* is more urgent than mine, a chronic and often treatable, but ultimately incurable form of lymphoma. The oncologist's original prognosis of my time from diagnosis through treatments to death turned out to be overly conservative and I rode, am still riding, the bell curve of probability, first traveling up and then down the sweeping arcs, and now along the thinning tail. Indeed, I worked for an-

---

* And a troublesome one it is. I will be discussing the reasons for its persistence and perniciousness and its commercial exploitation in a work of nonfiction, *In the Mouth of the Wolf*. The preface to that work can be found at http://www.ars-medica.ca/index.php/journal/article/view/13/50.

other nine years in scores of places around the globe before I reached the moment in Gage's life when this story begins.

But by then I was transitioning from investigator to writer and whatever discomforts I underwent in treatment were compensated for by my undergoing them in the company of my wife and in the comfort of my own home. My commute was no longer to my office downtown, but only to a converted bottom-floor bedroom. My lunch, just a short climb back up the stairs. A nap, just one more flight.

Although there is never a good time to undergo chemotherapy, my two years of treatment began during a busy period. I was putting the final edits on *Final Target,* finishing the first and second drafts and major edits of *Absolute Risk,* and writing the second Harlan Donnally novel. I was also investigating a death that occurred ten years earlier, one of my last cases.

According to the local police department, a young man in his twenties who had been found dead in a basement had been beaten by drug dealers a few weeks earlier and had died of his untreated injuries. During the intervening decade, no one had been arrested, no suspects even identified. The case was old, cold, and closed.

It had been many years since I'd worked in the tough parts of the Bay Area. My practice had developed into one that found me working more often in London, Kiev, or Chennai than in San Francisco, Oakland, or San Jose, and investigating this death meant for me, as for Gage in *White Ghost,* going to once familiar places and relying on people from the past to catch up to the present.

In searching the housing projects and skid-row motels and drug corners for witnesses, I found myself surrounded by death, and not only because of the reminders provided by my continuing visits to the Stanford Cancer Center. Driving around those streets was like walking through a cemetery, one not made up of headstones and crypts, but of sidewalks and corners, streets and alleys, front steps and backyards, empty lots and abandoned houses, each a reminder that many of those in the generation I once knew and on whom I had once relied to get me to the facts behind the tales were dead.

As I was talking to an old-timer outside the liquor store at Eight and Campbell in West Oakland, I thought of Stymie Taylor, a damaged man who'd spent much of his life in prison, but who many times knew someone or something that helped me get to the truth. I stopped in to visit his mother who had been at his bedside when he died. By then she'd outlived four of her children. She told me Sunday dinners had become a time of empty chairs.

Driving past a drug-dealing spot in East Oakland, I thought of Henry Scott, a cunning man who'd done a lot of bad in his life. I saw him last when he dropped by my office about a dozen years ago. I'm not sure why he came to see me and I'm not sure he knew why either. I was long out of his world, but by his walk and his talk, I understood the place he still held in it. I told him if he stayed in the Bay Area, he'd be a dead man; and a couple of months later he was, shot down outside a bayside nightclub.

And there were many more. Way too many more.

I passed the corner flower shop near the Sixty-Fifth Avenue housing project, within gunshot distance of hundreds of murders in the previous thirty years, and I remembered a sign I'd seen in the window in 1986: *Funeral Sale*. There are so many things wrong with that phrase, so disturbing anyone would even think it, I'll just let the image of that storefront speak the thousand words for itself.

I drove through the once infamous intersection of Ninety-Eighth and Edes, where in 1989 I had been trapped as men shot at each other from opposite corners. At least I'd had my car's sheet metal around me. The people running and ducking didn't. Six rounds were exchanged in seconds, the gunfight was over, and the shooters fled leaving nothing behind but lead and a memory.

Hairless, fatigued, pale, infused with chemotherapy drugs, and on the hunt for a witness, I walked into the courtyard of an apartment building where I had been told one was living. It was also where years earlier a drug dealer had me at gunpoint. It struck me that if he'd pulled the trigger I wouldn't have lived to die of cancer. I saw where I'd been standing and where he'd been standing, a dead strip of concrete on which there had occurred a live moment. I remembered his hand coming up out of his pocket and the look in his eyes.

They say cancer is the emperor of all maladies. At least on that day, it wasn't. It was a man with a gun.

In the end, it had turned out to be just another day in the life. He went his way. And I went mine.

Ultimately, I located witnesses who told me, and who later testified in federal court, that the men who had beaten the victim and caused his death weren't drug dealers at all. In truth, they were undercover police officers, and the homicide detective assigned to the investigation had known it almost from the start.

Based on the testimony of these witnesses and admissions by some of the officers involved, the judge later ruled that the department had engaged in a decade-long cover-up. The city's defense against the family's civil rights claim had been both absurd and immoral: its attorneys had made a statute of limitations argument that the victim's family should have discovered and exposed the police conspiracy sooner.

In fact, the injustice went far beyond the death and the cover-up. Not only did the detective remain in the homicide unit even after his role in the case became known inside the police department, but upon his retirement, the district attorney, the chief law enforcement officer in the county, hired him to work as an inspector in her office. And the lieutenant who supervised the officers, who was present at the time of the assault and who engaged in what the department admitted was an attempt to influence officers' reports of the beating, was assigned to head the internal affairs unit and promoted to the rank of captain.

I considered using the death of this young man as the basis of a Harlan Donnally novel, but unlike the mayors, city council members, judges, prosecutors, police chiefs, and city managers who served during these years, no reader of fiction would tolerate this kind of ending.

Some of Gage's thoughts in *White Ghost* are ones I had as I searched for witnesses, and they are at least some of the thoughts all cancer patients have as we carry on. Among other things, it meant thinking about time and what is worth spending it on and a reminder that the young man whose death I was investigating died at about the same time as I was first diagnosed. His life was stolen, beaten out of him by fist and boot, but mine remained—it still remains—my own to spend. And at least some of that time I chose to spend walking Graham Gage and Harlan Donnally, and their readers, through the landscape on which I have lived much of my life.

Acknowledgments

During a number of trips to Thailand over the years, I met with drug traffickers and members of syndicates who came together as investors in heroin in deals, along with those who laundered their money and the enforcers, political figures, and military officers who protected their operations. I also spent a good deal of time in Taiwan and China and met with government officials and owners of factories and trading companies involved in heroin and other smuggling.

For dramatic effect, I have portrayed real, but more extreme, symptoms of lymphoma as reflected in the clinical literature, but—unlike the characters Ah Ming, Eight Iron, Kasa, and Zhang—these should not be taken as typical. There has been substantial progress in lymphoma diagnostics and treatment, but it's still not specific enough to account for the disparate outcomes of patients with the same diagnosis, some surviving mere months and others, like myself, still alive after a decade and a half.

In recognition of the continuing resistance to the dictatorial rulers of the country, I have chosen to use the name Burma, rather than Myanmar, a name imposed by the military.

The death described in the Note to the Reader is well documented in court rulings and news reports.*

I am fortunate to have had the benefit of careful readings of the earliest version of this manuscript by Enid Norman, Seth Norman, and Chris Cannon and the careful readings of my medical condition by Doctors Ranjana Advani and Alan Yuen, and PA Katy Pose to whom I have dedicated this book.

To my wife, Liz, I dedicate me.

---

* Northern District of California, Docket No. C 09-01019 WHA, *The Estate of Jerry A. Amaro III; Geraldine Montoya; Stephanie Montoya, Plaintiffs, v. City of Oakland; E. Karsseboom; R. Holmgren; S. Nowak; M. Battle; C. Bunn; M. Patterson; T. Pena; Edward Poulson; Richard Word, Defendants.*

United States Court of Appeals, Ninth Circuit, Docket No. 10–16152, *The Estate of Jerry A. Amaro III; Geraldine Montoya; Stephanie Montoya, Plaintiffs–Appellees, v. City of Oakland; E. Karsseboom; R. Holmgren; S. Nowak; M. Battle; C. Bunn; M. Patterson; T. Pena; Edward Poulson; Richard Word, Defendants–Appellants.* "Court-Oakland Cops Stonewalled Beaten Man's Mom," *San Francisco Chronicle,* July 28, 2011.

About the Author

STEVEN GORE is a former private investigator turned "masterful" writer (*Publishers Weekly*) who combines "a command of storytelling" with "insider knowledge" (*Library Journal*). With a unique voice honed on the street and in the Harlan Donnally and Graham Gage novels, Gore's stories are grounded in his decades spent investigating murder, fraud, organized crime, corruption, and drug, sex, and arms trafficking throughout the Americas, Europe, and Asia. He has been featured on *60 Minutes* and honored for investigative excellence. He lives in the San Francisco Bay Area.

www.stevengore.com

THE P.I. GRAHAM GAGE SERIES

WHITE GHOST

An electrifying, harrowing new Graham Gage thriller that will leave readers hanging in suspense until the final shocking moments.

POWER BLIND

"Gripping. Relentless. Authentic. The year's best."
—Myles Knapp, *San Jose Mercury News*

ABSOLUTE RISK

Absolute Risk, like its acclaimed predecessor, is an international thriller for grown-ups: riveting, surprising, intelligent, and frighteningly believable.

FINAL TARGET

"*Final Target* is an action packed debut thriller with a unique plot and vivid characters."
—Phillip Margolin, *New York Times* bestselling author of *Fugitive*

THE DETECTIVE HARLAN DONNALLY SERIES

NIGHT IS THE HUNTER

From the author of *Act of Deceit* and *A Criminal Defense* comes the third book in the thrilling series featuring ex-SFPD detective Harlan Donnally.

A CRIMINAL DEFENSE

When Mark Hamlin, a defense lawyer with a slimy reputation, is found murdered underneath the Golden Gate Bridge, ex SFPD detective Harlan Donnally is unwittingly pulled back into the fray to solve the crime.

ACT OF DECEIT

A heart-racing masterwork of mystery, thrills, and suspense that introduces readers to a phenomenal new series protagonist, Detective Harlan Donnally.